KERRY J DONOVAN

ON THE ROCKS

VINCI

BOOKS

The Ryan Kaine series by Kerry J Donovan

On The Run

On The Rocks

On The Defensive

On The Attack

On The Money

On The Edge

On The Wing

On The Hunt

On The Outside

On The Lookout

On The Brink

On The Offensive

On The Charge

To Sergeant Douglas G. Campbell, who taught me how to climb and kept me safe—despite all my efforts to fall.

Vinci Books

vinci-books.com

Published by Vinci Books Ltd in 2025

1

A CIP catalogue record for this book is available from the British Library.

Paperback ISBN: 9781036701642

Printed and bound in Great Britain by Clays Ltd, Elcograf S.p.A.

Chapter One

Wednesday 16th September - Martin Princeton

Ben Craed, The Cairngorms, Aberdeenshire, Scotland

Still raining.

Martin opened his eyes a crack.

Rained all bloody night. Hour after sodding hour. Didn't let up for a single second, and he couldn't do a bloody thing to take shelter. He tried to move, but the pain wracked through his leg, hips, back. Everywhere.

Nothing but pain.

Dawn had brought hope, but it also brought heavier rain.

Used to love Scotland. Hated the pigging place now. Stupid country. Stupid weather. Stupid mountains.

Why didn't he stay home? Bloody idiot. He wanted to be with his mates. Wanted to run from the neighbours and their flowers and their Goddamned sympathy for Mum and Dad. Not for him though. Nobody asked how little Martin was doing. Nobody gave a toss about the baby brother. They left him to fend for himself. Bastards.

And where did he end up?

Up a mountain, alone, bleeding, and freezing to death.

A fuckup all my life. Everybody knows. Matty knew, but wouldn't say. Yeah, Matty knew.

Huge, crushing drops fell onto his face, into his eyes. The cold had numbed his skin, and the freezing air had sliced through his thin clothing.

So damned cold.

Why didn't he put on his heavy jacket when he had the chance? Too bloody stupid. That's why not. The other lads in the party, the ones with the muscles that made girls fawn all over them, didn't wrap up warm against the cold and the rain, so Martin hadn't either. Stupid idiot. They'd shamed him into it and now he was going to die alone in nothing but a pair of jeans, a T-shirt, and a light, summer jacket.

He'd been careless and the mountains were going to make him pay.

Overnight, the darkness had been total. No stars, no moon, no light. Nothing to see and nothing to hear but the wind whistling through the rocks, the hammering rain, and his pitiful weeping.

He tried not to cry like a girl but couldn't help it.

If dying alone in misery wasn't a good enough reason to cry, then what was? Besides, up here, no one could hear him. No one around to laugh at his blubbing.

Right on cue, a pulse of agony ripped up his left leg and

into his knee. It was probably broken, and it would end up killing him.

How long would it take to die? Would he last the day?

He knew people could survive without food for days, but the cold—the fucking cold.

He couldn't bear the thought of another endless night with nothing to focus on but the pain every time he moved and the blinding, screaming headache that clamped his temples so tight he thought his skull was going to explode.

Martin tried to keep still, but the shivering wouldn't let him. Each shudder fired electric shocks through his arm and leg. Music—his normal escape from the world—wouldn't come. Whatever he tried, he couldn't make the tunes play in his head.

He'd been on the rocks more than a day and nobody had come for him. Why not? Did anyone know he was missing? Had anyone raised the alarm?

What would happen to Mum and Dad now?

Again, he cried. Not from anger or self-pity but for what his death would do to his 'rents.

They'd already been through so much. Mum collapsed into Dad's arms when the police broke the news. Matty was one of the eighty-three people murdered by the madman, Ryan Kaine.

Ryan bloody Kaine.

Monster. Terrorist bastard. Fucking killer.

Ryan bloody Kaine killed Matty.

He killed Matt! Dear God.

At least he'd gone quickly. Always was the lucky one. Not like Martin. No, Martin was going to die alone on a bloody mountain. Exposure would get him, or gangrene. Painful and slow. And alone.

Matty, I'm so, so sorry.

The big brother who'd tormented and teased him all his life, but who'd have taken a bullet for him, would never come back. He'd never see Matty again.

Fuck.

He'd never see anyone again.

Should have stayed home. The desperation in Mum's eyes when he told her he was still going to Scotland despite Matt's death. He didn't ask. Didn't even bloody ask. Instead he'd been angry with her for insisting she walked him to school like he was a baby, too small to cross the road on his own.

"For God's sake, Mum. Stop crying. It's embarrassing," he'd said under his breath outside the school gates while the other lads stood by, trying not to smirk. "I'm only away for a couple of days. I'll be back in plenty of time for the funeral."

Why had he even said that? What was he thinking? She'd reacted as though he'd slapped her across the face. And he hadn't even apologised. He'd been a selfish bastard, didn't even say goodbye, and where was he now? Dying on a Scottish mountain.

Bloody idiot.

All because he wanted to see eagles up close.

Stupid, stupid, stupid.

To think he'd fallen for it.

What would Matty have said?

"You're a complete moron, baby brother. What have I told you about reading between the lines? Don't trust anyone! You fuckup. Fancy letting Mum and Dad down like this now I'm not here to save your sorry arse."

He'd have said it with a kindly smile and maybe ruffled

4

Martin's hair at the same time, but he'd have said it just the same.

Sorry, Matty. Sorry for being a fuckup.

A raindrop fell on the tip of his nose and ran into his mouth. He licked the water away. No chance of dying of thirst in Scotland.

Had a better chance of fucking drowning.

He sneezed. The movement shot a knife through his leg, his throbbing shoulder screamed, and the crushing vice around his head tightened.

Martin pushed his free fist into his mouth, bit down hard on the knuckles, and screamed in silence. Once again, he let the tears flow.

He stared up at the jagged edge of the cliff face in the distance, the one with its recently crumbled ledge.

If there were any search teams, would the broken rocks point them down to him? Could he last long enough for that?

Time passed slower than every single maths lesson he'd ever had with Ma Bancroft. Jesus, when would they put the old cow out of everyone's misery? She had to be pushing fifty.

Seconds, minutes, hours passed.

The rain lightened and finally stopped, but a heavy blanket of fog took its place.

Last night, before the sun set, the drubbing of a helicopter's rotor blades had given him brief hope, but the bloody thing had flown right over him without stopping. The spotters hadn't seen him, but why should they? The rocks hid him.

Maybe that helicopter hadn't been searching for him after all. Perhaps someone else was lost on the mountain.

Oh God.

They weren't coming. No one was coming.

He'd fucked up for the last time.

"Mum, Dad, Matty, I'm sorry I let you down. So, so sorry."

Martin Princeton closed his eyes to the cold, grey mist, clamped his arms around his chest, and waited for death.

Chapter Two

Heading North, A84, Near Bannockburn, Scotland

Two hours after crossing the border into Scotland, the fuel light on the dashboard flashed its angry, yellow, "Feed me, feed me" message. Ordinarily, Ryan Kaine would have gritted his teeth, but the exposed root of his broken tooth throbbed and made it impossible.

From hiring the Toyota Land Cruiser outside Luton, a full tank should have been more than enough to take him all the way to the foothills of *Ben Craed* and part of the way back again. But, despite the risk of speed traps, he'd been heavy on the throttle and the high motorway speeds had returned to bite him on the arse.

The dashboard's digital readout showed seventy miles

before the big SUV would start running on fumes, but the satnav told him he still had over one hundred to travel before he reached the Mountain Rescue Centre at Kinross Farm. The gas-guzzling monster drank diesel like a boozer hearing the call for last orders, and Kaine needed plenty in reserve for a fast escape if necessary.

No alternative, he had to risk a refuelling stop.

He slid a finger over the satnav's touch screen and ran the search. Twenty-five miles to the nearest petrol station. Enough tolerance to keep the speed reasonably high, but only just.

At Luton, Kaine had hired the only 4x4 in the shop. He didn't need the added traction on the motorway, but it would probably turn out handy in the mountains. And the way the weather ahead looked, his destination in the Cairngorms would be challenging without low range.

By the time he took the exit road off the A84 and turned into the BP forecourt, the miles-left-in-the-tank display showed three zeros. So much for the accuracy of the SUV's electronics.

Killian Services boasted a single-storey food court and shopping area, and a petrol station with four pumps, all in use. At 15:43, and with at least another ninety minutes on increasingly windy, uphill roads still to go, the rest stop couldn't have been better placed. He pulled in behind a tired-looking Volvo and waited with growing impatience for the grey-haired septuagenarian to climb from his car and work out how to operate the self-service pump. In normal circumstances, Kaine would have jumped out to offer help, but he needed to stay below the radar until his police contact, DCI Jones, had time to start the process that would clear his name.

He checked his injuries in the rear-view mirror—lump

above the left ear, left eye swollen almost shut, split lip, bruised cheek. Not pretty, and they were only the visible injuries. Stripped down to his briefs, he probably looked like tenderised beef.

Still, Adam Akers, the man who'd given Kaine most of the damage, had fared worse. Pinocchio hadn't earned his new nickname lightly. The thought of the man pleading with a plastic surgeon to reattach the tip of his nose made Kaine smile. The police would catch him soon if they hadn't already. No, poor, little Pinocchio was the least of Kaine's problems.

Kaine sat in the car, drumming his fingers on the steering wheel, and waited. He kept his head lowered. One sight of his face might have shocked the old boy at the pump into a coronary, and Kaine didn't need yet another death on his overburdened conscience.

Kaine stopped drumming long enough to search his pockets but came up empty. He'd finished the last of his sweets, the pineapple chunks, on the English side of the border and would resupply his energy fix in the shop when paying for the diesel, but only if the man ahead would ever finish topping up his bloody tank.

Yet again, he'd chosen the slowest lane. Why? The other one had already moved ahead by one car, and a showroom-polished, midnight-blue Mercedes Benz S-Class pulled alongside Kaine's Toyota. Two men wearing white shirts and ties with respectably short hair—one blond, the other dark brown—continued an animated conversation to the thumping, techno soundtrack blaring from the car's info-tainment centre. To obscure the undamaged side of his face, Kaine held his mobile phone up to his right ear and pretended to make a call. Fortunately, neither man paid him any attention.

While waiting for the old fellow to limp towards the kiosk, Kaine ran a continual search-sweep of the forecourt. There were two surveillance cameras—one on a pole with a two-seventy-degree view of the pumps, the other one at a lower level, above the door to the shop. Both covered the pumps and were fixed. He'd place good odds on there being at least one more inside the kiosk, pointing at the till—to prevent theft by the shop worker rather than the customers —and maybe a second surveilling the stock. He'd have to keep his face averted from the lenses, but the peak of his baseball cap would help with that.

The thirty-something Merc driver punched the car horn and rolled his hand forwards in an aggressive hurry-up, trying to antagonise a Sikh man at the pump ahead. The man turned his back and continued filling his Renault. Another shrill blast of car horn drowned out the rumble of road traffic for a moment, and the techno drivel increased in volume as the Merc's passenger window rolled down. The passenger poked his blond head through the opening.

"Hey, Gandhi. Pull your finger out o' your fucking arse-hole," he shouted, his accent pure Glasgow Southside. "We don't got all day tae wait for the likes of youse!"

The driver punctuated his younger mate's words with another long blast of the car's horn. They laughed.

Thirty pregnant seconds later, his Renault filled, the Sikh man returned the nozzle to the pump and struggled to lock his car's fuel cap under the glare of the two well-dressed bullies. The driver revved the Merc's powerful engine and rolled his car forwards until it all but rested against the Renault's rear bumper.

Along with the normal villains who passed into Kaine's sphere of influence, bullies rated high on his list of individuals to detest. He gripped the leather steering wheel tighter and tried to keep from jumping out of the car and having quiet words with the two halfwits.

The Volvo in front of Kaine finally moved, and he allowed the Land Cruiser to roll down the slight incline under its own weight.

The turbaned man slid into his Renault and drove his car into a bay in front of the kiosk, clearing the pump for the Merc. The Glaswegian watched as the Sikh and his wife entered the kiosk, an angry scowl darkening his round and spotty face. Kaine could almost hear the man's racist mind whirring above the ear-splitting noise pounding from his car's stereo.

At his pump, Kaine selected Diesel Super-Max and, keeping his head down and his back to the pumps, he started the fill.

The Merc drew to a stop on the other side of Kaine's pump. The driver killed the engine and, mercifully, the music died with it, leaving a light tinnitus ringing in Kaine's ears. The car's front doors clicked open and thumped closed, and the driver fiddled with the filler cap.

A shadow darkened Kaine's pump and its chrome side panels reflected a bulging, angry face.

Oh dear. Here we go.

The Glaswegian dug a forefinger into Kaine's shoulder blade, just about the only place on his body that didn't hurt.

"Fuck's sake, man. What happened to your coupon? Your face?"

Kaine paused for breath.

Can I never catch a break?

He considered ignoring the big thug, but that would have likely made the situation worse. Kaine kept the fuel flowing and turned the left side of his face to the young man, making a point to show the difficulty he was having trying to see through his part-closed eye.

"My wife gets angry when I forget to put the loo seat down."

The Glaswegian took a moment before getting the joke. He guffawed, slapped the same place on Kaine's shoulder, and turned to his mate.

"Hear that, Purdy?"

The driver looked up from his filling task.

"What d'you say, young 'un?"

Purdy's accent came from south of the border, down Manchester way.

"This southern softie lets his wife beat him into plum jam. D'ye see his chops?"

"I think you'll find he's joking, Georgie."

The backpressure of a full tank activated the off-lock on the nozzle of Kaine's pump. He withdrew it and tapped it against the filler tube.

"Is that right, pal?" Georgie asked. "Youse taking the piss out o' me?"

The man edged half a step closer to Kaine and blocked his way to the pump.

"Do you mind, son? I'm in a hurry."

"No, mate, I dinnae mind at all. I asked youse a question."

Kaine straightened, looked up through his good eye, and stared the man down.

Taller than Kaine by at least eight centimetres, Georgie's shoulder muscles rippled beneath the overtight shirt, stretching the seams. His collar and tie dug into his thick neck and, judging by the man's ruddy skin tone, seemed to cut off some of the blood flow to his head. It might have explained the man's slow response rate. His biceps bulged, and a trim waist and flat belly showed off hours of gym work. He had blue irises, pink eye, and rounded everything off with coffee-and-cigarette breath.

Lovely.

"A question, you say?" Kaine asked, keeping his voice down.

"Aye."

"What question was that?" Kaine considered a smile, but Georgie wasn't worth the discomfort.

"I asked, were youse taking the piss?"

Kaine sighed. Much more of the halitosis and bluster would put Kaine over the edge, and he couldn't spare the time to put the young blowhard in his place.

"Not at all, Georgie. But, come to think of it, I will need the loo before I drive off."

"Funny man, eh? Purdy," he yelled to his mate, "this man thinks he's a comedian."

"Behave yourself, Georgie. Can't you see the man's getting angry. Wouldn't want to rile him up or he might set his wife on us."

Georgie's forehead wrinkled again and his eyes rolled up in his head as though lost in thought. Whatever he saw in the sky must have explained the gag, and he barked out a loud laugh.

"Brilliant, Purdy. You're the comedian, not this pussy-whipped arsehole."

Georgie scoffed at Kaine, turned on his heel, and marched towards the kiosk.

Kaine replaced the fuel pistol into its holster.

"Sorry 'bout that, pal," Purdy said, without sounding the least bit contrite. "He's got anger control issues. A short fuse. You did well not to annoy him too much."

Purdy winked and added a contemptuous sneer.

Kaine jerked up his chin in a minimal acknowledgement of Purdy's half-arsed apology and headed for the kiosk. He pushed through the door and turned his face from the camera. On his way to the counter, he collected a cheese sandwich, a bottle of sugar-free lemonade, a chocolate bar, two individually wrapped slices of fruit cake, and a bag of pear drops. All to replace his swindling stock of energy.

Up front, Georgie stood aggressively close to the man in the turban and his tiny wife. He kept edging closer until the man, pushed up against the counter, had nowhere to go.

"Fucking holding me up again, Gandhi?" Georgie growled into the man's ear.

The acne-scarred young woman at the till watched the spectacle from behind her reinforced-glass security screen, but said nothing. Kaine marched forwards, stopped within arm's reach of Georgie, and smiled at the Sikh couple.

"Everything okay here?"

Georgie turned his head and smiled as though expecting to see Purdy. His grin mutated into a smirk.

"Hey, look. It's pussy-whipped short-arse."

Georgie showed his back to the Sikh couple and faced Kaine. Waves of highly spiced body spray leeched across the short gap between them, but Kaine held his ground. Showing weakness at that point would only escalate the aggression and the last thing he needed was to draw any more attention to his existence than he already had.

"Hello again, Georgie," Kaine said, playing nice when he really wanted to remove the man's head from his shoulders. "Why don't you leave this man and his wife alone and we can all be on our way. No fuss, no bother."

"You what?" Georgie growled, leaning closer and misting Kaine with yet more halitosis.

Reluctantly, Kaine backed up a couple of paces, giving

himself room to operate. Without looking away, he lowered his provisions onto a display shelf that held rows of greetings cards and a stock of keyrings. He flexed his fingers, keeping his hands open, but prepared for action.

In the convex mirror above and behind the till, Kaine watched Purdy enter. The driver turned away from the action and towards a vending machine offering canned and hot drinks.

Georgie looked at his buddy and then at Kaine, clearly trying to make a decision. A vein at his temple distended and his face turned an even deeper shade of red. Kaine began to worry the kid might stroke out. He considered advising Georgie to loosen his collar, but doubted the advice would go down particularly well.

In the mirror, Purdy fed two coins into the machine, pressed a button, and bent to collect his winnings—a silver can of cola. Still half-turned away from the till, he pulled the ring tab and took a long, noisy slug.

Georgie balled his hands into fists and cracked his knuckles. His jaw muscles tensed and his nostrils flared, bull-like. The only actions missing to complete the image were for him to snort and maybe paw the floor with his hoof. Kaine had to force himself not to grin at the performance. The big fool was posturing for his older mate, but Purdy still hadn't looked up to appreciate the show.

"Steady, Georgie," Kaine whispered, holding up his hands. "You really don't want to do this."

"I don't?"

"At least not in here. We need more room."

Georgie's forehead wrinkled. "We do?"

His puffy eyes swivelled in their sockets as though taking in his surroundings for the first time. In the mirror, Purdy lowered his drink and looked towards them. When Purdy sighed and shook his head in apparent disappointment, Kaine dared to hope the older man would talk sense into his young mate and diffuse the situation. He didn't really want to hurt the kid, but, never one to rely on hope over expectation, he turned and took a couple of sidesteps away from the counter. To defend himself properly, he needed to see both men simultaneously and neither in reflection.

The Sikh man hugged his wife, and the trembling shopkeeper reached for a phone, possibly to summon the police.

Bugger it.

Kaine didn't need more company. Things were moving fast, but not in a direction he would have chosen.

Purdy threw the lock on the front door, flipped the hanging sign from "Open" to "Closed", and swaggered towards them.

"What you doing, Georgie?" he said. "Causing all kinds of trouble without me?"

Great. Another fine mess.

Georgie's lips peeled back in a savage smile that exposed a set of perfect teeth so bright, he must have just had them whitened.

"This arsehole's interfering with the natural order of things, Purdy. He thinks I'm being too hard on these fucking towel heads. Thinks they need his protection."

Purdy kept approaching until Kaine held up his hand and showed his palm. All he needed was a pair of white gauntlets and he'd have been able to pass for a policeman on traffic duty.

"That's close enough, Purdy," he said, keeping his voice even and his tone pleasant. "Don't come any further."

The driver stopped five metres away, sniffed, and raised the can to his lips once more. He drained it in one long, glugging swallow and belched loudly when he'd finished.

Keeping his eyes on Purdy, Kaine spoke again. "Georgie, why don't you let the nice couple pay their bill and go?"

The kid's cheeks flushed so dark, they blended nicely with the Manchester United kit on the toy bear sitting on the checkout counter.

Purdy wiped his mouth with the back of his hand and dropped the can. It crashed onto the tiled floor, the sound rattling through the quietened shop. An oppressive silence stretched out, broken only by the muffled sobs of the Sikh man's wife. Purdy shifted his weight onto his back foot and crossed his arms, exuding an easy confidence.

"And if he doesn't?" Purdy asked, still smiling. "What happens then?"

The words of Kaine's drill sergeant back at his SBS boot camp—a grizzled, old, cliché of a man—rattled around his head. "When in a standoff and outnumbered, consider your position carefully. If you can, withdraw. If you can't, stick the knife in first."

"Do you have an alternative suggestion?" Kaine asked.

Georgie snorted, but said nothing and allowed Purdy to answer.

"I could kick your scrawny arse for upsetting Georgie, or let him have some fun and do it himself. What do you reckon to that?"

Kaine made a show of checking his backside. "Scrawny? I've never had that complaint before."

He scratched his week-old beard and pursed his lips as though considering Purdy's suggestion. Then, he nodded.

"That's an interesting proposition and you're certainly welcome to try, but do you mind if I make a counter proposal?"

Purdy shifted his weight again and uncrossed his arms,

preparing for action. He looked useful, as though he'd seen plenty of combat.

"Go ahead. Surprise me."

"Excellent. Why not let these good people get on with their lives? I'll pay their bill and mine, and then the three of us can go over to the café area and discuss the possible effects of Brexit on future trade negotiations with Europe. What do you say?"

Georgie finally found his voice again. "Are you a Paki-lover?"

Without dragging his focus from Purdy, the one he considered the real threat, Kaine said, "Oh dear, Georgie. You've got that so wrong." He half-turned to address the Sikh couple. "If you'll excuse me talking on your behalf?"

The man's grateful smile was enough to give Kaine permission. Kaine turned his attention to Georgie and spoke as though trying to educate a toddler, but kept half an eye on Purdy.

"Sikhism originated in the Punjab region, Georgie. That's India, not Pakistan, and your pejorative term is rather offensive. Very un-PC. If you insist on being a racist, at least try to ground your bigotry in fact. You ought to be ashamed of yourself."

"Huh?" Georgie's face crumpled in confusion.

"Care to explain it to him, Purdy?"

Purdy nodded. "Yeah, okay. He just called you a moron, Georgie. As it happens, he's right, but you're *my* moron and he's just earned himself a serious kicking." He jabbed a finger at the Sikh couple. "You two. Fuck off and count yourselves lucky. Don't show your filthy, black faces around here no more."

The Sikh man, arm around his wife's shoulders, stood tall and spoke directly to Kaine for the first time. "Are you going to be okay, sir?" His accent, precise Home Counties English, put Purdy and the halfwit to shame.

"Don't worry about me, Mr …?"

"Singh. Dalip Singh. My wife and I are grateful to you, sir. Are you sure we should go?"

"Please do, Mr Singh. These idiots won't hold me up for long."

Georgie snorted again, but did nothing more than force the couple to step around him.

Kaine waited for Mr Singh to unlock the door and hurry his wife outside before speaking again, this time to the woman behind her security screen. "Did you just call the police?"

She nodded. "Aye, but they won't get here for half an hour." She threw a hand to her mouth as though realising she'd said too much. "Sorry, I … mean they're on their way."

"Not a problem," Kaine said, running the timetable in his head. "Better call for an ambulance, as well."

Georgie cackled. "That's right. You're gonna need one."

Purdy shook his head slowly. "He means for us, Georgie. The fuckwit's still being a comedian."

In the courtyard beyond the window, a group of irate customers who'd been unable to activate the pumps, stood in a huddle. Mr Singh took centre stage, waving his arms and pointing to the shop. It looked as though he was trying to drum up support for a rescue attempt.

Kaine sighed. He'd only stopped for diesel and provisions, and things looked likely to escalate into a full-scale battle. Time to end the mess before the wrong people started getting hurt. He checked the time on the clock above the counter. The police would be ages yet.

"Tell you what, Georgie," Kaine said, deliberately

turning his back to Purdy, but keeping the mirror in view. "Why don't we save a bit of time? You tell me which one of you I should hospitalise, and I'll let the other play nurse-maid until the ambulance arrives. Sound fair?"

In the mirror, Purdy nodded.

Georgie threw a slow and telegraphed left cross at Kaine's jaw. Kaine jinked inside it, blocked the blow upwards with his right forearm, and snapped a stiff-fingered jab deep into the kid's sweaty armpit.

Georgie screamed and collapsed to his knees, holding his right arm stiff against his ribcage. The colour drained from his face. His eyes stared wide, and his mouth opened and closed in a desperate fight for air.

Kaine stepped around and behind Georgie, his back to the till and made ready for the attack, but a wide-eyed Purdy hadn't moved. Kaine ruffled Georgie's hair as though comforting an unruly schoolboy.

"Relax, Georgie," he said. "Don't try to fight it. I paralysed your axillary nerve, but it's not permanent. You're in shock right now, but you'll be able to breathe normally in a minute or two. … Maybe three."

Georgie slumped against the newspaper display. Tears formed on his lashes but they were not yet ready to fall.

Kaine forced his breathing to calm. Stunning the kid hadn't taken much effort, but the adrenaline had started to pump through his system, and he needed to keep his reactions under control or he'd end up doing Purdy some real damage. Despite everything, he didn't want to inflict serious pain if he could avoid it.

Purdy's hand shot into his jacket and came out carrying an ebony-handled switchblade. A flick of the wrist and a twist of the fingers exposed the stainless-steel cutting edge in all its shiny danger.

The shopkeeper screamed. Georgie panted, breathing again as his nervous system began to recover from the hammer blow.

Kaine stiffened and followed the arc of the blade as a grinning Purdy waved it ahead of him. He slid one foot in front of the other, advancing slowly.

Hell.

Kaine should have expected little else, but the dark-haired extremist might just have sealed his own fate.

"C'mon, fucker. Come see what Purdy's got for you!"

Step-by-sliding-step, the man edged closer, keeping his balance and presenting a much more dangerous proposition than the lumbering Georgie.

Purdy chuckled. "I'm gonna slit you wide open."

Kaine shook the tension out of his hands, grabbed a newspaper from the stand at his side, and rolled it into a stiff baton.

Watch his eyes, Kaine. Take your time.

He sucked in a deep breath and waited for Purdy to make his second mistake, drawing the knife being his first.

Chapter Three

Wednesday 16th September – Afternoon

Killian Services, A84, Perthshire, Scotland

Kaine didn't react to Purdy's advance but kept watching and waiting.

Although the man looked the part with his balletic chassé advance and his horizontal knife-wave, he'd already shown Kaine an opening. The racist bigot favoured a right-to-left swipe.

Purdy reached Georgie and glanced down. "You all right, boy?"

Georgie's lips quivered but no words emerged. He shook his head. The tears had started flowing, but some of the red had returned to his face.

Kaine held a finger in the air. "Very touching, Purdy. You have one last chance to put that knife away."

Purdy pulled in his chin and hunched his shoulders. His feral eyes locked with Kaine's. "Yeah?"

Kaine used the slight delay to calculate the distance between them. "Take one more step and you'll be wearing that knife."

For the first time since he'd pulled the switchblade, doubt showed on Purdy's expressive face. He'd expected a different reaction—he expected Kaine to cower in fear. The dark-haired Englishman looked from Kaine to Georgie and back again.

"Cocky fucker, ain't ya."

"Confidence isn't cockiness if it's justified. Look at the headlines."

With his left hand, Kaine pointed at a tabloid's above-the-fold headline, *The Hunt for Ryan Kaine Intensifies*. Purdy shot a glance at the paper and took a moment to register the full-face photo beneath the banner.

A moment too long.

Kaine lunged, drove his makeshift baton into Purdy's face, and continued his advance.

Purdy's head jerked backwards, and he threw out his arms for balance. Kaine dropped the paper, seized Purdy's knife hand at the wrist, and twisted up and in, towards Purdy's face. The wrist bones creaked and Purdy screamed.

The knife hit the floor.

Kaine butted him in the nose.

Purdy collapsed faster than Georgie had done and lay in a heap, blood pouring from a shattered nasal bone. He threw both hands to his face.

"You broke my nose," he squealed. "You broke my fucking nose!"

Kaine squatted in front of the bloodied man, picked up the knife, and pulled in a long, slow breath. It hadn't taken as long as he'd feared. He still had plenty of time to make a clean getaway.

"Now remind me," he said, holding up the knife and sliding a thumb across the blade to test its edge. "What did I say I was going to do with this?"

Purdy whimpered and tried to back away on his arse, but the heels of his shiny, leather shoes failed to gain purchase on the flooring. Kaine shot out a hand and grabbed the broken Englishman by the hair. He stood and dragged the bully up with him. Purdy's eyes never left the tip of the blade.

"Wallet," Kaine said.

"Huh?" Purdy grunted.

Georgie struggled, trying to use his good hand to push himself up from the floor. Kaine stamped on his fingers, breaking at least one. The kid squealed and dropped back down onto his backside.

"Stay where you are, Georgie, or I might lose my temper. You won't like me if I lose my temper. I turn a nasty shade of green."

Kaine removed his foot. Georgie pulled the damaged fist tight to his chest, and cradled it with the other hand.

"Now, Purdy," Kaine said, moving the tip of the blade towards Purdy's left eye, but resting the keen edge against his cheek. "I'll have your wallet."

The Englishman pulled his head back, straining against the grip Kaine had on his hair.

"A robbery? You're robbing us?" Purdy said, his words thickened by the blood flowing from his nose into his mouth.

Kaine lowered the knife and tested its edge on Purdy's

silk tie. The blade cut through it in one clean stroke. The severed end fell to the floor and coiled into a red-and-yellow-striped snake. The bigot may not have been able to handle himself in a knife fight, but he certainly knew how to keep the blade nicely honed.

"I asked for your wallet. Please don't make me search for it."

Slowly, Purdy stuck a hand into his inside jacket pocket and drew out a bulging leather wallet. He passed it over.

"Thanks ever so much," Kaine said. "Now, be a good little, racist bully and sit on the floor next to your mate while I have a quick look."

Purdy didn't move until Kaine touched the blade to the side of his neck and added a slight downwards pressure. The man dropped to the floor and leaned against his young partner-in-bigotry. The blood from his nose had formed a large Rorschach blob on the front of his shirt. Kaine saw a vampire bat sitting on a three-bar gate in the stain and wondered what the psychoanalysts would make of it.

"Excuse me, Ms ...?" he called to the girl behind the security screen.

"Mary," she called. "My name's Mary. Jeez, that was some fancy, kick-ass shit you did then. Kung Fu, yeah?"

"I got lucky. That car accessory display over by the route maps. Do you have any heavy-duty cable ties?"

"Aye, we've got all types."

"How long before the police and ambulance arrive?"

She glanced at her watch, frowning. "I don't know."

"Best guess."

"Maybe twenty minutes?"

Not long, but enough.

Before he could ask her to fetch the restraints, the front door burst open and Mr Singh rushed in, closely followed

25

by a powerful-looking, black man in an oil-stained boiler suit.

"Mr Singh, can you fetch me a packet of those cable ties, please? The big grey ones. I'm getting tired of guarding these two."

"I'll do it, man," the mechanic said. He selected the correct type and ripped open the packet as he approached the bloodstained battleground.

Purdy squirmed away as the man drew closer. "Get your filthy, black hands off—"

Kaine drove a thumb into the hollow between Purdy's jaw and earlobe. He grunted and slumped against Georgie, out for the count.

"Shut it. I've had more than enough of your racist claptrap."

Kaine checked the nail on his thumb. It needed trimming. Had it been much longer he might have sliced open Purdy's neck.

Mr Singh moved close. Kaine was pleased to see he didn't appear scared of him, only grateful.

"Did you kill him?"

"Who, Purdy?" Kaine shook his head. "Nah, but he'll have a thumping headache when he wakes. Georgie won't feel a whole lot better, either."

As if to confirm Kaine's statement, Purdy snorted and a bubble of blood popped out of one nostril.

Kaine watched the mechanic straighten their legs, move them until they were leaning back-to-back, and secure their ankles and wrists.

"Looks as though you've done that before," Kaine said.

The mechanic's nod caused his beaded cornrows to rattle. "Use them t'ings all the time at work. These two ain't going nowhere, bro."

"Thanks for the help. Mary there"—Kaine jabbed a thumb over his shoulder in her general direction—"says the police and ambulance are on their way. Can you give me a moment with Mr Singh?"

"No problem," the mechanic said, waving a hand. "I need to fill my rig and hit the road. You did good here. Got yourself some fancy dance moves."

Mr Singh's broad smile showed through his tightly rolled beard. "Please, call me Dalip. My wife, Banee, and I thank you for what you did." He thrust out a hand and they shook. "Thank you. You risked everything for complete strangers, and for that, you have our eternal gratitude."

Dalip looked down at the bound men and spoke again, this time more quietly. "If you wish, I will stay with these two until the police and ambulance arrive and explain what happened. No doubt, you will wish to leave."

His brown eyes, calculating behind his thick glasses, gave Kaine a knowing wink. Kaine's hackles prickled.

Damn it, he knows.

"Excuse me?"

Dalip bent and pointed at the tabloid in the display. He leaned closer and whispered, "The police are wrong about you, Captain Kaine. No one who saw what you did here could believe you are a bad man, a terrorist. And I'll shout that from the rooftops if I have to." He clasped Kaine's upper arm. "The surveillance cameras will tell the world what happened here. Go now, before the police arrive."

"Thanks, Dalip. And you are right, the police don't have the full picture yet, but they will soon. Can you give me a minute? I need a quiet word with Georgie here and then I'll be on my way."

"Very well. Banee and I will keep the young woman

company. I can see she's had rather a shock, and we still need to pay for our petrol."

Kaine ripped the thick wad of banknotes from Purdy's wallet and offered it across. "Should be enough there to pay for your inconvenience. I'm sure these two won't mind."

Dalip waved the money away. "That would be theft, Mr Ka—sir. I can't accept."

Kaine pushed the wad forwards again. "Okay, stuff it in the charity box on the counter. The British Heart Foundation needs all the support it can get."

"Now, that," Dalip said, his smile stretching wider, "is something I *can* do."

He beckoned through the window to his wife. She rushed through the entrance door and joined her husband at the counter, whispering a breathless, "Thank you," to Kaine as she passed.

Kaine risked knee ache and squatted beside Georgie, who glowered at him.

"How's the arm and the fingers?"

No reply.

"Don't fancy a chat? Can't say I blame you. Better just listen then."

He held the business card he'd found in Purdy's wallet for Georgie to see.

"Can you read, Georgie?"

The young man's eyes flashed with anger, which turned to fear when they met Kaine's dead-eyed stare. He'd been told of its power a number of times and once again, it proved effective.

"I asked you a question, Georgie."

"Yeah … I can read."

"Good, good. So can I. This card tells me your friend, Mr Archibald Purdue, is membership director for the

British Nationalist Movement. An objectionable bunch of fascists dressed up as a political party. Are you a member, Georgie?"

He nodded.

"Thought you might be. Where's your wallet?"

Georgie nodded to the back pocket of his trousers and Kaine found a business card in the near-empty folder.

"Now, listen to me, George Albert Hanley, Assistant Director of Membership, and listen carefully. I'm keeping these cards right here next to my heart." He slid them into the breast pocket of his polo shirt. I'm also going to take the contact details of that nice Sikh couple and the woman behind the till. Oh, and the big guy with the dreadlocks. You arseholes operate through intimidation, but if anything nasty happens to any of those four nice people, I'll know about it. If they receive threats or correspondence from the BNM—no, scratch that … if *anyone* so much as looks at any of them sideways, I'll be coming after you and Purdy here. Do you understand me?"

Georgie sneered.

"What's up, Georgie. Don't believe me?"

"You cannae protect them on yer own. The BNM is everywhere. We'll get them fucking wops and the nigger, and then we'll come for *you*. Next time we'll be tooled up."

Kaine placed his hand on Georgie's shoulder and squeezed the tender spot between the trapezius and the neck. The racist winced.

"You're coming after me, Georgie?"

"Yeah … we will," Georgie answered, eyes averted.

Kaine released his hold on the pressure point and Georgie whimpered. "You'll have to stand in line, son."

"Huh?"

"You'd better know who to look for, right?"

He opened the newspaper, dropped it in Georgie's lap, and patted the mugshot on the front page.

"Ryan Liam Kaine, at your service."

"Wha—"

Kaine slapped Georgie's cheek, slamming the side of his head against the display shelving. He leaned closer. Georgie's chin trembled and a damp patch darkened the crotch of his trousers, showing above the tabloid.

"That's right, Georgie. You can tell all your friends you came face-to-face with the most wanted man in the UK, and he let you live to tell the tale. Just remember what I said, though." He patted the business cards in his pocket and whispered, "*I know where you work, and I can find you any time I choose.*"

Georgie snapped his jaws together and closed his eyes, all fight gone.

"That's better, Georgie. Keep your mouth shut and you might just survive into old age."

Kaine stood. Time was flying, but before leaving, he had one more task.

"Mary," he said, approaching her security barrier. "The surveillance cameras in the courtyard, can you operate them from here?"

She made a face and shook her head. "They're broken. Have been for weeks. I told the owner, but he's such a tightwad."

"So you don't have pictures of my car?"

"You mean your Fiat?" Mary asked, making a point to look anywhere but through the main window. "No pictures, not a one."

"I thought you drove a Renault, like mine," Dalip said, waving Kaine towards the main door.

Kaine nodded his thanks to them both. He dropped

four of his own twenties on the counter, picked up his shopping, and hurried from the kiosk to his car.

On his drive through the forecourt, Kaine took a snapshot of each vehicle's number plate with his mobile for future reference, and threw a salute to the dreadlocked mechanic, who was still filling his tow truck.

As he rejoined the A84, the first drops of rain spotted the Land Cruiser's windshield and the sky over the distant mountains glowered with even more anger and menace than the two fools he'd left behind.

Chapter Four

Wednesday 16th September – Afternoon

The Cairngorms National Park, A9, Aberdeenshire, Scotland

Despite the energy boost he received from the petrol station sandwich and chocolate bar, Kaine struggled to stay awake for the final part of the journey. The sleep-inducing effect of the metronomic wipers was hypnotic, but even at full speed, they struggled to clear the deluge from the windscreen. He had to fight to keep his good eye open and tried to remember the last time he'd had an uninterrupted night's sleep. Five days? Six?

He tried lowering the driver's window, but the rain drove in on the slipstream and soaked his arm through in seconds, and the wet slap in the face actually stung. The aircon, set to Arctic winter, helped a little, but allowed condensation to cloud the windscreen. The going was tough, but his destination drew ever closer.

In the hour since leaving the petrol station, he'd had time to reflect upon the stupidity of his actions. Despite the relative ease with which he'd taken care of Georgie and Purdy, the fight had taken its toll in terms of energy expenditure. It had also given him another, albeit minor, injury to add to the growing list. He'd bruised his right thumbnail on Georgie's jaw. Fatigue and a near-blind left eye had thrown off his depth perception and affected his aim. If the fascists had been stiffer opponents, Kaine might have had to hurt them more seriously to compensate.

To make matters worse, his tongue kept worrying away at the gap where his right upper canine used to be. The exposed root still screamed every time he sucked in a draft of cold air or bit down on that side, but the dentist could wait. Martin Princeton, if he still lived, most certainly could not.

No doubt about it, he should have left well alone. Mr and Mrs Singh would probably have been okay without his intervention but, damn it, he could never stand aside in the face of such racism and bullying.

Kaine. You are a bloody fool.

He needed to keep below the radar a little more. If the police had arrived more quickly than Mary predicted, he might have been arrested. His actions at the service station could have jeopardised his mission, and he couldn't push his luck any further. Running around acting as the world's protector might have led him into more danger then he could handle, and he had a much more important task on his hands. Martin Princeton needed his help, and that had to take priority in the short term.

Kaine yawned and winced at the pain caused by such a simple action.

Exhaustion itself was a danger. He needed to stay awake. Talking to someone would help. The thought of calling Lara Orchard quickened his pulse. Bloody stupid. He'd only known the beautiful vet a few days and, already, the mere thought of her had the power to turn his insides into a quivering blob of jelly.

Yeah. Bloody idiot.

He looped the hands-free unit into his ear, called out the number, and the mobile's voice-activated system took care of the rest.

Lara answered immediately. "Ryan? Is that you?"

Kaine's heart flipped at the relief in her voice. Hell, but it was good to hear her.

"Of course it's me. Who else knows your number?" he asked with forced severity.

"Thank God, I've been worried sick."

"We only spoke a couple of hours ago. No need to fret about me, lass. Everything's good here. What about you?"

"I'm worried, but okay."

"Rollo still there?"

Kaine had detailed Rollo as her minder, knowing the highly skilled, former-SBS sergeant would protect her with his life.

"Yes, do you need to talk to him?"

No, I'd rather talk to you.

"Not necessarily. Any news from our friend, Mr Jones?"

She hesitated before avoiding the question and asking, "Where are you now?" Even over the crackling mobile phone line, worry clouded her voice.

"About half an hour from where I'm headed," he answered, checking the rear-view mirror for blue flashing lights, more from force of habit than any real expectation of being found in the middle of the Scottish highlands. He hadn't seen a speed or ANPR camera in over an hour. In fact, he hadn't seen another vehicle since leaving the A84.

Even when chatting with the woman who had stitched together the twenty-centimetre knife wound along his ribcage a week earlier, he couldn't lower his guard. He trusted Lara with his life and had done so more than once in their short relationship. No way would she knowingly give up his location to the police, but on an open line, he couldn't take any chances. His personal security rules had saved his life on numerous occasions in the past, and he wasn't about to relax them any time soon.

For the hundredth time, he scanned his surroundings, roads and air. The weather conditions—low cloud, mist, and heavy rain—ruled out helicopter search flights, and he'd not seen a single police patrol car since leaving Killian Services. Scotland's police resources, as stretched as everywhere else in the UK, couldn't flood so large an area with bodies, at least not in so short a time. His luck had held again.

He dropped a gear and made a left at the signpost pointing to Lower Glencrae. With a little over ten miles to his destination, the roads were familiar to him—and had been for over an hour.

"Have you been listening to the radio?" she asked.

"Yes."

"You heard the police have announced Sir Malcolm's arrest?"

"I did indeed. Our mutual friend, Mr Jones, moved more quickly than I expected."

Kaine pulled the Toyota tight into the hedge to allow a tractor pulling a trailer the size of a shipping container to pass him without removing one of the Land Cruiser's wing mirrors.

"So why don't you hand yourself in to the police?" Lara asked, urgency in her voice. "It'll be much safer for you."

"We've been through this, Doc. Mart—the boy's been missing nearly two days. Even though it's early autumn, the weather up here can change in a heartbeat. He needs my help. Clearing my name can wait."

Clearing his name came a distant second to finding Martin Princeton.

"What do you hope to achieve that the search teams can't?"

"I know this region better than most of the locals. I've lived on those mountains, and I might be able to help refine the search grid."

"But until the police have confirmed Sir Malcolm's reward has been withdrawn, you're still a target for any mercenary who thinks one million pounds is a good enough reason to kill you. Come back, Ryan. Go into police protection. Please, for me."

The worry in her voice changed to urgency and pleading. Kaine hated to refuse her anything, but Martin Princeton's needs outweighed his own. He'd been protecting himself for more years than he cared to remember, and he'd rather rely on his own skills of self-preservation than those of a few poorly trained, under-resourced, and under-motivated police officers. Besides, with the deaths of so many people on his conscience, saving Martin Princeton had become his first step along the road to some form of personal redemption.

As if redemption were even a possibility.

Whenever he closed his eyes for sleep, Kaine could see the fireball blooming in the sky over the North Sea, taking with it the lives of eighty-three innocent passengers and crew. No matter what he did or how hard he tried, he'd never be able to forget the pain or fully assuage the guilt of his mistake.

On the drive to Scotland, he'd vowed to spend the rest of his life protecting the families of the victims. Eighty-three families would have a guardian angel, even if they never needed one—even if they never knew it. Eighty-three families—*The 83*.

Giving the group a name strengthened his resolve. His job now revolved around protecting The 83, no matter the personal cost to him.

And his new job started with Martin Princeton.

A ninety-degree, right-hand turn nearly caught him unaware. He stamped on the brakes and yanked on the steering wheel before the Toyota could plough into the ditch opposite. His compromised reactions—a combination of fatigue and impaired vision—were starting to take their toll. He needed sleep and medical treatment, but they would have to wait.

"Ryan, can you hear me?" Lara asked, cutting into his thoughts.

"Yes, sorry. I'm concentrating. The weather's terrible and the roads up here are a nightmare."

"I … I saw the video recordings."

"Sorry?"

"Mr Jones showed me the film of those men torturing you. Ryan, it was horrible."

"You should try being on the receiving end."

He'd have tried to laugh it off, but the array of injuries, including the rib wound, made laughing an uncomfortable option.

"Ryan," she snapped. "This isn't funny."

"I know, lo—"

He was going to call her "love", but caught himself in time. What the hell was he thinking? He barely knew her. Damned weakness could get him killed.

Kaine tried again. "I'm not doing anything dangerous. Only going to offer the search team my advice."

The road narrowed to a pitted and frost-damaged single lane, the hedges bulging out into intermittent passing places. It climbed sharply as he pushed ever deeper into the foothills of the Cairngorms.

"What if someone recognises you? The police and press are all over the rescue centre. It's a huge human interest story. Rollo and I have been watching the news."

Kaine eased back on the accelerator as the road degenerated further. English minor roads were bad enough, but the extreme weather in that part of Scotland made the surface appalling. He'd driven on better-maintained vehicle testing grounds.

Although it hadn't seemed possible, the rain increased in force and the Toyota's wipers were unable to cope. The torrent flowed down the windscreen, obscuring the view and making the going ever more treacherous. It wouldn't do young Martin any favours for Kaine to run his car off the road. The random thought gave him and idea. A car crash would give him an excuse for looking so beaten up.

"The way I look now, my mother wouldn't have recognised me. Rest her soul."

"Ryan Lia—"

"No full names, girl. You know better than that."

After a sharp intake of breath, she spoke again, this time so quietly he struggled to hear her over the engine noise, the rain hammering on the roof, and the clicking squeak of the wiper blades.

"I'm coming up there. Leaving right away."

"No! Don't you dare. It's not safe. Stay right where you are with Rollo and Mr Jones. They'll protect you."

"So, it's okay for you to put yourself at risk but not me?"

She's finally getting the message. About bloody time.

"Exactly. I'm trained for this. You're not. Mr Jones, can he hear you?"

"No, he's in the kitchen making a cuppa."

"What's he like?"

"You've never met him?"

"Of course not. I've only spoken to him once and that was on the phone. What do you make of him?"

She took her time to reply, which made Kaine's warning antennae quiver.

"He's been interviewing Sir Malcolm most of the day, but won't tell me what the psychopath is saying. Mr Jones is quiet, doesn't say much, but doesn't miss anything either. I like him, though. Reminds me of my dad."

"Do you trust him?"

"Yes. Without a doubt," she replied, this time without hesitation. "The way he reacted when we watched the tape of your torture showed how much he cared. It affected him almost as much as it did me. I think he wanted to go back into the interview room and give Sir Malcolm some of the same treatment. He wouldn't, though. I can tell. He's too honest, obeys the rules. Rollo thinks so, too."

"Okay. If you and Rollo give him the all clear, he's okay with me. Hang on."

He stopped talking to negotiate another tight S-bend and the gnarled hedgerows finally peeled back to reveal a vista as stunning as he remembered, despite, or maybe because of, the howling storm. The dark grey-and-blue Cairngorms rolled up from a sea of purple-and-yellow heather and green moss, and the crags disappeared into grey mist and black cloud. Rain lashed the countryside, thrown down on the wings of an angry storm.

"Damn," he said, not meaning to say it aloud.

"What's wrong?"

"The weather's closing in. Anyone caught out in this without the proper protection is in real trouble."

Two miles distant in an elevated position, the lights from dozens of houses shone bright in the late-afternoon gloom. Lower Glencrae, with its five-hundred-odd residents beckoned. Three miles beyond that, over the next major fold in the Cairngorm foothills, stood Upper Glencrae. His destination, Kinross Farm, lay another mile further north.

The rain continued to lash the heather and shroud the hills, but occasional tiny cracks in the cloud allowed shafts of orange to flood patches of land in halos of sunny optimism.

At least the rain would keep the midges—little buggers —at bay.

"What are you wearing?" Lara asked, once more cutting through his musings.

"Sorry? Is this going to turn into one of 'those' calls where we discuss each other's underwear?" He smiled and stretched the cut on his lip.

"For God's sake, be serious for one moment, will you?" she growled.

Lara Orchard actually growled. Kaine nearly laughed out loud. God it was good to have someone who cared. He couldn't remember the last time he'd allowed anyone to peel back his protective layers. It was good. Scary, but good.

"The last time I saw you," she continued, "you were dressed as a burglar. When have you had the chance to change into mountain gear?"

Kaine risked tearing his eyes from the road for a second to take in his ensemble. Thin jacket, dark blue polo shirt, black chinos, and trainers. Possibly the worst-dressed mountain rescuer in the history of the discipline. More suited for a night-time pub crawl than a day-time scramble over granite outcrops.

"Don't worry, Lara. I'll do some shopping when I reach my destination."

"Shopping in the middle of the—"

"Lara. Don't say anymore. I'm sorry, but I have to hang up now. Please do exactly what Rollo and Mr Jones tell you. I can't be worrying about you while I'm up here. Okay?"

No response.

"Okay?" he repeated with more force.

"Okay," she said, obvious reluctance causing her to mumble.

"Thank you. I'll phone the moment I have any news. Bye."

He ended the call before she could say anything else and instantly regretted his abruptness. She was only trying to help and he'd shot her down. Somehow, he'd find a way to make it up to her.

Somehow.

Maybe the best thing would be to never see her again, but that would be horrible. Horrible for him if not her.

The conversation with Lara had given him an idea. To put it into operation, he needed to make another call, but it took some time to dredge up the number from his overtaxed brain. Eventually, he called it out to the device. He half-expected to hear a voicemail response, but the phone line clicked and the connection was instantaneous.

"'Allo? Qui c'est?"

"Sabrina? It's me, your old friend from this morning. Glad to hear you made it home in one piece. How's Paris?"

"Oh, *merde*. I did not expect to hear from you so soon. To answer your question, Paris is as beautiful as always and, of course, far superior to London."

Kaine managed a tight grin. Although she'd acted as much in her own interests as in his, the gifted, French IT specialist had been an unexpected and invaluable asset in his efforts to capture Sir Malcolm. Without her on his side, Kaine would have failed. He already owed Sabrina as much as he owed Lara, and he was about to increase the debt.

"Tell me, *mademoiselle*, do you have easy access to a computer and a decent internet connection?"

She sighed heavily.

"What do you require now?"

———

IN SPITE of being forced to slow the Toyota to a crawl, the narrow main street of Upper Glencrae rolled past in a swirl of rain-splashed houses and double-parked cars, and disappeared in Kaine's rear-view mirror in seconds. He dropped another gear and engaged four wheel drive for the final, steep climb into the gravelled parking area of Kinross Farm Mountain Rescue Centre.

He pulled in behind a spanking new, but mud-spattered Fiat Fullback. The slick beast would have had no trouble negotiating the track up to Kinross Farm, but at least half of the other vehicles parked nose-to-tail wouldn't have found it as easy. Equally muddy trucks and off-roaders stood interspersed with panel vans and campers, some with satellite dishes and long, raking antennae that whipped in the gale-force winds.

Police vehicles, parked at the front of the jam, had clearly been unable to bring order to the chaos. Kaine paused for a moment to take in the scene.

Externally, the place hadn't changed much in the years since his last visit. The three-storey, granite farmhouse with its low-slung blockhouses still seemed hewn directly out of the face of *Ben Craed*, Scotland's seventh highest peak. Apart from the biggest, *Ben Nevis*, he doubted many people outside the mountain climbing community could name any of the mountains in between.

Unless it had undergone a complete revamp since his last visit, the main office building comprised one large meeting room for lectures and operational briefings, lock-able storerooms at the back, a kitchen mess area, a small emergency clinic, and a shower block. If possible, he'd use both the shower and the clinic before becoming part of the search team. With luck, the well-stocked storerooms would come in handy, too.

Kaine eased the baseball cap onto his head, trying unsuccessfully to avoid the tender lump above his left ear.

Using the Fiat and the other tall vehicles as cover, Kaine climbed out of the Toyota and grimaced against the pain. After driving for the best part of ten hours—with just the one enforced stop for fuel and the fight—every muscle and joint in his body screamed against the sudden change in position.

He grabbed the large, military backpack from the rear seat—the spare Bergen he'd collected from his safe house in Camden—and slung it over one shoulder.

A mess of Jeeps, Range Rovers, Motorhomes, and high-sided media trucks stood between him and Kinross Farm. Six uniformed police officers, imposing in their reflective, yellow tabards and flat, peaked caps with their black-and-white-chequered bands, formed a human barrier between the press and the buildings. A portly, silver-haired police inspector stood on a step in front of the main door, addressing the gathering.

Moving gingerly and keeping his shoulders hunched against the rain and to hide from the massed ranks of the Fourth Estate, Kaine edged around the side of the crowd. The rain helped his cause as most of the media types sheltered beneath colourful golf umbrellas. Kaine kept his face turned from the police officers, but needn't have worried about being recognised. They had their hands full struggling to control the squabble of journalists who battled each other to win "the most ridiculous question of the day" contest.

One rain-bedraggled and heavily made-up blonde woman came up with the classic, "Is the harsh weather hampering your search?"

The question rendered the tubby inspector speechless for a moment, but Kaine didn't hang around long enough to catch his reply. He took a path that led around the side of Kinross Farm and ducked behind a stone outbuilding. No one shouted, no one stood in his way, and no one took any notice.

The back of the compound was deserted and Kaine relaxed a little. The short climb on loose chippings had loosened his joints and warmed his stiffened muscles. By the time he found the rear entrance to the main house, he was moving with much of his natural fluidity, or at least as much as he could reasonably expect given his discomfort and all his minor injuries.

As usual, the rear door was unlocked and would remain so until the team leader called an official end to the emergency.

Kaine pushed through the entrance and stepped inside, pulling the door closed behind him. He stopped and listened. The hubbub outside cut its way through the stone walls and double-glazed windows, but the words weren't clear enough to understand.

Ahead, the corridor stretched out for fifteen metres, two doors let into each wall. The ones on the left led to toilets and the clinic, the ones on the right guarded the storerooms —mountain rescue equipment in the first, clothing in the second.

Kaine turned the handle on the second door, it opened. He dived inside ... and crashed into a man-mountain, whose massive arms encircled a huge pile of clothing.

A scowl gouged deep grooves into the man's weather-beaten face. The huge man's bushy, red beard peeled back to reveal a set of teeth that wouldn't have embarrassed a grizzly.

"And who the hell might you be?"

Chapter Five

Wednesday 16th September – Early Evening

**Kinross Farm MRC, The Cairngorms,
Aberdeenshire, Scotland**

Rufus Redbeard stood at least six foot four inches tall. Kaine stepped back, giving the big guy space to breathe. He stood up straight, shoulders back, at a semi-formal attention.

"Staff Sergeant Peter Sidings," he said, forcefully. "Call me Peter. I'm here to help."

He thrust out a hand but the big man looked at the bundle in his arms.

Kaine held up his other hand and pointed at the clothes. "Need a hand with those, mate?"

Rufus' frown smoothed from a relief map of the

Himalayas into the gullies and channels of the mountain range out back behind Kinross Farm MRC. He turned sideways and nodded at a second bundle teetering on a stool in the far corner of the over-stuffed room. "Since ye asked, grab that wee stack and follow me."

Kaine edged his way past the giant and picked up his load—thermally insulated waterproof jackets and outer leggings, at least three sets of each. A quick glance around showed him the recent fundraising campaigns had been successful. Helmets, gloves, and mountain boots, all new, filled the shelves.

That was easy.

"These are nice," he said to Rufus' back. "Better than the threadbare rags you had last time I worked here."

The man stopped outside the door and allowed Kaine through before balancing his load on a raised knee and pulling the door closed. "Aye. A donation from a grateful patron. Bloody expensive kit it is, too. Saves us having to buy our own." He paused for a moment to study the man he must have taken for an interloper. "So, been here before, have ye?"

Kaine nodded. "A few years back. Is Big Sandy still around?"

The giant slowly shook his head. "'Fraid not. He copped it a couple o' years back."

Kaine had read of Sandy McAlister's death. He'd run into trouble during an apparently benign, low-altitude rescue a couple of winters back. Sandy's demise meant it was unlikely for any of the current crop of volunteers to recognise Kaine. At least that was the theory he'd been relying on since deciding to make his way to the highlands.

Rufus headed along the corridor towards the front of the building, but eased to one side to allow enough room for them to walk two-abreast. Kaine felt tiny beside the giant of a man, but the Scot's deep voice was melodious rather than threatening.

"That's terrible. Sandy was a fixture here," Kaine said and then kept quiet, waiting for the man to elaborate.

"Aye. A couple o' English fellows took a wee stroll in a blizzard without the proper cold-weather gear. Sandy died trying to drag them home."

"What happened to them. The English fellows?"

Rufus' gaze seemed to drift into a memory.

"Like Sandy, they didnae make it," he said, shaking his head slowly.

Kaine didn't feel the need to comment.

The corridor led to the kitchen. It had been refurbished since Kaine's last visit. Stainless-steel surfaces had replaced the elderly, bleached-pine originals. A huge urn of water steamed quietly in the far corner, and an elderly couple stood side-by-side constructing a healthy mound of egg mayonnaise sandwiches. Next to them, a thirty-something woman with flowing, auburn hair, muscular arms, and powerful thighs, spooned jam into small bowls that stood next to a huge pile of scones. Kaine's mouth watered at the thought and his stomach rumbled so loudly, he felt certain it must have echoed around the kitchen. As if to confirm his suspicion, the younger woman raised her eyes to look at him. Her mouth formed a sympathetic "O" as she caught sight of his face. She dropped the jam-covered spoon into the jar and rushed over to them.

"Drew McTay," she said to Rufus, or rather, Drew. "What are you doing forcing an injured man to carry such a load?" She wrenched the pile of clothes from Kaine's arms and placed them on an empty stool. They staggered and threatened to topple, but she steadied them with her hand.

Drew turned to study Kaine's face as though for the first time. "Bloody hell, now. I couldn't see yer face in the shadows back there. What happened to ye, man?"

Kaine spoke through the side of his mouth that had sustained the least amount of damage, trying to hide his missing tooth. "Mind if I explain it to Sandy's replacement? It'll save me having to repeat myself." He turned to the woman. "I'm sure it looks a lot worse than it is, Ms …?"

"Iona," she said, casting a twinkling-eyed glance at Drew. "Iona McTay. That brawn wi' no brains and no eyes is my big brother, Andrew. I have no idea what I've done in my life to deserve such a burden, but …" She dragged out a heavy sigh and relaxed her shoulders. "I'm told the Good Lord never gives us more than we can carry."

Drew groaned and dropped his load onto the stool beside the first one and used one pile to steady the other. "Ach, will ye listen to the shrew. I've been looking after her ever since she was in nappies, and she gives me nothing but earache."

The older couple, who had paused for a moment to check the commotion, looked at each other. The man raised his eyebrows and shrugged as if to say, "They're at it again." His partner nodded her agreement and they turned their backs and resumed prepping the food. They continued talking quietly, heads together as though deep in collusion.

Steam flickered up from a huge, stainless-steel pot on the stove. The enticing aroma of meat stew added to the welcoming ambience and once again, Kaine's stomach made its needs known.

Iona leaned closer to her brother and thumped his upper arm. "Away now and fetch Gregor, while I tend to this man's needs."

"Yes, boss," he said, winking at Kaine. "Right away, boss."

The big chap wandered towards the main office, complaining about his lot in life. Over by the sandwich counter, the elderly man ripped a length of transparent wrap from a holder on the wall and used it to cover the mini *Ben Nevis* mound of sandwiches. Kaine's stomach rumbled again. "Sorry Ms McTa—"

"The name's Iona. And was it your stomach giving off that hideous noise? When did you last eat, Mr …?"

Kaine fell into his well-rehearsed routine. "Staff Sergeant Peter Sidings. Peter, to my friends. And again, my apologies for the 'noises off'." He patted his guilty belly, making sure to avoid the tender and barely healed wound running along his ribs. "I had breakfast this morning and a sandwich during the drive, but … clearly, it wasn't enough." He tilted his head in the direction Drew had taken. "I don't hear much noise from the big room. Are those sandwiches for the reporters?"

"Not at all," she said, pointing him to one of the tables. "Those people can pay for their own grub down in the village. This food's for the police and the volunteers. We're waiting on a search team from Aberdeen this evening. They'll stay in the lodge overnight and make a start at first light. We cannae let them take to their beds without a decent meal inside them, now can we?"

"No, I don't suppose you can. What about the local search teams?"

"Some of them will stay out overnight, but the rest will be here by full dark."

Kaine checked the digital clock on the wall over the heads of the two cooks—18:53—and ran a quick calculation. With a maximum of three hours of daylight—less with the heavy cloud cover—he had no chance of doing anything worthwhile before dawn. He'd use the time to rest, recover, and wheedle his way onto one of the search teams.

"Coffee or tea?" she said, dropping a strong hand on his shoulder and "encouraging" him to sit.

If she'd used any more force, he might have broken the chair.

"Coffee please. White, no sugar."

"Coming right up. And ye'll have a bowl of stew and a sandwich or two?"

"Only if you insist," Kaine answered, adding the best smile he could manage without splitting his lip any further.

His mouth watered at the thought of hot food.

The older woman took command of the stew pot. She rescued a large bowl from the drying rack by the sink, ladled it full of the steaming stew, and walked it to Kaine's table. At the same time, her co-conspirator pulled three triangular sandwiches from under the plastic sheet, placed them on a side plate, and set it beside the bowl.

"That'll be forty pounds, please," he said, holding his hand out as though expecting to be paid in advance.

Kaine looked from one to the other and then at Iona, but she stared back at him through impassive, green eyes.

"No problem," he said, reaching into his hip pocket for his wallet.

The man's laugh started as a high-pitched rumble and burst from a thin-lipped mouth to blend with the gleeful titter of his partner-in-jest. Iona's formerly expressionless face broke into a grin bright enough to lift the gloom from the dull afternoon.

"Oh Peter. The look on your poor face, what we could see of it through all that bruising. I could swear you were thinking all the rumours of Scots being the meanest race on earth were true."

Kaine hesitated a moment before shaking his head. "No, that's not it at all, Iona. I was wondering whether the forty quid included a service charge."

His comment generated a belly laugh from the man and a screech from the woman.

"Did you hear that, Gretchen?" the old man howled. "A service charge. We'll have tae use that one next time."

Gretchen held her sides. "Aye, that we will, Jock. That we will. You're all right, Peter Sidings. You'll fit in well around here."

Jock? His name's Jock?

How much more Scottish could he be?

"That's Staff Sergeant Sidings to you, Gretchen. And don't you forget it," Kaine said. He would have added a wink, but the swollen left eye made it impossible.

Gretchen stood as tall as someone who barely tipped the measure at five foot nothing could manage and straightened her face. "Staff Sergeant indeed. Ye'll be expecting us to salute next."

Kaine shook his head again. "Absolutely not. Non-commissioned officers don't rate a salute. We're the grunts who do all the work, not the officer classes who sit around taking tiffin."

Out of sight of the laughing duo, Kaine pulled two fifty-pound notes from his wallet. He handed them to Iona and whispered, "Consider that a donation to the cause. I know how tough it is to run a volunteer service, and I've recently received a bonus."

Kaine thought of the millions of Euros sitting in his offshore account—money he'd coerced out of Sir Malcolm Sampson in return for sparing the man's worthless life. It wasn't exactly Kaine's money, but it *was* his to distribute as he saw fit. Donating to causes as worthy as mountain search and rescue seemed fitting enough.

Iona pocketed the cash and nodded her thanks. She poured herself a tea and sat across the table from him.

"Eat, man," she said. "Don't let it get cold."

Kaine grabbed a spoon and worked the mutton stew into his face past the cut lips, while trying to avoid the gap where his tooth used to be. Eating wasn't proving an easy task. If it had been less like a stew and more like a consommé, he'd have asked for a straw. But, if he was going to be any use in tomorrow's search, he needed to regain some of his strength. He continued eating through the pain barrier.

He managed another four spoonfuls of the delicious offering and one of the sandwiches, while watching the weather pitch and yaw through the wide windows. The cloud cover had lifted a little, but not enough for it to have stopped raining. The frustration of waiting for it to clear while a teenage boy lay lost and possibly injured in the hills did nothing to improve his mood or his appetite.

Iona sipped her tea slowly and hardly took her eyes off him. Her scrutiny became worrisome. Despite the injuries and the week-old growth of beard, did she recognise him from his broadcast mugshot?

"Is your jaw damaged?" she asked as though sensing his discomfort.

Kaine shook his head, relieved. Her visual examination had clearly been medical, not judicial. He tipped another spoonful of stew into his mouth and dabbed some spillage from his beard.

"It's just that you're not eating on the left side. I'm worried about damage to your facial nerves."

"You're a doctor?"

"Aye. Those bruises are recent," she said, leaning closer, her eyes narrowing. "Within the last twenty-four hours at the latest. What happened?"

Time to lie.

The truth certainly wouldn't help him gain the acceptance of the rescue community.

"Car accident in North Wales. A minor shunt, but the airbag failed to deploy. Looks worse than it is, but if you don't mind I'll save the explanation—"

"Until you have a chance to talk to the boss?" she interrupted.

"That's right. I don't want to appear rude, but that way will be more efficient."

She drained her cup and leaned back. "Understood. Finish your grub and come find me when you're ready tae get cleaned up. I'll find you a towel and some soap."

Kaine patted his Bergen. "I have supplies, but I'll need some wet weather gear for tomorrow." He let his eyes wander across to the pile of clothes on the stools.

"I'm sure we can kit you out … once you've spoken to Gregor."

"Gregor's the team leader?"

"That's right. Gregor Abercrombie. D'ye know him?"

Kaine scrolled through his memory banks but, thankfully, drew a blank. "Not as far as I know."

The door to the office opened and a man the size and shape of a small dump truck bustled into the kitchen. Although considerably shorter than Drew, he almost had to turn sideways to make his shoulders squeeze through the doorway. He nodded at Iona and the two old jokers in turn, and then focused his attention on Kaine. He sniffed as though unimpressed by what lay before him.

In Gregor's position, Kaine would likely have reacted in the same way. Kaine's dishevelled appearance wouldn't have inspired much confidence in a man leading the search.

"So, you're Sidings?"

Gregor's voice was surprisingly gentle, coming from a brutish face, but his eyes were intelligent, and didn't seem to miss much.

Kaine stood and faced him. They were about the same height, but that's where the similarities ended. Gregor Abercrombie looked wide enough to accommodate two of Kaine and presented as a symphony of grey—grey hair, grey beard, grey eyes, but ruddy cheeks.

"Staff Sergeant Peter Sidings," Kaine said. "Please call me Peter."

Gregor's huge mitt enveloped Kaine's offered hand, and Kaine braced himself for a hand-squeezing contest but was pleasantly surprised. The team leader's grip was firm, but not vice-like. He clearly didn't feel the need to demonstrate his strength to newcomers. Kaine took it as a good sign. The man might actually be prepared to listen to what he had to say.

"What happened to your face?"

His accent, educated and lowland, possibly from Edinburgh, was softer than the locals' harsher brogue and showed him to be a fairly recent arrival to the region. For him to have taken over from Sandy as leader of a tight-knit mountain rescue team showed promise. The man would definitely have needed skills or the locals wouldn't have followed him to the pub, let alone up a mountain.

"Car accident," Kaine repeated. "It delayed my arrival, or I'd have been here by midday."

Gregor took in the food on the table. "I see you've made yourself comfortable. Mind if I join you?"

He sat beside Iona without waiting for her consent. Kaine returned to his meal.

"Why are you here?" Gregor asked.

No preamble or bluster. Gregor's direct approach reminded him of DCI Jones, and Kaine appreciated it.

"To offer my help."

"What makes you think we need it?"

Iona turned her head to look at Gregor. The two cooks stopped all pretence at working and turned to earwig the conversation. Kaine only had one chance to make a first impression. He stared into Gregor's steely eyes. This was no time to pull his punches.

"The boy's still missing. You need all the qualified help you can find."

The door to the main office swung open again and Drew filled the doorway. He stood still, blocking the way of anyone who cared to interrupt.

Gregor's bushy beard rippled as his mouth formed a thin line. "I've never seen or heard of you before. In what way are you qualified?"

Kaine had a story prepared, but the details wouldn't hold up unless Sabrina had been able to work her magic. If she hadn't, and if Kinross Farm had been kitted out with a decent internet service since his last visit, they'd be able to expose his cover story in minutes.

Still, he didn't have much option if he wanted to help Martin Princeton.

"Back when Sandy was still in charge here, I was part of the team who ran the mountain preparedness course at HMS Whiteheath."

Gregor's eyes widened and the, "Bloody hell, now!" from Big Drew in the doorway generated the reaction he expected. Iona frowned and shot her brother a querying look.

Drew closed the door behind him and advanced into the kitchen-diner as though he was launching a full-frontal assault on a well-defended beachhead.

"You were in charge of The Beasting?" he demanded, excitement speeding his words.

He pulled one of the chairs out from under their table, dropped into it, and rested his elbows on the wooden surface. The unfortunate piece of furniture creaked in protest.

Jock and Gretchen drew closer. Kaine could almost hear their joint intake of breath.

"The Beasting?" Iona asked, one eyebrow arching.

Drew looked at his sister. "That's the selection process for the Special Boat Service. I've heard it makes the SAS selection programme look like a job interview at Pizza Hut. Is that true, Peter?" he asked, looking at Kaine with a degree of wide-eyed admiration.

Gregor's expression was more considered, more guarded.

Kaine nodded and toyed with his soup spoon as Drew continued his effusive explanation.

"Man, I've heard all sorts of stories about The Beasting. Five-mile sea swims in midwinter, scaling cliffs in full battle dress but without tethers, fifty-mile orienteering races through the night and against the clock. Are they rumours or the truth?"

Kaine needed to stay as close to fact as possible to make his real lies seem less like total fabrication.

"Some truth, some embellishment, but I can't go into detail. However, I do know this area well and I can prove it."

Gregor took up the challenge. "How can you do that at this time of the evening? Why shouldn't I just have you thrown out of here on your backside?" he asked with no sign of jest.

Kaine worked out the odds. Given the combined size and weight of the two men, and his own injuries, they might have a slight advantage over him, but he doubted it. He locked eyes with Gregor to make sure he had the team leader's undivided attention.

"Show me your search vectors on an OS map, and I'll talk you through the terrain of each area you've already cleared."

Drew bared his teeth in a smile. "This I've got tae see. And *you* might want to throw the man out o' here, Gregor, but ye'll be trying it on yer own. I'm no' inclined to go up against an SBS training officer who helped design and run The Beasting." His laugh, a cross between a roar and a cough, was entertaining and apparently heartfelt.

Gregor struggled to his feet and stood over Kaine. "Fair enough, Staff Sergeant Sidings—"

"Peter," Kaine said. "My friends call me Peter."

The grey-haired man nodded. "Do they, indeed. Come through to the big office and impress us all with your in-depth knowledge of this wee patch of Scotland."

Kaine let go of the spoon and raked his hands through his new beard. "Before I do that, there is one small problem."

"Which is?"

"I'd rather not show my face in public."

Iona spoke next. "Don't worry, Peter. You don't look that scary. People around here won't be put off by a few bruises."

"It's not that," he said, keeping his voice low. "It's not that, at all."

"What's the problem then?" Gregor demanded, clearly seeing his doubts confirmed.

Kaine pointed at the big man standing over him. "You know don't you, Drew?"

The redhead's mobile face showed confusion. "I do?"

"Who's out there?"

Kaine waited for the information to work its way into the large Scotsman's head. It took a couple of beats longer than Kaine expected.

"The police, you mean?" Drew asked. "Are you wanted by the police?"

Gregor's big hands clenched into fists.

Kaine didn't move.

Chapter Six

Wednesday 16th September — Early Evening

Kinross Farm MRC, The Cairngorms, Aberdeenshire, Scotland

"The police?"

Iona jumped up and backed away from the table. Drew stepped into the gap between her and Kaine to form an unnecessary protective barrier, but one Kaine appreciated. He'd have done the same thing if Lara or Sabrina had faced potential danger. Or anyone else, come to that.

Kaine eased his back into his chair and raised a hand to calm them. "No, I'm not worried about the police."

With the false name, the false cause of his injuries, and the misdirection of where he came from, he'd told nothing but a pack of lies since entering the building. He didn't enjoy misleading good people, but had no alternative.

"It's nothing to do with the long arm of the law, but everything to do with that pack of hyenas out there in the car park."

He waited for Drew, the man with the obvious military interest, to work out his meaning. It slowly dawned on the big guy and the clouds rolled across his face at the same time as a solitary shaft of sunlight broke through clouds.

"Aye, right. Of course," Drew said, clapping Kaine's shoulder. "SBS guys like to go incognito."

Kaine shrugged and added a little head tilt. "The first rule of Fight Club is …"

A beaming Drew finished the quote. "…you don't talk about Fight Club."

Gregor's big, grey head dipped once. Kaine assumed it was his version of a nod. "That's going to make things a little awkward for you."

"Sorry. I'd normally stay in the background or wear a ski mask, but this"—he waved a hand in front of his face—"makes it a little uncomfortable. Can you bring the map in here?"

"'Fraid not," Gregor said, shaking his head. "It's not a paper map. We have the terrain superimposed onto electronic whiteboards which are constantly updated with the latest satellite images showing the weather conditions. We also track the search teams' locations through GPS."

"You're kidding."

Things had certainly moved on since Kaine's last visit to the centre. The mention of a live internet feed sounded a row of alarm bells in his head, but he'd dived into the water with both feet and needed to complete the swim.

"You don't have one-to-1250 scale OS maps of the area?"

Gregor let out a growl. "Of course we do, but if you want an up-to-date sitrep, you'll need to see the screens. And while you're convincing me you know what you're talking about, I'll have Iona check your credentials." He nodded at the medic.

"Fair enough."

Kaine pulled out his wallet again and handed Iona his cover's business card and driving licence. "Currently, I'm Deputy Head of Transport Security for CSS. You might have heard of us."

"Conqueror Security Services?" Gregor asked. "The people who protect foreign dignitaries?"

"That's right. I'm just back from a job in the Irish Republic, which is why I was on the Dublin-to-Holyhead ferry. We docked at 05:25 this morning and some idiot towing a caravan cut me up on the A55, three miles west of Colwyn Bay. Hence my delayed arrival and all this."

Again, he waved a hand in front of his bruised face. Hopefully, he'd given them enough detail to sound convincing, but not enough for them to verify unless someone there had a contact in the North Wales Police Service. If they did, his game was up. He doubted Sabrina would have had time to plant the information into the North Wales Police's telephone logs.

Iona read the details on his business card, but made no move to leave. She was clearly interested in seeing him defend his grandiose claims.

Nobody moved or spoke until Kaine rubbed his hands together.

"Can we get on with it? I want to prove my worth so we can move forwards with a plan for tomorrow. Your search teams will be here soon, and Iona tells me you're expecting additional support from Aberdeen around now."

Gregor's beard bristled. "She did, did she?"

"And what's wrong with that?" Iona asked. "It's no' a secret. Inspector Gadget out there's just made the announcement to the media."

Her "Inspector Gadget" crack caused the Greek Chorus over by the food prep area to cackle loudly. Gretchen elbowed Jock in the arm and he cawed like an ancient crow.

"I take it Inspector Gadget is the … how shall I say this … the well-rounded police officer addressing the massed ranks of the Fourth Estate?" When Iona confirmed his assumption, Kaine continued. "Don't tell me he and his officers are playing any part in the search?"

Gregor snorted and said, "Not at chance, man. It'd be far too dangerous to let him or his men loose on the mountain. We'd end up with more lost souls to save than the poor lad. No. They're here to run interference with the media and to maintain crowd control. So long as we keep Inspector *Gaskell*"—he glared at Iona, daring her to laugh again—"in the loop, he's happy to stay out of the way."

"Aye, that's right," Jock said, drying his hands with a dishcloth. "Likes his moment in the limelight does Francis Gaskell. Same as his father and grandfather afore him. Always on their soapboxes that family. Shoulda been politicians."

"Too right," Drew said, "but he'll keep the press at bay, and that's a great help."

"Well then, Sergeant Sidings, if you've finished your free meal, let's get to work," Gregor said and headed towards the front office.

"Lead on, boss," Kaine said. "I'll follow."

Kaine stood with a damned sight more difficulty than

the older man seemed to, and the four of them headed towards the office. Kaine hung back to allow Iona to pass and followed her into a room that could have passed for the operations hub of a meteorological centre.

The basic footprint hadn't changed—a large L-shaped room, office tables and chairs to the left, and an open area in the centre for group gatherings and equipment maintenance when the weather outside was unwelcoming. Apart from that, the place was completely different.

The nerve centre of the operations room occupied the foot of the "L", which contained four desks, each with a flat-screen monitor and a keyboard—the absence of trailing cables confirmed full wireless connectivity. Two of the desks were occupied by a man and a woman wearing wireless headsets. Apart from the two comms people and the four of them, the office stood deserted.

To Kaine's left, a huge, floor-to-ceiling, touchscreen whiteboard covered the longest wall. It showed a topographical map of the region. As Gregor had promised, a direct link to the Met Office layered moving isobars and isotherms over the stationary map. The signs weren't good. The depth and power of the storm system showed no signs of weakening or moving away, at least not overnight.

On the wall adjacent to the main screen, another large whiteboard had been segmented into eight smaller windows. Each window showed a large-scale map of a dedicated search area, and each window had a designation from ST1 to ST8. The last three screens were blank, presumably set aside for the arrival of the teams from Aberdeen.

The IT and comms setup appeared to be state-of-the-art, one Sabrina would no doubt have salivated over. Someone had tapped into a good source of funding from somewhere.

"Blimey," Kaine said. "Things have changed. Last time I was here, you were relying on paper and pen. Where'd you find the money for all this? Have you become fulltime professionals since the Scottish Nationalists took power?"

Standing beside Kaine, Gregor scoffed. "Not at all. We're still independent volunteers and proud of it. All this" —he nodded to indicate the technology—"came from the one source."

"Impressive," Kaine said, hoping for more information to give him time to study the screens and generate a feel for the search operation so far.

Gregor held up a hand to keep them in place while he marched to the comms annex, allowing Drew to elaborate.

"Three winters back, a family got themselves stranded in a whiteout. Their teenage son broke his leg in a fall. Compound fracture of the femur. Deadly serious. The poor lad was in a bad way when we found him. Nearly bled to death. My wee sister saved his life." He nudged Iona, the pride in his voice obvious.

A red flush spread up from Iona's throat, adding much-needed colour to her pale cheeks. Kaine hadn't pegged her as the shy and retiring sort.

"Nonsense," she said. "I wouldnae have been able to do anything if you and Sandy hadn't found them and called in the helicopter."

"That's as maybe," Drew conceded, with some reluctance, "but it turned out the father owned an IT company. So rich, he made that tall guy from Dragon's Den look like a homeless beggar. He was that grateful we'd rescued his son, he donated all this equipment. He flew in a team o' technicians to install it, and his company maintains it for us, too. Truth is, we're probably the best-equipped mountain rescue centre in the whole o' the UK."

"Is the same man responsible for the spare clothing, too?"

"Indirectly," Iona said. "He now chairs the board of the fundraising committee and makes sure all his friends and business associates dig deep into their pockets. By the way, his son made a full recovery and wants to join the team when he's older."

Before she could add anything further, the image on the main screen dissolved away to be replaced by a larger version of the one depicted on the window marked ST4.

Kaine positioned himself in front of the screen and crossed his arms. He studied the picture and smiled. Gregor, or one of the comms guys, had removed the key and all the annotations and signs, not that it made a difference. Kaine recognised the almost-featureless surface from the shallow valley shaped like an exclamation mark in the top left corner. To test him further, the map had been rotated about thirty degrees to the west of magnetic north.

Sneaky beggars.

He half-turned towards Gregor, who stood to Kaine's left and the swollen eye made him difficult to see.

"That's *Tha Fearann Còmhnardi*," Kaine said. "The Flat Lands. Nothing there but rolling meadow, gorse, and the odd shallow bog. A simple flyover in a helicopter would clear that segment, if you could put one in the sky in this weather. Failing that, at this time of the year, you'd probably be able to cover most of it in a four-by-four. Why do you have a team over there?"

Gregor appeared at his side. "The chopper's been grounded most of the day."

"Doesn't answer my question. That search area should have been cleared by now. If this is another test, you're wasting all our time."

Gregor signalled to the female comms officer and a different image appeared on the screen; this one labelled ST2. The grid showed the section of folds to the northeast of The Flat Lands. The closely packed contours indicated a steep slope ascending to the north. A kidney-shaped puddle in the northwest quadrant gave Kaine all the confirmation he needed.

"That's *Dubhaig Loc*, Kidney Loch. It's shallow, but dangerous. And that"—he pointed at the slope indicated by the contours—"is the northwest slope of *Ben Craed*. No school teacher in his right mind would take a bunch of teenagers anywhere near those slopes. It's asking for trouble."

Another signal from Gregor brought up window ST3. A trio of peaks set in a rough isosceles triangle at the top right of the image made identification easy.

"*Tha Na Trì Uaigealta*, The Three Hags. They're evil. Tricky to climb even for an expert. Plenty of loose scree and prone to rock falls. What would a school party be doing anywhere near that serious climbing territory?"

Gregor turned his head towards the comms area and drew his fingers across his throat. The image on the big screen reverted to its original configuration. If anything, the storm front looked deeper, angrier. It still hadn't moved.

"Okay, Peter," Gregor said, breaking out a rueful smile. "You've convinced me. You clearly know the area."

"Usually, a search team leader would be happy to have another experienced hand in an operation like this, but your face says otherwise. Is there something you're not telling me?"

Gregor flashed a glance at Drew and Iona before locking eyes with Kaine. "The information we have is the boy might have ditched the school party intentionally."

"Why?"

Gregor didn't reply straight away. Kaine repeated his question.

The Scotsmen averted their eyes, leaving Iona to answer. "We need to face the possibility that Martin Princeton left the group with the intention of committing suicide."

The floor beneath Kaine's feet seemed to fall away and he threw a hand against the screen to steady himself. The image beneath his palm wrinkled and diffused as though he'd pushed his hands into a puddle of water. That Martin would want to kill himself after what had happened to his brother seemed plausible, even likely given the circumstances, but it hadn't entered Kaine's mind during his long drive north.

Bloody hell.

Had his action in the North Sea resulted in the loss of yet another innocent life? Did he have one more death on his conscience? Despite having cleared his name in the eyes of at least one member of the police force—if not in the eyes of the deity Kaine's mother used to pray to every Sunday morning—his culpability might never end.

Kaine considered the possibility for a moment and the slow, concrete weight of guilt filling his stomach threatened to engulf him. Here was one more death that he could never expunge from his soul.

What could he do? Leave and search for redemption elsewhere? The questions and consequences swam through his head.

"So, you're treating this as a recovery operation?"

Gregor shook his head emphatically. "Absolutely not. Without a body we treat this as a standard S&R scenario. We act as though Martin Princeton is still alive until we know for certain he isn't."

Blood rushed to Kaine's feet to fill the gap left by the disappearing floor. He took a couple of quick breaths to settle himself before asking what he considered the obvious question.

"What makes you think Martin's suicidal?"

"From what his teacher and his classmates told us."

Of course, the teacher.

Kaine berated himself silently. Fatigue had played a part in his mind-set. He should have asked to see the teacher straight away. Kaine knew how stress affected recall and what could be more stressful to a teacher than losing one of the kids in his care? After taking course after course on interrogation techniques, Kaine knew how to elicit information from even the most traumatised or reluctant interviewee.

"What did the teacher say? Is he the one who pointed you to The Three Hags?"

Kaine spread his fingers over the touchscreen to zoom in on the map. The contours brought a refreshed image of The Three Hags into focus. His mind rolled back to the days he and Rollo—his climbing buddy of choice—had spent mapping out a training climb for the more capable recruits. He'd enjoyed the technical complexity of the challenge, but the thought of a lone teenage boy being anywhere near the place was difficult to contemplate.

"Does Martin Princeton know how to climb?" he asked.

Gregor shook his head. "According to Mr Bartholomew, the teacher, young Martin was adequate on the school's indoor rock wall, but not competent. Apparently, he instructed the boys to stay within sight of the camp, keep in pairs, and not to attempt any climbing."

"If they were supposed to stay in pairs, why's Martin the only one missing?"

"Aye, and teenage boys always do as they're told, right?" Drew said, a deep growl rumbling through his massive chest.

Anger flashed through Kaine's belly at the teacher's apparent lack of control over his charges. Already, he knew his next move.

"How many boys were in the party and how many teachers? The news reports didn't give out many details."

"That's right. We're holding back that information. Mr and Mrs Princeton are on their way and we don't want to upset them any more than they already are."

"Understood. So? How many were there?"

"Six boys, Mr Bartholomew, and his teaching assistant."

A small group. Controllable. Not too bad. Kaine had imagined a much larger, more unwieldy party. Assuming Bartholomew had any kind of intelligence and physical presence, a six-to-two ratio ought to have been easy enough to manage. At least in theory.

"The news said they were on a geography field trip?"

"Aye, that's right."

"Geology or botany?"

"Botany," Gregor answered. "They were associated with the Nature Scotland programme and tasked with mapping the flora and fauna of a specified area. The boys had no reason to do any real climbing."

Kaine cast his mind back the best part of three decades to when he was Martin Princeton's age. If he'd been anywhere near a mountain, depressed or not, he'd have found the challenge too much of a draw to ignore. The question had to be asked. Was the lad as much the adventurer as the fifteen-year-old Ryan Kaine?

"What emergency equipment did the boys carry?" Kaine asked.

Although appearing to focus his attention on Gregor, he didn't fail to notice Drew tapping Iona on the hand in which she held Kaine's false business card and driving licence. Without a word, she sidled away to one of the empty desks in the communications enclave and started tapping at a keyboard. Her typing speed suggested one who knew her way around an internet search.

Damn. All down to you now, Sabrina.

Gregor turned to Drew. "You spoke to Bartholomew last. What did he say?"

The big man's upper lip curled. "Usual stuff. Wet-weather gear. Map and compass. Rations and water. And of course, all o' the boys had mobile phones. Not that there's a mobile phone mast within thirty miles of their campsite. Ye'd be surprised at how many complaints we receive about the lack of a mobile signal here."

Kaine shook his head. No, he wouldn't. From what he'd seen of the younger generations, most of them behaved as though losing a phone or internet connection would stop their hearts from beating.

"How did the teacher … what's his name again?"

"Kurt Bartholomew," Gregor answered.

Kaine wondered why the name sounded familiar but couldn't bring the memory to the surface. He continued his questioning. "How did Bartholomew contact you to raise the alarm?"

"See that?"

Gregor pointed to a door in the far corner of the room. In Kaine's day, it led to a musty storeroom but, given the centre's wealthy benefactor, it could conceivably house a sauna and spa bath.

"That's where we keep our rental comms equipment on charge. Anyone who needs one can hire a satellite phone before taking off into the wilds. For educational groups it's a mandatory requirement of their insurance cover."

"Bartholomew had one of your satphones?"

"Aye. There's an emergency 'hot' button linked directly to our control centre and the call automatically relays the phone's grid coordinates. It's accurate to within ten square metres. Despite the chopper being grounded, we had a team at the location within ninety-five minutes of receiving the call."

Gregor pointed to the small, red cross in the centre of the map on the large screen. It was marked PZ, and the time stamp showed the call as being received at 09:13:53.

"That's where we found Mr Bartholomew and the rest of the lads. We designated it as Point Zero and set up a standard grid search pattern using it as the point of origin."

Point Zero corresponded to a position in the top right quadrant of the ST1 window. It located the party at about six kilometres southeast of Kidney Loch.

"How long had the boy been missing before Bartholomew made the call?"

Gregor and Drew exchanged another glance before the team leader answered. "Two and a half hours."

What?

Kaine took a moment to let the information sink in. "So, Martin was missing for nearly five hours before you even started the search?"

He ran a quick calculation in his head. An untrained individual over such rough terrain could average no more than two miles per hour. "By the time you started, the search radius could have been around ten miles."

Again the two men shifted glances. This time they added some foot shuffling.

Gregor cleared his throat. "Not necessarily. The boy was

missing from his tent when Bartholomew called him to breakfast. He could have got up in the middle of the night and wandered off at any time."

Kaine puffed out his cheeks before remembering how painful it would be. He winced but tried to hide it. It wouldn't take much of a show of weakness on his part for Gregor to withdraw support for him joining the search teams in the morning, and he wanted to be up and out at first light. Assuming the boy still breathed, he'd already suffered one night's exposure to the Scottish Highlands' weather and, unless the forecast improved dramatically, he was about to endure a second. Irrespective of his physical condition, the boy would be hard put to survive a third.

The best Kaine could hope for was that Martin had holed up somewhere, uninjured and sheltered from the worst of the weather. Even so, the next day would mark the search team's last realistic chance to find Martin Princeton alive. He wanted—needed—to be part of the search.

"Why did the teacher take so long to raise the alarm?"

Gregor jerked his wide shoulders in what Kaine could only interpret as a shrug. His expression beneath the beard remained impassive. "He and the boys set off in pairs to search for Martin. Apparently, he'd been known to wander off on his own although, up to that point, he'd always stayed within shouting distance of the camp. I've talked to Bartholomew. He liked to give the boys room to breathe and, given Martin's recent loss"—again the broad shoulders twitched—"you know his elder brother was one of the victims of Flight BE1555?"

Kaine nodded. He couldn't bring himself to speak through a suddenly dry throat.

Drew broke the brief silence. "Canyouimagine what it was like for a teacher to lose one o' his students? Especially one like Martin who's going to be the centre of a media shit storm." He lowered his voice at the use of the mild cuss word and shot a look at Iona, whose eyes remained glued to her computer monitor. "The man would have been terrified. Probably hoped to find the lad by himself and save his blushes."

Kaine ground his teeth, ignoring the spike of pain. "Trying to save his job, more likely. That's bloody irresponsible. What did you make of him? I mean, what's this Bartholomew like?"

Gregor paused for a moment before answering. "Drew spoke to him more than I did, but he seems genuinely upset. Said he had the other boys to consider or he'd have been out with the search parties yesterday. The police interviewed him, and they've checked him out as thoroughly as they can. There were no warning flags."

"Any chance I can have a word with Bartholomew and the rest of his party?"

"The boys are under police protection. We sent them home on a bus last night with the teaching assistant, Gavin Atkinson. Bartholomew refused to go. Says he wants to stay and help. Also wants to talk to Mr and Mrs Princeton when they arrive tomorrow. I have no idea what he'll say or how they'll take it, but it shows commitment. He could easily have skedaddled with the rest of his party."

"I'd still like to talk with him. Maybe I can help jog his memory. Help narrow the search zone. Part of my work has been involved in training people on interviewing techniques. Now he's had more time to think, he might have remembered something since yesterday morning. Would that be okay?"

"I don't see why not," Gregor answered.

"Where is he?"

"We gave him a room in the accommodation block. I guess he's trying to gather himself before meeting the Princetons."

"The accommodation block's in the same place it's always been?"

Drew jerked a thumb towards the rear door. "Aye. Same building, but with slightly better decor and comfier mattresses. He's in room number five at the far end of the men's block."

Before Kaine could head out, Iona returned from her computer. She carried a small, paper notepad and, from her relaxed attitude, Kaine could tell Sabrina had found the time to work her electronic magic.

Kaine forced the tension from his shoulders. He hadn't realised he'd been holding them so stiff.

Iona addressed Gregor directly, but the rest of the people in the room could hear her. "According to the Conqueror Security Services website, Staff Sergeant Peter Sidings is a fully vetted employee. Peter here has MoD and EU security clearance, and is a highly qualified instructor in defensive driving techniques."

She raised the notepad and read out the details. "His bio states that he's had two tours of Iraq and three of Afghanistan, one leading the protection team for Bruno Di Marco, the MD of Ventini Construction. Apparently, they're the firm that won half of the civilian contracts to rebuild Kabul."

Drew seemed convinced. "That's an impressive CV."

"The website has an in-depth bio and a good ID photo."

"I guess it doesn't look much like me at the moment?" Kaine suggested.

"Not a lot," Iona answered, smiling. "But it's definitely

you. Again, she turned to Gregor. "Peter is who he says he is. I'm convinced, but I do have one slight question mark," she added, glancing sideways at Kaine. "I cannae find any mention of an accident involving a car and a caravan on the A55. I'd have thought that would have merited a local news report or two."

Kaine pressed a hand against his cheek before wrinkling up his face.

"I'm afraid there won't be a police report," he said as sheepishly as he could manage. "The other driver and I didn't inform the police."

"Why not?" Gregor asked. He didn't appear persuaded by Sabrina's seeded information.

"For crying out loud," Kaine said, lowering his voice to a stage whisper, "I'm in charge of transport security for high-profile dignitaries. How would it reflect on the firm if it came out I was involved in a traffic accident? I'd be a bloody laughing stock."

Drew and Iona nodded, seemingly satisfied, but Gregor clearly wanted more. Kaine obliged.

"I'm afraid I broke the law by not reporting the accident, which is another reason I'd rather not meet the good Inspector Gadget until these bruises start to fade. There wasn't much damage to the other driver's caravan, and he shunted us both onto the hard shoulder so we didn't hold up traffic." Kaine paused for breath and shrugged. "My company offered to pay the guy off and, considering the accident was his fault, he jumped at it."

The doubt in Gregor's eyes melted away and with it, Kaine's worry. Sabrina had done exactly what she'd promised and yet again, his debt to her grew.

"Are we good?"

Kaine addressed his question to Gregor, who nodded.

A relieved Kaine tried to keep his face stone-like. "It's nice to be a trusted member of the team," he said only half in jest. "Now, if you don't mind, I'd like to ask Kurt Bartholomew a few questions."

He couldn't wait to meet the man entrusted with Martin Princeton's safety.

Chapter Seven

Wednesday 16th September – Early Evening

Kinross Farm MRC, The Cairngorms, Aberdeenshire, Scotland

"When did you last actually see Martin Princeton?" Kaine asked as gently as he could, not wanting to come across as the hard-boiled inquisitor and have the man clam up.

"Um ... two nights ago, a little after eleven o'clock." Bartholomew's hesitant response appeared to indicate fatigue mixed with the desperate need for accuracy. "That was the last time I actually saw Marty. I did hear him and his tent mate, Aiden Murphy, chatting into the night, but they stopped around one o'clock. After that, I ... I must have fallen asleep."

Kaine had found Bartholomew where Drew said he'd

be and, despite the red eyes and haunted expression, the man cut an impressive, if dishevelled, figure. Six foot two, shaggy, blond hair, square jaw with a three-day fuzz of stubble—he could have been the blueprint for the rugged mountaineer-surfer. The thing that set him apart from the "cool dude" image were his dark blue eyes—eyes that carried a world of pain, and maybe a continent of guilt.

When Bartholomew answered Kaine's knock and called him into the small room, the teacher had been standing beside his bunk bed staring dejectedly through the double-glazed windows. Kaine doubted the magnificent mountain view through the glass held much appeal and imagined that the man felt the same sense of loss and hopelessness Kaine had felt on learning of Martin's disappearance.

What surprised Kaine as much as anything was the man's plummy accent. Judging by the teacher's surfer looks, Kaine had expected a Cornish or an Aussie's Gold Coast twang, but heard refined Home Counties. More than that, the second he saw the teacher, Kaine realised why the name Kurt Bartholomew had been so familiar. Years earlier, he'd seen the man's triumphant face smiling out at him from the centrefold of *Climber's World Magazine*.

If he'd had the opportunity, Kaine would have asked Sabrina to produce a complete dossier on the good-looking teacher, but for the moment, he'd go with his gut. And his gut said the blond man was hurting.

"What's Martin like?"

Bartholomew lowered his gaze and took a moment to gather his thoughts.

"Marty's a good lad. Special, you know? A gifted student academically. Not much of an athlete, but he was great in the field."

"In what way?"

"He'd do anything for anyone. A real asset to the team. Collecting samples, tabulating results, writing reports, doing all the background research before we left school. The other boys on the field team would look up to him even though he was a year younger."

"The news reports said Martin is fifteen. That puts the other boys at sixteen?"

"Yes, they're in Key Stage 4. That's for pupils aged between fifteen and sixteen."

"Half a dozen teenagers could be a bit of a handful. I'm told you had an assistant."

He nodded. "Yes, I did. Gavin Atkinson's been with me for five years. Reliable. Solid. He helped me marshal the little beggars. You're dead right. Field trips can be a nightmare for a solo teacher," he said almost dismissively, a sad smile forming on the handsome but aging face.

"I understand Mr Atkinson returned to England with the boys."

"That's right. Someone had to supervise them, and I wanted to be here for when Mr and Mrs Princeton arrive. Not looking forward to that, I can tell you."

Bartholomew jumped as a heavy gust smashed a torrent of rainwater against the glass. He half-turned away from Kaine and stared at the storm still raging over the mountains. Three branches of forked lightening shot from the clouds and a near-simultaneous fusillade of thunder showed how close they were to the storm's centre.

"God, I'd hate to think how he must be feeling out there alone in that. Always assuming … Oh God, what have I done? I shouldn't have let him come on the trip. I can't imagine what his parents must be going through. He was my responsibility and now he's—"

"We don't know what's happened. He might have found

shelter. There's no point beating yourself up about things just yet."

"Ah, yes, right. Sorry. My head's all over the place."

"Do you have any idea what happened?"

Bartholomew filed the rough end of his right thumbnail across the edge of his teeth. He'd bitten the rest of his nails to the nub and had started munching away on the skin around the nailbeds. Each fingertip looked red and raw—he'd drawn blood more than once.

He shook himself as though trying to wake from a bad dream. "Remind me again why you're asking all these questions, Mr …?"

"Sidings," Kaine said. "Peter Sidings. As I said earlier, I used to work in the area. I'm hoping to help focus tomorrow's search."

Without removing the digit from his mouth, Bartholomew said, "Good. The others haven't been able to find any trace of him, and I'm starting to lose hope." He paused long enough to spit a piece of chewed skin on the floor before adding, "Marty idolised his brother, Matty. Losing him in that air crash tore the lad apart inside, you know?"

Bartholomew seemed to be losing concentration. Kaine tried to bring him back on point. "How was his mood the evening before he disappeared?"

The teacher stopped biting his thumbnail long enough to rub his eyes and then raised them to look at Kaine almost for the first time.

"Who exactly are you? You're not police. Not dressed like that."

Kaine introduced himself again and stretched the truth a shade further. "Gregor Abercrombie brought me in for my local knowledge. I'm here to help find Martin. Are you okay with that?"

"Of course. I'll do everything I can, but"—he leaned closer, eyes narrowing—"have you been in a fight?"

Kaine shook his head. "Car accident."

"You look familiar. Have we ever met?"

Shit. What were the odds?

Kaine had been lucky in the "who'll recognise the suspected terrorist" stakes, but it was only a matter of time before someone linked his battered face to the police wanted photo. Considering his mugshot had been all over the media for the best part of a week, his not being recognised so far had been something akin to a miracle.

He tilted the left ear towards the teacher as though to hear him better. Not for the first time since his beating, Kaine was grateful for the swelling and the bruising.

"We might have come into contact. Until a few years ago, I lived nearby. Climbed these rocks most evenings in the summer."

Kaine's time at HMS Whiteheath had forced him to climb in the damned mountains through the winter, too, but he had no intention of expanding on his work history, not to Bartholomew. To the teacher, he'd keep his military background quiet for as long as possible. One link might lead to another, and Kaine couldn't afford to take the risk.

The teacher raised his chin in a sharp nod. "That's probably it. We may have passed each other on the face of *Ben Craed*. I've been climbing in the region since I was a boy. I held my first school field trip up here nearly a decade ago." A shadow crossed his face that had nothing to do with the weather battering the mountains. "This is the first time anything like this has ever happened. Please believe me. I run a really tight ship. The boys are safe in my care. At least, I thought ... Oh Lord, what am I going to do?"

The last words formed a prayer, his hands clasped close to his mouth in supplication. Bartholomew's breath caught in his throat, and he wrung his hands so hard his skin creaked.

Kaine had a hard time watching another man battling tears, but his emotional threshold had been lowered recently. He totally understood exactly what Bartholomew was going through.

"Is Martin a good climber?" he asked, intentionally using the present tense.

Bartholomew sniffed and wiped his eyes with the heels of his hands. "Sorry 'bout that. Embarrassing. But in answer to your question, no, not really. Marty was okay on the indoor rock wall at school, but shied away from the real stuff. Didn't have the nerve for it, you see. But that's okay." He sighed. "Mountaineering isn't for everyone, is it?"

Kaine's mind conjured an image of a bunch of pubescent schoolboys running around a mountainside goading each other into taking ever more dangerous risks. Not the happiest of thoughts.

"How did the other boys treat Martin's aversion to climbing? Any taunting? Bullying?"

Bartholomew stiffened. His gaze met Kaine's and was fixed in a glower. "Absolutely not, Mr Sidings! The school doesn't tolerate bullying of any kind. If I thought any of my boys capable of such behaviour they would most certainly not have been invited on the course. And ..."

He paused to take a deep breath and rubbed a calloused hand over his mouth.

"And?" Kaine prompted.

"I told you earlier, the boys got along really well. In fact,

I was proud of the way they supported Marty in his time of need. As I said, Marty idolised his elder brother and took his death really hard. Of course, we had the usual high jinks and banter, but it was well-natured, and Marty usually gave as good as he got. And I never tolerated any shenanigans when we were close to anything dangerous."

A warning chimed in Kaine's head.

"I thought you kept the boys well clear of any danger."

"Of course I did, but nowhere in the highlands is ever completely safe. As a mountaineer, you'd know that."

Kaine was forced to agree. He'd seen highly skilled and well-equipped marines suffer accidental injuries in the most benign of conditions. He didn't envy Bartholomew's attempts to herd a group of teenage boys in the triple shadow of The Three Hags.

The second mention of the dead brother not only deepened Kaine's sense of remorse, it also sparked a question. "Given that Martin's brother passed away so recently, I'm surprised his parents let him out of their sight."

The teacher nodded, the hairline creases at the corners of his eyes deepened and added a decade to his age. Kaine revised his estimate. He and the powerfully built Bartholomew were probably of a similar vintage. But whereas the weather and battle scars had etched Kaine's face to show every one of his forty-odd years, in a kinder light, Bartholomew could have passed for a much younger man.

"It shocked me, too," Bartholomew said. "I taught Matty Princeton, Marty's elder brother, for years. Watched him develop into a wonderful athlete and a top-class student. The headmaster and I co-sponsored his scholarship into Cambridge. The world lost a born leader when Matty died."

Kaine didn't need the schoolteacher to remind him of the true cost of his shooting down Flight BE1555. Every dead passenger and crew member was a tragedy Kaine would live with forever. He clenched his jaw. Pain exploded up through the root of his broken tooth. Kaine's eyes watered. It wasn't much of a penance.

Bartholomew continued. "I expected Marty to give up his place on the team, but he was adamant. At the behest of his parents, I tried to convince him to stay home, but he wouldn't change his mind. Now I can see why."

During the last sentence, the teacher's voice faded to a whisper, and he lowered his gaze to his hands once again. Kaine thought he could detect a slight tremor in the chewed fingers.

"What do you mean?"

Without looking up, Bartholomew answered. "I think Marty intended to … to commit suicide. He grew more and more reserved as the days passed." The gaze lifted and the ocean-blue eyes locked on Kaine's. "We put it down to sadness at Matty's loss, but I think it was more than that. Much more. Depression, anger, pain. A death in the family affects us all in different ways, Mr Sidings."

"I know," Kaine answered with feeling.

"I tried counselling the boy, you know? Took him under my wing and kept him apart from the other lads at times and it seemed to work. As I told the police and the search teams, I thought I'd reached him. That last night, he took part in the campfire discussions and even joined in with the singing. Young Fitzwilliam brought out his harmonica and Allenby has a wonderful blues note to his voice. I really did think Marty had turned the corner."

Bartholomew turned his back to Kaine once more. He

placed his hands on the windowsill and rested his forehead against the glass.

"Mr and Mrs Princeton will be here in the morning. I have no idea how I'm going to face them. I gave them my word I'd look after their boy. Their remaining son."

Tears fell. Kaine looked away and gave the man a chance to gather his thoughts.

Two sets of headlights raked the courtyard. Cameras flashed and spotlights turned. The background gabble of the media people increased in pitch and volume, their voices raised in question.

Kaine joined Bartholomew at the window and looked towards the courtyard car park. Two long-wheelbase Land Rovers pulled to a crunching stop behind the line of police SUVs. Four officers dressed in full police uniform disembarked from each vehicle. One member from each team opened the rear doors and distributed backpacks. Once in possession of their kit, the men barged through the ranks of reporters and entered the main building. None stopped to answer the questions thrown at random by an increasingly agitated press corps.

The gloom of an earlier-than-normal dusk had leaped forwards since Kaine first entered the dormitory block. It wouldn't be long until full night descended. Fortunately, irrespective of cloud cover, full dark wouldn't last longer than nine hours or so. They didn't have long to plan the next day's search strategy. Nor did he have much time for rest and recuperation.

Bartholomew gave no indication he'd noticed the arrival of the new search team. In other circumstances, Kaine would have given the upset man longer to recover, but he didn't have the luxury of time and neither did Martin Princeton.

"Who discovered Martin was missing?"

Bartholomew jerked as though someone had prodded him in the ribs. He straightened but kept facing forwards as though he might be able to find the boy by staring through the glass.

"Marty's bunkmate, Aiden," he said. "Aiden Murphy."

"What time was this? First light?"

"No, a little later. I woke at sunrise, a little after six o'clock, and lit the fire for breakfast. Then I roused the lads. I like to get an early start, but you know what teenagers are like. I'd have had more chance trying to coral a pack of cats. Aiden popped his head out of his tent and asked where Marty was. Nobody had seen him that morning. Aiden noticed his bedroll was empty but thought Marty had woken early. It was his turn to make breakfast."

"You must have been worried."

"Not really. Not at first. We all thought he'd gone to relieve himself. Marty wasn't one to take a leak in public and the campsite backs onto a small granite tor. We use it for privacy. Dig a hole, add composting material. Environmentally sound, you see. We take all our refuse with us and dispose of it responsibly. I demand that from the outset. The school takes its ecological responsibilities seriously, you know? The head wouldn't allow us to go on the field trips unless he was absolutely convinced of our environmental credentials. In the first year at school, I run a complete module on environmental care in the wilderness."

Kaine allowed Bartholomew to ramble. He didn't want to interrupt the man's flow for fear of missing something important.

"Anyway," Bartholomew continued, "when I'd made breakfast, porridge served the Scottish way with salt and no sugar, Marty still hadn't returned, so I sent Gavin—Gavin

Atkinson—to go fetch him. When he returned alone, that's when I started to get worried."

"Is that when you used the satellite phone?"

Bartholomew's shoulders dropped and he lowered his head. "I should have. I know I should have, but ... God, why didn't I call then instead of wasting all that time?"

Kaine agreed with him, but kept it to himself. He knew what it was like to feel guilt. If he hadn't destroyed Flight BE1555, maybe Martin wouldn't have gone missing.

"What did you do after Atkinson raised the alarm?"

Bartholomew raked his fingers through his wavy, blond locks and stood taller. "I organised the boys into pairs and sent them off in cardinal points of the compass."

Kaine bit back an angry retort. In sending out random search teams, he'd not only wasted time and risked more injuries, he'd also destroyed any trail Martin might have made when leaving the camp.

Nice one, Bartholomew. Call yourself a mountain man?

"Why did you do that?"

"I panicked a little. Thought maybe Marty had fallen in the dark. Wanted to check the immediate area before raising a false alarm. I know it was wrong, but ..."

Bartholomew punched the safety rail of the top bunk. It creaked, but held together. It must have hurt, but the teacher didn't seem to register the blood oozing from the split skin on his prominent knuckle.

"I ... made sure the boys all stayed within sight and shouting distance of each other, but after an hour, we found no sign of him. Nothing. So I blew the whistle to call off the search and we gathered back at the campsite. That's when I called the MRC, the Mountain Rescue Centre."

Kaine recalled the Point Zero time stamp on the big

screen in the main office: 09:13:53. A good two and a half hours after sunrise. So much time wasted.

"What was the weather like at the time?"

"Sunny and mild with a light, southerly breeze." He nodded at the black-and-grey storm raging beyond the window. "No hint of that in the forecast. Bloody Met Office dropped the ball on that one."

"Did Martin take his backpack?"

Bartholomew stared at Kaine for a moment, a question forming in his eyes before answering. "Of course he did. It's one of my intractable rules. Whenever anyone leaves camp, they have to take their emergency pack with them. Even if it's only to go to the latrine. As you know, weather in the mountains can deteriorate in minutes."

"So, Martin has his emergency pack with food and warm clothing?"

A flash of hope shone in the teacher's eyes. "Yes, yes. He does. You're right. I'd forgotten about that. Despite the storm, he might have taken shelter to ride it out. I've been so worried, it ... slipped my mind."

A smile lit Bartholomew's face. In that moment, Kaine could see how such a man might produce loyalty and hero worship in a school population. He could see how a distraught Martin might have preferred to spend time roughing it on a mountain with his friends and favourite teacher rather than with his grieving parents. Teenagers could be so heartless.

Kaine asked the million-pound question.

"Do you have any idea where he might have gone?"

Bartholomew closed his eyes and sighed.

"I've been sitting here on my own in the quiet running through every place Martin had been during the trip. You say you know the area, Mr Sidings?"

Still keeping his bruised and battered side to Bartholomew, Kaine tilted his head. "Pretty well."

"You ever been to Kidney Loch?"

Kaine nodded. "I have. Why?"

"On our third day the weather was so hot, one of those rare days of high sun and vicious midges, we took the afternoon off to swim. Marty was in his element. He's on the school swim team. He clearly loved the loch. It was the first time he could show off to the others, I had to call him back or he'd have swum across at the widest point, which is over—"

"Eighteen hundred metres," Kaine said.

Back in the day, Kaine had swum the same lake dozens of times, as had the recruits he'd beasted.

"Yes, that's right. Just over a mile. I didn't want him out in the middle. If he'd encountered any difficulty he'd have been on his own." He lowered his head. "I never did learn how to swim properly, and the other lads were worse than me."

"So, you think Martin might have headed to Kidney Loch?"

Again, a slight shrug of the strong shoulders preceded his response. "It's possible. I mentioned it to Gregor Abercrombie and he called in a team with more experience of searching mountain lakes."

"The guys from Aberdeen?"

"Yes, that's right. The *Ben Craed* Mountain Rescue Team doesn't really have the need. Apart from a few streams, Kidney Loch is the only open water within their normal search area."

Kaine nodded again. "They've just arrived."

"Is that what all the commotion was about a couple of minutes ago?"

"Yes. Is there anywhere else Martin could have gone?"

"I can't think of one. He certainly wouldn't have gone anywhere near the mountain."

"You like Martin, don't you?"

"Yes," he said, the reply emphatic and fast. "He's a fine lad. Always eager to please. Would do anything for you."

A dark idea formed and rattled around in Kaine's over-tired head. He studied Bartholomew closely but found no real reason to mistrust the man who seemed genuine enough, although wracked with guilt. He didn't want to give it voice, but a kid's life was at stake and he couldn't risk it to avoid upsetting the man's feelings.

Kaine deliberately changed the subject to access the teacher's gut reaction.

"Naming Zelda's Smile was a hell of an achievement."

"What?"

Bartholomew chewed the cuticle on his left thumb and spat out the dead skin in an automated action he probably didn't realise he was doing.

"I read the article in *Climber's World Magazine*."

"You did?"

"Very impressive."

The teacher puffed out his chest. "Took me a couple of years to plan the route and seven attempts before I finally cracked it."

"Wonderful. You must have been ecstatic."

The man's eyes shone bright. "I was indeed. Worried, too."

"How come?"

"I completed the climb during the last week of the season, just before the weather closed in. Early September, 2007. Had to wait seven long months before I could climb it again with independent witnesses. And every day from

February 2008 onwards, I expected to hear that someone else had claimed it. You see, I started at St Thomas' Grammar a week after cracking the climb. Had to wait until the Easter of '08 to return here. Tense times, I tell you. Tense times indeed."

Kaine managed a tight smile before the split on his lower lip forced him to stop.

"I can imagine. Never been in that position myself."

Although he'd broken dozens of climbs in his career, both solo and as part of a team, he'd been required to keep them all secret.

Bartholomew spat out another cuticle and made a fist. "It was my one chance to gain immortality."

"Really? There are still plenty of unnamed climbs up here, and you were still a young man in 2008. Probably close to the height of your powers."

The teacher's eyes locked with Kaine's and for the first time, he saw something in them he didn't like. Aggression? Petulance? He couldn't tell, but it was almost as though the teacher took Kaine's words as a challenge.

"No, no, you don't understand. The immortality wasn't for me, but for Mother. I wanted the climb named after her before she passed away. She was ill, you see. Brain tumour. Terminal. But I did it. Officially, I cracked Zelda's Smile on Good Friday, March 21, 2008."

The proud smile again lit his face.

"The pupils must have been awestruck to find a celebrity on their teaching staff."

Bartholomew's smile faded. "Possibly, but I generally keep the climbing side of my life to myself. The only reason I agreed to that *Climber's World* interview was to prove to Mother they'd named a climb after her. They don't give out certificates, you know?" He paused to wipe a tear from his eye. "Mother was so proud. I think she died a happy woman."

"And your father?"

"Father passed many years earlier. When I was still in prep school."

"So, no one at school knows you named a climb?"

Another sad smile formed.

"They do now. I have it on my CV and had to declare it when the headmaster approached me to reinstate the geography field trips."

"These field trips were the headmaster's idea, not yours?"

"His initiative, exactly. But he didn't have to work hard to convince me. Look at that," he said, nodding towards the darkening view. "I mean, who wouldn't want to spend time here? Magnificent. The boys love it here, too. It's a wonderful learning environment."

Someone knocked on the door. Bartholomew answered, and it opened to Iona. She stayed in the doorway.

"Mr Bartholomew," she said, her strong, Scottish voice filling the enclosed space, "are ye up to taking supper with the team? You'll be needing to keep yer strength up."

The teacher pushed away from the window and stood tall. His mop of hair brushed one of the rafters. "I've lost my appetite, but I do need to eat something. Thanks."

He took two paces towards her before stopping and, almost as an afterthought, turned to face Kaine.

"Mr Sidings, do you have all you need? Are you finished with me?"

Kaine returned the man's flat stare. "Yes, thanks. You've been of great help."

Bartholomew nodded and Iona stepped aside as he

ducked through the low doorway. She waited for him to leave before speaking.

"Mr Sidings, would you like to take a shower before I treat those cuts?"

"Sounds like a plan. I'll let the hubbub die before interrupting the proceedings."

She crossed her arms. Her corded biceps would have been the envy of many a young man. The woman had power to spare and a pleasant, if wide and bucolic, face.

"Well, I dare say Gregor will be happy to have your input, but I doubt he'll let you join the search. There's no insurance cover for ye and he won't want anyone slowing the men down."

Kaine smiled and wondered whether the combined forces of the Kinross Farm and Aberdeen Rescue teams contained anyone capable of stopping him.

Especially when he had a horrible feeling they were searching in entirely the wrong place.

Chapter Eight

Wednesday 16th September – Evening

Kinross Farm MRC, The Cairngorms, Aberdeenshire, Scotland

By the time they stepped outside, all daylight had leached from the sky. Only the lights bleeding through the farm-house windows illuminated the car park. Of the reporters and their entourage, there remained no sign. They must have decamped to their individual hives to write their copy and file their reports.

On the short walk between the accommodation blocks and the main building, Kaine detected a distinct let up in the rain. Despite that, by the time he dived through the rear door to the main building, he'd once again been soaked through to the bone. Bartholomew ignored Kaine and Iona, and continued into the kitchen.

Kaine removed his cap, swiped the rain from his hair and beard, and stood still, dripping a puddle onto the flagstone floor.

Iona removed her hat and coat and hung them on a hook in the hallway.

"Hold on there a moment," she said. "We don't need to be mopping up after ye."

She tutted at Bartholomew's trail of wet footprints before diving into the clothes store and returning with two fluffy, white bath towels—no doubt another gift courtesy of their wealthy benefactor. She also handed over a neatly pressed lumberjack shirt.

"It's a medium and should fit. You're no' the biggest man I've ever seen."

Kaine draped a towel over his head to catch the drips falling from his hair. "Good things, small packages."

"It doesnae always work that way," she said, clapping his shoulder and letting out a throaty laugh.

By the time he pulled back the towel to check her expression, she'd left to join the noisy throng in the kitchen. He took the opportunity to visit the rest room and tidy himself before having to brave the search teams and whoever else had joined the party from Aberdeen.

He closed the rest room door behind him and threw the bolt. Anyone who saw the full extent of his injuries and all his healed scars would soon see through his lies. He peeled off his sodden jacket and T-shirt, and exposed the damage.

The knife wound running along his ribs had healed pretty well since he'd received it the morning after he'd shot down Flight BE1555—thanks largely to Lara's veterinary skills and her prowess with needle and sutures. He removed the plaster dressing and touched a finger to the wound. Red and highly sensitive, but no serious discomfort. He'd finished the full course of antibiotics and saw the lack of swelling and redness as a really good sign. One recent wound down, but so many more to deal with.

He took a fast, but revitalising shower and stepped out of the cubicle, bracing himself against the cold. The mirror over the sink showed him what the others had been reacting to since his arrival at the MRC. Not a pretty sight, his reflection almost made him gasp, and he'd been expecting it. No wonder they all looked at him as though he'd lost a fight with a mincing machine.

Purple bruises covered the left side of his face—eye, cheek, and jaw. The one above the eyebrow had already started showing green around the edges—a good indication of the fast-repair mechanism he'd been gifted with at birth. The swelling around his cheek had diminished, too, and allowed him to form a smile that looked less like a lopsided grimace. The left eye, though, was still problematic. Puffy and engorged, he still had trouble seeing much through it. Not brilliant for depth perception, but by morning it would have improved enough not to hold him back during the search.

Fortunately, impacted vision notwithstanding, the recent damage was largely cosmetic. Even at his best, he'd never make anyone's Top 100 list in the beauty stakes, but he'd recover, and more quickly than most. Another positive, after the stiffness born of sitting in the car for the best part of a day, he had a full range of movement in all his major joints and no serious muscle damage. After a full night's rest and a healthy breakfast, he'd be fit and raring to go by dawn's first light.

He dabbed his face with his discarded T-shirt to avoid

staining the nice towels, and felt a million times better than when he entered the bathroom. After drying off with the second towel, he buttoned himself into the warm, woollen shirt. The transformation from half-drowned, badly beaten warrior, to dry, half-beaten car crash survivor was complete.

The only thing to ruin the good vibe was the jagged shaft of pain he suffered each time he touched the exposed root of his broken tooth with his tongue. If Iona was half the medic he hoped, she'd have something to deaden the pain until he could find a decent dentist.

Satisfied he'd done the best cosmetic repair job possible given the available resources, Kaine rolled the T-shirt into a tight ball, dropped it into an accommodating swing bin, and prepared to run the gauntlet of mountain rescuers' eyes.

With no idea who he'd face in the main office, he was taking a huge risk of exposure, but he'd made the decision and couldn't back down.

He picked up the damp jacket, draped the first towel around his neck, and stepped into the corridor.

Man up, Kaine. Time for the show.

He bypassed the silent kitchen and stood in the deserted hallway, his undamaged ear pressed against the closed door to the main office. He could clearly make out Gregor holding forth against a murmuring crowd.

A low-pitched, English voice Kaine didn't recognise asked how likely it was that Martin had headed for Kidney Loch.

"You've seen the area we've already covered on the search grid," Gregor answered. "From what Mr Bartholomew tells me, Martin wouldn't have gone anywhere near the mountain. The only place he could reasonably be is the loch. It's why we called in you and your team. And thanks for coming so quickly, by the way."

"Well, it wouldn't be the first time we've had to pull *Ben Craed*'s spuds out of the bonfire!" the first man said to hoots of derisive laughter from a boisterous crowd.

Kaine smiled at the good-natured banter between two friendly but separate groups. He recognised the natural tension of men preparing for an operation for which they feared a negative outcome. In Kaine's military past, his men would be expecting to suffer battle casualties, but the men on the other side of the door were expecting to find the corpse of a drowned teenager.

Drew's voice cut through the growing din. "Ye wee beggars have already munched your way through a week's rations, and you'll no doubt be wanting breakfast afore ye head out in the morning. Is that not payment enough?"

Gregor, Kaine assumed, silenced more raucous laughter with the rap of knuckle on wood.

"Okay," he called out, "it's getting late and it'll be an early start in the morning. In answer to your question, Lewis, you can see the location of our search teams on the screens. They'll continue working their grids at first light, while we target the loch. And on a positive note, we've just had the latest weather report. The Met Office assures us the helicopter will be able to take off by mid-morning at the latest."

An appreciative background hum greeted the news.

Gregor spoke again. "Mr Bartholomew, is there anything you'd like to add before I send everyone away to their beds?"

The legs of a chair scraped on the flagstone floor and the room descended into a hushed silence.

"I ... I don't think so. As I said, young Marty showed no interest in the mountain and preferred to act as the team's curator. He'd often stay close to the camp while the rest of us collected our samples. I have no reason to think he'd go anywhere near *Ben Craed*. And I'd like to ask a favour, if I may."

"Ask away, lad," Gregor said, with some hesitation as though he knew what to expect.

"Will you let me join the recovery team?"

Kaine stiffened.

Recovery team?

When had the search and rescue become a recovery operation? Kaine had heard enough. He needed to act or the boy's slim chances of survival would disappear down to nothing.

He pulled back from the door and grabbed the handle, but it opened almost in his face. Iona, eyes wide, nearly bumped into him.

"Peter, I wondered what was taking ye." She smiled and looked him up and down. "You look much better for a scrub and a brush up, and the Scottish plaid suits ye."

Kaine plucked at the front of the red-and-black-chequered shirt. "Fits perfectly. Thanks for the loan."

She examined his face. "The swelling's going down nicely, and the bruises are already fading. Are you certain your accident was only this morning?"

He coughed out a short laugh. "I'd hardly make a mistake about that, but"––he rested a hand over the sensitive area at the side of his mouth and grimaced––"there is one thing though."

"Aye?"

"Do you have anything to ease the pain of a broken tooth? This bloody thing's driving me nuts."

"Nae bother. Come away wi' me to the clinic, and I'll find you some clove oil and painkillers. It'll help until you can get to a dentist."

"Thanks, that would be great. Apart from that, all I need's a good night's sleep in a comfy bed."

The way her eyes danced made him think he'd made an improper suggestion, but she appeared more amused than offended by the idea. He'd have been flattered, but had other things on his mind and, once he'd finished in Scotland, a damned attractive veterinary surgeon to catch up with.

He jerked his head towards the office and quickly changed the subject. "What's going on in there? Sounds as though they've already given up on Martin."

"Have you been peeping in through the keyhole?"

He snorted. "Nope. I stuck my ear against the door panel like any self-respecting eavesdropper. Didn't want to interrupt the planning session. Not happy with what I heard, though. When did they decide it was a recovery operation?"

Her lips pressed into a narrow line and her brows furrowed. "Nobody's given up on the boy. What you heard is experienced people hoping for the best, but preparing for the worst. It's wet and it's cold, and the wind-chill factor overnight is going to make the perceived ambient temperature fall to well below freezing. It's hard to believe anyone left exposed out there without the proper equipment could have survived, especially one who's depressed."

She wasn't seeing the whole picture. Before facing a roomful of strangers, Kaine needed someone on his side, and Iona was his one best chance.

"Martin took his emergency pack. That's not the action of someone who's suicidal. It's the action of a person in control, and one who knows what he's doing."

"So why did he wander off?" Iona asked.

"I don't know. Maybe he needed time alone. He's just

lost his brother, remember. Despite what Bartholomew said about the way the other lads treated Martin, I know how teenage boys can behave. They could have been brutal and easily hidden it from the teachers."

She shook her head. "I met them. They didn't strike me as being that way. They seemed genuinely worried for their friend."

Or worried they'd bullied him into running away.

"Oh, I forgot for a moment. You were part of the team who arrived at Point Zero yesterday."

"I was. Me, Drew, Gregor, and Alec Groom," she said, looking directly at him once again. "Alec's in charge of Search Team One. He's been on the ground since the start."

"What did you see?"

"Sorry?"

"Describe the campsite to me in as much detail as you can."

"Why?"

He gave her a thin smile.

"Humour me. Please?"

She took a moment before speaking again. "Four two-man ridge tents and two singles—one for each teacher. The spare tent housed the provisions. They were set in a semi-circle in the lee of the prevailing weather and gathered around the cooking fire. It was neat and orderly. As well-maintained as any bivouac I've seen on the mountain."

"What about clothing and equipment? What were the boys wearing?"

She closed her eyes as though trying to cast her mind back a day. "They all wore the same mountain-ready gear. Good quality stuff. Same colour and manufacturer. It almost looked like a school uniform, but designed for the mountains. Expensive hiking boots, too, and a strong, wet-weather outer layer."

"Anything else? Did you look inside the tents?"

"Of course. We've had so-called 'missing kids' playing pranks on us and hiding just for the kicks, but this wasnae like that. Not at all. You only had to take one look at the boys to know it wasnae a joke."

"Sorry, I had to ask. You understand?"

"Aye, but we're no' amateurs, Mr Sidings."

Kaine smiled. "Peter, please. Call me Peter. What was the atmosphere like in the camp. Desperation? Panic?"

"Close to it, but the way Mr Bartholomew and Mr Atkinson marshalled the boys was very impressive. They could have easily broken down, but the boys rallied to them, Mr Bartholomew in particular. They were respectful, you know?"

"Okay. Understood. What happened when you got them back to the centre?"

"By that time, Inspector Gadget and his men had arrived. He and my big brother interviewed them as a group, and I treated two of the boys for cuts and bruises."

"The boys were injured?"

"Not really. Nothing more than a few minor scrapes. The worst thing was a dislocated little finger. The lad had tripped and hurt his hand during the search for Martin."

Kaine nodded, taking it all in and trying to picture the scene. A bunch of teenage boys led by two adults, scrambling around the foothills of a mountain in search of a missing friend was hardly the most inspiring of pictures. Why hadn't Bartholomew mentioned the minor injury during their chat?

"Before you led the party away, did you strike camp?"

"No. As I said, the weather was turning bad and we

wanted to get the boys to safety before it got any worse. After Gregor calls off the search we'll send a team up to clear the site and store the gear at the centre until the school can arrange a collection."

"Did you notice any climbing gear anywhere? Ropes, harnesses, hardware?"

"No. None of that, but I didn't look in all the tents. You'll have to ask Drew."

"Will do. Given the chance."

Kaine didn't like the thoughts rattling around in his head. With Bartholomew a world-class climber—according to the article in *Climber's World*—it didn't seem likely he'd visit the mountains and not bring any climbing gear. If only for safety reasons.

Kaine added another item to his agenda—search the campsite and the surrounding area.

"One more question," he said as she started to edge past him.

She stopped, almost within touching distance. The healthy smell of the outdoors, fused with coffee and a light perfume, filled his nostrils.

"Yes?"

"I understand the boys were sent home last night after they'd given their statements."

A brief nod. "That's right. They were agitated and we are no' running a crèche."

"Who made the decision to send them home?"

"Inspector Gadget okayed it. Said he'd done with them and they'd be better off away back home."

"You said the inspector okayed it. That means someone else made the suggestion. Was it Bartholomew?"

Another sharp nod. "Aye, it was. You could tell how

worried he was for their state of mind. Why are ye asking these questions?"

Kaine shrugged. "No reason. It's just a pity the boys aren't still here. I'd love to have spoken to them. They would have been closer to Martin than Bartholomew or Atkinson and might have remembered something today they forgot yesterday."

"Mr Bartholomew was quite insistent. I think he wanted to get them home so he didn't have to look after them and could join the search tomorrow."

"Really? That's interesting. He told me he was sticking around to talk to the parents."

Her left eyebrow raised into an arch. "You can see why he wouldnae want to do that, can't ye?

Kaine didn't respond. During his time in the military, he'd made more than his fair share of uncomfortable visits to the grieving relatives of lost comrades. He'd hated every single one, but would never have dreamed of shirking the responsibility. On the other hand, Bartholomew might see the act of searching for the missing boy as the same form of redemption for which Kaine aspired.

Damn it to hell.

Trying to double-guess another man's motives fell way outside his training and expertise. For preference, give him a beach assault against heavy artillery, or a night patrol behind enemy lines any time.

Iona must have seen his wince as discomfort. She tapped him on the arm and pointed to a door at the far end of the corridor.

"Come wi' me. I'll find you that clove oil."

He followed her into a compact, but well-appointed, treatment room. Apart from the spectacular and Biblical view through the small window—lightning flashes bathed the mountain crags in electric, blue-white forks—the clinic reminded him of the one in Lara's peaceful farmhouse. At least it had been peaceful before some very bad men had destroyed the place and nearly taken both their lives.

Iona unlocked a wall-mounted unit and handed him a small cardboard box containing a bottle of super-strength paracetamol.

"No more than one tablet every four hours, okay?"

"Yes, Doc."

"And dab the oil on your fingertip and rub it into the damaged tooth and gum. It might sting a little to begin with, but … I reckon you're used to taking punishment."

Kaine broke open the box and dry-swallowed a pill. He cracked the seal on the bottle of clove oil and followed her instructions. His eyes watered when the oil hit the spot, and he grunted.

"Bloody hell, Doc. Thanks for the warning. As usual with you medics, the treatment is almost as bad as the injury."

After a moment or two, the sharp ache faded. A massive relief after a day of throbbing pain.

She leaned closer and studied his injuries, eyes narrowed as Bartholomew's had done earlier. Her fingers reached up to touch the bruise on his lower jaw. Kaine jerked his head away.

"What on earth's going on here?" she asked, backing away and casting a sharp glance at the door.

Kaine's internal alarm rang out loud, warning blasts. He should never have let her get so close in such a well-lit room. The dark hallway and low ambient lighting had hidden his face a little, but the bright lights of the clinic had shown her something. Did she recognise him from the police bulletins?

"What's wrong?"

He forced his arms to relax and opened his hands. The last thing he wanted was to subdue an innocent woman.

She pointed at his chin. "Your beard hid it from me earlier, but that bruise on your chin isn't from hitting a steering wheel. That's from a fist. You've been in a fight."

Relief washed over him, and he allowed his shoulders to fall. He gave her an apologetic smile and, to prompt a little sympathy, dabbed more clove oil into his mouth.

"Guilty as charged. I'm so sorry to have fibbed, but I didn't want you guys thinking I was a hothead. Thought it might scupper my chances of being allowed onto the team."

Iona leaned against the wall and crossed her arms. The action caused her breasts to bulge. Kaine studiously avoided looking at the opening of her polo shirt and the enhanced cleavage.

"So what happened. You were in a fight, no' a car accident?"

Kaine pulled in a sharp breath and let it out as a sigh.

"No, it *was* a car accident, and it *was* in North Wales, but it didn't involve a caravan."

"Go on."

She relaxed a little and stopped throwing calculating looks at the door. Kaine lowered his head and stared at her boots, a safer alternative than looking higher.

"An arsehole in a BMW cut me up during an overtake and we had what racing drivers call a 'coming together'. Basically, the moron crushed my front, offside wing and shunted us both into the hard shoulder."

Iona's expression changed from concern to that of a scolding schoolmarm. "And that's when ye decided to jump out o' the car and teach the man a lesson? Road rage was it?"

She stopped short of wagging her finger under his nose, but not by much.

Despite his aching fatigue, Kaine was delighted he'd been able to think on his feet and come up with another lie at short notice. Again, he hated the subterfuge, but when circumstances demanded it, he could spin yarns with the best of them.

He looked up through hooded brows and reprised the apologetic smile. "Not me, Iona. I promise. The guy—a huge bloke, built like a heavyweight boxer—came at me as though the incident was my fault. He threw the first punch through my open window while I was struggling to remove my seatbelt."

Her eyes opened wide. Kaine guessed—hoped—they held sympathy.

"That's terrible. What happened next?

"He threw another punch ..."

"And?"

"I ducked and he broke his hand on the top of my head. Here"—he removed his cap—"you can feel the bump."

She reached up and prodded the quail-egg-sized mound.

"Ouch. Take it easy, Doc. I've been in the wars."

She withdrew her hand. "So, he hit you twice and you did nothing?"

Kaine replaced the cap and wished he hadn't when the brim grazed the injury and sparked yet more sharp pain. He doubted he'd be able to find many places on his body that didn't hurt to touch.

Bloody hell, did he need a long rest.

"The bloke took one look at his busted hand and backed away. Have you ever seen a big bruiser cry? Not a pretty sight. After that, I called my company and they smoothed things over. Last I heard, the man was on his way into surgery."

"No police involvement?"

"Yes, I called the ambulance and the police, but my company, CSS, has some pull with the Home Office, and we weren't going to press charges, so the local police let the matter drop."

Kaine shut his mouth to stop shovelling the bullshit. Iona seemed satisfied with his explanation but he didn't want to push his luck too far.

"Okay," she said. "What do you want to do next?"

"Mind if we check out what's happening in the office? I'd hate to be side-lined from tomorrow's operation."

He didn't tell her he wanted to keep a closer eye on Bartholomew.

Chapter Nine

Wednesday 16th September – Evening

Kinross Farm MRC, The Cairngorms,
Aberdeenshire, Scotland

The office turned out to be emptier than Kaine expected. Gregor, Drew, and a fit-looking police officer he'd not seen before, were gathered in front of the big screen, heads together, locked in quiet discussion. The female communications operator had left her post, presumably for a break, along with the others he'd heard earlier. Bartholomew sat behind a vacant desk next to the male comms operator, a phone pressed against his ear, apparently listening intently. His eyes followed Kaine all the way as he and Iona crossed the floor and interrupted the three-man huddle.

Kaine did his best to ignore Bartholomew's silent and brooding inquisition and focused on Gregor.

"There you are, Peter," Gregor said on their arrival and turned to the new man. "This is the fellow I was telling you about. Staff Sergeant Peter Sidings, this is Inspector Lewis Elliott, head of the Police Scotland Dive and Marine Unit. They've come all the way from Aberdeen to help us poor mountain folk." Gregor added a smile to lessen any perceived insult.

Heart thumping, Kaine shook the inspector's hand, half-expecting the young officer to shout, "Gotcha!" and slap the cuffs on him.

Before that moment, Kaine had no idea Scotland's main dive rescue team was a police unit. As a member of the Special Boat Service, he'd never had cause to use civilian diving facilities.

Elliott's grip was firm and, mercifully, his gaze rested on Iona. He released Kaine's hand and beamed at her, his bald pate shining under the energy-efficient light bulbs. Elliot was just about the only man Kaine had seen since arriving in Scotland not to sport a full beard. Probably related to maintaining a good seal for his facemask. Divers rarely grew beards when on active service.

"I'm very pleased to meet you, Staff Sergeant Sidings," Elliott said, his strong Devonshire accent, with its rolling Rs and extended OIs, an interesting counterpoint to the local dialect. "Mr Abercrombie tells me you're familiar with the area and are keen to help. That right?"

Until that point, he'd given Kaine little more than a cursory glance, his focus remained fixed on Iona. Her body heat radiated across the short space between herself and Kaine. She and the young cop clearly knew each other on a more than professional level.

Ah, young love.

"That's right," Kaine answered.

He kept his chin tucked in but he needn't have bothered. Elliott only had eyes for the doctor.

Kaine continued. "I'll do all I can, but will make sure to keep out of your way."

"That face looks nasty," the cop said, finally taking time to glance at him.

"Glad my mother isn't around to hear you say that. She used to think I was handsome."

Kaine braced himself for the interrogation.

"Gregor, are we all set for tomorrow?" Iona asked, coming to Kaine's rescue.

He silently thanked her for it.

Elliott deepened his chest and tightened his abs into a decent six-pack. "Evening, Iona. How"—he swallowed—"how are you?"

Kaine eased away and caught the embarrassment in the medic's demeanour. She flushed under the cop's appreciative gaze.

"I'm fine, thank you, Inspector Elliott. How's your new girlfriend?"

Elliott's face crumpled into a pained grimace. "Iona, I ..." He glanced at Drew, as though asking permission to talk to the big man's baby sister.

Iona didn't seem to appreciate the gesture and turned to the team leader. "Gregor, are ye gonna answer me?"

"Aye, we're all set," Gregor answered, his tone neutral. "The rest of Inspector Elliott's team is in the main barn checking their dive equipment. They're fed and watered, and will be ready to leave at first light."

Iona dipped her head in a short nod. "Good. In that case, I'll go check my medical equipment in the clinic."

She nodded to Kaine and the others before turning her back on Elliott and stomping away.

Elliott spoke directly to Gregor. "Are we done here, sir? I need to talk to her. She's mad at me."

"Ya think?" Drew said, his ironic tone and bunched cheeks showing amusement at the young cop's discomfort.

"Yes, we're done," Gregor answered, shaking his head in disappointment.

Without another word, Elliot hurried after the angry medic.

"She caught him dancing with a police colleague at the Midsummer *Ceilidh* and jumped to the wrong conclusion," Drew told Kaine by way of explanation. "A real hothead, my wee sister."

Kaine opened his hand as though to say he understood, but brought the conversation back to his reason for being in Scotland. "What's happening with the existing search teams?"

During the strained greetings, he'd been studying the wall screens for signs of movement and was disappointed to see that three of the windows remained blank.

"They're camping out and will pick up from where they left off tonight," Drew answered for Gregor.

Thank God for that.

Kaine wondered what had happened to change their minds. From what he'd overheard earlier, he'd been worried Gregor might have wound down the search to focus everyone's attention on the loch.

"Excellent. Have you allocated me a role?"

"I have indeed," Gregor answered.

Kaine drew a hand through his embryonic beard. He'd only been growing it for a week—for disguise rather than aesthetics—but it had yet to bed in. Were it not for the other discomforts, the scratchy whiskers would have driven him mad.

"You're an ex-military man. Yes?" Gregor asked.

"I am," Kaine said, slightly worried by the change of subject. "And proud of it."

Where's he going with this?

"Have you ever done any tracking?"

Kaine nodded, relieved. The tension of leading a double life was making him jump at shadows. "Yes, I've done my fair share. I taught a high-intensity fieldcraft module for a while. I can track well enough."

"I hoped you might say that. Tomorrow morning, do you mind starting from the campsite at Point Zero? See if you can pick up the lad's trail?"

Kaine tried to make it look as though he was considering the task rather than wanting to bite Gregor's hand off. He waggled his head for a moment before replying. "It won't be easy. From what I've heard, half of Scotland has traipsed through the area since young Martin went missing. But yes, I'll happily give it a shot."

He'd been intending to visit the campsite anyway. Now he had Gregor's formal approval, things couldn't have worked out better.

Drew bellowed and slapped Kaine on the shoulder with a force that threatened to dislocate the joint.

"Excellent," he said, voice booming, "and assuming she's still talking to me, I'll make sure Iona sets ye up with some decent wet-weather gear. You'll freeze to death if ye go out there in that rig."

In the comms enclave, Bartholomew replaced the handset in its cradle and stood. He hovered behind the desk for a moment before striding to the group, eyes still fixed on Kaine, one step away from a glower.

"Mind if I butt in, chaps?"

Gregor turned to him. "Of course. Do you have something useful to say?"

"Tomorrow, is it all right for me to tag along with Mr Sidings? I might be able to help. After all, I was the last person to speak to Marty. I might see things I missed before, now I've had a chance to … ah, centre myself. You know, time to think."

Bartholomew threw out a disarming smile, but Gregor's beard bristled again. It seemed to do a lot of that when its owner was talking to an Englishman.

Kaine broke the silence and fired a question at the teacher. "You say you were the last person to speak to Martin?"

Bartholomew's eyes rolled towards Kaine and hovered in all their ice-blue chilliness. "That's right."

"But you told me he shared a tent with a lad called … what was his name?"

"Aiden Murphy," Bartholomew said and shook his head impatiently. "Yes, yes. Of course he did. I meant I was the last responsible adult to talk to Marty. Sorry, I'll try to be more accurate in future."

Kaine stared at the chiselled teacher, who took a half-pace backwards.

"What might you have missed?"

Bartholomew shrugged. "I won't know until I see it. Don't forget, I know that area intimately, as did my boys. And I need to help." Again he turned to the team leader. "Please don't make me stay here twiddling my thumbs. You need all the expertise you can get. You know that."

With obvious reluctance, Gregor relented. "Okay, you can go with Peter. I'm sure he'll appreciate your company and your insights."

"Thank you," he said and shot a wary glance at Kaine. "Are you okay with that?"

"It won't be a problem. Not to me," Kaine answered, making eye contact and not breaking it until Bartholomew blinked first.

With a minor victory won, Kaine turned away from the teacher.

"Iona tells me there's been an improvement in the weather forecast."

A white lie perhaps, but Kaine didn't want them to know he'd been earwigging their conversation. People didn't take too kindly to eavesdroppers, and he doubted Iona would give up his secret. She did seem to have other things on her mind.

Drew answered, a great, big smile on his bushy face. "Aye. We've had good news there. The Met Office expects the storm front to weaken overnight. They say the chopper should be able to fly by mid-morning, but it'll be at the very edge of its operating envelope. High winds expected."

"That is wonderful news," Bartholomew said, rubbing his hands together. "It means you'll be able to shuttle the divers to the loch and get them in the water before noon."

"Aye," Drew agreed. "Just as long as the weather people aren't talking nonsense. That storm doesnae look like its fixing to ease up any time soon."

They turned to face the window in time to see another double-fork of lightning stab at the mountain.

"I pity Marty being outside in this," Bartholomew said. "The wind-chill alone will be devastating."

Kaine was fast growing tired of the teacher's pessimistic attitude. "You never know, he might have found himself some shelter. There are plenty of nooks and crannies on the southwest slope."

Bartholomew rounded on him, eyes ablaze. "Jesus, man. Why don't you listen to me? Marty would never go anywhere near the mountain. The kid was timid. Frightened of his own shadow. He'd get a nosebleed climbing the stairs."

The sudden outburst took Kaine by surprise and, if their shocked expressions were any indication, Gregor and Drew felt the same way.

"Nevertheless," Kaine said, keeping his tone even, "I don't think we should rule anything out. Losing his older brother might have changed him, made him stronger. I've seen similar reactions in my work."

Bartholomew deflated as though someone had let all the air out of him.

"I'm so sorry," he said, head lowered. "I really don't know what happened. The strain has been enormous since Marty disappeared. As I'm sure you can imagine."

He rubbed his face with both hands as though washing away the anger. A deep breath later, he raised his head.

"Mr Sidings is right, of course. We can't rule anything out. If there's the slightest chance that Marty's still alive somewhere …"

He let the sentence trail away. A distant expression floated over his face.

Drew's short, coughed laugh caught Kaine's attention.

"It seems like baby sister's made up wi' yon Elliott. Good job he and his lads are away tomorrow, or I'd have to act as chaperone."

Iona arrived from the kitchen. Her shy smile lit the room as she marched towards the group. She raised a finger at her brother. "Not one word out o' you, Andrew McTay, or I'll brain—"

"Oh my God!" Bartholomew yelled and jumped backwards.

Eyes wide, he jabbed an accusatory finger at Kaine.

"Now I remember where I've seen you before. You're Ryan Kaine. You're the bastard who shot down Matty's plane!"

Chapter Ten

Wednesday 16th September – Evening

Kinross Farm MRC, The Cairngorms,
Aberdeenshire, Scotland

Kaine shot out a hand, grabbed Iona's left wrist, and yanked her towards him. Off balance, she stumbled, and he staggered under her solid weight.

"Get off me!" she screamed, and twisted and wriggled to break his grip.

Kaine threw his free arm around her neck and held her tight against his chest. Her heart thumped wildly as she struggled to free herself.

Drew roared and took a pace forwards.

Kaine shouted, "Don't move!"

Drew stopped dead, raised his massive fists, and bared his teeth. "Leave her alone, ye wee bastard!"

He edged forwards, but Gregor stretched out an arm to hold him back. Bartholomew watched the action, eyes and mouth wide, arms thrown out to the side as though for balance.

"I don't want to hurt anyone," Kaine said, backing towards the kitchen door. "Please don't do anything stupid."

Iona tried to bite his forearm, but Kaine dug the heel of his thumb into the pressure point on her wrist. She yelped and stopped struggling. He relaxed his grip, eased the pressure on her neck, and pushed his mouth close to her ear. "I won't hurt you, I promise. Please stop struggling and we'll both get out of this unharmed."

She relaxed and he took her whole weight, at least seventy kilos of bone, muscle, and raw, animal power. The heel of her boot raked down his left shin. He stopped himself from shouting out. Any sign of weakness or hesitation and they'd be on him and then he might have to really hurt someone. Iona's booted heel scraped down his shin again.

Kaine tightened his grip around her neck, released her wrist, and wrapped his arm around her waist. He yanked her off her feet and took her weight on his hip to protect his vulnerable shins. Her arms and legs flailed. A moment later, fingers reached for his face, nails—cat's claws—searched out his eyes.

"Stop that, woman," he whispered. "You'll only force me to hurt you. I'll let you go the second I'm out of here."

As he backed away, Drew and Gregor crept forwards, maintaining their distance. After five more steps, he bumped into the wall and risked a quick look behind. They'd missed the door by three feet. Two sidesteps later, he released her waist and scrabbled behind him for the handle. He found and turned it.

The door opened and they tumbled through. He slammed it shut and slid the bolt across. As promised, he let her go. She fell to the floor and scrambled away from him, ending up against the leg of a table.

"Are you okay?"

"What d'ye care?"

"I care," he answered, scoping the kitchen, relieved to find it empty. "And I am sorry. Stay there and you'll be fine. Remember this. My only reason for being here is to help find Martin Princeton. That's all."

Kaine left her on the floor, snatched up the Bergen he'd left earlier, and raced to the far door. He entered the rear corridor at full pelt. Behind him, panicked voices raised the alarm. The corridor seemed endless, but was ten metres, no more.

The noises behind grew louder, more strident. Fists hammered on the kitchen door. With luck, in their panic, no one would think to take the long route around the outside of the building and block his exit. He hurried past the clothing storeroom. No point wishing he could stop and suit up against the weather. He'd have to improvise.

Already, a plan was forming. If he could escape the building and reach his car before they raised the full alarm—

Behind him, the crash of splintering wood told him Drew had breached the paltry kitchen defences.

"I'm okay," Iona yelled. "Go get him!"

She'd recovered enough to give him away. No long term effects from his roughhousing—a relief and a good sign.

Heavy boots thumped over flagstones.

Kaine reached the rear exit, turned the handle, yanked

open the door, and raced out into the night. An icy wind sliced through his plaid shirt and he hadn't taken three paces before the lancing rain had soaked him through.

Which way to the car?

Think, man. Think.

Lights flickered on around him, shattering the darkness with blazing white squares and destroying his night vision. He raced forwards, half-blinded, eyes straining to find an escape route, ears open for sounds of pursuit.

The gravel at his feet sloped downwards, towards the car park. Breathing hard, he angled to the right, past low bushes, ducked left, and smashed into something wide and soft. A man grunted. Air exploded from him as they crashed to the ground, in a rolling, tangled mess.

The man met Kaine's automatic, "Sorry, mate," with, "What the fuck?" and a waft of whisky and smoker's breath. Kaine rolled off the marshmallow man, found his feet, and raced on.

Behind him, the cry of help was drowned out when a wailing siren broke through the growing uproar.

Move, keep moving.

Run. Hide.

He needed a place to hole up. A place to think.

One hundred stumbling, fractured paces later, he found a low wall, dived behind it and crouched down in the deep shadows. It took all his willpower not to suck in loud gasps of air. Despite his lungs' desperate need, he controlled his breathing—something he learned years earlier, in dive school. He counted four heart beats in, eight out. As his heart rate slowed, so did his breathing.

All around him, chaos reigned. Men and women yelled questions, others answered. No one took charge.

Kaine was in the middle of a farm that had been

converted into a mountain rescue centre not a military compound. Most of the people were volunteers, mainly farmers and office workers, not prison wardens. They knew little about finding someone who wanted to remain hidden, and that, Kaine could use. The police might be a problem, but they were disorganised and would take time to pull their act together.

The car park lay somewhere off to his left, down the hill, but the volume of noise from that area told him the siren had roused the journalists. They would have his mugshot—the bruising wouldn't help anymore—and would be baying for the story. What would it be worth in career terms to the media hack who helped capture the notorious terrorist, Ryan Kaine?

He waited, biding his time, hoping for a lull to give him an opportunity to reach his Toyota.

People ran, backlit by the temporary media floodlights and the illuminated windows. Rain pelted his back. The first gut-wrenching shiver tore through his body. The memory of his North Sea swim—only a few days earlier— threatened to freeze him to the spot, but adrenaline surged through his system, giving him a boost of warmth. He yawned, part of his body's fight-flight response to pull in more oxygen to fuel his muscles.

Minutes passed.

He needed the jacket from his Bergen but couldn't risk moving until the immediate furore died.

More shouting carried above the siren, this time close and drawing closer. Kaine curled into a tighter ball and hugged the shadows for warmth and security.

The car alarm cut out and voices broke through the new silence. Shouts, orders, calls across the open spaces. Dozens of people, mainly men, searched the area.

"Where'd he go?"

"Who?"

"Ryan Kaine?"

"Who?"

"Ryan bloody Kaine, the killer. He's here."

"You're fucking kidding."

"No I'm not. He's bloody here I tell you. Drew told me."

The men attached to the voices, dressed for the foul weather, passed within feet of Kaine's bolthole but carried on towards the farmhouse.

If he could find one man alone, Kaine might risk an attack to borrow a warm coat, but taking on two or more men would likely force him to play rough. He'd rather suffer the conditions than hurt another innocent.

"What the hell's Ryan bloody Kaine doing here?" the first man said, curiosity overcoming his worry and his voice fading as the two hurried away.

"Who the fuck knows? He's just attacked a reporter. Jumped out and beat him to a pulp. Someone said he was after the missing boy."

"Why would the arsehole want to kill Martin?"

The pair turned a corner and Kaine missed the rest of the conversation. Already the rumours were running wild. Muddled whispers starting out with Kaine as a terrorist and ending up with him as a random attacker and potential child-killing monster.

The rain fell, battering his back and shoulders, hammering on his cap, and running in rivulets from the peak. Despite the confusion, he'd never reach his car without being recognised and, from what he'd just heard, they wouldn't let him give himself up without a pitched battle. Although the police he'd seen hadn't been armed and he hadn't seen any firearms on show, Kaine doubted there was a farm in the UK without at least one shotgun. He didn't need to come up against a panicked local with a twelve-gauge. God knows who might get hurt in the crossfire.

Shit. Where will it end?

Chapter Eleven

Wednesday 16th September — Andrew McTay

Kinross Farm MRC, The Cairngorms, Aberdeenshire, Scotland

Drew McTay fumed. He'd never felt so helpless. He wanted to crush the English bastard with his bare hands, but the man had Iona and, with Gregor holding him back, Drew could do nothing about it. She fought, though. Kicking and biting and scratching, the way she used to do when they were bairns.

Good girl, leave yer mark on the murdering savage.

Ryan Kaine, in Scotland? For God's sake, why?

As Kaine backed towards the door to the kitchen, Gregor dropped his arm and allowed Drew to follow, but the teacher just stood there, watching. Useless git. Arrogant,

English pricks coming up here, thinking they owned the highlands.

"Leave her alone, ye wee bastard!" he yelled, but Kaine ignored him.

Drew needed one opportunity, just one.

Try picking on a man, then we'll see how tough y'are.

Without lowering his eyes, Kaine let go of Iona's waist and searched for the handle. He cracked open the door and they tumbled through.

Drew raced forwards, but Kaine threw the bolt before he could reach it. He could have smashed the bloody thing open with a well-placed boot, but the swinging door might have hurt Iona, and besides, Kaine was a desperate and dangerous man. Who knew how he'd react to a direct attack?

With Gregor at his shoulder, but the teacher nowhere close, Drew slapped on the door with an open hand.

"Iona? Are ye all right, girl?"

He stopped banging and pushed his ear against the wooden panel.

"Drew, I'm fine."

She sounded shaken, but unharmed.

Thank the Good Lord.

"Get away from the door. I'm coming through."

"Wait, I can—"

Drew no more than leaned against the door and it collapsed inwards in a splinter of groaning wood. Iona sat on the floor, four feet from the doorway, breathing hard and rubbing her wrist, but scowling fit to murder a home-grown, English terrorist. He'd seen the expression on her face so often as a kid, he almost laughed in relief at her sass.

"Are ye okay, sis?"

He reached down and heaved her to her feet, but she waved him away.

"I'm okay," she shouted. "Go get him!"

"Are you sure?"

"I'm fine, ye big barmpot. I did him more damage than he did me. Get after him. I'll go fetch Inspector Gadget. Don't let him get away."

Gregor took the lead through to the back, but the open rear door told him they were too late. The bugger was away in the dark.

Drew burst into the night, struck by the cold and the wet. What was the killer wearing? A thin, cotton shirt and jeans? He'd freeze to death if he stayed out all night. Good bloody job, too.

Gregor stood in the lee of the building, sheltering from the lancing wind and bent forwards, breathing hard.

"Are ye okay, man?" Drew asked.

Gregor nodded. "Just winded, that's all. Which way did he go?"

"No idea, he could be anywhere." Drew stood tall, searching the darkness. The centre's lights shone through the uncurtained windows, but did nothing to help find the wee bugger.

Gregor straightened, colour flushed his face.

"Should we start searching?" he asked.

"No' much chance of the two of us finding him in the dark. We need more lights and all the men." Drew kept his eyes open, aching to step out, but knowing how pointless it was with no torch and being poorly dressed. "Why's that lunatic coming up here pretending to be a staff sergeant? What in God's name's he after?"

Gregor shook his head and pointed to the centre's open doorway. "Let's get in out of the rain and wait for Francis

Gaskell. This is a police matter and he can take charge. I don't want anyone stumbling around in the dark risking injury if Kaine's as dangerous as the police and press are saying."

"What d'ye mean 'if'? He attacked Iona, for God's sake!"

"I know. I saw him, too."

They stepped into the dry and hurried through to the kitchen. Finding it empty, they continued to the main office. Bartholomew had returned to the comms corner, the phone handset once more attached to his ear.

"Where's Iona?" Drew asked Craig Conroy at the desk. "I thought she was going to raise the alarm?"

As if she'd heard him, the siren in one of the centre's Land Rovers howled into life, its wails cutting through the evening's silence. Drew stared through the west windows. Lights flicked on in the dormitory block, doors opened, and torchlight cones snapped on all around the car park. One set of halogen lights broke the gloom, and then another as the reporters fired up their lighting rigs, no doubt praying for a story to fill the empty pages and the screen time.

Silhouettes filled doorways, faces appeared in windows, raised voices yelled over the alarm, and, no doubt, confusion filled minds.

The siren cut off. Iona left the car and raced back to the office, shoulders hunched against the rain. She burst through the door and stopped when she spotted him and Gregor. Her eyes searched the room.

"Find him?"

Drew snorted and shook his head. "No need for the sarcasm. He's still out there somewhere. Are ye sure you're all right, lass?"

"I told you I'm fine. Stop your fussing."

"Why the siren?"

"Gadget wasnae answering his phone and his room was empty."

"Probably schmoosing the reporters," Gregor said. "He's never happier than when his name's in the papers."

Lightning flashed and illuminated Inspector Gaskell in the open doorway. He stood beneath a huge golfing umbrella—BBC Scotland logo to the fore—his uniform jacket buttoned skew-whiff. The police officer who represented the might of Police Scotland looked like a badly packed sack of spuds.

Probably the most superstitious policeman in Scotland, Gaskell collapsed the umbrella and shook it out before crossing the threshold.

"Where's the fire?" he demanded.

Gregor gave him the bullet-point outline, and Gaskell's jaw hung open throughout.

"Well?" Gregor asked when he'd finished and Gaskell hadn't responded. "What should we do?"

"I-I don't ..." Gaskell paused, and then shook himself from his stupor. "Kaine? Ryan Kaine here in Upper Glencrae? ... Okay, okay. First thing ... road blocks. Do we know what car he drives?"

His puffy, little eyes searched them for an answer, but received none.

Gregor spoke up. "There's only one track out of the MRC and down to the village. Get your men to park across it."

Gaskell raised a finger. "Aye. Aye, right. Good idea."

Lewis Elliott arrived, his soaked T-shirt sticking to his ripped torso. Iona gasped, raced to the door, and threw herself at him. He hugged her tight. Elliott's eyes found Drew, who nodded his permission. Iona took him to one side and started talking. Elliott's face darkened and his jaws set tight, facial muscles bunching. Drew knew exactly how the Englishman felt. If either of them found Kaine, the police would need DNA to identify the bastard's body.

Drew left Gaskell issuing instructions to his men via his personal radio and signalled for Gregor to join him by the big screen. Bartholomew still talked into his phone. Who the hell could the man find to speak to so late in the evening?

He read the clock on the whiteboard. 22:18. Was that all? It seemed so much later.

"What's on your mind?" Gregor asked.

"We need to do something about Kaine."

"What do you suggest?"

"We're a search team, yeah? Why don't we start searching?"

Gregor shook his grey head, exasperation written in every crease and fold on his weathered face. "We look for people who want to be found. From what I've heard on the TV and radio, Kaine's a military expert. Every police officer in England has been looking for him for days, but somehow, he gets past them all and turns up here." He paused for a moment and shot a glance at Gaskell, who was talking with Elliott and a uniformed sergeant Drew had seen around, but couldn't name.

"This could get complicated and dangerous," Gregor said, the worry in his voice obvious. "We need to leave the manhunt to the police and concentrate on finding the boy in the morning."

Drew raked his wet hair away from his eyes. Fear for Iona and anger at Ryan Kaine had driven Martin Princeton clean out of his head.

Shame on you, Andrew McTay.

"But with Kaine out there and dangerous we need to

protect ourselves. I reckon we should at least set up a watch."

Gregor's mouth opened, but before he could say anything, the volunteers arrived, dressed for a night outdoors. Drew smiled. He'd always known he could rely on his people. Elliott's crew fell in behind—six men and two women. They, along with Gaskell's officers and the volunteers, would be more than enough to keep Kaine at bay and the farmhouse safe.

Probably.

Gaskell stepped alongside Gregor and they turned their backs to the crowd.

"I've stationed my men and two cars at the entrance to the car park. No one's left the area by car since the alarm. This fellow, Kaine, is either still on site, or has taken to the hills. Agreed?"

He looked at Gregor and Drew for confirmation.

Gregor answered. "Agreed. What now?"

"Given who we're after, this is beyond me and my officers. I'm going to call Chief Inspector Murray at HQ. He'll want a full emergency team here by morning along with an ARU. The nearest one's in Aberdeen. Trouble is, they'll not be able to reach us for hours. In the meantime, can I count on your people?"

Gregor took a breath before answering. "We're civilian volunteers, not police officers. I don't really want any of my guys tangling with a madman like Kaine. You can ask for volunteers, but I'm not happy to have people wandering around the place. And what about the reporters?" He nodded in the general direction of the car park.

Gaskell stood taller, the light of opportunity shining in his eyes. "I'll give them a statement as soon as I've spoken to Chief Inspector Murray. We need to keep a lid on this or the whole world will descend on the place and we'll be dealing with a riot."

The media had gathered in the courtyard between the car park and the main buildings. Their rumblings and shouted questions increased in volume and annoyance with each passing minute.

Drew stared through the window, his anger and frustration growing. An image seared itself onto his brain. It was sharp and clear, and it refused to fade—Ryan Kaine's arm wrapped around Iona's throat.

Wait 'til I catch up with you, wee man. Just you bloody wait!

Chapter Twelve

Wednesday 16th September – Night

Kinross Farm MRC, The Cairngorms, Aberdeenshire, Scotland

Kaine held his position in the deep shadow thrown by the drystone wall for over an hour before moving to a new location—in the gorse and heather seventy-five metres above and to the west of the MRC. It was a perfect, if sodden, spot to observe the activity but remain hidden. The lightweight, waterproof jacket he'd retrieved from the Bergen repelled the worst of the rain, but did almost nothing to keep him warm. The wind carved through the thin material as though it didn't exist and he shivered away much of his energy reserves.

From his nest, Kaine had a sniper's view of the centre

and its surroundings. He could make out most of the court-yard, some of the car park, and, through the intervening trees and bushes, even a few of the well-lit houses in Upper Glencrae. Most importantly, his vantage point gave him a good view of the kitchen and main office through the large, ground-floor windows.

It didn't take long for someone—no doubt Gregor—to gain some manner of control over the proceedings. Pairs of men began patrolling the areas bathed in light, presumably worried Kaine would launch a single-handed attack on the place.

Kaine could see the irony. While he hid under a bush, freezing his nuts off, others were terrified he planned to start murdering them in their beds. Just the thought of curling up beneath warm covers was enough to weaken his resolve.

Why didn't he simply walk down the hill and hand himself in? After all, a nice, warm, dry police cell would be so comfortable.

Yeah, right.

And between bouts of beating him with rubber hoses, they'd listen to his theory on where to find Martin Prince-ton. Sure they would. Far-fetched? Perhaps, but in spite of their training, police officers were only human. During his military service, Kaine had seen plenty of well-trained, battle-tempered soldiers turn on their captives.

By 00:15, the reporters had migrated to the flat, gravel area in front of the rescue centre. They stood under umbrellas or awnings, preparing to phone stories in to harassed newspaper editors, or beam the news directly into the nation's homes. The twenty-four-hour news cycle was alive and well, and on full view in front of his eyes.

Inspector Gadget's six uniformed officers had manoeu-vred two of their SUVs to block the route from the car park to the village. Not that the road block mattered. Kaine had no intention of going anywhere until he'd done all he could to find Martin Princeton.

If he'd wanted to, Kaine could have escaped the area by car at any time. The road block wouldn't have stopped him. The village beyond it contained plenty of rich pickings. He could have had his choice of getaway cars. In any event, six unarmed constables didn't form much of an obstruction, especially since Inspector Gadget made them stand guard in the open. Kaine could have overpowered them all easily enough, if he'd wanted to.

Not yet ready to act, he awaited his opportunity.

The rain hammered on his back and shoulders, and dripped from his cap down his neck. It made his life uncomfortable in the short term, but what of Martin Princeton?

Without Kaine, the boy could die if he wasn't dead already. The rescue team was searching in all the wrong places. Of that, Kaine was almost certain. So, what could he do?

As he lay in the gorse, a plan formed slowly.

Before reaching his risky decision, he'd considered and rejected a number of options, including setting off on foot in search of the boy, but that wouldn't work. Ignoring his lack of proper clothing, without decent night vision equipment, he wouldn't be able to cover more than a few miles before daybreak. Not far enough to reach his target area and, with his notoriety, the police would throw up every search helicopter and send out every available officer in the region to run him to ground. Forget Martin Princeton, the search for a mass murderer would take priority.

Damn it.

Even acting with the best of intentions, he'd inadvertently hampered Martin's chances of rescue.

He'd already discounted the second option of giving himself up to the police, and with both running and handing himself over off the table, it left very few alternatives.

The option he chose—using a third party as his mouthpiece to point the search teams in the right direction—was fraught with risk but an obvious solution. The who and the how had yet to be decided.

One person came to mind, but while reaching her without running into trouble would be challenging enough —convincing her to help might prove impossible.

At 00:32, the main door opened and the general murmur in the courtyard erupted into a roar. Cameras flashed, lighting rigs trembled, and two dozen heads turned to face the front.

Gregor Abercrombie and Drew McTay stood either side of an impressive-looking Inspector Gaskell. At least he might have looked impressive if Drew or Gregor had warned the inspector his tunic buttons were misaligned.

Gaskell stood tall and tried to straighten his jacket front.

"Ladies and gentlemen," he shouted, his voice carrying to Kaine on the back of the strong, easterly breeze. "Thank you for being so patient. As you'll be aware, we've had a suspected sighting of Ryan Kaine, the person responsible for shooting down Flight BE1555." He cast his eyes around his audience and tacked on the word, "Allegedly," almost as an afterthought.

The cameras threw another volley of flashes at the police officer, who squinted against the blazing lights but managed a confident smile. After they'd settled down, he continued.

"We've not been able to absolutely confirm the sighting, but have decided to act accordingly. I'm sure I don't really need to say this, but I will, so listen carefully. Ryan Kaine is a highly trained and deadly killing machine." Gaskell punctuated the rabble-rousing speech by waving an index finger in the air. "On no account should anyone attempt to detain him alone. Am I making myself perfectly clear?"

The lights flashed once more. Gaskell nodded, apparently pleased at his speech's reception.

Voices rose from the gathering. Question overlapped question and morphed into a cacophony of white noise. Drew and Gregor exchanged looks of disgust. Kaine smiled. The inspector had a nice way of keeping things cool and of pouring oil on troubled waters. No wonder Iona had no time for the heavy-boned policeman.

Way to go, Inspector Gadget.

Near as damn it, the man had just set light to the oil and sent the villagers out to hunt the monster.

A woman called out, "Are we safe?"

A man added, "Is it right he attacked and seriously injured one of your volunteers?"

"What are you doing to catch him?" another man yelled.

A fourth shouted, "You've blocked us in here! I've got a deadline to meet and a mistress to service!"

That claim received hoots of laughter from the rowdies and another wag in the crowd shouted, "And while you're there, I've an appointment with your wife, Hamish!"

Gaskell harrumphed and patted his hands in the air. "This is no joking matter. You ought to be ashamed of yourselves. We have a lost boy out there and a suspected terrorist running around in the dark. You all have access to the internet for Kaine's identity photo so you know what he looks like. Be vigilant."

Gregor leaned forwards and tapped Gaskell on the

shoulder. He covered his mouth with a hand and said something Kaine couldn't make out. The reporters kept shouting, and their questioning became more and more raucous.

After Gregor finished talking, Gaskell scratched one of his chins and turned to face the crowd again. He raised his arms in the air and waited for silence. It took a few seconds.

"We'll get nowhere if you all keep shouting at once. Let's have a bit of order here, eh?"

He paused again and the crowd noise dropped to a thunderous rumble.

"That's better." Gaskell cleared his throat. "So, Mr Abercrombie has just given me an updated description of the terrorist ... sorry, of the suspect. It seems that Ryan Kaine has grown a beard and has a bruised and swollen face."

The man with the extra-marital appointment threw a hand in the air, but didn't wait for Gaskell to acknowledge it before speaking. "So, we're looking for a man who looks like he's gone ten rounds with Anthony Joshua?"

More raucous laughter suggested at least some of the hoard had been sampling the local tipple.

Drew lunged forwards, barging Inspector Gadget aside. "What the hell's wrong with you? Ryan Kaine killed eighty-three people on that plane and attacked my sister earlier tonight. He's a dangerous man! If you're no' going tae help find him, at least keep out of our way."

Kaine stiffened. Had he miscalculated his restraining techniques on Iona? An acid guilt ate away at the lining of his stomach. If he'd hurt the doctor, he'd never forgive himself. Kaine hugged his chest to stop himself shivering.

Smug grins dropped from faces and a sombre mood rippled through the more sober members of the crowd. Another hand shot up, this one belonged to a TV reporter, a woman. "He attacked your sister? Can you give us some details? We haven't seen an ambulance coming or going. How badly hurt is she?"

Drew jerked his neck and pulled back from the edge of the step as though the sudden realisation that he'd spoken to the media, and through them to the world, had become too much to take.

"She's not hurt, but is badly shaken. She's inside being looked after by … friends."

Kaine let out a relieved breath which condensed around his head. His abdominal wall cramped and his arm and leg muscles tensed. He fought the drive to shiver by force of will alone and conserved his last remnants of body heat by curling into a ball and wrapping the jacket tighter around his body.

It didn't work very well.

His body heat leached into the air around him. Anyone shining a light in his general direction would see steam rising around a shaking gorse bush and discover a fugitive a few degrees away from hypothermia. If the crowd didn't disperse soon, Kaine would be forced to take desperate action or give himself up to Gaskell.

"What exactly happened?" the same female TV reporter called.

Drew turned away, clearly unable to face the lights. He looked at Gregor, who nodded his support and spoke for him.

"Kaine used Dr McTay as a shield to make good his escape, but apart from being shaken up, she's uninjured and will be staying here to help with tomorrow's search for Martin Princeton. Remember him? He's the Search and Rescue Team's first and only priority. As for Ryan Kaine,

I'm sure he's miles away by now. And before you ask, Dr McTay will *not* be doing any interviews."

Gaskell stepped forwards and took control once more. During Gregor's speech, he'd managed to sort out his buttons and, with a straightened tunic, he appeared more confident in his role.

"Any further questions?"

"When can we leave, Inspector Gaskell? I really do have a report to write and copy to send."

"My men will release your vehicles one at a time, but you'll need to undergo a thorough search. Ryan Kaine is a resourceful man and, although we think he's long gone, we can't be sure. I won't take the risk of him having broken into one of your vehicles. I'm asking you all to be vigilant and to stay in groups."

"What's your next step?" the same reporter asked.

Gaskell paused for a moment.

Kaine could understand his reluctance to answer. He'd be weighing up the value of keeping the reporters calm and onside, against tipping his hand.

"I've asked for volunteers, and the excellent folk in the mountain rescue team have been helping my men to secure the area, at least for tonight. As you can no doubt see, we've set two-man teams to patrol the centre for security reasons only. It's too dark and too dangerous to send anyone outside of the lights to search, but I agree with Mr Abercrombie. If Ryan Kaine has any sense, and I'm certain he does, he'll already be miles away from here. He'll be out in the open right now, running for his freedom, but"—he smiled as the cameras flashed again—"never you mind. We'll catch the man as soon as it's light enough and clear enough to send up the helicopter. He'll not get far at night over this terrain.

It wouldn't surprise me if we find him tomorrow, lost and begging for rescue."

A venerable reporter, with a grey beard, bushy enough to rival the one Gregor sported, waved an old-fashioned notepad. "So, you'll be cutting the size of the search team to chase down Ryan Kaine? Is that it? Do you not care about the boy? Or are you more concerned with being part of the team that captures Ryan Kaine?"

Murmurs of disgruntled agreement rippled through the crowd.

"Fraser Monroe," Gaskell growled, jabbing a pudgy finger at the elderly reporter. "That insinuation is beneath even you. We've had our disagreements in the past, but this isn't the time to air them. I've just this moment got off the phone with Chief Inspector Murray at headquarters and apprised him of the situation. He knows how thinly we're spread here and has called in the Serious Incident Command Team. They will be here by first light. He has also authorised the deployment of an Armed Response Unit. They're coming from Aberdeen and will be here by nine o'clock tomorrow morning."

"And the army?"

"That's a distinct possibility. The SIO—that's the Senior Incident Officer—will make that determination when he arrives and has all the facts at his disposal. We must remember one thing. Although Ryan Kaine is dangerous, he is only one man and, as I've already said, there's no reason to assume he's still anywhere near Kinross Farm."

Another hand barely reached shoulder height before its owner shouted, "Why did he attack Billy Dougherty?"

"Who?"

"My cameraman."

"Oh, I see." Gaskell dug a finger between his neck and

shirt collar, trying to ease the strain, and again the cameras flashed. "My sergeant is currently interviewing Mr Dougherty, but your friend's a little vague on the details."

"If I know Billy," a different wag in the crowd called out, "he tripped over a stone on his way to the bushes. The man ne'er could handle his whisky."

More laughter greeted the claim, but Kaine had heard enough. The imminent arrival of an ARU from Aberdeen, while not surprising, put a serious time constraint on his schedule. On top of that, movement inside the well-lit office gave him the opportunity he'd been waiting for.

Time to go, Kaine.

Moving slowly to work the cramp out of stiffened muscles, Kaine kitty-crawled from beneath the bush and struggled into his Bergen.

With one eye on the continuing press conference and another on his destination, he clambered thirty metres uphill and deeper into the darkness before stopping. He stilled his breath to listen and counted to fifty before climbing unsteadily to his feet. He swayed against the head-rush and waited for the dizziness to pass.

The driving rain and howling wind had done a great job of masking his sounds and keeping the people away. On top of that, the uphill crawl through knee-high grass and moss had loosened his joints and warmed him through. He was ready for action and focused on his plan.

He set off down the hill, taking a circuitous route, and headed back to the centre.

Chapter Thirteen

Wednesday 16th September – Iona McTay

Kinross Farm MRC, The Cairngorms, Aberdeenshire, Scotland

Iona cupped her hands around the mug of warm, milky chocolate, thoroughly enjoying its comforting taste and Lewis' close attention. A warmth built in her belly that had little to do with the chocolate, but lots to do with his proximity and his concern. Not that she'd let on too easily. A girl had her methods, and playing it cool in the face of his anxiety was working well. She had him exactly where she wanted him, and she was not about to lose her advantage.

"You sure you're okay, love?" Lewis asked, a lost-little-puppy look on his handsome face.

Lord, she could just eat him up.

"For the one hundredth time, Inspector Elliott, I'm perfectly fine. And stop calling me 'love'. I'm Dr McTay to you. And don't you dare forget it."

"Good God, Iona, how many times do I have to tell you, Ellie Strachan kissed *me*. I didn't kiss her back, and you've got to know that. Damn it, girl, I've loved you since the first time I clapped eyes on you, and I … God, you could have been hurt tonight. When I think of that bastard with his hands all over you, I could tear his heart out."

He kneeled in front of her, hands on her knees and eyes brimming.

She took pity on him and covered his hands with hers.

"He didn't hurt me, Lew," she said quietly. "In fact, now I've had time to think on it, Kaine seemed genuinely upset. He actually apologised when he let me go, and he looked as though he meant it."

"But he's a killer. Think of all those people on that plane."

Iona closed her eyes and tried to associate the man she'd known for a few hours as Peter Sidings with the actions attributed to Ryan Kaine. She found it difficult, but not impossible. During her psych rotation in med school, she'd been exposed to dozens of patients with sociopathic and psychopathic tendencies. Some she'd diagnosed easily, others had taken a little longer. It usually had something to do with the eyes, the way the patients looked at her. A slight disconnect between the words and the apparent human empathy.

Although he'd lied from the start, she understood why. Kaine hadn't exhibited any of those pathological abnormalities in his actions or reactions. In a clinical setting, Iona would have sworn the man was well-balanced and normal.

High-functioning and driven, even. She didn't see him sitting on any of the DSM lists.

For Peter Sidings, or rather Ryan Kaine, to have fooled her so completely was not only frustrating, it was deeply disappointing.

Darn it, what had she missed? He'd seemed so genuine. Quietly spoken, he appeared focused only on the missing boy.

"A penny for them?"

Iona smiled. She could rely on Lewis to throw out a cliché when she needed to hear one.

"My thoughts are worth much more than that, Inspector."

He lowered his head and kissed the back of her hand. She jerked it away and checked the kitchen, relieved they still had the place to themselves.

"Lewis," she barked. "This is no' the time or the place. So unprofessional. There's a killer on the loose and people will be in and out of here all night."

"Fuck 'em," he whispered, but scanned the room before doing so. "You've had a shock and I'm comforting a dear friend."

She rested her hand on his once more and relaxed.

"So, what are we going to do?"

"What … you mean?" His gaze fell on the hallway leading to the accommodation block.

"Don't be ridiculous. We can't slope off and play house when there are things to do."

He sighed. "I suppose you're right. But we're going to take a rain check, aren't we?"

She pushed forwards, kissed his cheek, and struggled to her feet. Lewis stood, too, and looked at her through loving eyes. Lord, he was handsome and strong. She allowed him to wrap his powerful arms around her, and she felt safer than she had since the attack.

Lewis lifted her chin and arched an eyebrow in question. "Aren't we?"

"We most certainly are," she answered, pushing him away. "But for now, we have work to do."

He shook his head emphatically. "Oh no, Dr McTay. You're going to rest. We need you wide awake in the morning."

"But Gregor and Inspector Gadget called for volunteers to patrol the centre," she said and patted her chest. "I'm a volunteer."

He gripped her upper arms, lips compressed. "Now listen to me for once, woman. With all those people involved in both searches tomorrow, there's bound to be the odd accident or two and we'll need a fresh, clear-eyed medic."

She frowned and once again heard Granny McAdam saying her face would stick that way. "I know that, but—"

"What if we find the boy alive but injured? And what if someone finds Kaine and he puts up a fight? We might need you to run triage. And don't forget the boys from the Armed Response Unit. Some of those guys make Jesse James look like a pacifist. And besides"—he squeezed her arms for emphasis—"I want you safe in your room until morning. Please?"

"Are ye always going to be this bossy?"

He sighed. "When we're married, we'll discuss most things equally, but when it comes to your safety, I rule. Is that clear?"

Her mouth dropped open. "What was that? What did you say?"

He sighed again, this time more heavily. "I said, when it comes to your safety—"

Iona broke free of his grip and slapped his shoulder. "No, before that. The bit about when we're married."

Lewis' sheepish smile screwed up his face and created the dimples she loved.

"You will marry me, won't you?"

She stood, open mouthed, trying to speak, but unable to form the words.

"Well?"

Breathe, girl. Breathe.

"I ... You chose a fine time to ask."

"I'll propose properly later with the full package—restaurant, down on one knee, engagement ring, the lot—but can I take that as a yes?"

"Yes. Of course, yes!"

Heart fluttering wildly, she attacked him with a mad kiss before breaking away when a trio of his teammates burst through the door from the office. They broke out a raucous cheer and launched into spontaneous applause.

One shouted, "Go get her, Inspector."

Another whistled through his teeth.

Grace Jackman, the team's only woman, said, "And once again the man with the officer's pips wins the hot chick."

Lewis' face flushed bright crimson. He lost the dimples, but didn't push her away.

"Pack that in, you guys. That's my fiancée you're talking about."

Grace broke through the mêlée of backslaps and congratulations and pulled Iona to one side.

"Can I see the ring?" she asked, eyes bright.

"Haven't got one yet. He sort of asked me accidentally. Spur o' the moment kind o' thing."

"How on earth does anyone propose by accident? You

make sure he gets you a nice ring. A huge solitaire. Men can be so damned cheap." She smiled and dragged Iona into a back-slapping hug. "I'm kidding, girl. Lewis Elliott's a true diamond. One of the best men I've ever known. If I were straight, I'd marry him myself."

Tears threatened to leak from Iona's tired eyes. So much excitement was almost more than she could take. After what had been the most traumatic event in her life so far, the night was ending on such a high note. She sucked in a deep, long, and wholly satisfying yawn.

Lewis appeared at her side. "Okay, that's enough. Go report to Inspector Gaskell. We have some patrols to support and Dr McTay needs her bed."

His angry scowl cut short another lewd cackle and the party dispersed.

"Come on now, girl," Lewis said. "I'll walk you to your room."

He took her gently by the elbow and escorted her through the rear corridor, across the open space to the accommodation block, and showed her to her room.

After another kiss that could have continued for an hour longer as far as Iona was concerned, he left her at the threshold, wanting more.

"Sleep tight, love," he said. "I'll wake you with a coffee at oh-six-hundred."

He smiled and ran a gentle finger down her cheek and along her chin. In other circumstances she'd have pulled him into the room, but he had his duty, and she did need her rest.

She watched him hurry away to join his team before sighing and closing the door softly. It clicked shut and she reached for the light switch.

Within minutes she'd stripped off her clothes, pulled on

one of Lewis' extra-long T-shirts, and crawled into bed without washing her face or brushing her teeth—more of Granny McAdam's cardinal sins. The pillow was soft, the bedding fresh, and her mind filled with thoughts of missing teenagers, fleeing fugitives … and wedding plans.

A COLD, calloused hand clamped over her mouth. Another pressed down on her shoulder, pinning her into the bed.

"Don't move. Don't scream," a man whispered.

She opened her eyes and stared into the implacable face of a killer—Ryan Kaine.

Oh God, no!

Her heart tried to smash its way through her ribcage, blood roared in her ears, and the dark room started spinning. She tried to kick out, but the tangled bedding held her legs in place.

Chapter Fourteen

Thursday 17th September – Pre-Dawn

Kinross Farm MRC, The Cairngorms, Aberdeenshire, Scotland

For the second time in a few short hours, Kaine laid his hands on the same innocent woman and hated himself for it. She struggled and kicked, but the covers restricted most of her efforts and saved him from yet another gouging.

She fought him, eyes wide, screaming beneath his hand and trying to bite it, but he held firm until she stopped struggling and slumped back into the bed.

Kaine allowed her ragged breathing to recover before easing the pressure on her mouth.

"If I let go, will you scream?"

Kaine couldn't see much in the dark, but her eyes glistened in the fractured light showing through the part-closed curtains. Except to struggle for breath, she didn't move to respond.

"I'm taking a big risk here, Doctor. Please answer me. If I take my hand away, will you scream?"

Her head twitched. He took it as a no, but when he removed his hand, she sucked in a huge breath and he covered her mouth again.

"Iona, please listen." He spoke quietly, pleading, trying to calm her. "I know you're terrified and I'm truly sorry, but I have no choice. If you scream and someone comes to help, I might be forced to hurt them, and I really don't want to do that."

He cast his eyes around the room, searching for weapons she might use but found nothing to cause concern.

"Now, once more. I'm going to release you. Please don't make a sound. Give me five minutes to explain myself and then I'll leave. I promise. Okay?"

This time, the nod was more definite.

No doubt about it, Kaine was taking a hell of a chance, but he needed her and couldn't think of an alternative. He let her go and stepped back into the middle of the room. She scrambled to the corner of the bed, pulled the covers over herself, raised her knees, and curled into a tight ball. She stared at him, panting, terrified—a wild animal caged.

"Thank you," he whispered and stood, hands raised in surrender.

For a full minute they stayed locked in position while her breathing recovered and she adjusted to the situation.

"Please don't hurt me," she whimpered. "I-I've just gotten engaged."

As soon as the words tumbled out, she threw a hand to her mouth as though astonished at her revelation.

Kaine nodded. A couple of hours earlier, from his position outside in the cold, staring through the kitchen window, he'd guessed the young, English cop had proposed. What else could have elicited such a raucous and spontaneous response from his team?

"Congratulations," he said, unable to think of anything more original. "I hope you'll be very happy."

Pitiful, but he genuinely was delighted for her. If his life had turned out differently, maybe he and Lara would ... No, bugger it, no point wishing for miracles. If he hadn't fallen foul of a plot to kill innocent civilians, he and Lara would never have met. Not in a million years.

How had his life come to this? Terrifying an innocent woman in her bed hadn't been a part of his game plan when he'd made the snap decision to head for Scotland. But, as the saying went, no battle plan ever survived the first shot.

"I'm guessing Inspector Elliott just proposed?"

"Yes, how did ye know?"

"The way you looked at each other when he arrived, the attraction was obvious. Then he wouldn't leave your side all night after I'd ... made my escape. Can't blame him, though. If someone had treated the person I loved that way, I ... well, you know."

"You've been watching us?"

Kaine nodded, grabbed the only chair in the room from its spot under the window, and placed it against the door. "Mind if I sit? It's been a long, tiring few days."

As he collapsed into the hard-backed chair and sighed heavily, she scrunched into a tense ball.

"Please try to relax, Iona. I'm really not going to hurt you."

She pulled an arm out from under the quilt and pointed to the pile of clothes on the floor.

"Pass them to me."

He did as she asked and averted his eyes while she dressed beneath the covers. Once satisfied, she slid to the edge of the bed, and pushed her feet into a pair of flat shoes. She stared at him, arms crossed tight to her chest, her body held stiff.

"How did ye know where to find me?"

"I could give you a load of bull about my Holmes-like detective skills, but I've been here before, remember? I wasn't lying about everything. This room was always set aside for the resident medic and ... well, your name's on the door."

He grimaced at his pitiful attempt at humour.

"What d'ye want wi' me?" she snapped, clearly not falling for his charm, and he couldn't blame her a whole lot. "Am I a hostage?"

"No. You're a messenger."

Kaine tried to relax the cramp from his shoulders. After spending fifteen minutes indoors and out of the rain, the building's warmth had finally started to work through to his bones, and his clothes steamed gently. He must have looked a real mess—a terrifying mess.

"What did you just say?"

He dipped his head in a tired nod. "I'm here to give you a message to pass on to your friends before I skip town."

Her eyes flashed with rage and she spoke through clenched teeth. "You couldnae have left a note?"

Kaine relaxed a little more. Anger was a better look on her than fear. She was a strong woman and would soon recover.

"My notebook and pen are in my hire car. It's a Toyota

Land Cruiser, by the way. Although no doubt your Inspector Gadget has identified and impounded it by now. At least he should have done. A simple process of elimination, and he's had more than enough time. Unfortunately, not having my car has left me in a bit of a pickle. No mobile phone, no dry clothing, no provisions."

"My heart bleeds for you."

"Thank you."

She sniffed. "I was being facetious."

"So was I."

Iona didn't return his half-hearted smile.

"What's the message?"

"I'll get to that in a sec, but first I need you to know that I am not a terrorist."

Her upper lip curled into a sneer. "What are ye then, a 'freedom-fighter'?"

He had to admire her spirit. Most people in her position would have been quivering wrecks. Iona McTay reminded Kaine of another woman whose life he'd barged into unannounced and unwanted. A woman to whom he owed his life.

"It's a long story, Iona, but I am a wronged man."

"I'm not interested in hearing your pitiful excuses. Please get out of my room and leave me alone."

"I promise to do just that, if you'll listen to what I have to say. I can't give you all the details, but I was on my way to the police to give myself up when I learned of Martin Princeton's disappearance."

"So you just had to come up here to help us poor, useless Scots. Is that it?"

Kaine covered a yawn with his hand. She yawned in sympathy.

"In a manner of speaking, yes," he answered. "Earlier,

when I told you I knew this area, it was the truth. And since my chat with Bartholomew, I have had an idea where you should focus tomorrow's searches."

The sneer disappeared to be replaced by a sarcastic smile. "And you expect me to believe that? You were actually going to hand yourself over to the police and you're only here out of the goodness of your heart?"

Kaine puffed out his cheeks and instantly regretted the pain it caused.

"Whether you believe it or not, it's the truth."

"Why don't you do that now?" She waved a hand in the direction of the main building. "Inspector Gaskell and the others are through there in the main office. All you have to do is shuffle along and put your hands in the air."

Kaine sighed. "Believe me, Iona, I'd love to do just that. I've been awake for most of the past week. Nothing looks more inviting right now than that bed you're sitting on."

She leaned away, her expression wary.

"Don't worry, Doctor. Your honour is safe with me."

She sniffed. "So why don't you hand yourself over?"

"I made a promise to help find Martin, but I can't do that from a police holding cell."

"Who did you promise?"

Kaine glanced at his watch: 03:22. Less than three hours until dawn. As expected, his approach was taking too long, but he needed Iona's help, and she wouldn't offer it without at least part of the story.

"Myself."

"Ha! You expect me to take a promise made by a terrorist, to himself, seriously?"

"I'm no terrorist, but I hope so, yes."

"Care to explain yourself?"

Asking questions was a good sign. Perhaps he was starting to make a connection, and by God, he needed one.

"The Princetons have already lost one son, and I have to help get Martin back. After that, I'll hand myself over to the authorities. That's it."

"I don't believe ye."

"Can't say I blame you, but ..." He pointed to the phone on her bedside table. "Is that a landline? Can you dial out?"

Her brow creased in confusion, but she nodded.

"Good. When I'm gone I want you to get hold of a Detective Chief Inspector David Jones of the Midlands Police. He's based in Birmingham. From what I've heard, he's a workaholic. You might even find he's still in the office."

"At this time o' night?"

"He's in the middle of a rather important investigation, but if he's at home, convince the night operator to make him call you."

"And why would they do that?"

He tried another lopsided smile but his cheek grated against the inside of his mouth, irritating his exposed root. He risked dragging his eyes away from her long enough to dig the bottle of clove oil from his pocket.

Iona winced as he applied the salve and sucked in a sharp breath.

Excellent.

Her empathy was a good sign and reinforced his hope. Perhaps he could convince her to help after all.

"Why would I want to call this policeman?"

"DCI Jones is the man I planned to hand myself over to. He knows the full story of Flight BE1555. He also knows the real person responsible and that I'm an innocent man."

So far, that was the only real lie he'd told her this time around. He wasn't innocent, not by a long way, but she wasn't ready for the full story. The world probably wasn't ready for the full story.

"So this DCI Jones, he can clear your name and call off a nationwide search?"

Kaine shook his head. "Not on his own, but he has all the evidence he needs for the authorities to charge the real culprit."

"How d'ye know that?"

"Because I handed it to him." He waved a hand at his face. "This happened while I was gathering the evidence."

"Not a road rage thug, then?"

"No," Kaine answered. "A different kind of thug. A smarter, more devious kind of thug. Richer, too."

"You seem to attract the attention of angry blokes. I can see why."

"This beating happened while I was chained to a chair. But it's a long story, and I don't have the time right now. Please wait until I'm gone, then call DCI Jones. He'll vouch for me."

"Why hasn't he made a public announcement? Why is every cop in the UK still hunting for ye?"

He shrugged. It was difficult and his shoulders were heavy, but he managed the impressive feat by force of will alone.

"There's a little thing called the rule of law. I imagine he has to jump through all sorts of legal hoops and, strictly speaking, it isn't even his case. As I said, it's a long and complicated story, but DCI Jones happened to come highly recommended by the only policeman in the country I would trust with my life. A man called Giles Danforth, but that's a different story."

"So, I contact this DCI Jones and he convinces me you're a good man and I should trust you. What then? What d'ye want from me?"

"Nothing much. Nothing onerous, I promise."

"Go on."

Kaine groaned as his broken tooth jabbed a red-hot poker through the middle of his head.

"Just a sec."

He dabbed another drop of oil onto his tooth and closed his eyes against the flaring pain. He still had an hour before he could pop another painkiller.

"Why me?" she asked quietly. "Why d'ye choose me? And why did you attack me in the office?"

The pain diminished to a dull, throbbing ache. How would he cope when the clove oil ran out?

"It was the only way I could escape without hurting anyone. If I hadn't grabbed you, that big brother of yours would have tried to stop me, and I might have had to hurt him."

Her expression changed from surprise to disbelief. "You were worried about hurting Drew? Have ye seen my big brother?"

"Exactly. He's a powerful man, and I wouldn't have been able to play as nice as I did with you."

She scoffed. "You call that playing nice?"

"Your arm, does it hurt?"

"I ..."

She looked down at her left hand, flexed her fingers a couple of times, and made a fist. Then she pulled back the cuff of her shirt to expose the wrist. Pale skin, no bruising. She rotated her wrist back and forwards, and flexed the fingers again.

"No, no it doesn't hurt at all."

He nodded.

"During our little … dance, I compressed the nerve between the radius and ulna bones. Painful, wasn't it?"

She scowled. "You don't have to tell me that."

"But perfectly harmless if it's done by an expert. You see? No bruising. Didn't even leave a mark. It was the safest way I knew to stop you breaking my shins with your bloody climbing boots. It's also the reason I wrapped my arm around your waist and yanked you off your feet."

"You'd have deserved it," she said through a grudging smile.

"No doubt."

The smile looked good on her. It reminded him of the one she gave Lewis Elliott after his proposal.

Outside in the hall, a door creaked open and clicked shut.

Damn it.

Heavy footfalls pounded on the wooden floorboards, growing louder as they approached. Kaine put a finger to his lips, praying Iona would keep quiet and the footsteps would keep going, but they stopped outside the door, and someone rapped gently.

Kaine held his breath.

"Iona, it's me, Drew," he said, using a stage whisper. "Are ye okay, sis?"

Kaine eased to his feet but kept his eyes glued on Iona. He shook his head and pushed out desperate, pleading vibes. He mouthed the word, "Please."

She opened her mouth and Kaine saw the end of his freedom and the end of Martin Princeton's life. He wasn't going to fight a good man like Drew McTay, nor was he going to risk hurting the brave medic. He slumped his shoulders and allowed his arms to drop.

Iona spoke, her voice quiet and apparently slurred with fatigue. "Drew?"

"Aye, sis. How are ye?"

"Trying to sleep, man. Why can't ye leave me alone?"

Drew laughed quietly. "That's ma wee sister. Tough as nails and twice as sharp. See you in the morning. And don't fret yourself, I'll be keeping my eye on yon Englishman. Lewis Elliott's no' allowed anywhere near your bedroom until *after* you're hitched. Ye hear me?"

"Goodnight, Drew," she said, her delivery one of enforced patience.

"Night, sis. Sleep tight. I won't let the Englishman bite."

Drew's chuckle and clomping footsteps faded and Kaine exhaled slowly.

"Thank you, Iona. I appreciate that."

She glared at him for a moment before speaking. "Don't make me into a fool. So, you know where Martin is?"

"I think so."

"Can ye tell me?"

"Do you climb?"

"What? Mountains? Where are ye going with this?"

"Humour me. Do you climb?"

"Don't be daft, I value my hide. Climbing's for thrill seekers and idiots, and I'm neither. Drew is, though. He loves all that macho malarkey."

"Thought he might. I doubt there's many search and rescue volunteers around here who don't climb."

She leaned forwards, searching his face for clues. "So? What of it?"

"Before I answer that, can I ask a question?"

"Another one?" she asked.

He took it as her agreement.

"What did Kurt Bartholomew do after I … left the office?"

Iona closed her eyes in thought.

"Nothing."

"What exactly do you mean by 'nothing'?"

She rested her elbows on her thighs. "Exactly that," she said. "He didn't do anything at all."

"Interesting. I'd have expected him to join in the search for me. Especially since he raised the alarm in the first place. Didn't he offer to help find me?"

"No."

"What about a phone call?"

"Yes, he did use the phone, but that was *before* ye left. All he did after raising the alarm was sit in a chair. As far as I could tell, he was just listening and watching. I don't remember him saying anything at all."

Kaine imagined the scene for a moment. Everyone would have been rushing around, trying to find him, yet the teacher did nothing. Why? The answer came in a flash of anger.

Bloody hell!

Kaine leaned forwards. This time, Iona didn't flinch.

"Was he looking at the screens?"

After another brief pause, she answered, "Ye know, I think he was. Yes, yes definitely. I thought he was lost in thought, shocked. You know how shock effects people in different ways?"

"I do. Was he watching the big screen or the one segmented into windows?"

"Both, I think. Why?"

Kaine cast his mind back to his hiding spot in the gorse. He'd been able to see into the office through the big, horizontal window, but the comms alcove and the screens had been hidden by the junction between the side wall and the gable end of the MRC.

The revelation hit him with the force of a baseball bat to the gut. He hadn't actually seen Bartholomew since his escape from the office!

Kaine jumped to his feet and grabbed the chair. Iona jerked up her arms in fear. He held out a calming hand and put the chair to one side to free up access to the door.

"Oh hell. Bartholomew, where is he now?"

"Last I heard, he was heading for bed. We gave him one of the single rooms in the men's dorm."

"I know. I visited him."

"Why? What's wrong?"

"I need to check on him."

Kaine darted through the door, turned right, and hared along the corridor. Iona followed hard on his heels.

Chapter Fifteen

Thursday 17th September – Pre-Dawn

Kinross Farm MRC, The Cairngorms, Aberdeenshire, Scotland

Kaine and Iona reached the door at the end of the hall at full pace. Kaine surged through, scanned the area for patrolling guards, and crossed the narrow, open-air strip between the buildings. He stopped before opening the door to the men's dorm. The wind sliced through him, undoing all the good work the warmth in Iona's room had achieved. At least the rain had stopped. Overhead, a dozen stars pricked the blackness, and a waxing, crescent moon picked out the leading edge of the cloud bank. The forecasters had been right, thank God. By morning, the weather should be clear enough for the chopper to fly.

"When we reach his room, you knock and ask if he's okay. Say you're worried about him after all he's been through."

"What for? He needs his rest."

"Humour me. I'm betting he won't answer."

Iona hesitated and shot him a look that asked, "Why am I doing this?" before nodding and opening the front door. A corridor stretched into the darkness. It matched the one they'd just raced along, right down to the wooden flooring, the frosty, white walls, and the landscape posters of *Ben Craed*.

Kaine raised a finger to his lips and they padded over the creaking floorboards, stopping at the third door on the left. She knocked.

"Mr Bartholomew, it's me, Iona McTay. Are you okay?"

Silence.

She waited a moment before repeating the performance, but a little louder.

Kaine waited fifteen seconds before trying the handle. It turned and the door squeaked open.

"Damn," he said, "I knew it."

Kaine stepped fully into the room, the replica of Iona's, and pulled her inside after him. He threw open the curtains to allow in some background light and sat on the edge of the bed. The room hadn't changed much since his earlier visit, only now, it was empty of clutter. Bunk beds, side table, dining chair, empty locker, and nothing else. Bartholomew had packed his clothes into his rucksack and scarpered, and Kaine suspected he knew where.

Iona pulled up the chair and sat facing Kaine, their earlier roles reversed.

"How come ye knew he'd be gone?"

"Premonition. Guesswork. Who knows?"

"Where's he disappeared to?"

"My guess is he's looking for Martin. I think he saw something on the screens in the main office that triggered a memory."

Or worried him.

"Why didn't he tell anyone? For crying out loud, we all want to find the boy."

Kaine considered his response. He couldn't risk voicing his real suspicions. At best she might think he was trying to divert attention away from himself and onto the teacher. At worst, she might think him delusional and give him away for his own protection.

He hedged.

"I don't know. Maybe he feels responsible and wants to find the boy on his own. To become the hero of the hour. Maybe he's worried the focus of everyone's attention will be on the hunt for me rather than the search for the boy. Either way, he's gone, and I need to find him."

Her eyes widened. "You're going after him?"

"Too right I am."

"In the middle of the night with the whole country after ye, you're just going to wander off over hills and search for a man who's looking for a boy who's been missing for the best part of two days?"

"I am."

"You're a lunatic."

"Quite possibly."

"You'll fall into a rabbit warren and break your leg. I've seen it happen often enough."

"I've completed a few night manoeuvres in my life and have lived to tell the tale. Besides, I'm going part of the way in the centre's spare Land Rover."

"Really?"

"Well, I hope so. It'll help me catch up to him by dawn. By the way, I don't suppose the centre has any surveillance cameras?"

"Of course not. We're in the middle of nowhere and nobody around here would steal from us."

"Pity. I'd like to know how much of a start Bartholomew has on me. I'd like to intercept him before he reaches the campsite."

"Why?"

"So I can follow him without having to play the tracker. I'm adequate at most fieldcraft skills, but I'd hate to risk Martin's life because I followed the wrong boot prints."

Kaine slapped his hands to his knees and pushed himself upright. His joints creaked as he stood. God above, he was tired.

"Right then, I'm off to find Martin Princeton, but can I ask one more thing before I go?"

She stood and faced him. "Ask away."

"We're about the same size. Might I borrow a jacket? It's perishing outside."

"If I said no, what would you do?"

"As I'm not a thief, I'd have to go out in that weather and risk freezing to death. Would you want that on your conscience? What about your Hippocratic Oath?"

"Ryan Kaine, you're a conman."

She placed one hand across her waist, raised the other to her chin, and tapped her lips with a finger as though deep in thought. He waited patiently, not wanting to force her hand.

Eventually, she nodded.

"Drew and I keep a complete change of clothing in the old Land Rover. You could take Drew's but you'll be swimming in it. Better off taking mine."

"For swimming, I prefer a wetsuit," he said, "but I'll happily borrow your coat."

"What size shoes do ye wear?"

"Tens."

"Drew takes a size eleven. You'll find his spare boots in the pack with the clothes. Ye can hardly go climbing the mountain in those trainers."

Riches indeed.

"Thank you. You think of everything."

She reached for the door handle.

Kaine dropped a hand on her forearm and held her back. "Where do you think you're going?"

She plucked his hand away. "The garage is on the other side of the centre. You'll need my help to reach it through the patrols. I know a quiet way."

He shook his head. "Uh-uh. Too risky for you. If they find us, the police will accuse you of aiding and abetting. Besides, exfiltrating a confined space is what I'm trained for."

"But this isn't a military compound and you don't have time to crawl around in the dirt. The sun's going to be up in a couple o' hours. I can help ye."

Damn. Her logic made complete sense.

"Okay, you lead, but if we're caught, say I forced you to help, okay?"

The sense of *déjà vu* was overwhelming. He'd said pretty much the same thing to Lara only a week earlier. How many more people would he be forced to involve in his troubles?

Iona led the way along dark paths, between outbuildings, stopping when danger appeared, and continuing when the route was clear. As a nocturnal trailblazer, she was a natural.

In a narrow crawlspace between two rickety sheds, she dropped to her knees and he followed her lead. The heavens opened again and the rain fell with even more force than before. For once, the weather took Kaine's side. Anyone out and about would be keeping their heads down during a thoroughly miserable vigil.

Iona beckoned him closer and pointed across the way to a brick barn.

"That's the garage, but it's open ground. Wait here while I open the doors and start the engine. We'll take the old Defender. It's a temperamental, wee beastie, but I've always had the knack."

Before he could stop her, she crept out from the shadows and strolled along the overgrown, concrete path leading to the garage as though her actions were the most natural thing in the world.

She'd covered no more than ten paces before a man stepped out from the shelter of an old shed and a torch snapped on. The cone of light sliced a funnel into the dark, illuminated the heavy rain, and shone in her face. Iona threw up a hand to shield her eyes.

"Who's that?" the man shouted.

Kaine didn't recognise his voice, but guessed it belonged to a man in his seventies at least. Old enough to be Jock's contemporary, but taller and carrying a few kilos more weight.

The torchlight picked out the dark metal of a double-barrelled shotgun. Mercifully, the barrel pointed at the ground and stayed that way.

"Alastair, is that you? Bloody hell, man. You nearly gave me a heart attack. Get that light out o' my eyes, and don't you dare raise that old shotgun."

The old man lowered the torch and shone it at her feet.

She was still wearing her indoor shoes. Her feet had to be soaked through. If Alastair noticed the inappropriate footwear, he didn't comment.

"Iona?"

"Aye, it's me. What d'ye think you're doing skulking around here in the middle o' the night?"

Alastair stood a little taller. "I'm on patrol."

"Oh for goodness sake. Does anyone know you're out here?"

The old man sagged a little under the weight of her crushing glare. He lowered his gaze.

She pressed home her advantage. "What about Flora? Does she know you're out here in the driving rain?"

"No. She's safe in bed while I'm protecting the village."

"Playing at soldiers, more like."

She marched forwards, grabbed his arm, and eased him towards the downhill path.

"Away ye go home afore ye catch your death. I've enough on my plate without having to treat a silly, old man for pneumonia."

The elderly guardian stuck out his chin. "Stop treating me like an invalid, woman. I've been a farmer all ma life. A little lost sleep never did me any harm. And what are you doing out and about? Shouldn't you be recovering from your ordeal?"

"What ordeal? Don't believe all ye hear from the media people. Ryan Kaine hardly touched me. And I certainly don't need a foolish, old man wandering around in the dark with a loaded shotgun. Away back home with ye."

"You didn't answer my question. What are you doing out and about?"

She stood, hands on hips, head shaking. "If ye must know, I'm still on call despite all the excitement. Maggie

McGovern's fretting about her condition. Claims to be having contractions, which is completely ridiculous given she's only six months gone. Now, are ye going to detain me any longer, or would you like to come along and hold Maggie's hand while I give her an examination? A full, *internal* examination."

Even in the poor backwash of the torch and the farmhouse lights, Kaine could see the blood drain from the old man's craggy face.

"No, no, no. That's okay. I'll be away to my bed. Tell Maggie I wish her and her bairns well. All six o' the wee ankle-biters."

Without another word, he took off down the path towards the village as though the hounds of hell were snapping at his heels. Kaine grinned into the dark. His respect for the young medic grew. She'd done well. Without her intervention, he'd probably have stumbled into the old man and his gun, and the situation might have dissolved into disaster.

Iona signalled for Kaine to stay put and disappeared around the corner of the old barn. Seconds later, the metallic creak of rusty hinges and the rumbling cough of an old, diesel engine told him she'd made good on her promise. He jumped out from his hiding place and raced across the open space as Iona reversed the Defender into the rain.

Iona kept the lights off and the engine idling while he closed and locked the double doors. Kaine ran around to the driver's side, but she shook her head.

"Jump in the passenger seat. I know the way. I'm driving."

"No, it's too dan—"

"Don't just stand there jabbering, man. Jump in before this old beastie wakes the whole centre."

Again, he could see her logic and, despite the inherent danger, he needed to trust her. After first removing his water bottle, he lobbed his Bergen in the back, dodged around to the front of the Rover, and climbed inside. She slipped the clutch and pulled away before he had time to fasten his seatbelt, and he bounced around on the poorly upholstered passenger's seat.

"Take it easy on the throttle, Iona. I'm battered enough already."

"Don't start telling me what to do. I'll drive any damn way I choose."

"Sorry, Doc."

"So ye should be."

He let her settle for a moment before asking the question he couldn't ignore any longer.

"Why are you helping me?"

"I have no idea, but if ye keep questioning my motives, you can get out and walk."

"No, no," he said, locking the seatbelt into place. "I'm good here, thanks."

Iona pointed the battered, old wreck uphill and kept going without lights until they'd dipped into a hollow, rounded a hillock, and were well out of sight of the centre. Only then did she activate the sidelights.

"Can you see anything out there?" he asked, familiar with the difficulty of driving over rough terrain without the benefit of full beams.

Her eyes shone in the green light emitted by the dashboard.

"I can see well enough. Lived here all my life. Don't often drive at night, but I'll keep the full beams off for a wee while. I'll need them for the tricky part, though."

Finally restrained by the seatbelt, Kaine relaxed a little

and allowed her to concentrate. She drove well, but the gears kept crunching when she shifted between first and second, and he took it to be mechanical failure rather than driver incompetence. The Land Rover had to be at least fifty years old and that was being conservative. The occasional mechanical glitch was only to be expected.

After a couple of miles being rattled around the cab, Kaine recognised the terrain.

"Taking us up *Wee Burn*?"

"Aye. It's no' the fastest route up to the campsite by car, but it'll get us there ahead of him. That's assuming that's where he's headed."

"You've driven *Wee Burn* before, I take it?"

She nodded. "Aye, but never at night. Too dangerous. And I imagine the storm will have increased the flow a touch."

"Probably, but I've never seen it impassable. Just take it slower, use full beams and all the spots, and we'll be golden. Wake me if you need my help."

"You're really going to try to sleep while I bounce this *auld* crate over rocks and boulders and who knows what else?"

Kaine yawned and stretched out his arms.

"Sorry, but I haven't slept properly in days. I'm exhausted and need some shuteye."

Kaine slid the passenger seat as far back as it would go, braced his feet against the dashboard, and rammed his backside hard against the backrest. He closed his eyes as Iona dipped the front, offside tyre into the fast-flowing water.

Before long, Kaine's rocking, bouncing world grew distant and slowly fell silent and still.

Chapter Sixteen

Thursday 17th September — Early Morning

Ben Craed, The Cairngorms, Aberdeenshire, Scotland

The ocean swell calmed to a gentle rocking, the boat's outboard motor dropped to idle, and something sharp jabbed Kaine in the ribs. An oar? A paddle?

Leave me alone, for God's sake.

He tried to ignore the discomfort but it happened again. He cracked open his eyes and squinted against the pre-dawn half-light. Iona jabbed him again and smiled, her eyes shining.

Not a boat on the ocean. An ancient Land Rover on a mountainside. Kaine blinked. Rubbed his tired eyes, gently.

"That was fantastic," she said, excitement in each word. "Driving along a burn at night is so exciting."

Kaine straightened the crick out of his neck and arched his back. Joints clicked and stiff muscles protested, but he didn't have long to loosen up before he needed to start moving.

She'd parked the big, old tank facing north. The mountain, backlit by an angry haze, loomed over them, ominous and imposing. He popped a painkiller, washed it down with some water from his canteen, and dabbed some clove oil on the root before saying anything.

God, how he hated the taste of cloves.

"Told you it was a doddle. Nice work, Doc."

"What now?"

Kaine glugged some more water, taking care not to wash away the foul-tasting clove oil.

"No time to sit around gassing. I need to load up and be on my way, soon as. Oh, and you said I could borrow a jacket?"

"It's in the back under the seat."

"Thanks."

He opened his door and slid out into the sharp, morning air, hunching his shoulders against the lessening drizzle. His feet sank into the moss before it compacted enough to take his weight. Moving fast through the boggy surface would be a killer, but the ninety-minute sleep had worked wonders and he was raring to go.

Kaine lifted his face to the sky and let the rain freshen his skin. It felt good. The place looked good, too. He smiled and tried to remember the last time he'd seen the beautiful mountain at dawn. Shame his return had to be for business, not pleasure.

"The camp is about three and a half miles that way," Iona said, pointing to *Ben Craed*'s west-facing foot.

He shot her a withering look before adding a wink which worked, at least partially since the swelling had diminished.

"Thanks ever so much, but I keep telling you I've been here before."

Once or twice.

A light, south-westerly breeze chilled his exposed skin, but that was no hardship and pleased Kaine no end—it would keep the hated midges at bay. A bloody good job, considering the punishment his face had taken since he'd become a fugitive, coupled with the fact he didn't have a Tilley hat or face net.

Kaine sloshed through the clinging moss to the back of the Land Rover. Her jacket was a perfect fit and he took a moment to luxuriate in its warmth. He thanked her again and retrieved his Bergen. It contained his portable life— spare clothes, emergency kit, bedroll, and one or two other items that might come in useful later in the day.

He threw the Bergen over one shoulder and worked the other webbing strap into place, shrugging and shucking until he found the sweet spot. The waist strap needed cinching tighter. Since he'd been dodging the police, he'd shed maybe four kilos of body mass he could ill afford to lose as it depleted his energy reserves and lowered his thermal insulation. The Bergen's stock of cake and energy bars, and the boiled sweets he'd bought at the petrol station, would suffice in the short term.

He retraced his steps to the passenger door, sinking further into the moss under the added weight.

"When you get back to the centre, make sure you tell

everyone I forced you to drive me here, especially your fiancé. No doubt he'll be up and about by now wondering what's happened to you. One more thing. Tell Drew and Gregor to come look for me at Zelda's Smile."

"Zelda's Smile? What's that?"

Not that he doubted her in any way, but she'd just confirmed her lack of a climbing background. Any serious climber in the region would remember the day they named a new route. Their celebrations would be tinged with envy for the route's conqueror. After all, who wouldn't fancy immortality?

"If Drew doesn't know, he's no serious climber. Will you pass on my message? Please?"

"Zelda's Smile. Okay."

"Thanks for everything."

He took another deep breath and prepared to leave, but she held out a hand. "I'm going to ask once more. Why not come back with me and tell Drew in person?"

"There's no time. Your Inspector Gadget forced the issue when he mentioned the armed police. They'll be here in a couple of hours and some of those guys have a reputation for being a trigger-happy bunch. It'll be safer for me out here on the mountain. It's pretty much my home territory, and I'll be able to see them coming."

"Come back and I'll make sure you're safe. The police won't shoot if I'm with ye."

"No, I'm sorry, Iona. It's too dangerous. I can't risk your safety. Martin needs help, and I'm the only one who knows where to look."

"Kurt Bartholomew's out there. He's searching, too. Maybe he'll find the boy."

"Maybe he will."

177

And that's another thing I'm worried about.

"What's Martin Princeton to you anyway?"

"Absolutely nothing. I've never even met the lad or his family."

"Is it because his brother died aboard Flight BE1555?"

Kaine swallowed. The mental image of the explosion in the sky over the North Sea still had the power to rip open his guts and spew their contents over his boots.

"Yes," he said, lowering his eyes. "Call DCI Jones, he'll explain everything."

Hopefully.

She picked up the satphone clipped to the holder on the dashboard and wagged it at him. "I'll ring him the moment I reach open ground. The signal in this particular valley is patchy at best."

Kaine nodded. "Take care, Iona McTay-soon-to-be-Elliott."

She swatted a hand at him and wrinkled her nose. "I'm a modern woman, Mr Kaine. I'll be keeping my family name."

"Fair enough. Goodbye, Iona. Thanks for everything."

Kaine turned away and headed for *Brus Creig*—the near-vertical finger of rock, the tor behind which Bartholomew had set up his camp's latrine—and wondered whether he'd ever see her again.

He didn't look back when the Land Rover's gutsy engine roared into life.

The breeze off his left shoulder helped Kaine keep up a punishing pace, and he took a swig from his canteen every fifteen minutes. Despite the drizzle and the low temperature, exercising at or near his anaerobic threshold was hot, thirsty work. During his time as an SBS training officer, he'd "binned" many a rookie who'd collapsed as a result of dehydration. The service considered failing to maintain one's fluid electrolyte balance a sackable offence. SBS personnel's most important weapons weren't their Colt C8s or their sidearms or their transport—they were their minds and their bodies. Neither worked efficiently without water.

Four miles dragging through soggy, undulating terrain at a five-percent gradient took its toll on his lungs, back, and thighs, but he continued the relentless cadence.

At 06:36, the sun broke through the darkly boiling clouds and lit the summit of *Ben Craed* with a pale yellow halo. Under different circumstances, Kaine would have stopped to revel in the beauty, but he lowered his head and drove forwards, planting one foot in front of the other, climbing ever higher.

As the altitude increased, the moss turned to grass, and then to gravel and rock. The underfoot conditions improved and his speed increased. His immediate target—a rocky outcrop with a flat top—grew ever closer.

With ten metres to go, and making sure to keep his head below the rim of the rock wall, Kaine stopped. He removed the Bergen, took a couple of deep breaths and another sip from his canteen, and retrieved a pair of Zeiss binoculars from one of the side pockets.

Moving as silently as possible over the gravelled surface, he crawled to the edge of the outcrop and climbed the two-metre face up to the gently sloping plateau, before dropping to his belly and shimmying the rest of the way to the leading edge.

The rough, granite rocks abraded his palms as he crept forwards and poked his head over the lip. Kaine tried to ignore the discomfort of the rough rock pressing against the tender scar on his belly.

Ahead and below him, a wide, grass-covered valley

stretched out between his plateau and another low range some two hundred metres away. In the shadow of the distant range, four two-man tents and two singles formed a semi-circle grouped around a ring of scorched stones that retained the blackened remains of a campfire. The layout was exactly as Iona had described it the previous evening, and it looked relatively undisturbed.

Had he arrived ahead of Bartholomew?

Kaine ignored the binoculars for the moment and took in the whole panorama.

To his left, the relatively flat plain dipped gently south-westwards towards the rippling lowlands and would eventually lead to Kinross Farm MRC and Upper Glencrae. To his right, three parallel gullies—like scratches from an eagle's talons—had been gouged out by retreating glaciers during the most recent ice age. They started at a thirty-degree incline and grew ever steeper until reaching the near-vertical slopes of the mountain, which scraped the sky as a blue-grey jagged monument to the forces of nature. At irregular intervals, horizontal striations in the rock formed narrow, weathered paths. The paths enabled careful and skilled climbers to reach the upper slopes by a direct but more technical route than the ones on the southern face used by tourists.

Kaine couldn't see it from his present position, but after two hundred increasingly steepening metres, the first two grooves would merge into a single, narrow cleft, which, in turn, led to a false flat spot, some six hundred metres below the summit.

The third notch, the one furthest away, led indirectly to the base of Zelda's Smile.

Kaine flipped off the lens caps and raised the binoculars to his eyes, focusing on the campsite. Despite the lenses being coated with a non-reflective film, he cupped his fingers around the lens pipes to prevent any chance of the low sun reflecting off the glass and giving him away.

The binoculars' 10x50 magnification brought one of the smaller tents into sharp focus. The camouflaged, all-season, ridge tent—clearly Bartholomew's—stood out in contrast to its cut-price brethren in quality, and must have set the teacher back at least fifteen hundred pounds. It wouldn't have disgraced an expedition to the Himalayas and showed how seriously the man took his mountain excursions.

Kaine quartered the campsite with the binoculars. It looked untouched, battened down, and sodden. No sign of the teacher. He'd reached the place first.

Excellent.

The rain eased, falling more as a light, summer shower than the previous night's autumnal deluge. The storm had just about run its course at last, but a stiff wind buffeted the peak of his cap and picked at his jacket, causing it to billow at the back. Kaine bunched the material to his chest to stop the movement drawing any attention and tried to make himself comfortable on the unforgiving, granite slab.

During his short, but hectic, trek to overlook the campsite, Kaine had debated his next move. He rejected beating the information out of the teacher, although he'd been sorely tempted. His remaining choices had been relatively simple. Ignore Bartholomew, strike out for Zelda's Smile, and gamble he'd guessed right, or wait and hope the teacher would lead the way.

Kaine chose option two. He could afford to wait half an hour to load up on food and recover from his exertions. If Bartholomew didn't show within that time, he'd head out and pray he'd made the right call.

While maintaining his vigil on the valley below, he

settled down to wait and ran the other information through his head.

According to the screens in the centre, the search team, ST1, had bivouacked overnight halfway between the school campsite and *Dubhaig Loc*. Unless they changed course for whatever reason, ST1 wouldn't be a factor in the upcoming day's events. Kaine would be on his own until Bartholomew arrived and until Iona passed along his message. Whether Gregor and Drew would act on the information remained to be seen.

Kaine took a tentative bite out of a granola bar he'd rescued from the Bergen and chomped on the crunchy mess, trying to ignore the sharp pain that pulsed through his tooth every time he chewed. He washed it down with a glug of water and dabbed another drop of clove oil to the wound.

Within minutes, the pain subsided and the food and enforced rest improved his outlook on life. He *could* do this. He *would* find Martin Princeton.

He rewrapped the remains of the bar, stuck it in a pocket for later, and popped a pear drop into his mouth as much to mask the hateful taste of cloves as for the sugar hit.

Never a man to crunch his boiled sweets—he valued his remaining teeth too much—he usually timed how long he could make them last. Twelve minutes was a good average for a pear drop. This time though, he ignored the game and wore away the sugar coating with his tongue, and soon released the sharply sweet flavour. Sugar gave him energy, and the flavour gave him pleasure. Little things, but important in the overall scheme of his life.

Five minutes later, the sweet had all but disappeared. Not a good sign in terms of his record, but the sugar rush further improved his mood. The rain stopped, sunlight filtered through the broken cloud, and, for the briefest of moments, Kaine managed a smile, despite the raging toothache.

During his makeshift breakfast, Kaine kept scanning the area downhill from the campsite, concentrating on the direct and gentle route Bartholomew would have taken from Kinross Farm.

Off to his right, movement in the heather caught his eye.

Once more, Kaine raised the binoculars. The small figure of a man wearing a dark green jacket picked his way up the slope, leaning forwards, head bowed, facial features hidden beneath the brim of a Tilley hat. A head net saved him from the midges which, protected by the lee of the ridge, would be flying and nibbling away at anything with a blood supply. The newcomer scrambled towards the campsite, hands and feet working in unison, making good time. A skilled mountain climber.

"Hello there, Kurt, my man," Kaine muttered into the wind. "I've been waiting for you. Where are you headed from here?"

One hundred metres from the tents, Bartholomew dropped to one knee and waited, head turning, scanning the scene. Seconds later, and clearly satisfied the place was empty, he continued to climb.

"Suspicious, or what?" Kaine muttered.

When he reached the flat land, the teacher stopped again, chest heaving, breath expelled in a cloud of condensation. In the dark shadow of *Ben Craed*, the frigid air caused his body heat to rise up in a fog of steam around him. He stood tall, head canted to one side, his left ear cocked in the direction of where ST1's bivouac was supposed to be. He lifted the face net and turned towards Kaine's outcropping.

Kaine held his breath and locked his body stiff. Even at a distance of sixty metres, any movement would likely give him away. Slowly, he adjusted the focus on his field glasses and studied the teacher's face, but he struggled to read the expression behind the searching eyes and open, gasping mouth. Bartholomew had clearly raced up the hill from the centre to reach the campsite and now struggled to recover.

"Yep, it's a tough climb. Not as fit as you thought you were, are you? So what now?"

Kaine maintained his observation post, binoculars to his eyes, watching, waiting.

After scouting the campsite, Bartholomew dived into his tent and emerged seconds later, carrying something Kaine couldn't identify. He hurried towards the base of *Brus Creig* —the grass-topped column of rock that erupted from the moss at an angle of about ten degrees off the vertical and canted to the northeast.

Kaine expected the teacher to disappear behind the tor to relieve himself. Instead, he dropped to his knees at its base. With his back to Kaine and his hands hidden, Bartholomew leaned forwards and started moving his arms as though scratching at the ground.

"What the hell are you doing?"

Kaine wormed his way back from the edge, dropped to the ground, and raced three hundred metres northwards, uphill along the foot of the outcropping, hoping to find an unrestricted view. He climbed back up to a point further along the plateau and, breathing heavily, raised the binoculars once again.

Bartholomew, now almost in quarter-profile and with hands visible, was digging away at the edge of a flat slab of rock with something long and metallic—a climber's pole. He worked the soil and moss away from the edge of the rock, clearly trying to dig a hand-hold.

No doubt about it, he was trying to work the rock loose.

"What's under there, Bartholomew?"

Oh Jesus.

Chapter Seventeen

Thursday 17th September – Iona McTay

Ben Craed, The Cairngorms, Aberdeenshire, Scotland

For the first time since Ryan Kaine woke her, Iona had time to think. God above, what had she done?

By helping a fugitive she'd broken the law. What had Kaine called it? Aiding and abetting? She licked her ash-dry lips. What sort of sentence would they give her for helping him escape? The image of sitting in a prison cell for years on end, unable to visit or even see her beautiful mountains, tightened her chest and made it difficult to breathe.

Back in her room in the middle of the night, Kaine's story had sounded so plausible, but in the crystal-clear light of a cold morning things seemed so stark, so different.

The potholed track—no need to drive the burn in the early-morning light—dropped away at a steeper gradient, forcing her to concentrate on the drive rather than her predicament. She slipped into second gear and the Land Rover's box crunched in complaint, as usual. The poor, old thing either needed a gearbox rebuild or to be put out to grass.

After leaving Kaine on the mountainside, Iona had spent the whole journey rehearsing her story, but she'd never been good at lying. Drew would see right through her lies and evasions the moment she opened her mouth, so she needed to get him alone. She'd tell him the truth and trust him to keep quiet. As for Lewis, his role as fiancé would be at odds with his role as a police officer. How could she look at him and lie so soon after agreeing to be his wife? That was no way to start their life together.

"Oh dear God."

The low sun cast sideways shadows that hid some of the worst of the trail. She kept missing the proper line. Often-times, the Land Rover bottomed out on the springs and bounced her clear out of the seat despite the safety belt. The dashboard clock showed the time as twenty-five past six. Would anyone have missed the truck yet? They would surely assume Ryan Kaine took it to make good his escape. But Alastair would likely be up already. He might have called Gregor and said he'd seen her by the old barn. They'd have discovered her empty room and would have roused the whole centre.

Oh hell! Things were going from bad to worse.

Lewis and Drew would be terrified for her. They'd think Kaine had attacked her again. How easy it would be to blame things on people accused of wrongdoing, even without evidence.

The track levelled off and the wild gorse and heather gave way to meadow grass. Kinross Farm appeared from behind a low hill, and a hive of people turned as she leaned on the horn. No point in trying for a stealthy arrival with the raggedy, old engine loud enough to raise the dead. She'd announce herself as the released hostage.

Three men broke away from the group and ran towards her, Lewis, Drew, and Gregor. Her lighter, faster fiancé—darling man—left the other two far behind.

When they were no more than twenty metres away, she jammed her foot on the brake pedal and the old truck juddered to a sideways stop. Lewis yanked open her door and threw his arms around her.

"Oh Jesus," he cried into her neck. "I thought he'd taken you. We were about to start a manhunt."

He stopped talking to plant a kiss on her mouth so hard, it crushed her lips against her teeth.

"Where've you been? I was terrified."

"Darling, I'm okay. I really am. He didn't hurt me. Didn't lay a hand on me."

Although not strictly true—Kaine had placed a hand over her mouth to wake her—it made her point, and the concern on Lewis' face diminished a fraction. They kissed again, this time with less ferocity and again, she felt loved. She had to fight back the onrushing tears.

Drew and Gregor arrived and stood, clearly delighted, but at the same time embarrassed, at the wanton show of affection. Shocking. Well, hang them. She'd hold onto her fiancé for as long as she darn well pleased.

"You certain you're okay?" Lewis whispered. "He didn't do anything?"

She caressed his cheek, unused to the feel of stubble on his normally smooth skin. "Positive. Don't make a fuss."

"What happened, sis?" Drew asked, finally stepping in front of Gregor and easing Lewis aside. "We were worried for ye."

Iona shot a glance towards the rest of the crowd in the courtyard. Inspector Gadget lolloped across the field, struggling to wade through the shin-high grass. His normally ruddy cheeks had turned beet red with the effort, and she could hear his panting breaths from dozens of metres away.

She looked at each man in turn before locking eyes on Lewis.

"The four of us need to talk in private."

Drew's frown caused his bushy eyebrows to form a dark red mono-brow. "What's going on, sis? I don't like the sound of that one little bit."

Iona waved at the Rover's rear compartment. "Jump in. I've a message from Ryan Kaine and you all need to hear me out."

She faced front, revved the engine to drown out their vocal objections, and waited for the rear doors to open and close before slipping the clutch and pointing the old truck towards the courtyard at the rear of the MRC. She ignored Gadget's wheezing calls for her to stop.

———

STANDING in a circle in the quiet of a locked meeting room in one of the outbuildings, the men listened to her story in silence, but only after she demanded they hear her out with no interruptions.

"So, what d'ye reckon?" she asked after bringing them up-to-date.

She expected Drew to speak first, but Lewis opened with, "Why's he after the teacher?"

"He didn't tell me," she answered and then turned to Drew, "but he said you should look for them both at a place called Zelda's Smile."

Drew and Gregor exchanged puzzled glances.

"Why's he going all the way up there?" Drew asked.

"You've heard of it?"

Drew and Gregor nodded, while Lewis shrugged and shook his head.

"Kaine said ye would. Care to enlighten Lewis and me?"

"It's a short, but monstrously tricky climb on the north-west face of *Ben Craed*. Not many people outside of the climbing community will have heard of it."

"Clearly Ryan Kaine has," Lewis said, his brooding eyes drilling a hole into her heart. "Do you have any idea what he's playing at?"

Iona took a breath. "The only feeling I got from him was a desperate need to rescue Martin Princeton."

"And he thinks Bartholomew knows more than he's letting on?"

"Aye," she answered, nodding. "And the fact the teacher's gone missing seems to confirm Kaine's suspicions, no?"

Lewis rubbed the creases out of his forehead. "Why should we trust anything Ryan Kaine says? He's a liar and a bloody terrorist—"

"*Alleged* terrorist," she corrected.

"Okay, Kaine's an *alleged* terrorist who broke into yer room in the middle of the night and forced ye—"

"No, I volunteered to take him to Point Zero," she interrupted again, trying not to sound guilty.

While Gregor huffed and Drew growled in exasperation, Lewis grasped her upper arms in a fierce grip, his eyes locked onto hers. "Now listen to me, girl. As far as anyone outside this room is concerned, Ryan Kaine *forced* you to take him up the mountain against your will. And that's an end to it!" He broke eye contact to confirm the statement with Drew and Gregor, who both nodded. "If anything other than that gets out, you could be in serious legal trouble. Do you understand me?" He emphasised each word of the last sentence.

She blinked under his loving glare. "And you're prepared to perjure yourself for me?"

"Yes, girl. We all are."

Gregor nodded, but she could feel his reluctance. She doubted he'd ever done anything illegal in his life.

Drew tugged at his beard, trying to force it into submission. "This English detective, what's his name again?"

"DCI Jones."

"Aye, Jones. Did he confirm what Kaine told ye?"

She lowered her gaze and shook her head. "I couldnae get through last night and the satellite signal on the mountain is patchy today. I-I didn't want to keep stopping on the drive back because I knew how worried you'd be."

Lewis draped an arm around her shoulders. "Worried? I was bloody terrified. We all were. Don't you ever do anything like that again, hear?"

She leaned against him. "I promise. Don't be mad at me. I believe everything Ryan Kaine told me. Cannae explain why, I just do. Deep down, he's a good man trying to rescue Martin Princeton. You're a police officer. Can you use your clout to call this DCI Jones chap and see if he confirms Kaine's story? Don't you have passwords and things?"

He smiled and kissed the top of her head in a gesture

she'd think patronising if she saw it in a movie, but in life she found it adorable.

"We don't all have secret handshakes, love, but I'll see what I can do. West Midlands Police, you say?"

She nodded. "DCI David Jones."

"Okay. Let's see what the man says. Is that live?" He pointed to a phone on one of the desks.

"Aye, of course it is," Gregor said, finding his voice at last. "Dial zero for an outside line."

Lewis crossed to the far side of the room, leaving her with Drew and Gregor. She looked up at her brother. "So, Zelda's Smile. Tell me about it."

He raised his shoulders and kept them raised for a moment before letting them drop and adding a sigh for good measure.

"Not much to say really. A treacherous climb that novices should avoid at all costs. There's a tricky overhang halfway up, but the main problem is the loose scree covering most o' the handholds."

"Have ye ever climbed it?"

"Aye. I finally succeeded last summer," Drew said. "Took me five attempts. A difficult pitch, and that overhang's a killer. Why's Kaine so interested in the Smile?"

"I don't know. He didn't say, but he didn't strike me as a man who'd be interested in something that wasn't relevant to his mission."

"Assuming his mission *is* to save Martin Princeton and not add him to his tally of *alleged* victims?" Gregor said, a thunderous expression darkening his face.

"Gregor," she said, "I was with the man for a good wee while. The only sense I got from him was a need to find the boy. During the drive, Kaine said something about an article in *Climber's World* from back in 2008.

Drew, you have a subscription, do you remember the article?"

"From 2008? Hardly. I'll go fetch them from my collection."

He hurried from the room, and Gregor locked the door behind him. The meeting was starting to take on the feel of a group plotting a bank raid. Iona found herself simultaneously worried and excited. She'd never admit to the excited part, not openly, and definitely not to her fiancé.

Would she ever get used to calling him that?

Lewis ended his low-voiced phone call and turned to face them. He sat on the edge of the desk, a thoughtful frown made him look even more sexy. She loved his action-man persona, but the man-with-a-brain guise was even better.

"Well?" she demanded, annoyed at his reluctance to speak. "What'd he say?"

Lewis crossed his arms and leaned back. "DCI Jones was unavailable and the civilian manning the phones would only put me through to the senior duty officer. A tight-lipped bugger, but he did promise to pass my details along. Hopefully, he'll be in touch soon. The SDO did let it slip that Jones and his team were involved in what he called an 'investigation of national significance' yesterday morning." He narrowed his eyes and stared pointedly at Iona. "That's a police euphemism for any terrorist-related operation. And since nothing significant hit the news yesterday related to Birmingham, I reckon we can give Kaine the benefit of the doubt. At least for the time being. What happened to my future brother-in-law?"

Before she could answer, Drew rapped on the door, "Come on, let me in. It's cold out here."

Gregor turned the key and Drew entered, armed with a

thermos, a tube of plastic cups, and a plastic bag that had to contain the magazines.

"That was quick," she said.

"It's a quarterly and I keep them in date order."

"Of course ye do." She smiled at her over-tidy brother.

He handed the thermos and cups to Lewis, commandeered a chair from a stack in the corner, and placed it next to a table. Lewis distributed the coffees while Drew took his seat and opened the inside page on the first copy. He read the index of the winter edition, closed it, placed it on the table, and repeated the performance for the spring edition. The summer volume took his fancy.

"Aye, here it is."

Iona and Lewis stood over his shoulder as he scan-read the opening paragraphs. Gregor stood alongside her, eyes squinting as he took in the stunning, colour images of the same ragged wall of rock taken from a number of different angles. The main photo contained a younger-looking Kurt Bartholomew, smiling brightly and striking an heroic pose with a deep blue sky behind him. Inset into the main photo, an action shot showed him hanging from the rock by a red-and-yellow-speckled rope. Iona had to admit, the younger Bartholomew looked magnificent. There was a man at the peak of his powers—the mountain conqueror. A far cry from the bearded, haunted man she'd watched prowl the centre for the previous day or so.

Lewis stood close, their hips touching, as she savoured her coffee and his warmth. Drew finished reading and summarised the salient points.

"It says here, Bartholomew soloed the new climb on Good Friday, 2008. It's the upper middle section of the northwest face of *Ben Craed*. Seems he named it Zelda's Smile after his mother."

Lewis sipped his coffee and pointed at the picture showing Bartholomew hanging upside-down, clinging to the rock by his fingertips and one booted foot.

"Looks like an animal of a climb."

"Aye, so it does," Drew agreed. "And it is."

"You've really climbed that?" Lewis asked.

The left side of Drew's mouth lifted into his trademark, lop-sided grin. "Like I said. It's tricky to solo, but not so bad if you study the route in advance now it's mapped out."

Lewis winked at Iona and shook his head. "Rather you than me, man. I'll stick to my nice, safe dives into freezing, Scottish waters."

"Soft southerner. What my sister sees in ye is a mystery," Drew said, slapping him on the shoulder and causing him to spill some of his drink over the floor.

"It's my good manners and English charm, you big, hairy goon."

Gregor grunted. "This is all very good, but what are we going to do about Kaine?"

He turned to Lewis for advice, but her fiancé shook his head.

"We have to report this to Inspector Gaskell. I'm a police officer, sworn to uphold the law. What else can I do?"

Gregor spoke again, this time to Iona. "If Kaine's about to be exonerated, why didn't he give himself up and explain all this in person?"

"I don't know," she answered, "but you saw his face. He said he was nearly beaten half to death when collecting the evidence to clear his name."

"Nothing to do with a car accident?" Drew said.

"No."

"So, we've already caught him in more than one lie. Why should we believe him now?"

Lewis held out his hand for quiet. "Let's think about this for a minute. If Kaine lied to Iona, and he *is* a terrorist, why would he risk capture by walking into the middle of a search operation? There are more than a dozen police officers at the centre right now, not to mention all the volunteers. On top of that, we have a pack of reporters baying for a story. I'd have thought this was the last place on earth a fugitive would choose to hang out. By now, a real terrorist would have left the country or laid low to plan his next attack. He wouldn't come to a place where a stranger with a beaten face would stand out a mile."

Gregor tilted his head. "You make a decent point."

"From what he told me," Iona said, "I don't think he's the least bit interested in his freedom except as far as it would harm his chances of finding the boy."

"Okay," Lewis said with the finality of a man who'd made a decision. "Here's my suggestion. We hold off talking to the inspector until I've heard from DCI Jones, and when we do, we all say Iona drove Kaine against her will. Agreed?"

Gregor and Drew nodded immediately. Iona tried to stop herself from crying in appreciation. Neither man would lie for anyone else.

"Meanwhile," Lewis continued, "I'll move ahead with the plan to search Kidney Loch in case Kaine's got it wrong, and you guys organise a team to head right out to that hellish climb." He pointed to Drew and Gregor first, then tapped a finger on the magazine page for emphasis. "Agreed?"

Drew's instant, "Works for me," beat Gregor's, "Aye, okay," by a hair.

"And me?" Iona asked.

"You, my darling," Lewis said, "are staying right here

unless and until we find someone in need of medical treatment. I don't want you anywhere near the mountain when the Armed Response Unit arrives."

"Why not?"

Lewis hesitated for a moment before answering, worry creasing his handsome face. "Didn't tell you before, but I know the man in charge of the armed unit, Inspector William Cody. They don't call him Buffalo Bill just because of his name."

Iona's stomach flipped.

"Does he deserve that nickname?"

Lewis' pained expression did absolutely nothing to alleviate the acid that had started eating away at her stomach.

"Remember that police shooting on the London Underground a few years back? The one where the innocent, Chilean student was shot dead? Buffalo Bill led the team. He transferred to Police Scotland after a tribunal and a court case exonerated him."

"So, Kaine was right to be worried for his life?" Gregor asked. "Darn it. The last thing we need is a gang of heavily armed police running around the mountains with a search under way."

As though to underline his fears, a police siren's angry wail broke the outside stillness.

"Oh hell," Lewis said, taking Iona's hand. "The posse's arrived."

Chapter Eighteen

Thursday 17th September – Morning

Ben Craed, The Cairngorms, Aberdeenshire, Scotland

Kaine squeezed the metal body of the binoculars so hard his knuckles cracked. He wanted nothing more than to shimmy down the far side of the plateau, race across the valley, and find out what the teacher was up to. Ignoring the knife thrust of pain, he ground his teeth and waited.

Bartholomew's heavy breathing and frustrated curses echoed off the rock face and reached Kaine's ears, carried on the strong breeze. He was trying to move a two-metre-long slab of granite and was clearly surprised at the difficulty of the task.

Why would he expect to lift a rock that looked as though it had been in the same position since the end of the last ice age unless he'd already done so recently? Kaine creased his mouth into a grim smile as the answer came to him.

"Not such a knowledgeable mountain man, are you, Kurt?"

The heavy rain over the previous few days would have settled any recently moved rock deeper into the soil's substructure, creating a vacuum seal with the sodden peat moss. To lift it, Bartholomew would need an extra pair of hands or something to give him a mechanical advantage.

The teacher grunted, stopped digging, shouted, "Fuck it," and turned to look at the campsite. He slapped the heel of his hand against the vertical face of *Brus Creig*, leaving a muddy imprint, and jumped up. He raced down the hill to his tent, worked the zip to the front opening, and dived inside. He reappeared in seconds with a short-handled, fold-away shovel, probably the one the boys had used to dig the latrine.

The teacher obviously had the same idea as Kaine. He slogged back up to his diggings, found a loose stone nearby, and placed it near one corner of the slab. He jabbed the blade of the shovel between the slab and the smaller rock and, using them as lever and fulcrum, leaned his full body-weight against the handle of the shovel.

A couple of seconds passed before the gloopy mud released its hold and the slab shifted. It rose, and the rock and soil parted, making a loud, wet slurp. With the suction seal broken, Bartholomew released the shovel and hinged the rock to the vertical with both hands.

Kaine craned his neck, but he couldn't see into the hole left by the raised cover.

Bartholomew reached in, scooped out some loose mud, and stopped. He sat back on his haunches and turned his head to the sky. His shoulders slumped. Once again, he dipped a hand into the hole.

Once more, Kaine held his breath.

Bartholomew's hand came out gripping a large, grey sack. A sack covered in rich, black mud and dripping water.

Kaine released his pent up breath as a relieved sigh.

If it were light enough for Bartholomew to lift with one hand, no way could the bag contain the remains of a teenage boy.

Bartholomew stood, checked his surroundings again, and pulled on the top edge of the rock. It fell back into place. Muddy water sprayed out as it landed, splattering the foot of *Brus Creig* and Bartholomew's trouser legs.

"What do you have there, Kurt?"

As though to answer Kaine's question, the teacher, eyes still furtively scanning the area, upended the sack and the contents fell into the moss—a bulky coil of ultra-light-weight, mountaineers' rope, and a smaller bag that clanked as it hit the ground. Given Bartholomew's background, Kaine would've laid good odds on the bag containing protection equipment—spring-loaded carabiners, nuts, tricams, and quickdraws. Everything a mountaineer would need to tackle any climb on *Ben Craed*!

Damn his eyes.

The bastard had lied to everyone. He'd sworn blind that he and the kids had no interest in climbing. They were simply there to collect biological specimens for geography class.

Yeah, right.

No wonder Kaine's gut had reacted so badly the moment he'd met the teacher in his quiet, little dorm room.

Kaine's built-in bullshit detector had fired off warning shots he couldn't ignore.

The one thing Kaine had left to decide was his next move.

Should he run into the campsite and revisit his earlier, rejected plan of beating the truth out of the lying piece of crap, or wait to see what the bastard did next?

Before Kaine could make the decision, Bartholomew stuffed the equipment bag into his rucksack, hefted it onto his back, and draped the rope diagonally over his shoulder. Then, without a second look, he turned north and headed up the mountain towards the three claw grooves.

"Which one, Kurt? Are you going to prove me right?"

Kaine lowered the binoculars, the bright, morning light making them unnecessary. Bartholomew wasn't going anywhere Kaine wouldn't be able to see him for at least half an hour. The downside of the open terrain meant that following the teacher would expose Kaine to the risk of being spotted himself. On the other hand, Bartholomew had no reason to suspect Kaine would be anywhere near the mountain.

Yes. He would assume Kaine had struck out in a bid for freedom and wouldn't be within ten miles of *Ben Craed*.

"Think again."

If Bartholomew took any route other than to the north, Kaine might lose him for a while, but he was willing to bet every penny he had on the teacher heading straight towards Zelda's Smile.

Kaine clipped the lens caps back on the binoculars, stuffed them into his side pocket, and slithered backwards away from the plateau's edge. He retrieved his Bergen and climbed parallel to the ridge, heading for a saddle, some five hundred metres above. Once he reached the break in the ridge, he'd descend into the next valley and follow which-ever trail Bartholomew took.

Optimistic for the first time since arriving in Scotland, Kaine charged up the hill, setting a furious, lung-bursting pace—one, from experience, he knew very few civilians would be able to match. Judging from the way Bartholomew had handled the climb into the campsite, he was confident of overtaking the teacher and, with his local knowledge, he knew exactly the right place to engineer a meeting.

BLOWING HARD, Kaine scrambled over the loose rocks, hand-over-hand, the toes of his borrowed mountain boots digging into the crumbling surface, teasing out each purchase. Occasionally, stones and gravel broke loose and tumbled towards the valley floor. He sacrificed caution for speed, and silence for the opportunity to forge ahead of Bartholomew.

The twin drivers—fear and anger—pushed him forwards. Fear of failure and what it would mean for the boy's chances, and anger at Bartholomew for knowingly leaving a pupil to die alone on the mountain. Both fed strength into his arms and legs. Up he climbed until he reached the saddle, only then did he pause for breath.

Kaine shook off his Bergen again and jammed it into a cleft between two rocks. It slowed him down, restricted his mobility. He'd return for it later.

He scrambled up the last few metres until his eyes reached the narrow fissure in the rocks. The wind ruffled his hair and freeze-dried the sweat on his brow. He controlled his breathing. If he'd estimated the distances correctly, Bartholomew would be below him, but close—close enough to hear heavy breathing and, if the wind changed direction, smell Kaine's heated sweat.

On the windward side of the mountain, scrambling footfalls and muffled curses reached Kaine's ears. With very little space separating him from Bartholomew, Kaine's anticipation grew. He'd wait until the man passed by instead of jumping out and risking a startled fall. Not that he cared what happened to the teacher. He just wanted Bartholomew alive long enough to answer a few simple questions and close enough for Kaine to take the rope and the protection equipment the man had stuffed into his rucksack.

A terrified scream echoed off the rock walls. The scream combined with the scraping rattle of rock tumbling on rock and the crack of breaking bones. The yell cut short.

Christ, what?

Kaine squeezed into the V-shaped cleft, dragged himself through the narrow gap between two rough slabs, and craned his neck out in time to see dislodged stones tumbling downhill, but nothing else.

He leaned out a little further, locking himself in place by splaying his legs and clamping his boots against the sides of the cleft.

"Bartholomew?" he yelled.

The teacher didn't respond.

Kaine twisted and looked up the slope in case the wind had played tricks on his ears. Nothing but empty, sloping rock.

"Bartholomew, where are you?"

He edged further out, shielding his eyes with a hand, and peered downhill.

Some twenty-five metres below, a knuckle of granite jutting out from the cliff—*Craed's Fist*—created a shadow so deep Kaine couldn't see what it hid, but a wide blood smear led into the darkness. Bartholomew's blood.

The splash of red stood out in stark contrast against the greys, whites, and blues of the mountain and the cloud-dotted sky.

Apart from the howling lament of the lancing wind, Kaine's world fell silent.

Chapter Nineteen

Thursday 17th September — Iona McTay

Kinross Farm MRC, The Cairngorms, Aberdeenshire, Scotland

Iona stared through the kitchen window and watched the big police wagon bounce up the farm track and slide to a stop in the middle of the courtyard. It threw up a mist of spray, and a hail of gravel shot from the rear tyres. Riot bars, in the retracted position above the windscreen, circling blue lights, and fading sirens gave it the aggressive air of an irritated hornet bracing for an attack.

Five black-clad police officers—all men—jumped from the van and fell into line, standing at attention. A sixth man, small of stature but large of presence, climbed from the front passenger seat, and walked slowly to the front of his crew.

"At ease, men."

The men stamped their legs apart and took a stance that looked anything but easy or relaxed. They listened, faces stern.

"Weapons and equipment check at the double. Pack enough supplies and equipment for an overnight operation, and be prepared to move out the minute the chopper arrives. ETA sixty minutes. Fall out."

The men stamped to attention, snapped a right turn, and rushed to the back of their vehicle. They started unloading rucksacks and weapons, and speaking in some form of military code Iona couldn't follow. The leader, presumably the man Lewis called "Buffalo Bill", spun away and marched up to Inspector Gadget, who'd shown some sense and stayed well out of the way of the quasi-military troop.

Iona opened the window to hear the conversation between the cowboy and the would-be politician.

"Gaskell?" Cody asked.

He didn't offer his hand.

"That's right," Gadget answered, smiling and apparently unfazed by the slight rebuff. "And you'll be Inspector Cody? I'm in command here until the superintendent arrives with the Serious Incident Command Team. Which might be some time since they're having trouble negotiating these narrow roads."

Cody sniffed and swiped at his chin with the back of a gloved hand.

"I'm afraid you're under a bit of a misapprehension, Gaskell. The man we're after is a suspected terrorist, known to be armed and extremely dangerous. According to the rules of engagement, at this time, the senior *armed* officer is in charge until the suspect is apprehended or incapacitated. Until a more senior officer arrives, I'm in charge here. Now, I take it you've set up an incident room?"

Gadget's eyes narrowed, his cheeks reddened.

"Yes," he said, pointing to the building behind him. "I have indeed."

"Good. Take me to it and give me a full briefing."

Cody stomped through the main door, followed by a blustering Inspector Gadget.

Incapacitated?

Iona turned to Drew, who looked at her, anger darkening his face and said, "That wee man's only been here a few seconds and already my guts are in a knot. This isn't going the way we want it to."

"Did you hear him say 'incapacitated'?" Iona asked. "The man's already talking about shooting Ryan Kaine. Can you see why he didn't want to hand himself over to the likes of 'Buffalo Bill' Cody?"

The office door opened and Lewis rushed in. He raised the mobile phone in his hand as he approached.

"DCI Jones returned my call."

"Well?" Iona demanded, desperate to have her instinct for Kaine's honesty vindicated. "What did he say?"

Lewis creased up his face. "He's a close-mouthed bugger. Came out with the usual 'I can neither confirm or deny' bullshit, but he did want to know why I was asking about Ryan Kaine."

Iona tried not to react, but her disappointment must have shown. Lewis held her hand and she tried to absorb a little of his strength.

"He was talking on his office line and the call would have been recorded. Given that this is a national investigation with potential terrorist links, even if he wanted to tell me something sensitive, he couldn't."

"So we're back where we started?"

A knowing smile stretched the edges of his mouth. It was both infuriating and delightful.

"You have something, don't ye?"

The smile broadened enough to deepen his laughter lines.

"When we're married I won't be able to keep any secrets from you, will I?"

"And why would ye want to? C'mon now. Tell me."

He squeezed her hand and addressed both her and Drew. "Before he ended the call, DCI Jones said he had friends in Aberdeen and he wished me luck in finding Martin Princeton."

The excitement in Lewis' eyes was clear, but she couldn't fathom the reason behind it.

"Don't you see?" Lewis asked.

"See what?"

"I gave Jones my name and told him I was based in Aberdeen, but I didn't say anything about the lad."

"So?"

He squeezed her hand again, this time more forcefully.

"If Jones hadn't talked to Kaine, how did he know the man would be up here trying to save the boy? Also, if he knew Kaine was here, why didn't he alert the local police?"

Relief flowed over her like a warm shower after a cold day on the mountain. "Because Jones believes Ryan Kaine is innocent," she breathed. "I was right to trust him, wasn't I?"

"Yes, I really think you were, love."

Drew coughed theatrically. "D'ye mind leaving that lovey-dovey nonsense for later?. The chopper's on its way. If we don't take first dibs on it, yon cowboy's gonna be on the mountain before us and that's the last thing anybody needs."

"What was Kaine wearing?" Lewis asked Iona.

"My spare jacket. It's grey and inconspicuous."

"Aye," Drew said, "he's only a tiny, wee man, about as tall as the cowboy. The way the papers were talking about him, you'd think him a Nessie-sized monster."

Iona couldn't help smiling at the way the "tiny, wee man" chose to avoid facing Drew for fear of doing him damage. She couldn't tell Drew what he'd said or her idiot brother would consider it a challenge. She didn't fancy seeing the altercation. The complete certainty with which Kaine delivered the statement told her it had nothing to do with bravado and everything to do with the man's ability.

IN OTHER, less fraught circumstances, the scene that greeted Iona when she, Lewis, and Drew entered the main office would have been laugh-out-loud hilarious. Gregor and Buffalo Bill faced each other, practically standing toe-to-toe, each wearing a scowl, shouting over the other and looking angry enough to come to blows. Inspector Gadget stood off to one side with his back to the room, talking into a telephone. He spoke quietly, but his red neck and ears, and his posture, indicated embarrassment rather than anger. She'd known Gadget long enough to be surprised the thick-skinned blowhard was capable of such an emotion.

The two angry men, of similar height, but with Gregor twice as wide, fell silent as Drew and Lewis approached them. Iona kept her distance.

"Do we have a problem, Gregor?" Drew asked, standing head and shoulders over them both.

Gregor, breathing hard, tore his eyes from his quarry and faced Drew. "This officious eejit is demanding first use of the helicopter, and he won't take no for an answer."

Not to be outdone, the cowboy craned his neck to look up at Drew. "As I've already said, this is a police matter. I am commandeering the helicopter until such time as the fugitive, Ryan Kaine, is in custody or—"

"*Incapacitated*," Drew growled, leaning closer, as intimidating as Iona had ever seen him. "Aye, you made yourself perfectly clear when you arrived, but this is *my* farm and *my* land."

He emphasised each word by jabbing a forefinger into his chest and was so impressive that in Cody's place Iona would have been quaking in her boots. The one weakness in Drew's statement was that their family had donated the farm and all its land to the National Trust back in the '90s to avoid paying inheritance tax. Everyone in the room knew it except for Cody, but no one would dream of gainsaying her brother, not while he was in one of his assertive moods.

Drew allowed the silence to drag out for a while before continuing. "The search for Martin Princeton takes priority over yer range war. D'ye get me, wee man?"

Cody opened his mouth to speak but Drew raised a finger under the cowboy's nose. "There's no argument here. The helicopter is military, not police, and their duty is clear. Finding the boy's the top priority, but … I can offer a compromise if ye'll hear me out."

Iona stiffened. Why would Drew offer to compromise with the aggressively officious, little worm? She shot an enquiring glance at Lewis, but he just shook his head and shrugged.

The cowboy chewed on his bottom lip. His hands clenched into fists and held tight against his thighs. The engorged veins on his temples warned of high blood pressure that might require medication, but Iona wasn't about to suggest he attend one of her clinics on hypertension. Not yet awhile.

"Okay," the cowboy said, his voice sounding strangulated. "I'm open to compromise. What do you have in mind?"

Drew moved away from the cowboy and tapped his finger on the screen with the Point Zero "X".

"D'ye see that?"

Cody drew closer to the screen and nodded. "Yes."

"Kaine released my sister a couple of miles southeast of that spot." His finger traced a line to the point where Kaine and Iona parted ways. "Yer truck will never make that journey. If ye like, we can let ye have our spare Land Rover and a driver. He'll get ye there within three or four hours. Jock O'Dowd knows this area better than anyone alive. He's a tracker too and will point ye in Kaine's general direction."

Iona covered her smile with a hand. Although Jock did know the area as well as anyone on the team, his driving skills made Mr Magoo look like Lewis Hamilton. As for a four-hour trip, she and Kaine had covered the same distance at night in a little over ninety minutes.

Drew had just given Ryan Kaine a chance to catch up to Bartholomew and maybe find the boy. She'd never been more proud of her big brother than at that very moment.

Lewis leaned close and whispered, "My God, he's helping them find Kaine. Why are you smiling?"

She shushed him. "I'll tell you later."

IONA KEPT in the background for the following hour while the police around her checked and packed their equipment.

The armed officers announced their readiness first, and they looked the part. Each man carried a heavy-looking backpack, an evil-looking machine gun, and a pistol in a holster attached to a utility belt that made Batman seem under-resourced. They fell into line in the courtyard once more, standing to attention, the backpacks on the ground at their feet. Iona had to admit they were an impressive, if terrifying, sight. The cold self-confidence each man exuded made her fear for Ryan Kaine and confirmed that his decision to act on his impulse for self-preservation was the correct thing to have done.

From what she could tell, none of these steely eyed men would hesitate to take the shot if Kaine fell under their gunsights.

Buffalo Bill Cody stood front and centre, a general inspecting his troops, grandstanding for the amassed media that spread out around the car park, fighting for the best view and the killer shot.

"Okay, men," the cowboy shouted, making sure everyone in the crowd could hear. "You know who we're after. Ryan Kaine is a terrorist—"

"*Alleged* terrorist," Gregor barked his interruption.

The cameras flashed. Buffalo Bill's jaw muscles rippled.

"Yes, right. As I was saying, Ryan Kaine is an *alleged* terrorist suspected of killing the eighty-three passengers and crew of Flight BE1555." He paused for effect and allowed the cameramen and women to capture his square-jawed greatness. "He's evaded capture for the past eight days and we're going to find him right here, right now. I don't need to tell you how dangerous he can be. He's a trained killer. A marksman."

Iona had to bite her cheek to stop herself shouting out in Kaine's defence.

Cody continued. "All I'm saying is, be careful out there. We don't know Kaine's intentions, but we do know his *alleged* crimes. Now, fall out and muster around the back near the Land Rover. Dismissed!"

His men shouldered their backpacks and marched around the side of the building. Drew nudged her in the back with his elbow—his way of saying goodbye.

She looked up at him, squinting against the glare of the bright morning sky. "What was the point of that man's grandstanding?"

"No point at all, sis. The arrogant, wee beggar clearly likes the attention. He's after taking down a national fugitive and hoping to get his name in the papers. I've seen his type before."

"I don't like this, Drew. All those guns on the mountain. Someone's going to get hurt, and I'll have to treat them."

Lewis stood close, keeping his voice low, lips barely moving as he spoke.

"I know what you mean, love. Things could get out of hand very quickly." He turned to Drew. "Does Jock know what we want?"

Drew tucked in his chin and matched Lewis for volume. "Aye, he's taking them along the northeast track, avoiding the smoother and more direct northwest lane. He'll lead them a merry dance, but cannae do more than delay them for a couple o' hours. And with all the rain we've had recently, Kaine will have left a trail even Jock could follow."

Iona nodded her agreement. "Kaine's footprints will be clear until he reaches the rocks on the lower slopes, but he knows an armed team's after him. He'll be careful."

Behind the MRC, a diesel engine rattled into life. It

died, chugged, and rattled again before settling into a smoother, less asthmatic rumble. The second gear crunched, the engine noise grew to a crescendo as the old Land Rover climbed the hill towards the rear paddock, and then the cacophony slowly diminished.

"That's the posse on its way," Lewis said, unable to mask the sarcasm. "When's that bloody helicopter due?"

Gregor detached himself from Gadget's clutches and joined them on the porch. The four of them stood in a huddle, ignoring the reporters who made their growing annoyance clear with ever louder demands for a statement other than the platitudes that had started spewing from Gadget's flapping lips.

"Are you still planning to dive the loch?" Gregor asked Lewis.

"No choice. It's what we're here for and what we're trained to do. In any event, we'd be a liability scrambling about on the mountain. Besides"—he scratched his chin, a faraway expression softened his features—"Mr and Mrs Princeton will be here soon, and I'm not going to be the man who tells them we can't be bothered to get our feet wet to find their boy. There's a chance Kaine's wrong and—"

Iona reached out, but Lewis shook his head.

"Yes, I know," he said, almost sighing. "If the boy *is* in the lake we'd be nothing more than a recovery team, but at least the parents would have a body to bury this time."

A short while after the rattling clatter of Jock's diesel engine faded into the distance, the regular, drubbing thump of the Sea King helicopter's rotors chopping the air replaced it.

Lewis tipped her a swift salute. He, Drew, and Gregor hurried towards the helipad, leaving her to stare up at *Ben Craed*'s apparently benign face.

Good luck, Kaine ... Ryan. Bring the lad back home safely.

She sighed. A forlorn hope. Ryan had no more than six hours before the ARU caught up with him. In that event, she hoped Ryan would give himself up without a fuss, but deep down, she knew he wouldn't.

Chapter Twenty

Thursday 17th September – William Cody

Ben Craed, The Cairngorms, Aberdeenshire, Scotland

William Cody, fingers curled through the Land Rover's grab strap, seethed at the geriatric driver's dithering. It had taken less than half an hour of being bounced around in the cab for him to suspect he'd been stitched up by the giant with the red hair and his grey-bearded leader. The useless bloody Gaskell had been of no help. A bunch of fucking highland inbreeds the lot of them. Dim-witted arseholes. Same accent, same vacant expression, same blankness behind the eyes.

"What the fuck's wrong with you, man? We should have reached the drop off point an hour ago."

"There's no call to use that language wi' me, son," Jock said quietly as he crunched into a lower gear with all the finesse of a man hitting a block of metal with a lump hammer.

The wizened, old fossil licked his lips and stared through the mud-spattered windscreen, deep in concentration as the old truck bottomed out in yet another bloody rut. The speedometer needle flickered around the ten-miles-per-hour mark and rarely hit fifteen.

Christ, it might have been faster to walk.

"How far away are we?"

Jock eased his foot off the throttle pedal before turning his head to answer. The Land Rover slowed even further. Cody wanted to scream. In the back, his men took the opportunity to chill. How they could snooze in such conditions was anybody's guess. Moronic Scotsmen. Each one of them had shit for brains.

"We'll no' be long now, Sergeant Cody. Just at the foot of yon bump," Jock said, jabbing an arthritic index finger at the northwest slope of the mountain. The bloody thing looked no closer than it had done when they left the damned farm.

"It's 'Inspector' Cody, and you said the same thing two hours ago."

"Aye, so I did, and you're starting tae sound like a wee bairn wi' your 'Are we there yet, Daddy?'. Can you no' see I'm doing you a favour, son? Walking all this way wi' that heavy equipment would have tired you out. Have you done much high-altitude marching?"

"Of course we have."

He wanted to yell at the man, tell him to put his foot on the bloody accelerator, but bit his tongue in case the geriatric fool took offense and turned back the way they'd come.

"And this is hardly high altitude. We're less than four thousand feet up. My men and I have trained in the Alps."

"Okay," the Scot said. "There's no need tae be so tetchy, son. Nearly there."

Jock faced forwards, squinted into the damp brightness, and screwed up his face in concentration. To Cody, the expression looked a little like a smug and toothless grin.

———

THEY CRESTED the brow of a steep hill and the driver slammed on the brakes. He knocked the Rover into neutral and yanked on the handbrake.

"Here y'are, sir. Told you I'd get you here safe and sound."

Cody surveyed the God-forsaken landscape. A moss-covered meadow sloped steeply upwards into the grey-black mountain. In the middle ground, a green-and-purple wasteland stretched out in front of a rocky bar that ran northeast from the mountain and dipped to the southwest. He recognised the topography from the screen in Kinross Farm's office and from his large-scale OS map.

The point where Kaine had released the McTay woman—his team's destination and starting point—lay on the other side of a stream, bursting its banks with runoff from the storm. Cody gritted his teeth against the sunlight glinting on the water.

"You're fucking kidding me, aren't you?"

"What d'you mean, son?"

"We've got to cross that river?"

"That's *Wee Burn*. The storm turned the only other route into a quagmire. If we'd tried that way, we'd ne'er have gotten through."

"How come Kaine and the doctor managed it?"

Jock's expression suggested he was trying to explain the basics of highland weather to a simpleton. "The storm surge is running full flow now. *Wee Burn*'s not so wee this morning."

"What do you expect us to do?"

Jock frowned. "Isn't that obvious, son? We'll have tae ford the stream and climb the rest of the way tae the start point. I'll be right wi' you after I've donned my waders. They're in the back wi' your men. Don't suppose you packed your own?"

The Scotsman's brown-toothed smile was either one of encouragement or sarcasm, but Cody couldn't be sure enough to take offence. Fucking thick Scots and their impenetrable accents. Half the time, he couldn't understand a word the buggers said.

He twisted in his seat to face the back.

"Okay men, out you get. Load up. I want us ready to move out in five minutes. Sergeant?"

The tall sergeant, Walter Townes, lifted his cleft chin. "Yes, sir?"

"Full weapons and comms check," Cody said, tapping his throat mic. "I don't want anyone losing touch up here. No telling how anyone finds their way around in this wilderness."

He shot an angry sideways glance at Jock, but the driver had crawled out the door and was easing the kinks out of his back, apparently oblivious to Cody's aggression.

While his men ran through their pre-launch drills, Cody hit the transmit button on the satellite phone he'd taken from one of the comms monkeys at Kinross Farm. The system buzzed. An instant response that shocked the hell out of him. At least someone in the country was awake. He half-expected the bloody kit to fail.

"*Inspector Cody,*" the young voice said, his English accent like a breath of fresh air. "*I have your location on my screen. Is everything okay, sir? Over.*"

Thank fuck for someone with sense and professionalism.

"That's an affirmative. I'm reporting in and testing the communications equipment. Have there been any fresh sightings of the target? Over."

"*Not a one, sir. But I'm to tell you Superintendent Ingram-Howe of the Serious Incident Command Team has arrived and would like to speak to you. Over.*"

"Better put him on, then. Over." Cody ground his teeth. The last thing he needed was more idiot brass interfering with the real work. He'd met Ingram-Howe before and the man had done nothing to change his mind about Scotsmen or senior officers. A waste of space, the bloody lot of them.

The line fell silent for a second before clicking into life again. "*Inspector Cody? Over.*"

"Yes, sir. Over."

"*Superintendent Ingram-Howe here. I need a situation report. Over.*"

Of course you do, you buffoon.

"We're about twenty minutes away from the spot where the target released the doctor, sir. Over."

"*Very good, Inspector. I've had a chance to interview Dr McTay and she's convinced the, ah, target is trying to find the missing boy. Over.*"

"Is that right, sir? Over," Cody asked, not believing a word of it.

"*Yes. You have good maps of the area, I assume? Over.*"

Like he'd march off into the fucking wilderness without the requisite maps and satellite tracking.

Such a clown.

"Yes, sir. Once we're on the target's trail, we'll be in a better position to confirm his destination. I'm not saying the doctor's mistaken, but the target is a cunning bas—ah, individual. No one can be sure he didn't lie through his teeth. Do you have any more information or instructions, sir? Over."

"*Only that the diving team has arrived at the loch. Over.*"

"Yes, sir. I heard the chopper flying over us about an hour ago. Over."

The bloody thing had practically wagged its tail boom in derision as it flew past. The Jock bastards were laughing at him.

Ingram-Howe continued as though he hadn't been listening. "*They've set up a base of operations and will be searching the banks for signs of the boy before they start their dives. Over.*"

"Thanks for letting me know, sir. Over."

Now, fuck off and let me get on with my bloody work.

"*Unfortunately from your perspective, the search for the boy must take priority. You're on your own when it comes to finding the target. Over.*"

"That's for the best, sir. If you don't mind my saying. Kaine's dangerous. No telling what he'll do when cornered. I'm happy not to have a bunch of civilians getting in the way. Over."

"*Good point, Inspector. Good point indeed. Over.*"

"With your permission, I'll brief my men and be on my way, sir. Over."

"*Right you are, but I want hourly reports. Over.*"

"Yes, sir. I'll call on the hour every hour, satellite signal permitting. One final thing, sir. When will the helicopter be available for a flyover? I haven't seen hide nor hair of it since its second flyby. Over."

"Ah, yes. I should have said. The, ah, Coastguard reported a container ship in trouble in the North Sea. I'm afraid you'll be without air support for the rest of the day. Over."

Fantastic. When were you going to tell me, you useless prick?

"That's … unfortunate, sir. Over."

"Yes, hardly ideal, I know. I considered countermanding the order to redirect, but there are dozens of men aboard that ship and, to be perfectly honest, Kaine's a lower priority. Furthermore, the boy's been missing for three days. We're probably looking at a recovery operation right now. Over."

"Understood, sir. Cody, out."

Cody disconnected the call before he could say anything that might put him in trouble with the Super. He breathed in the chill, fresh air. It smelled of musty damp and sickly sweet heather. Give him the gritty air of London over the vicious acid out in the bloody mountains any time.

He rubbed his hands together, trying to recover some mobility into his fingers after they'd cramped from hanging onto the grab strap for so bloody long.

Things were bad, but could have been worse. With any luck, taking down Ryan-fucking-Kaine would be his passport back to the big time. The scuttlebutt radiating up from his friends in London suggested no one of any consequence would mind if Kaine didn't come back breathing. Secrets within secrets. Nobody wanted dirty laundry washed in public.

"Suits me," Cody mumbled.

He turned to his men. They'd lined up at the front of the Land Rover. Jock, engulfed from feet-to-chest in rubber waders, stood to one side, a patient smile on his weather-scoured face.

"Sergeant, are we ready to go?"

Townes nodded. "Aye, that we are, sir."

"Okay, let's go find ourselves a killer."

THE STREAM TOOK LONGER to ford than Cody expected. The bitter, waist-high water froze his nuts and chilled his belly. His arms ached from carrying his gear high over his shoulders. Fortunately they only had to wade thirty paces at their crossing point. Had it been much wider, he'd have had to rig a safety line and waste even more sodding time. Although the fast-running water had the power to knock them off their feet and send them tumbling into the rocks below, he and his men made it to the far bank without serious incident.

On the far side, dripping wet, they set off after Jock, who maintained a leisurely pace up the slope towards their target start point.

Two hundred metres from the stream, they reached the tyre tracks made by Kaine and the doctor that morning. They didn't seem any deeper than the tracks their Land Rover had just dug into the moss on the other side of the stream. The revelation confirmed his suspicion that the driver and his cronies back at Kinross Farm had screwed him and his team over. Why the fuck would they do that? Why would they hamper the search for a terrorist, for fuck's sake?

Shit.

No point crying about it now, but if Kaine escaped as a result of their actions, he'd throw the blame on the inbreeds and maybe even try charging them with obstruction.

He'd love to see how they liked those apples.

The ancient Scot stopped at a point where the tyre tracks had churned up the moss with a three-point turn. He bent over at the waist, walked in a semi-circle, and stopped again. He pointed at the ground and then at a point halfway up the green slope to a break in the rocks.

"There y'are, Inspector. See his footprints? They're heading straight for yon notch in the rocks. The saddle. You cannae see it from here, but the other side o' yon ridge you'll find the school campsite. Search Point Zero. That's where your man was heading, just like he told Dr McTay."

Cody took one look at the ground. A blind man could have seen the footprints made by Kaine's boots. Jock's input was a bloody crock. Jock the Crock. Fuck. All that time wasted. Most of the fucking morning.

Still, that wouldn't matter. They'd catch Kaine soon enough.

Cody had read Kaine's dossier on the way from Aberdeen. Although a former captain in the Special Boat Services—a special forces unit renowned for their fitness and ferocity—in his early forties, Kaine had to be way past his prime. How far could he have travelled over rough, mountainous terrain in four hours? Five kilometres? Six? Maybe less if he had to stop and hide to avoid the search teams.

Cody looked at his men. Despite their heritage, they were half-decent police officers, highly trained, fiercely fit, and proud. With any luck, they'd catch up to the terrorist before sunset.

"Mr O'Dowd, thanks for all your help. We can take it from here."

Jock dipped his head. "Oh aye, that you can. I'll be on my way back to the centre. They'll maybe need my help afore the day's out. I'll say farewell for now. Take care on the mountain. *Ben Craed* can be an unforgiving soul. And Mr Kaine knows his way around."

He tipped his cap and strolled back down the hill towards the Land Rover.

Stupid, old fucker talked as though the mountain were a living creature. For as long as he was marooned in this rural backwater, Cody would never be able to understand the Scottish mind. Backwards. Stupid. Inbred.

He strapped on his backpack, shouldered his Colt C8 carbine, and gave his team the once over. The clowns looked as ready as they were ever going to be.

"Okay, men. Let's ship out. Sergeant Townes, lead on. Follow those tracks up to that cleft in the rocks. Stedman?" He nodded to the next man in line. "Keep your eyes on the satnav. I want to know where everyone is at all times."

Firearms Officer Reece Stedman gave him the thumbs up and hit a button on the touchscreen of the device strapped to his forearm. They struck out up the slope, with Townes maintaining a strong pace.

Before they'd covered three hundred metres, the rattle-thud of an elderly diesel engine echoed through the valley below them. Jock O'Dowd had reached the Land Rover in good time. The downhill run would have helped, but judging from the old boy's leisurely stroll, Cody hadn't expected to hear the engine start up until they'd reached the notch. He stopped and turned.

The Land Rover started moving, but instead of making a U-turn and heading back the way they'd come, O'Dowd drove up the hill another fifty metres and then turned left, heading straight towards the stream.

"What's he doing?"

Barely slowing, the Land Rover drove straight at the far bank, dipped into the stream, and crossed to the near bank. The whole way across, the fast-flowing water barely reached the wheel arches.

"You fucking bastard!" Cody screamed.

Townes appeared at his side, shaking his head.

"Bugger. We could have avoided that bloody soaking."

"Sergeant Townes. A master of the understatement. I knew he'd been delaying us all the bloody time."

"Why would he do that?"

"No idea, but I'll have a word with the old bastard after we've got Ryan Kaine's head ready to mount on a fucking wall plaque."

Townes' mouth stretched into a thin smile that didn't reach his washed-out blue eyes. "Strange people these highlanders. They never did make a lot of sense to me, sir."

Cody nodded.

Never a truer word.

"Better get a hurry on, Sergeant. I want Kaine in the bag by sundown."

And as far as Cody was concerned, it might just as well be a body bag.

Chapter Twenty-One

Thursday 17th September – Early Afternoon

Ben Craed, The Cairngorms, Aberdeenshire, Scotland

Kaine wriggled backwards into the cleft until he found enough room to flip over and reverse direction. He shuffled back out, leading with his feet, until they dangled over the edge.

The granite, although rough to the touch, was slippery with runoff water and moss, and offered precious little in the way of traction. Taking great care, he grasped the ledge with both hands, flipped onto his back, and allowed gravity to pull him towards *Craed's Fist*, digging his heels and fore-arms into the rock to act as brakes.

As he slipped closer to the *Fist*, the gradient flattened

until his descent slowed enough for him to sit up and slide the rest of the way on his backside.

Once he'd reached the deep shadow, Bartholomew's fate became clear. The teacher lay in a twisted mess, wedged into a fissure between the cliff face and the *Fist*. His head rested on a boulder, seemingly intact, but his legs dangled in space, the left foot rotated outwards at an unnatural angle. The shattered point of his shinbone poked through the red-painted trouser leg. Blood ran into his boot and flowed over the scree nestled in the crook of the fissure. At least the teacher's chest moved and his eyelids fluttered.

From a distant visual examination, Kaine wouldn't have thought it possible, but the man still lived. He still breathed.

Kaine shimmied closer. Underfoot, stones dislodged and rippled down the slope. He slowed, balancing the need for haste against the risk of driving a loose rock onto the teacher's head and finishing the job his own rushed careless-ness had begun.

Bartholomew's eyes opened, focused, and bugged wide.

"Kaine! Oh Jesus. Don't … no, don't kill me. Please don't—"

He lifted his head, but his face creased in pain and he lowered it back onto the boulder.

"Don't move or you'll fall. I'm coming to help."

Kaine kept his voice authoritative but calm. A large stone moved beneath his foot. He stopped moving.

"Bartholomew?"

"Yeah?"

"I'll be there in a second, but you need to do something for me."

"What?"

Bartholomew's eyes blinked open for a moment before rolling up into his head. The precarious nature of his position, caught between an approaching Kaine and a drop to his death, fought with his desire to survive.

"Oh God. Please don't let me die."

"Shut up and keep calm."

Panic would stimulate the teacher's heart rate, raise his blood pressure, and increase the blood loss. One good thing —the cut on his leg flowed, it didn't pump. Not an arterial bleed, but in such conditions, life-threatening nonetheless.

Bartholomew's right forearm looked broken, but the left arm seemed whole.

"Can you move your left arm?"

"Yes, I-I think so."

"Cover your head with it, but move slowly. I don't know how secure you are."

"Why should I cover my head?"

"I'm moving over loose rock. You need to protect your head in case."

Bartholomew's arm twitched and he cried out.

"I think my collarbone's broken. It hurts."

"Tough. Protect your head or risk concussion or worse. It's your choice. You're leg's bleeding badly, and I need to staunch the flow."

Kaine's own position wasn't exactly secure and he had no time for the man's self-pity.

Bartholomew raised his arm over his head, whimpering the whole time.

"Please hurry."

Kaine kicked the loose stone away from the edge and watched it skitter and bounce down the slope, missing Bartholomew by a few centimetres. He kept descending and stopped when he'd drawn level with the teacher's head. Leaning tight against the mountain face, he assessed the teacher's situation—serious. Potentially fatal.

How unfortunate.

"Okay, lower your arm. Things look pretty stable up above. You should be safe enough for the moment. What happened?"

"Huh?"

"How did you fall?"

His lower lip trembled. "Stupid mistake. I was rushing and missed my footing. Slippery as hell up here … all that rain."

Moving with great care, Kaine sidestepped lower down the slope, leaning against Bartholomew. As he slipped between the teacher and the rock, he passed his hands over the man, checking for less obvious injuries along the way, but found nothing. He found no weapons either.

No value in being careless.

"Okay, you seem to be wedged pretty tight in here, which is good. Don't struggle and you'll probably be okay."

"Everything hurts. I can't move my other arm and my fingers are growing numb."

"Suck it up, man. You're lucky to be alive."

"Why are you helping me after I … I exposed you?"

"It's what I do," Kaine said, straight-faced.

"But you're a … a"—Bartholomew whimpered as Kaine tested his pelvis for damage—"terrorist. All those people on that plane."

"Yeah, right."

Kaine studied Bartholomew's legs from a closer vantage point. The blood flow had lessened, perhaps because the man's heart rate had fallen, but the danger was obvious.

"The next part's going to hurt, but there's no alternative."

"What … what are you going to do?"

"Your left tibia's broken. Fibula too, probably.

Compound fracture. I need to stop the bleeding and splint it or you won't last until rescue gets here."

"Oh God."

"Ready?"

"No."

Kaine reached forwards, wrapped his arms around Bartholomew's thighs, and pulled upwards, folding the teacher's legs into his waist. The pitiful creature screamed through the whole process. Kaine had treated dying men in war zones who reacted with more stoic courage.

He folded Bartholomew's legs into a more comfortable position and leaned them against a shelf of rock.

"Well done," he said, trying to avoid the tang of sarcasm. "Now I need to stem the bleeding."

Taking care not to nudge the damaged leg, or dislodge Bartholomew from his perch, Kaine twisted at the waist.

"I don't have anything to bind that wound. I need your rucksack. This'll be tricky."

Kaine removed the Fairbairn-Sykes dagger from its calf scabbard. The keen edge took seconds to slice through the webbing straps, but his patient snivelled and whimpered the whole time.

"Shut up, or I'll leave you here to die."

"S-Sorry, but … it's … agony."

Snot leaked from Bartholomew's nose and ran into his mouth. He spat it out. Tears fell.

Kaine grabbed the front of Bartholomew's jacket and pulled him forwards, ignored yet another piteous scream, and slipped the rucksack out from beneath him before easing him back.

He jammed the rucksack into a flat spot above the teacher's head, worked the top clip loose, and scrabbled around inside. His fingers found cloth and he tugged out a T-shirt and a sweater.

"This'll do."

The dagger made easy work of slicing the thin T-shirt into bandage-sized strips. He used the sweater to bind the wound and stem the blood flow, and the strips of cotton to tie the man's legs together at knees and ankles. Not the best splint job Kaine had ever managed, but with nothing else to hand, he'd at least stabilised the break. He straightened out the freshly bound legs and propped them up on a bar of rock, keeping them above the level of Bartholomew's chest.

"That might keep you from bleeding out too quickly," he said without emotion.

Kaine worked his way back up the slope past Bartholomew's head, until he reached the rucksack, where he found a canteen in the bottle pocket. He unscrewed the lid, held the container up to his nose, and sniffed. He didn't recognise the smell.

"What's this?"

"Mainly water, but … with an …isotonic additive. K-Keeps the body's electrolytes in balance."

Kaine shook his head. Plain water would have done a similar job in a cool climate—water, and a hunk of Kendall mint cake. He handed the canteen to Bartholomew who drank noisily, gagging after the second swallow.

"Thanks," he said and offered it to Kaine.

Kaine sipped. It tasted of salty sugar. Not unpleasant, but not necessary. He replaced the top and set it on the ground out of Bartholomew's reach.

"C-Can I have s-some more … please? Thirsty."

Kaine ignored the plea and turned his attention to the rucksack once again. It didn't take long to find the grey bag with the climbing gear. He also found one of the rescue centre's satphones. It seemed to have survived the fall well enough, but the signal strength registered zero.

"C-Call the helicopter. I-I need … a hospital."

Kaine shook his head. "No signal. I'll have to find an open spot higher up."

"Hurry."

Kaine shot out a hand, grabbed Bartholomew's clothing again, and brought their faces close together. The teacher closed his eyes and flinched as though expecting a blow, but Kaine did nothing more than remove the climbing rope from the man's shoulders and let him drop again. Bartholomew's head bounced as it connected with stone. Again, he whimpered.

Kaine gave the rope the once-over—Diamond Blue, 9.6mm thick, single cord, and, given the weight, between eighty and ninety metres long. Its six kilograms was light by military packing weight standards and wouldn't prove too difficult to lug the rest of the way up the mountain.

He leaned closer to the injured man. "I'll go for help when you've told me the truth."

"Truth? I … I have been—"

"Lying bastard," Kaine shouted, pushing the rope into Bartholomew's face. "You told everyone at the centre you never bring any climbing equipment with you on these school trips."

Bartholomew raised his hand and again, his lower lip quivered.

"I didn't lie, not … not t-technically," he whined, unable to meet Kaine's hot glower.

The colour had drained from his face, and his skin had become translucent, absorbing the bright daylight, but reflecting none of it back.

"E-Every Easter I spend at least a … a week up here on

my own," he continued in an emotionless monotone as though Kaine was not there. "Revisiting the scenes of previous glories, before Mother passed. A-A s-sort of pilgrimage."

Bartholomew dropped his hand to his chest and stared up, no doubt studying the clouds swirling around the mountain's peak. Tears flowed and he wiped them away with the heel of the same hand.

"I bury the rope, carabiners, and the other gear here all summer to save me lugging it up every visit."

Kaine scoffed. "You leave all that expensive equipment to rot in the ground all summer?"

"It's perfectly okay. Safe under that slab and I change it every year … s-so there's no problem with … wear and tear."

Kaine wasn't buying it. "You expect me to believe that crock? Replacing a rig like this every year would cost a fortune. How much does a secondary school teacher earn these days?"

Bartholomew swallowed and held his hand out for the canteen. Kaine shook his head.

"Keep talking. Time's wasting."

"I … I'm not into teaching for the salary. I have independent means. Father came from money and M-Mother died a rich lady. I don't want for much. I'm a teacher and good at it. This equipment is nothing to me. I'd rather replace it as new each year than … risk it failing during a climb. Believe me, I've seen what happens to climbers when their equipment fails."

So had Kaine.

"Why did you dig this lot out today? What are you doing up here?"

Bartholomew raised his head and looked at Kaine for

the first time since he'd treated the injury—pained surprise etched on the man's pallid face.

"To … to save Marty, of course. I need to save the boy."

Kaine stiffened. Had he misread the teacher's motivations?

"Explain yourself."

Bartholomew took a moment before responding, his breathing stronger and more consistent. "When I … exposed you back at Kinross Farm things started to spiral out of control, you know?"

"No. Tell me," Kaine said and made a point of letting Bartholomew see him checking the time. 13:53. "Better hurry, though. I don't have long."

"When you used Dr McTay to help you escape, everyone went batshit crazy. They started searching the farm and growing more and more berserk. The press people acted as though they … as though they all had a hard-on, desperate to be in on the story of … hunting you down." He swallowed and continued. "And then that idiot, Inspector Gaskell, called his boss and announced they'd called in the armed unit from Aberdeen." He paused and held out his hand for the canteen. "Please? I'm gasping."

Kaine relented and handed the canteen over.

Bartholomew took a mouthful before continuing. "Everyone seemed … more interested in finding you than poor Marty. I tried to talk to that man with the grey hair and beard, the leader of the volunteers."

"Gregor Abercrombie."

"Yes, yes, Abercrombie. I … I tried talking to him. Tried to make him see that saving Marty was more important than catching you, but he waved me away. And that's when I saw it on the screens. You know … the screens with the … little windows showing each of the search teams?"

Bartholomew's story didn't match Iona's, and Kaine knew which person he believed, but he humoured the injured teacher.

"What about the windows?" Kaine asked.

"Well, looking at the maps all together made me see that focusing the search on Kidney Loch might be … the wrong thing to do. And then … and then I remembered what we talked about in my room."

He took another swig of his concoction and offered it back, but Kaine refused. The water in his Bergen would suffice for the rest of the day.

"Keep going," he urged, tapping at his watch.

"It reminded me of Marty's hero worship of Matty." Bartholomew panted. "Marty w-wanted to prove himself to his … dead brother. It started me to … thinking."

"What did you come up with?"

"I started wondering whether … I'd gotten it all wrong. Maybe I'd misinterpreted Marty's mood as depression rather than … well, determination." He blinked twice and stared at Kaine through deep blue eyes. "You see, Marty has never been interested in my stories about climbing the mountains, but this trip he … he started asking questions and the other boys encouraged him, so I … well, gave in and showed them all the route."

"You did what!"

Kaine allowed his hand to form a fist. He'd guessed right.

"No, no … it's not what you think, Mr Kaine. I only *showed* them to the … base of the route, and I t-talked them through the simple mechanics of the climb." He looked around him and shuddered. "I took them the long way around. Didn't come this way, it's far too … d-dangerous for novices. I chose the *Craed's Fist* route today to

... reach Marty faster. Bloody b-backfired, didn't it? Fucking ironic."

He coughed, took another deep glug from the canteen, and tightened the lid.

"C-Can I ... ask you a question?"

Kaine nodded.

"Were you watching me when I dug out my climbing gear?"

"Yes."

"What did you think I was doing?"

"At first I thought you'd buried Martin and wanted to move the body in case the police brought up cadaver dogs. Then I saw you empty the bag."

"Did you see me ... p-praying?"

"You looked up to the sky, but I didn't know what you were doing."

"I was praying for forgiveness."

"Why?"

The teacher's lower lip trembled again and, once more, tears fell. This time he didn't wipe them away.

"I needed forgiveness for letting Marty down. I ... I should have known he ... he wasn't suicidal. He's too strong-minded a boy for that. When I dug up that bag I knew for definite Marty had been on his way to climb Zelda's Smile."

"Why?"

"Because ... I ... I keep two sets of gear in that sack. Two ropes and two bags of ... protection equipment. There was only one set left!"

Kaine studied the teacher for a while, trying to decide whether or not to believe him. He'd spent so long thinking of Bartholomew as the villain of the piece, he was having a hard time changing his mind. Not that it mattered. He couldn't help both the teacher and the pupil. Kaine had his objective. Bartholomew would have to take his chances with the rescue team. The experienced climber had screwed up by moving too fast over terrain that deserved to be treated with respect. He'd have to suffer the consequences.

With the satphone, both Bartholomew *and* Martin had a chance, but only if Kaine got a hurry on.

"Do you have a space blanket in the rucksack?"

Bartholomew shook his head. "D-Don't carry one in the summer."

"Everyone should carry a space blanket irrespective of the season."

"I-I know. I'm an idiot."

Kaine still couldn't make up his mind about the teacher. Was he a fool or a liar? He knew a way to find out.

"I've not been this way before. I think I saw a split in the trail up ahead. Which is the fastest way to your climb, west or east?"

Bartholomew closed his eyes and sank back into the layer of gravel. "East. You'll find a near-vertical chimney. It's narrow enough to straddle. The west funnel starts off climbable but halfway up it becomes glass smooth and ends in a stopper. Impassable. No, take the east fork and you'll be at the foot of Zelda's Smile within the hour."

Lying bastard.

Kaine took hold of the equipment, draped the rope over his shoulder, and scrambled to his feet.

"Okay, I'm off."

"Don't leave me, please," he cried, grabbing Kaine's trouser leg at the ankle.

Kaine kicked the grip loose. "I'm here for the boy. If you keep still, you'll be okay until the rescue team gets here. I'll call them as soon as I'm in the clear."

"You're leaving me here to die!"

Kaine dropped to one knee and pushed his face close to Bartholomew's.

"Shut your snivelling mouth. Without me, you'd be dead already. You're lucky I'm actually here to *save* Martin. I know these rocks better than you ever will. If I'd followed your direction and taken the eastern chimney, I'd have ended up stuck in a hole. What the hell's wrong with you? What really happened to the boy?"

Bartholomew's face creased up. "I ... no. I'm confused. You're wrong."

"We'll see. If I'm wrong, we're all in trouble, aren't we. I'll get stuck in a funnel and won't be able to call for help for any of us."

He patted the teacher's cheek, harder than strictly necessary, said, "Don't go away now," turned, and started climbing.

"Come back. Don't leave me here to die. Come back, you bastard. You fucking bastard!"

Bartholomew's strident curses echoed through the swirls and hollows of the mountain face, fading as Kaine increased the distance between them.

Chapter Twenty-Two

Thursday 17th September – Early Afternoon

Ben Craed, The Cairngorms, Aberdeenshire, Scotland

By the time Kaine had scrambled carefully back up to where he'd left his Bergen, he was blowing and sweating hard. The treacherous footing had slowed him down. It was easy to see how Bartholomew had fallen in his rush to reach the boy. The only thing Kaine had yet to determine was the teacher's true intentions. His actions had been bloody suspicious, though.

In Bartholomew's position, Kaine would have kicked up merry hell back at the centre. Would an innocent man really barrel off on his own solo search for a missing boy, ignoring all the potential help available to him? Not that it mattered a hoot. Bartholomew was in no condition to affect proceedings.

With no possibility of finding the answer, Kaine cut off the thoughts and concentrated on his climb. He dislodged more small rocks, but didn't bother to warn Bartholomew. As far as Kaine was concerned, for whatever reason, the teacher had left one of his pupils to die. The man deserved everything coming to him.

Kaine retrieved his Bergen, strapped it on, resettled Bartholomew's rope, and set off again, climbing a near-vertical gradient that took on the shape and feel of a ski jump ramp.

Fifty metres later, the incline levelled off into a flat, horizontal shelf that gave him a safe place to pause for a breather. He took the opportunity to drink, polish off the rest of the half-eaten granola bar, and test the signal on the satphone—still no joy. Breath restored, he turned west and started climbing again.

The shelf followed the contours of the cliff face, snaking in and out like a pencil-thin, Alpine pass, inclining ever upwards. At irregular intervals, the face would fold in on itself and turn a sheer corner at a ninety-degree angle or more. Without taking care he could easily plummet to his death.

Twenty minutes into his ascent, with the wind whistling through the crevices and carrying with it Bartholomew's howls of fear and rage, the shelf narrowed so much it almost petered out altogether. It forced Kaine to face the cliff wall and crab sideways.

The shelf angled upwards and narrowed further until he was walking on the toes of his boots and searching for handholds to keep himself pinned into the face.

A fifteen-metre crab-shuffle brought him to another

sharp turn. The cliff canted fifteen degrees away from vertical, pushing him into the granite and making his position a
great deal more secure.

After two more sidesteps, his left hand met empty air as
the cliff-face shot back and away like the corner of a
skyscraper. He turned his head and his eyes found nothing
but blue sky flecked with fluffy, grey clouds that appeared so
close he thought he could reach out to touch them. The
optical illusion probably had something to do with the crystal-clear highlands air, so recently washed clean by the two-
day storm.

Kaine found two pinch holds, clung tight, and leaned
his upper body out from the granite. For the first time since
leaving Bartholomew, he twisted to his right and looked
down. In the distance, part-hidden in shadow and shrouded
in a light mist, he could just make out *Craed's Fist*, but not
Bartholomew.

Kaine looked beyond the *Fist*. The patchwork quilt of
greens, yellows, and purples hundreds of metres beneath his
feet, spread out as far as the horizon, east, west, and south.
It looked so soft and inviting that for half a second, Kaine
wondered what it would be like to simply step off the rock
and let the air take him. Let gravity pull him to the ground.
Let it take away his guilt, his dishonour.

Man up, Kaine. There's a boy to save.

The eighty-three innocent people he'd killed deserved
better than his suicide. Their families, The 83, deserved
more.

He paused, hung limpet-like, kissed the gritty rock, and
tasted salt and moisture. The Bergen's straps cut into his
shoulders. At certain angles, it acted as a sail, caught the
wind, and did its best to pluck him from the cliff face.

Mercifully, the ledge widened to a full fifty centimetres

as he rounded the corner and found an area protected from the wind. Ahead of him lay Scooter's Chimney, a crack wide enough to climb with relative ease and the feature Bartholomew had tried so hard to hide from Kaine.

From experience, Kaine knew the vertical chimney led to the mountain's false summit, *Sgian Dubh Còmhnard*— Dagger Plateau—which led directly to the top of Zelda's Smile.

Kaine allowed himself a grim smile of his own. Not far to go, only the chimney to scale, and then a relatively simple and flat, five-hundred-metre stroll to his destination.

He took a moment to study the crevice, trying to work out an optimal route for a feature he'd not climbed before.

Seventy or eighty metres tall, it started wide enough to use a back and foot brace, but tapered into a narrow cleft at its upper third, no wider than his shoulders—a squeeze chimney.

He'd scaled more difficult climbs, but that was back in his glory days, his prime. Whether he could manage it after a week with very little sleep, and the stress his body had endured, he'd soon find out.

The howling wind seemed to mock his hesitation.

Kaine removed the Bergen and dropped it to his feet. He couldn't carry it during the climb, nor could he leave it.

He uncoiled the rope to ensure it wouldn't tangle, and tied one end to the Bergen's shoulder straps and the other around his waist.

Kaine placed the backpack near the chimney's hearth and flattened his back against the left wall. He jammed his left heel into his buttock, and placed his palms on the rough granite on either side of his hips.

"Okay, Kaine, old man. Let's see if you can remember how this works."

After a deep breath, he straightened his right leg and rammed his foot against the opposite wall, the rubber tread of his climbing boot giving good traction. Easing the pressure off his back, he drove up with his hands and left leg, and slid upwards. His back scraped against the granite. He made half a metre with the first thrust, but the action stressed his rib injury, and sharp pain shot into his chest and left arm.

Kaine eased the counter-pressure on his hands, back, and foot, and slipped back to the chimney floor. He rested for a moment. Why was it more difficult than he remembered?

Come on, man. Get on with it.

He swapped legs and tried again, leading with his right leg, a less-familiar and less-comfortable position. It took a few repetitions to learn the new action. At first, he needed to talk himself through each step, each foot placement, each progression. He started by working through the moves in turn—hands up and lever; right leg straighten; left leg brace; push, heave, and rest.

After ten repetitions the routine became more fluid and automatic. After fifteen, he rested, locked into position, quads trembling, sweating a river. The perspiration softened his palms and the textured stone abraded his skin, but the stone was forgiving—the perfect non-slip surface.

After thirty repetitions he looked down.

Twenty, maybe twenty-five metres below, the Bergen, made smaller by the distance, seemed to grin up at him in encouragement. The Bergen carried Kaine's survival gear, his life. For some reason, the familiar, inanimate object gave him strength.

The thought made him grin.

There he was, shimmying up a mountain pipe risking

his life to find a teenager who was probably already dead. On top of that, he was being chased by a bunch of cops armed to the teeth with submachine guns, and the only thing that gave him comfort was an inanimate, waterproof backpack.

Bloody fool.

A bubble of laughter caught in his throat. He fought it down, unwilling to expend the energy needed to force it through his mouth. Hysterical laughter might literally be the death of him.

Two-thirds of the way up the climb, the gap between rock faces contracted and restricted his progress. He had to change his body position and convert into a squeeze-climb.

After a short search, he found a good foot hold, lowered his left leg, and waited for the circulation to recover. Returning blood flow made his foot tingle in a sweet torture. He wiggled his toes and flexed and extended his ankle until the pins and needles faded.

Come on, Kaine. Stop your malingering.

He cracked on.

Using a combination of heel-toe leverage and judicious hand holds, he slithered upwards inside the narrowing gap. Progress slowed to a snail's ripple.

The rest pauses became longer and more frequent as his strength ebbed. His lungs were scorched raw by the sharp air, and the muscles in his arms and legs burned.

Two metres from the top of the climb, a sound. Up ahead, something moved!

The electric prickle of premonition stopped Kaine mid-movement. He snapped a glance at the opposite wall and froze.

Bloody hell.

The big, yellow eye of a golden eagle regarded him with

imperious malevolence. The eye stared at him from behind a black, white, and yellow beak, its curved hook tapering to a vicious, menacing point. The bird, less than a metre from Kaine's head, could have ripped off his face, and Kaine, jammed into place inside a narrow column of stone, couldn't have done a thing to prevent it.

Kaine held his breath.

The eagle's beak opened and stretched into something that could have passed for an avian yawn.

"Hi there, Goldie," Kaine whispered, with his heart hammering loud enough to echo through the chimney. "I really hope you've already eaten today."

Goldie tilted its head as though wondering whether the intruder warranted its attention. Kaine tried to make himself appear small and unappetising.

"Don't mind me, girl. I'm just passing through."

The raptor screeched, Kaine yanked his head back, feathers brushed his face, and the huge creature leaped from its eyrie and took to the sky. Two beats of its massive wings were enough to settle it into a glorious, relaxed glide.

Kaine waited for his heartbeat to slow. He'd seen plenty of wildlife documentaries in his life, but a TV close-up did eagles no justice at all. He vowed never to take Attenborough's cultured and knowledgeable delivery for granted again, but in future, he'd watch wildlife from the comfort of a leather recliner.

Come on, Kaine. You don't have all day.

With quads and calves on fire, sweat dripping down the back of his neck, and teeth gritted, he squirmed upwards. The flat shelf at the top of the climb appeared, he stretched his left arm up, found the lip and pulled.

Once more!

His right heel found a notch in the rock. He pushed up,

added a final kick and flipped over the wide ledge. He belly-crawled over the lip and lay still, gasping the fresh mountain air, a sopping, trembling spent force, but he'd done it!

He'd made it past the worst test.

Kaine closed his eyes, blew cool air on his rubbed-raw palms, and waited for his heart rate to slow and his breathing to recover.

Recovery took longer than it used to. Age, the injuries, and fatigue were taking their toll. He stared at his butchered hands, the product of sweaty skin, abrasive rock, and the lack of climber's chalk. Still, he'd recuperate quickly enough, assuming he could ever find time to rest.

Short breaths in, long breaths out. In through the nose, out through the mouth. The swimmer's recovery.

The trembling in his arms and legs diminished as his body repaid its oxygen debt. Food and water would help, but his rations were running low and, with any luck, Martin would need more than his fair share.

Although he wanted nothing more than to lie in the sun and let the air dry the sweat from his face and hands, time raced on. He rolled onto his back, sat up, braced his right foot against a jutting boulder, and heaved on the rope.

Hand over hand, each movement taking more skin from his hands, the Bergen—his and Martin's lifeline—drew closer. When his grip finally failed, he resorted to a rowing action, wrapping the rope around his hands, keeping his arms straight and leaning back to his full extension. As though working out in the gym, he counted each rep.

At seventeen, the top of his beautiful Bergen appeared over the rim. After one last, grunting heave, the pack popped into his lap. He hugged it like an old friend.

"Hi there, buddy," he said, panting. "Good to see you again."

He grabbed one of the water bottles and sucked down three healthy mouthfuls. Each tasted like the finest vintage Champagne. Flat Champagne, but delicious nonetheless. The same side pocket as the bottle gave up one of the fruit cakes he'd bought from the petrol station—slightly stale but still edible.

Kaine slumped against the bag, nearly drained, but couldn't afford any more recovery time. He scrambled to his knees, but dizziness forced him to stop and wait for the headrush to clear.

Unsteady on his feet, Kaine dug out Bartholomew's satellite phone and hit the power button. Still no bloody signal. Damn it. If the teacher's fall had broken the thing they could all be in real trouble.

He looked up and scanned the area. A relatively flat plateau stretched out to the south and east. Directly in front, it rose sharply to become the final rise to the summit. To the west, the flat rock became yet another narrow, upwards-sloping ledge, this one led to the top of Zelda's Smile and, if miracles still existed, Martin Princeton.

With the satphone on and held at head height, he rotated slowly through three-sixty degrees. Due south, he found a signal. A signal!

He held his position, hit the red emergency transmission button, and prayed.

Chapter Twenty-Three

Thursday 17th September – Iona McTay

Kinross Farm MRC, The Cairngorms, Aberdeenshire, Scotland

Gregor's incessant pacing was starting to drive Iona up the wall, across the ceiling, and back down the other side.

His usual stoic calmness had given way to monosyllabic responses to the questions he didn't actually ignore. No doubt he'd have preferred to be out on the mountain with Drew and the others. One day soon, his heart condition would stop him working altogether, but her treatment was at least staving off the inevitable.

The sole high point of the day had been the arrival of the overbearing and obnoxious Superintendent Ingram-

Howe and his Serious Incident Command Team, but only because it meant the enforced absence of the useless lump, Inspector Gadget. The man spent his time locked in toadying conversation with his superior officer in their Command Centre—a big trailer bedecked with satellite dishes and covered in Police Scotland decals.

Iona had suffered an intensive, two-hour interrogation by a pair of detectives who pumped her for information on Kaine. She gave them little, pretending to have been too traumatised by her experience to remember anything.

Despite the influx of a dozen uniformed officers, as far as Iona could tell, their only contribution to proceedings had been to push the media pack a few paces further away from the centre. Welcome though that was, it didn't seem particularly vital in the wider scheme of things. A show of force, no more.

Shortly after making an appeal for calm to the same reporters he'd pushed away, Ingram-Howe instructed his uniformed officers to form a cordon around the centre. She presumed the action was meant to prevent Kaine from doubling back and killing them all where they stood.

Daft fools.

Ingram-Howe and the detectives had clearly ignored her assertions that Kaine's only apparent desire was to save the boy. As usual, no one listened to the voice of reason. As least they hadn't arrested her for helping a wanted terrorist, which at one stage, the older detective—a hatchet-faced man with tobacco-stained teeth and a slight cast to his right eye—had threatened.

She felt useless until she was required to treat one of the constables who'd tripped over a root and twisted his knee. Iona took a few minutes to brace the injury and organise an ambulance to take the unfortunate man to Aberdeen

General for a precautionary scan. In other circumstances she'd have been amused by the reporters' frantic reaction to the medical evacuation. One tabloid journo yelled, "Is he another of Ryan Kaine's victims?"

Lord above, for some people, Kaine had taken on the combined persona of Hannibal the Cannibal, Cyrus the Virus, and the Bogie Man. He'd be accused of stealing babies from their cots and selling them to the circus next.

Minutes stretched into hours, and Iona spent the quiet time with her eyes fixed on the search screens.

She focused on two of the eight signals superimposed on the monitors. Drew's and Lewis' teams—ST3 and DT1, respectively.

Worryingly, the Armed Response Unit didn't show on the map. Buffalo Bill hadn't activated his satphone for a while. Where on earth was he?

By late morning, Lewis and his team had set up a dive base on the loch's southern bank. She'd eavesdropped on his informative twelve forty-five report to Ingram-Howe.

Apparently, while two divers remained at base to set up their scuba gear, Lewis and the other three had searched the banks for signs of the boy.

"*Sorry, sir,*" Lewis had said, breathing hard and sounding depressed. "*We found no signs on the bank. I'm reluctant to commit my people to a dive without more evidence that Martin was ever here, but—*"

"There's no point in you being there without getting your feet wet," Ingram-Howe interrupted, ignoring the correct radio protocols. "We need to demonstrate to the world we're doing all we can to find the boy. Over."

"*To the press you mean, sir?*" Lewis said in little more than a stage whisper. "*Elliott, out.*"

"Inspector Elliott!"

Iona smiled at Lewis' reaction to his superior's media-savvy eye. It wouldn't do him any favours in terms of career progression, but would earn him a warm reception when he returned to her arms.

The helicopter's second and final local trip of the day had deposited Drew's team between the loch and the southwest foot of *Ben Craed*—its slightly more accessible face—shortly before noon. He and his team had started up the main trail and climbed steadily towards the base of Zelda's Smile, much to Superintendent Ingram-Howe's annoyance. The senior police officer didn't seem to appreciate Drew's insistence on listening to the second-hand advice of a suspected terrorist. In a terse, three-way satphone conversation, Drew had maintained his cool, but Gregor had played his "rescue takes priority over police search" card.

"That beggar is worse than Buffalo Bill. He's looking for glory and doesn't mind who he stamps all over to get it," Gregor said to Iona in a quiet moment after Ingram-Howe had stormed off to the mobile unit in a childish huff.

"It makes Ryan Kaine's case for him, doesn't it?" Iona replied. "When I think I actually tried to convince him to hand himself over to those people … It makes me shiver."

Apart from Lewis and his dive team, in Iona's mind, the police had become more of an enemy than Ryan Kaine would ever be.

She turned to study the big screen. "Any idea where the posse could be?"

Gregor tapped the screen over Point Zero. "They won't be far from the campsite. Did you see the body armour they were wearing and all that weaponry they were carrying? Hardly lightweight. I doubt they'll be moving all that quickly."

Iona frowned. "I think we need to warn Drew that we've lost sight of Buffalo Bill."

"I'll give him a call, tell him to take care, but you know your brother. He won't back off if there's a chance of finding the boy."

She had to agree. Drew could be a pig-headed fool. The big, brave lump.

A flickering on the big screen, nothing more than a darkening in the pixilation, drew her eye.

"What was that?"

The blemish disappeared.

Gregor replaced his headset and switched on the mic. "Craig. Did you catch that?"

Craig Conroy, the senior comms operator on duty, responded quickly. "Aye. We had a flash signal from one of our satphones, but it's not registered to any of our teams. In fact, it should still be in its charging bay. Don't know what's going ... hold on, the signal's back and holding steady."

Another red dot appeared on the screen a few miles north of Drew's marker. Craig added the designation ST9 and said, "Whoever it is just hit the emergency button. Here y'are." He hit the speaker button on the system.

"...*to Kinross Farm, are you receiving me? Over.*"

A spike of electricity fizzed through Iona's body.

"It's Ryan Kaine!" Iona said. "I recognise his voice."

Gregor nodded and took over the mic from Craig.

"ST9, this is Gregor Abercrombie. Receiving you loud and clear, over."

"*Great. Do you have a fix on my position? Over.*"

"Aye, of course," Gregor answered, staring at the window on the screen. "You're on Callie's Bluff, directly above Scooter's Chimney. You know there's an armed police unit on the mountain? Over."

Iona signalled for Craig to enlarge the image on the big screen and gave him the thumbs up when the map zoomed in enough to encompass the signals ST3 and ST9. The first was closing in on the second, which itself was stationary, but close to the area she now knew to contain Zelda's Smile.

"*Don't worry about that for now,*" Kaine said, so calm he might have been out for a Sunday stroll in the park. "*I found Kurt Bartholomew. He's had a fall and is in a bad way. Compound fracture of the left tib-fib. He's lost a lot of blood. I've done what I can for him, but he'll need airlifting out, over.*"

"No can do, ST9. The helicopter has been redirected to an emergency in the North Sea. Over."

"*Okay, understood,*" Kaine said. "*Bartholomew's jammed in the crook formed by the cliff and Craed's Fist. He's safe for the moment, but I doubt he'll survive for long without proper treatment. Over.*"

Gregor leaned closer to the screen, pointed to a spot below and to the west of Scooter's Chimney, and said, "I know exactly where you mean. We'll pass your message to Drew's team, ST3. They'll have to change course. I doubt they'll reach the *Fist* for at least two hours. Over."

He signalled to Craig's partner, Gillian McTavish, who nodded and started speaking into her headset.

"I'll also direct the nearest teams to support ST3," Gregor added. "Trouble is, nearest vehicular access to that spot is back near the loch. It'll take a while to get someone up there. What about you, ST9? Are you still heading for Zelda's Smile? Over."

"*Yes. I need to check it out before taking my leave of Scotland. Over.*"

"But the armed police—"

"*I'll worry about them when I have to. Bartholomew let something slip, if you pardon the pun. I think he had something to do with*

Martin's disappearance. I'll call again when I've found the boy. ST9, out."

The ST9 tag blinked from the screen and at the same time, the main doors opened. Inspector Gadget entered the room at his chest-out, belly-in, self-important best. He led a civilian couple, surrounded by uniformed police officers. Of Superintendent Ingram-Howe, there was no sign. Dealing with the little people was clearly beneath him—delegation being the prerogative of the senior officer.

Arrogant prig.

Iona recognised Martin's parents from the TV news reports.

Mrs Princeton was short and slim, but her puffy, red eyes and the tissue dabbing her nose told of her suffering. Mr Princeton stood round-shouldered, as though he didn't have the strength to pull them back and himself upright. His thinned lips and gaunt features betrayed a desperate need to hold himself together for the sake of his wife. Iona's heart lurched at their pain, but she could do nothing for them. She tapped Gregor's shoulder.

"I'm useless here. I'll take the old Land Rover and drive to Lewis at Kidney Loch. I'll be ready for Drew when he's recovered Bartholomew. Is that okay?"

Gregor covered his mic. "It could get dangerous up there, lass. Think of those idiots with their guns."

"Are ye going to try and stop me?"

His beard bunched but couldn't hide a wry smile. "I wouldn't dream of it, lass, but take Jock with you and stay safe."

"I'd rather be up on the mountain than here with you and the Princetons. I know how you love dealing with distressed family members. I'll go find Jock and grab my gear. Good luck."

"Don't forget a satphone. There should be a couple left."

Iona signed out a phone, ST10, and headed for the rear exit. She refused to make eye contact with the Princetons and barrelled through the door before Gadget could drag her into something she didn't want to handle.

Chapter Twenty-Four

Thursday 17th September – William Cody

Ben Craed, The Cairngorms, Aberdeenshire, Scotland

"…the evil, old bastard set us back three hours, sir. Over," Cody said, struggling for breath as his team maintained a fast, uphill pace into a slicing headwind.

"*Who? Over*," Ingram-Howe asked.

"The driver, Jock O'Dowd. Over."

At 13:15, he'd been late to make his report—via his unit's satphone, not the one issued by the MRC—but he didn't give a shit. Ingram-Howe could stuff his fucking timetable up his arse.

Cody fell back into the role of "tail-end Charlie" and made sure none of his men could earwig the conversation.

He didn't want them knowing how much difficulty he was having keeping up. His vision had started to grey at the edges, a sure sign of over-exertion. Not a good example to his men, and certainly not helpful if it came to a firefight.

He considered calling a halt for rest, but they'd already lost too much Goddamned time.

"*Are you saying he deliberately delayed your arrival at Kaine's last known position? Over,*" Ingram-Howe asked.

Too right he did, the miserable geriatric.

"I'll never be able to prove it, sir, but that's exactly what I'm saying. Over."

"*Damned locals think they're above the law,*" the superintendent growled before adding, "*Over.*"

Cody couldn't argue the toss on that one.

"Bunch of fucking inbreeds, sir. Pardon the language. Over."

"*Not to worry, Inspector. We'll keep this conversation off the record, if you understand my meaning? Over.*"

Cody had a good indication of what the Super meant, but he needed the protection of clear operational instructions.

"No, sir. You need to spell it out to me. Over."

"*You want me to spell it out, Inspector Cody? Okay, so hear this. Ryan Kaine is a suspected terrorist wanted by every police service in the UK. What do you think it would do to Police Scotland's position in the next round of budget negotiations if we were to take in the man when the English have failed? Over.*"

"Understood, sir. But there is a slight problem. Over."

"*Which is? Over.*"

"Given his track record south of the border, he's unlikely to come quietly. Over."

"*Probably not, but listen to me carefully. If you use your best judgement, you'll have the backing not only of the Chief Constable of*

Police Scotland, but you'll also have the full support of the UK govern-ment. Our full backing, no matter the outcome. Hear me? In fact, people in certain quarters have let it be known they would prefer it if Ryan Kaine were never able to testify in a court of law. Do I make myself clear now, Inspector Cody? Over."

"Crystal, sir. Over," Cody answered without hesitation.

He stopped walking, allowed the men to pull further ahead, and dragged in some much-needed oxygen.

"Excellent. There's no further need for hourly reports. I wouldn't want them to interfere with the pursuit of your target. Don't contact me again until after you have Kaine in the bag. Ingram-Howe, out."

Cody cut the comms link and simultaneously shut off his mobile's digital recorder. He allowed himself the briefest of smiles. Ingram-Howe had just given him tacit permission to kill a known terrorist, and it paid to have protection. There was no telling what the Super's "off the record" comment actually meant in practice.

He'd been fucked over once after a shooting incident, and he wasn't going to let it happen again. No, Kaine's death would be his ticket back to the big time and the recording would guarantee it. He deserved to be in London, not in Scotland—the UK's toilet.

The wind eased to a gentle breeze.

Finally, things had started looking up.

Chapter Twenty-Five

Thursday 17th September – Early Afternoon

Ben Craed, The Cairngorms, Aberdeenshire, Scotland

Kaine powered down the satphone, tucked it into one of the Bergen's side pockets, and started coiling the rope. During the operation, he checked the fibres for damage. It seemed pretty sound, but it wasn't as though he had any alternative but to use it.

He wrapped the last metre of rope around the middle of the coil and secured it using the ties at the bottom of the Bergen. After a quick series of stretches to loosen his calves, thighs, and back, he threw the bag onto his shoulders, cinched up the waist belt—taking care to avoid the still-tender knife wound—and struck out on the final part of his climb.

A heavy bar of dark cloud rolled in front of the sun and robbed the day of its recently accumulated heat. Kaine reached the next bend in the route, a spur in the rock face which buckled into another fold, this one far narrower than the chimney. It rose almost vertically to end in dark sky. He pushed on, leaning into the granite, but still able to walk without the need to crab sideways. The ledge finally petered out and ended in a flat wall that canted away from him at a forty-five-degree angle.

All day long, the drying wind had made the rock climbable without the need for protection. Bouldering techniques—palming, toeholds, and pinch holds—were all he needed to clamber up to the next level, another false flat, this one unnamed.

The sun poked out from behind the clouds, and the wind died to a whisper. Kaine paused for a drink. He dribbled water onto a cloth and wiped his hands and face free of sweat and accumulated grime. The skin on his palms stung like the devil, but that wouldn't slow him down. He'd had worse injuries in his life.

Kaine took a moment to check his position.

The mountain dropped steeply away from his feet and the land spread out to the horizon in the same rolling mass of green-clad hills and patches of purple and yellow. To the west, the northern shore of Kidney Loch peeked out from the side of the cliff face. At a distance of four miles out and half a mile down, he wouldn't have been able to see the divers even if they'd made their base on that shore, but he found some comfort in knowing Drew McTay and Iona's fiancé were within calling range. If he did find Martin alive, they'd be no more than a couple of hours' climb away.

Chivvy on, Kaine. Not far now.

He pushed away from the face and climbed on, the going made easier as the surface levelled into a gentle, upwards gradient. A few hundred yards and one more easy climb and he'd reach his destination. He estimated thirty minutes, no more.

It took twenty-three.

Kaine, breathing easy, slipped out of the Bergen once more. He placed it on its back and settled it against a jutting rump of rock, pressing it down hard to make sure it wouldn't topple. After lugging it three quarters of the way up *Ben Craed* the last thing he needed was to lose the blessed thing.

Stretching out ahead, the two-metre-wide ledge looked pristine—its surface washed clean of tracks by the storm. It showed the scratches and scuffs of previous human visitors, but none of them looked fresh. The north face of the mountain didn't lend itself to the casual day tripper. Only serious climbers ventured so far up and, since Bartholomew had conquered the final unclimbed route, they had lost interest in one of Scotland's minor mountains. The country still boasted plenty of unclaimed routes to attack and name, most of them in the far north, many along the ragged coast.

Kaine followed the ledge for another few metres, looking for signs of … what was that? Scuffmarks. Pieces of cliff had crumbled under the weight of something heavy, something that had been too close to the edge.

Excitement flared as did anxiety.

Kaine dropped onto his front and popped his head over the ledge. The cliff face fell away into nothingness.

He edged further out. Dislodged dust and stone clattered and bounced off the wall and skittered into the distance.

An overhang dropped away beneath him, canting inwards for forty metres before jutting out again to form a serrated ridge. After that, the cliff fell far away to a valley floor.

Something black melted into dark grey rocks—a bundle of rags fluttering in the breeze. He couldn't make out any details.

Kaine scrambled backwards, taking care not to disturb any more stones. Heart pounding, breathing deeply, he raced back to the Bergen, grabbed the Zeiss binoculars and the satphone, and returned to the ledge. He dropped onto his front and crawled out once more.

Binoculars to eyes, he rolled the knurled nut to adjust the focus. The image sharpened—into a body. Unmoving, crumpled, but a body.

Forty metres below, on his back, eyes closed, skin deathly pale, but protected from the worst of the elements by the saw-toothed ridge and the overhang, lay Martin Princeton!

Christ Almighty!

"Martin!" he yelled. "Martin Princeton! Can you hear me?"

Nothing.

No movement, no flickering eyelids, no twitching lips. Nothing but the whispering wind and the scudding cloud.

Heart racing, Kaine scrambled back from the ledge. He reached into his jacket, ripped out the satphone, and hit the red button.

Chapter Twenty-Six

Thursday 17th September – Gregor Abercrombie

**Kinross Farm MRC, The Cairngorms,
Aberdeenshire, Scotland**

Gregor Abercrombie avoided Mrs Princeton's tear-filled eyes, unable to find the comforting words she needed to hear. Sure, he'd mumbled the normal upbeat platitudes, but as usual, they did as much good as spitting on a fire. Instead, he focused his delivery on Martin's father, the silent type who appeared impressed by their electronic setup and paid close attention when Gregor described what was happening on the search screens.

Mr Princeton's focus roved from the big screen to the split screen windows and back again.

"I see you've spread your search teams wide,"

Princeton said, his voice dry and scratchy, presumably from lack of sleep, "but why the focus on the lake, and"—he pointed at the activity on the big screen—"what's going on there? All your teams are marked ST. What's DT1?"

Gregor scratched his beard. How was he supposed to answer that? The police should have briefed the parents on the situation, including the hunt for Ryan Kaine.

Standard operating procedures usually dictated that the locator tags be removed from the screens whenever any civilians entered the office. Rescue volunteers didn't want family members to know where they were focusing the searches in case one of them tried to join in the search. Having fraught and desperate people scrambling over the mountains wouldn't help matters. Unfortunately, in this instance, Craig had been distracted and the tags had remained in full view. He held up a hand in apology, but Gregor let it pass. They were all feeling the strain. Two days with minimal sleep compromised the best people, and Craig happened to be one of the very best.

"You weren't told?" Gregor said, turning to Gaskell who'd eased away from the couple, for once in his life trying to make himself inconspicuous.

"Told what?"

"We've had some new information—"

"What new information?" Princeton's demeanour changed in an instant from quiet hopelessness, to loud anger. "Answer me, man!"

Gregor held out a placatory hand. "DT1 is a dive team from Aberdeen. They're here to search that loch."

Mrs Princeton clutched her chest. "Why? What would Martin be doing near a lake?"

"Mr Bartholomew suggested Martin might have … I'm

sorry, I think you need a proper explanation. Inspector Gaskell? This is your area of expertise, is it not?"

Princeton's lips formed a thin gash, a man on the edge of losing control. He rounded on Gaskell, who took another backwards pace before finding a spine and standing taller.

"What's going on, Inspector? And why are so many of the police here armed?"

"If you and Mrs Princeton will follow me to the Incident Room," Gaskell said, hesitantly, "we'll give you a full briefing."

Princeton took his wife's hand and escorted her from the room. The poor woman didn't appear to know what was happening. Her glazed eyes were lost in an internal hell which Gregor could barely comprehend.

Lord save her from the Devil's work.

He closed his mind to the couple's grief and focused on the only thing he understood and could control—the people on his screens.

The ST9 signal flared again, holding steady a few points north of its earlier location. He snapped his head around to Craig Conroy at the comms desk.

"Is it him?"

"Aye."

"Put him on speaker."

"*Kinross Farm, are you receiving me? Over.*" Kaine's words burst through the speaker, this time his voice was faster, more animated.

"Loud and clear, ST9. This is Kinross Farm receiving you full strength, over."

"*I've found him. I've found Martin Princeton! Over.*"

Gregor froze. The office fell silent around him. He signalled for Craig to patch it through headphones only. He didn't want the Princetons getting wind of the next part. Gregor grabbed a spare set of headphones and clamped them over his ears.

"ST9, repeat that, over."

"You heard me, Gregor. I found the boy, over."

"How is he? Over."

"Can't tell from here. I'm at the top of the Smile, and the boy's about forty metres below me, tucked into an overhang. No one could have spotted him if they didn't know where to look. He seems to have fallen from the upper ledge, but he's not moving. Over."

"Understood, ST9. I'll let ST3 know where he is, over."

"How far away are they? Over."

"About ninety minutes. You can leave the rescue with us, over."

"That's a negative, Gregor. If he's still alive he may not have ninety minutes. I'm going down there to see what I can do. Over."

"You've done all you can. Remember the Armed Response Unit. They're bound to find out where you are. Over."

"Makes no difference. I'm staying with the boy. ST9, out."

The ST9 icon blinked off. At the control desk, Craig shook his head.

"Have you called Drew?" Gregor asked Gillian.

"Aye. He's climbing as fast as he can, but as you said, he's more than an hour from ST9, and there's ..." She winced.

"Bartholomew?"

"Aye, they're going to reach him first. If he's as badly injured as Kaine said, they'll not be able to leave him."

"Damn it. Who else do we have in the area?"

Craig zoomed out the large screen until the other signal flags appeared in shot. The nearest, ST1, was on the eastern side of the range, and even though using an easier, faster route, they were still at least three hours' hard climb from Kaine's recorded position.

"Where's Iona?"

"ST10," Craig said, nodding to the appropriate window. "She's about five minutes from the loch, but not answering her phone."

"Contact Inspector Elliott. Tell him what's happening. She'll be wanting to go and help her brother, and I don't need her climbing that mountain on her own, or with Jock. Inspector Elliott's likely to be the only one who can stop her."

"Good idea."

Craig nodded to Gillian who made the call to the loch.

"What of Mr and Mrs Princeton? Are you going to tell them?" Craig asked.

Gregor sighed. "I'd rather wait until we know the lad's condition, but I suppose they have a right to know."

"If you tell them, you'll have to let the police know who told us. And Gadget's gonna let his friends with the guns know where they can find him."

"Don't you think I know that? Damn it, man. Did you see the look on Mrs Princeton's face? Poor woman deserves to know what's happening. I need to call that state-of-the-art mobile unit of theirs and tell them we have some news. Perhaps if Superintendent Ingram-Howe learns that Ryan Kaine found the boy he'll maybe call off his attack dogs."

Craig scoffed. "Is that likely?"

"As likely as Gadget being voted in as MP in the next general election, I'd imagine. Better put me through to that stuffed shirt anyway."

Gregor allowed his eyes to settle on the large screen.

What happened during the following few hours would likely live with him for the rest of his days. He turned his back on the others and made the sign of the cross.

Pray God the boy's alive, and Ryan Kaine sees the next sunrise.

Chapter Twenty-Seven

Thursday 17th September – Early Afternoon

Ben Craed, The Cairngorms, Aberdeenshire, Scotland

"Martin?" Kaine called over the buffeting wind. "Don't know if you can hear me, son, but I'm on my way down to you."

His words echoed off the rocks and bounded away into the void.

In the few minutes since Kaine first spotted the lad, his limp body hadn't moved. The binoculars showed him in an awkward position, on his back with his right arm pinned beneath him and his left draped across his chest, not unlike the position Kaine had found Bartholomew lying in.

Irony knew no limits.

Martin's legs were out of sight, hidden by a jutting rock, no telling their condition. Whatever the situation, it would take skill for the rescue teams to reach him either from below or above, and even if the chopper had been available, the overhang made a winch lift impossible.

Kaine didn't have time to worry about that for the moment. He had to establish the boy's condition, and he couldn't do that from where he lay.

As Kaine prepped his descent, he chatted to the boy the whole time, trying to keep Martin's spirits high. He knew from personal experience the psychological lift an injured man received when hearing from his rescuers.

"There's no natural anchor point up here so I'll need to make one. Be with you soon. I promise."

Kaine searched the cliff face behind him for a good location for his fixing nuts. He released the rope from the Bergen and unfurled it. In the bag of climbing metalwork he found a spring-loaded double cam, with a heavy-duty webbing loop and a stainless-steel hoop washer. A slim and lightweight device on which to risk his life, but he had precious little alternative. The cam fitted perfectly inside a two-centimetre, diagonal fissure and locked into place with a satisfying snap. He gave it a sharp tug. It felt firm, no slippage, no deflection in the rock.

A smaller crack two metres away accepted a five-millimetre safety nut and created a strong, second anchor point, onto which he attached a carabiner. He slid the lead end of the rope through the carabiner and tied it with a bowline-on-a-bight to equalise the tension between the two anchors. As long as he kept his weight on the working side of the rope, the knot would hold tight. Remove the weight, and the knot would loosen and allow him to recover the rope for the second part of the descent. At least that was the plan. He scrutinised the arrangement, checking for kinks. It all looked pretty good.

"Martin," he yelled, "I've fixed the belay point. Won't be long now."

With no harness available, Kaine sliced three metres from the free end of the rope, tied a Swiss Seat rappel harness, and secured the free ends in place with a couple of half hitches. A second carabiner snapped through the waist loops, completing the rig.

Not the most comfortable harness he'd ever worn, but it would have to do.

"This thing pinches in all the wrong places, Martin. Hope you appreciate what I'm risking here, but I'd make a terrible father anyway."

Kaine found a winged, figure-of-eight descender in the kit, attached it to the harness carabiner, and was finally ready to roll.

Working solo, he wouldn't have anyone on belay—anchoring him using another rope if things went wrong—but he wasn't going to wait for the police to give him a helping hand. Martin had waited long enough for help.

Kaine took stock.

Five minutes from nothing to a two-point belay, harness, and descender had to be some form of mountaineering record. Perhaps he should call the people at Guinness?

Kaine wrung his hands together to test the skin. Sensitive. Too sensitive. He made makeshift, fingerless gloves from a pair of socks, and tied the loose end of the rope to the Bergen before lowering it carefully over the side.

He counted off the marks on the rope as the Bergen

dropped towards Martin's position—thirty-eight metres. His estimation hadn't been a mile off.

"Hear that scraping, Martin? That's my backpack. In it, there's food, water, and a space blanket. We'll soon have you nice and warm."

He leaned his full weight against the belay and bounced. The anchor points took the strain without any deflection. Everything looked good to go.

Okay, Kaine. You can do this.

He turned his back to the edge, twisted at the waist to look down into the chasm, and released some of the tension on the descender, forcing himself not to grip the braking end of the rope too hard. That way led to blisters and cramped fingers, the twin dangers faced by the rookie during an abseil. With his feet planted firmly on the point of the ledge, he leaned out until his legs were horizontal and his body was at right angles to the mountain face. He released the brake rope slowly.

Dangling in the air, with the overhang taking the rock face further away, he allowed the rope to slip through the descender.

The drop took no more than thirty seconds before his feet found the ledge beside his Bergen. It appeared solid enough, and he let out a relieved sigh.

Standing three metres above and six metres to Martin's left, Kaine locked the rope into the descender with a bight, and a single safety hitch. The pressure on his thighs and groin from the harness cords eased and the blood started flowing to his legs once more. A shop-bought harness was uncomfortable enough but, given the chance, the jury-rigged assembly would saw through his thighs and end up crippling him. He tried to ignore the pins and needles tingling in his feet and took in the scene below.

From the top of the climb, Martin looked bad enough, but from close up, things looked even worse. With pale skin and blue lips, he lay on his back, face exposed to the elements. He had a nasty gash on the top of his head. The blood had congealed and blackened in his matted hair.

Martin's lower left leg hung out in space, but his right leg had been snagged by a narrow crack in the rock. The unnatural angle of his foot suggested a dislocated ankle at the very least. Although it looked extremely painful, the rock probably held him in place and may have saved his life.

"Martin? Can you hear me?"

No response.

Kaine studied the boy's position, trying to decide the best way to approach. Up and over, or down and under?

Martin's head rested against a wall of granite that climbed steeply for six or seven metres until it canted outwards to form the overhang. It gave a little room alongside the boy for Kaine to stand.

Beyond the crack trapping Martin's ankle, the shelf dropped away abruptly and near-vertically. For Martin to find himself in that position, the only place on the climb large enough to hold him, could be classed as miraculous. If he'd fallen half a metre on either side, he wouldn't have stopped until hitting the rocks in the valley below.

The wind howled, trying to pluck Kaine from the mountain. He shot out a hand to steady himself. Another gust rustled Martin's thin mountain jacket … but, no. Not the wind.

A slight rising of his chest as Martin breathed.

He breathed!

Bloody hell. He's alive!

Nothing could have prepared Kaine for the joy of seeing the young man's chest rise. In the days since he'd shot

Flight BE1555 out of the sky, Kaine had been fighting to survive and had little spare time to find a reason for hope. But, hanging from the side of a Scottish mountain, he wanted to laugh, cry, scream, howl into the rocks, but that might have terrified the kid off the ledge. Instead, he just grinned.

"Martin? If you can hear me, don't move, okay? You might not know this, but you're stuck on a ledge about sixty metres up from the valley floor. Don't move. Understand?"

Slowly, the fingers on Martin's left hand clenched into a fist and rotated, the thumb extended. The boy heard and, what's more, he understood. The blow to his head looked serious, but Martin remained aware of his surroundings. Things were looking up. Now all Kaine had to do was find a way to get close and to lower them both to safety.

Easy peasy.

"Okay, Martin, that's great. Really good. The mountain rescue team will be here in a little while, but I'm going to come and check you over. Okay? But remember, don't move, and don't try to watch what I'm doing."

Martin gave him another shaky thumbs up. His chin twitched and tears formed in the corners of his eyes. The boy's highly charged emotional state might lead him to forget his situation and cause a disaster. Kaine had to reach him fast. Up and over was the quicker alternative.

Decision made.

"Right, here I come."

He hoisted the Bergen to his shoulders, but kept the rope tied as a safety backup. The added weight didn't help with the chafing, but with an end in sight, Kaine could put up with the discomfort for a little while longer.

He released the lock on the descender and walked backwards down the rock face until he was level with the boy.

"Nearly there, Martin. Hold on, mate."

Stepping gingerly, making sure not to disturb any of the rocks surrounding the boy, Kaine edged closer, paying out the rope a little at a time. This wasn't the point to rush. He had no way to tell how precarious the boy's hold on the mountain really was.

Gravel shifted underfoot. A larger rock moved. Kaine paused, adjusted his feet, and continued, hardly daring to breathe.

Three more metres.

Two.

Touching distance.

The flat rock beneath Martin held firm. Finally … he'd made it.

"Okay, Martin, I'm here and you're going to be safe."

Although he'd found a decent position alongside the boy, Kaine needed more space to work. He slid a lock-nut-with-tail into a crack in the rock wall and hung the Bergen from it with another carabiner.

Losing the weight of the pack made breathing more comfortable, and eased the pressure on his legs. How good it felt to be free of the constriction.

Kaine worked the Bergen's catches to release the top flap. He found the plastic bag inside, ripped it open, and removed the gold space blanket. First things first. Warm the boy, check his wounds, then give him water and food.

Gently, he wrapped the blanket around the boy's torso

The sense of doing something constructive after so many days of running for his life and defending himself from attack, couldn't be beaten. It took a second or two for Kaine to realise the background sound he heard was him humming an old Beatles song, *Good Day Sunshine*.

Where had he dragged that tune from?

Didn't matter. Life, at last was, if not exactly good, then better.

He dribbled water onto Martin's cracked and parched lips. The boy's eyes flickered open. The pupils constricted against the light and seemed to find focus.

"Who … are you?" he asked, his voice ragged.

"I'm Ry—I'm from the Kinross Farm Rescue Centre. Here to help. You should feel the warmth from the blanket pretty soon. How about some food? Fancy a little fruit cake?"

"P-Please."

Martin's eyes rolled up in his head before opening again when Kaine pushed a small piece of fruit cake under his nose. The boy opened his mouth and started chewing.

"Pretty good, yeah?"

Martin tried to raise his head, but winced and let it rest back against the rock. His tangled hair, stiff with dried blood and dust, hung in drapes over his face, a spider's web of thick strands. Gently, Kaine pulled a curl away from his forehead to expose a ten-centimetre gash at his hairline, between his ear and what would be a centre parting.

"There's a cut on your scalp, but are you hurt anywhere else?"

Kaine had seen far worse head injuries from a serious fall. The head laceration didn't look too grim, and Martin appeared lucid. He likely had a concussion, but the medics would deal with that later.

"The doctor at Kinross Farm will want to give the cut a thorough cleaning. You'll probably need some stitches, but it won't show much below the hairline. On the bright side, this'll be a good look for you, mate. Girls go for guys with scars big time. Or so I'm told."

A thin smile tugged at the edge of Martin's lips, and

already the space blanket and the cake were starting to work their magic. Colour had returned to his face, and his lips had changed from light blue to pale pink.

Martin swallowed the cake before answering. "My … my leg. I can't move it."

Kaine confirmed the security of the Bergen before untying the rope and slipping the end under Martin's lower back. He groaned at the movement.

"Sorry, mate, but I need to make sure you're going to stay where you are. Wouldn't want you taking me over the edge with you. What would that do to my standing in the rescue community, eh?"

He grinned and added a wink to deflect Martin's attention as he formed a double loop and tied it securely around the boy's waist.

"There you go, mate. Safe and sound. Now, let's check you over."

Kaine stood and leaned further out towards the edge of the ridge.

"Your right leg's trapped. The ankle might be broken or dislocated. Can't see any blood from here, but I'll deal with that in a minute. What about your arm? Any pain?"

"Sh-Shoulder," he said and nodded, no more than the tiniest dip of the chin. "C-Can't … feel my hand."

"Okay, I'll sort your arm first and then take care of that leg."

He slid a hand under the space blanket and across the boy's clavicle. Although the collar bone appeared intact, the ball joint at the head of the humerus bone stood shockingly proud of its socket in the shoulder blade. A shoulder dislocation was one of the few injuries Kaine had yet to suffer, but he could well imagine the pain it produced.

Kaine eyeballed the ropes and all the anchor points before risking the next part.

"Sorry, mate," he said, keeping his tone light and confident. "This next bit's not going to be fun, I need to straighten your arm. Ready?"

"N-No."

Kaine leaned against Martin's chest to stop him shifting sideways, pushed his right arm under the lad's neck and braced the injured shoulder. He gently rolled Martin onto his side, away from the precipice. Sweat popped out on the boy's bloodied forehead. He grunted, clenched his teeth, but didn't cry out.

Good lad.

Kaine compared the boy's reaction to the way Bartholomew squealed at every twitch. Martin was made of stronger stuff.

"Sorry, but this can't be helped. I need to straighten your arm. After that we can think about getting down from here. Ready for the next part?"

Martin scrunched up his face and nodded against Kaine's arm.

"This might hurt a little."

Kaine braced the injured shoulder from the back and reached his free hand down and behind to grab the pallid wrist. It would hurt, but improving blood flow was essential, and he couldn't wait a moment longer. He took hold of the wrist, freed the arm, and brought it around to the front. The joint popped back into position—the wet squelch sounding like the drumstick being pulled from a roast chicken.

Martin screamed and passed out, which was probably for the best, considering what Kaine had to do next. Dangerous, but he couldn't leave the boy exposed any longer. He had to free the leg and lower him to the safety of the valley floor, and the lad would be better off out of it.

Martin's right forearm and hand were grey, the blood circulation had clearly been compromised, but Kaine felt a slight pulse at the radial artery. Time would tell whether he'd regain use of the arm, but at least the boy would survive—assuming Kaine could lower him to the valley floor safely.

Kaine used two T-shirts from his pack to strap the arm to Martin's side. He then leaned across the boy's body to assess the leg injury. A mess. The next part was going to be really harsh.

"Sorry, Martin, but I need to check your circulation before releasing your leg. Ready?"

The lad made no response. Not a bad thing.

As gently as possible, Kaine removed the boot, checked the foot's colour—white, not black, a good sign—and tested the pulse behind the ankle bone. Thin and thready, but present. Apart from the unnatural deflection of the joint and the heavy swelling, the signs appeared good. Next for the difficult part. Using the weight of his own body to keep Martin pressed into the narrow shelf, Kaine grasped the trapped leg with one hand and yanked it free.

Martin groaned, but didn't wake.

"That's the worst over, mate. Now I'm going to get you down to safety so the rescue team can carry you out of here. After that, you've got a real treat. A rather attractive doctor is going to stabilise you before taking you to hospital. Lucky, lucky boy."

Kaine used his last T-shirt to tie the boy's legs together and was finally ready for the tricky part.

He stood and took a moment to make sure he'd done all he could.

Everything now depended on the knots he'd used to tie into the double anchor at the top of the climb. If he'd buggered them up in his haste, they'd both be stuck on the ledge until Drew's team arrived, or worse still, the Armed Response Unit.

Kaine settled himself into position on the foot loops, released the pressure on the descender, loosened the guide rope, and tugged.

Chapter Twenty-Eight

Thursday 17th September – William Cody

Ben Craed, The Cairngorms, Aberdeenshire, Scotland

Cody clambered upwards, three men behind him, Sergeant Townes and Stedman up ahead.

Despite the cool wind blowing at their backs, it was hard, sweaty work. Even though the firm footing was a nice change from the sucking, cloying moss, trudging forwards was a tough, back-breaking effort. While their heavy packs, weapons, and body armour were great for urban environments, for a mountain trek they couldn't have been more of a bloody liability.

What the fuck was Ryan Kaine doing? He had the

whole of the world to hide in yet he'd ended up in Scotland chasing after some missing schoolboy. What for?

Nothing in the man's service record or police file suggested he had a "thing" for young boys. The man had no close family, no young relatives. As far as his personnel file showed, the last time he'd had any association with kids was before he left school.

Captain Ryan Kaine was a highly decorated military officer with an honourable discharge from the marines and no history of madness. Despite that track record, he'd shot down a civilian aircraft, killed dozens of people, and now hunted the brother of one of those self-same victims. If that wasn't a sure sign of a rabid animal, Cody didn't know what would be.

Maybe the former-SBS Black Ops officer had a latent form of PTSD. The most mild-mannered and innocent of men could break down and turn violent, and Ryan Kaine was certainly neither mild-mannered nor innocent. Perhaps he'd developed an irrational grudge against BrightEuro Airlines, the operator of Flight BE1555. Perhaps they'd double-booked him on his last package holiday to the Algarve. Maybe a cute flight attendant had rejected his advances or spilled his in-flight coffee into his lap. Stranger things had caused highly strung ex-soldiers to snap.

Either way, the nutcase had to be stopped. And he, William Cody, was ready, willing, and more than able to complete the task.

"Okay," he shouted. "Take a five-minute break. Light up if you need to."

The men found the nearest suitable place to sit and formed a loose circle in the rocks, keeping their eyes and ears open for signs of the target. While in the middle of a live operation, none would or should ever truly relax.

In the year since he'd taken over the unit, Cody had managed to pound some sense into them, but they'd never be as good as the team he'd created in London. The Scots weren't bright enough to be really good. Too damned emotional. Too damned soft.

"Sergeant Townes?"

"Yes, sir?"

"How far have we come?"

Townes took the tablet from Stedman and clambered down to Cody, breathing easily, apparently untroubled by the exercise or the tough conditions. The thick sod was finding the terrain too fucking easy. Wouldn't have surprised Cody if the Glaswegian's mother had mated with a mountain goat. Either that, or he was too bloody stupid to know when to be knackered.

Townes drew alongside and held up the tablet for Cody to see.

"Just under three and a half miles, sir."

"That all? We left the campsite ninety minutes ago."

Townes nodded and pulled in a deep breath. "Tough going up here, sir, and this equipment's not built for yomping up all these hills."

Tell me about it.

"How far to the ridge?" Cody asked, pointing to the thin line of grey on the horizon.

The sergeant consulted his screen. "A little under two miles."

"Really? Looks closer."

"That's 'cause the air is thin and clear up here and the sightlines are open. You're too used to all that smog down there in London." Townes smiled in a bid to lessen any perception of an insult. "Suck that fresh, Highland air into your lungs, sir. Do you the power of good."

"Don't give me that bollocks, Sergeant. This stuff's so fucking cold and clean, it's scorching my throat. We're still over an hour away from that notch."

Their position was marked as a fixed X at the bottom of the screen. Andrew McTay's locator beacon showed as a flashing, red dot towards the top.

"See that? McTay's on the move. He was supposed to be searching the lake, but he started up the mountain, and now he's changed course again. I told you the big, bearded arsewipe was hiding something."

Townes' thin lips twisted into something that could have been a smile or a grimace. Cody could never tell.

"Aye, sir. That you did. Touch of pure genius when you had Stedman plant that tracker on him."

Cody ignored the compliment and tapped McTay's marker. "What's he up to?"

"No idea, sir. He's headed for the north face of *Ben Craed* now. It says in the guide"—he slid his finger across the screen and activated a search engine—"the north face 'boasts some of the most technically demanding climbs in the whole of the Cairngorms. A must see for all serious mountaineers'. "

"Makes my question even more relevant. What the bloody hell's McTay doing? Do you think he's in direct contact with Kaine?"

"No chance. Their satphones are two-way only. Linked directly to Kinross Farm. Keeps the bandwidth down and ensures they maintain the satellite signal even in the shittiest weather. It's one of the reasons why they need those comms techies. No, sir, my guess is Abercrombie's talked to Kaine and passed a message on to Mr McTay."

Fucking people. What are they doing?

"How detailed is that map? Can you plot a route to intercept McTay's party?"

Townes screwed up his face. It looked as though he'd bitten into a thistle.

"Not a chance," he said. "We could head up any one of those gullies and meet a dead end. Then we'd have to double back on ourselves and lose even more time. The system's mapped and stored their route. It's accurate to within ten metres. Our best bet is to cut across that ridge and strike out for the area west of the loch until we cross McTay's trail. We'll be able to follow him easily enough after that."

"Okay, better get a shuffle on then. I want to be within firing range the moment McTay meets up with Ryan Kaine."

"Assuming he's heading to Kaine."

"Oh, he is. I can feel it in my aching bones." Cody picked up his pack and settled it onto his shoulders. "Okay, people, up you get. I want to hit that ridge in forty minutes. At the double. Move!"

———

DESPITE CODY'S CONTINUING words of "encouragement", it took over an hour to reach the rocky outcrop separating one valley from its neighbour. They took another ten minutes to locate a safe place to scale its broken surface, by which time, they were all blowing hard—Townes included—and temporarily useless as a fighting force. None of them, not even Patel, their number one marksman, could have hit the side of a barn at twenty paces with a rocket launcher. Not even if it was lit up with a laser-targeting imager.

As they approached the ridge, he'd given his men instructions to move into silent-running mode, using hand signals to issue final instructions. He tapped his fingers to the top of his head. They gathered around him and he spoke quietly.

"Take another rest and check your equipment. Sergeant Townes and I are going to scout the ground on the other side of that ridge. With me, Sergeant."

He and Townes scrambled up yet more loose gravel and popped their heads over the top of the crest. Each had field glasses and trained them on the expanse of broken water spread out half a mile below them. White topped waves driven on the wind broke against the mud-grey shoreline. Dots of movement and the sun's reflection on the lake's southern bank caught Cody's attention. He adjusted the focus on his glasses and the dots became the small figures of men, three in the water, and three on land. Those in the water wore shiny, black wetsuits and carried air cylinders on their backs. Their land-based colleagues tended to a cart loaded with diving equipment.

"Looks like they're packing up, sir," Townes muttered.

"They can't have finished already. It's only been a couple of hours and that lake's pretty big. They've either found the body, or called off the search. Can you see a corpse?"

With his eyes still glued to the field glasses, Cody felt rather than saw Townes shaking his head.

"No, sir."

"Me neither. So, if they've called off the search, someone else must have found the boy. Yes?"

"Makes sense to me, sir. I guess that answers the question why McTay's team is on the mountain trail and not heading to the lake."

Cody lowered the glasses and turned to his second-in-command, smiling, unable to hold down the rising excitement. "And you know what that means?"

"Ryan Kaine found the boy?"

"I'd put money on it. It also means those arseholes back at Kinross Farm have definitely been holding out on us. C'mon, let's get moving."

Cody flipped onto his back and scrambled down the slope to the men, his spirits soaring.

"Huddle up," he said and dropped to one knee.

He waited until they'd gathered around. They'd all recovered their breath. Each man looked alive, excited, and ready for the next phase.

Sometimes, miracles actually did happen.

"We're reaching the end game here, people. I want to remind you what we're up against. Ryan Kaine killed eighty-three people on that plane, and he's still free and clear. Basically, the bugger's been laughing at every cop in the country. But he's here now, and we're going to have him. Understood?"

The men nodded and looked at each other in turn, their expressions ranging from grim determination to smiling anticipation. Cody could almost smell the adrenaline in the waves of sweat emanating from hot and excited bodies.

"A word of warning, though. Kaine is dangerous. A killer. You've all read his profile. If he makes a threatening move, don't hesitate to shoot. The woman he abducted, Dr McTay, swears he isn't armed, but those buggers at Kinross Farm have been lying to us since we arrived. We can't trust a word any of them says. I'm telling you here and now, Ryan Kaine isn't getting away. None of us wants his escape on our jackets. I don't care if we pull him off this mountain in a fucking body bag. Do I make myself clear?"

He stared at each man in turn. All nodded without hesitation. One added a, "Hell yes!"

Townes made a fist and pushed it into the centre of the huddle for the rest of the men to bump. Cody didn't join in. He didn't give a toss about that kind of bullshit.

Cody clapped Townes on the shoulder. "Sergeant, over to you."

"Thank you, sir."

Townes held up the tablet so everyone could see the map clearly.

"Stedman and I've been tracking this marker since we left Kinross Farm. McTay's team changed course a little while ago. The boss and I think they're heading for a meet with Kaine and Martin Princeton. They're a good way ahead of us. We need to get a scurry on, but keep the noise down. We don't want to scare Kaine away. Got me?"

A quiet chorus of, "Yes, Sarge!" rippled around the group.

"Stedman," Cody said, "you've done your stint as point man. Take the sweeper role for now. Patel, make sure you're good to roll. I reckon we might need your particular skillset before too long."

Patel's white teeth shone bright through his dark beard. "Yes, sir. I'll be ready."

"Okay, men. Eyes peeled, ears open. Kaine's time for laughing at us ends today."

As does the fucker's life.

Chapter Twenty-Nine

Thursday 17th September — Afternoon

Ben Craed, The Cairngorms, Aberdeenshire, Scotland

Twenty-five metres to go.

Kaine teased out more of the rope and walked backwards down the mountainside with Martin dangling beneath him from another makeshift harness.

The relief Kaine had felt when the rope slid from its anchor points and coiled easily around his upper arm had been tempered by the worry for the boy's condition, but he needn't have feared. Despite his youth—or maybe because of it—Martin was improving by the minute. He clearly came from strong stock.

"You'll be down on firm, flat ground in a minute, lad. *Hang* in there!"

Martin grimaced, but it had nothing to do with pain. Kaine couldn't help groaning along with the lad after resorting to such a naff pun.

Martin's lips moved, and Kaine had to stop descending to hear him say, "Don't give up your ... day job."

The lad looked up and their eyes met.

"Yeah, sorry."

As they dangled in space, Kaine couldn't get over the rapid improvement in the boy's condition. A little warmth, food, and some minor medical treatment, and he'd improved beyond all expectation. The positive psychological effect of rescue would have been a massive boost for the boy. He even helped during the descent by using his good hand to hold himself away from the cliff.

Pale, sweating, and clearly in pain, Martin refused to shout out whenever he swung in the wind and collided with the hard stuff.

Fifteen metres.

The ground slid up to meet them. With two metres to go, Kaine locked the descender and studied the boulder-strewn surface, looking for a good place to land. A flat, smooth area of rubble and grey dust was set off to his right and Kaine stepped around a vertical ripple in the cliff and let out a little more rope.

Seconds later, Martin landed as gently as a feather on a waterbed. As the boy's weight came off the rope, the carabiner attaching them to each other loosened. Kaine unclipped them and the boy settled onto his back, his face creased in pain, and his eyes squinting against the bright sun.

"Okay, Martin?"

"Aces. It's … good to be down on the ground. Thought I'd be stuck up there … 'til Christmas."

"I'll be right with you. Don't go rushing off and getting lost again. Don't think I'll bother searching for you next time."

Martin stretched out a weak grin. "You really aren't … the least bit funny."

"Agreed."

Kaine spotted another relatively flat patch of ground a little to the right of the boy. He planted both feet against the cliff face, bent at the knees, and pushed off. At the same time as he swung out, Kaine released the descender, sailed through the air, and landed lightly on his feet five metres from Martin's head.

"Okay, Martin. Time to call in the cavalry. I'm guessing you don't fancy spending another night under the stars?"

"Stars? What pigging stars?" Martin said, his voice gaining in strength all the time. "Apart from that tiny patch of blue sky up there, I've seen nothing but black and grey clouds. Hate this bloody country."

"Rubbish. This is one of the most beautiful places on earth. Not the mountain's fault you fell off the top ledge."

Martin's shining, blue eyes lost a little of their lustre and he turned his head away. "Not my fault, either," he mumbled, almost too quiet for Kaine to make out.

"What was that, Martin?"

"N-Nothing."

The lad blinked and a tear squeezed from between his closed lids.

Clearly, something was eating at the boy, but Kaine didn't feel he was ready to be pressed. Whatever was worrying the lad, others would be in a better position to tease it out of him—perhaps his parents.

"Got any more of that cake?"

"Typical teenager. Only been on the ground five seconds and you're already hungry. No, 'Thank you for saving my life'?" Kaine said, grinning.

Martin turned to face him once more. He took a stuttering breath before saying, "Sorry. I ... do appreciate everything, but I'm starving. Do you have any more food, please?"

Kaine stretched his mouth into a wide beam and dug into the Bergen. He found a honey-and-nut energy bar.

"You okay eating nuts?"

The boy held out his good hand. "Yes, thanks. I could eat the leg off a horse. That what my dad always says. Me and Matty both."

Another cloud of sadness slid across Martin's face, but Kaine didn't need to hunt for the cause of that one. Bile rose to his throat. He may have found the boy, but the cause of Martin's emotional pain rested firmly in Kaine's lap. He couldn't think of a single thing to say that might alleviate it.

Kaine tore the wrapping from the food bar and tucked it into Martin's hand. "Suppose you want the last of my water, too?"

"Unless you have a beer or some *Irn Bru*."

"Now who's being funny. You're too young for beer, and your teeth are too precious to risk on that sickly, orange stuff. Besides, I only arrived in Scotland yesterday. Haven't had time to stock up on the local delicacies."

Martin devoured the food bar in three ravenous mouthfuls, barely taking time to chew. The boy's healthy appetite was a positive sign, and it gave Kaine hope for the boy's future. He took a sip of water, passed the flask across, and dug inside the Bergen for the satphone.

"So, if you're not a comedian," Martin said once he'd swallowed his food and drained the flask, "what are you?"

"Just a volunteer passing through."

He powered up the phone and checked the signal strength—a full three bars. Miracle piled on top of miracle. At least he wouldn't have to leave the boy, who seemed desperate for his company. And who could blame him?

"Not a boxer?"

"What?"

"Your face. Either you've been in a fight, or you've fallen down your own mountain."

Kaine put a hand to his cheek. With all his exertions, he'd almost forgotten his injuries—all but the broken tooth which still throbbed enough to drive him as nuts as the energy bar Martin had just demolished.

"An argument with an angry man."

"One man did that to you?"

Kaine snorted and shook his head. "Not really. It started with two, but neither man is bragging about it now."

"When I first opened my eyes and saw you, I nearly wet myself. You're a scary-looking dude. Thought you were a banshee, or whatever they have up here. Don't tell my parents I'm a cry baby."

"You're no baby, Martin. The way you helped on the abseil down here when you must have been in agony. Never seen anyone so brave."

"Who are you? I need to know your name."

Jesus, how can I answer that?

"I'll tell you later. First, I need to contact the rescue centre. Your parents will have arrived by now. They'll be desperate to hear you're alive."

Kaine pulled away, but Martin grabbed his wrist and squeezed tight. He could have broken the grip easily enough, but it might have jogged the boy, and he'd caused the lad enough pain.

"You're Ryan Kaine, aren't you? I recognise you … from the news reports. You killed Matty. You killed my brother!"

Kaine tried to look away, but the hate in the young man's eyes speared him through the heart with the same accuracy as the surface-to-air missile he'd launched from the middle of the North Sea.

In that moment, halfway up a Scottish mountain, he couldn't lie. Martin deserved the truth. The full, unadulterated facts, told by the man who'd killed his brother.

"You did, didn't you? You blew up Flight BE1555."

Martin delivered the words with a flat, unemotional tone, the tears rolling down his young face, lower lip and chin quivering. Kaine's eyes watered as he nodded. His throat constricted and he found it almost impossible to breathe. This was so hard. He'd faced armed men on four continents intent on doing him and his men untold harm, but none had turned him into a trembling bowl of jelly in the way Martin was doing.

Man up, Kaine, the kid needs the truth.

Under Martin's intense, hate-filled eyes, Kaine lowered himself and sat cross-legged on the stony, windswept valley floor and started talking.

"This isn't going to be easy, Martin, but I'm so sorry. I did launch that rocket, but I was set up by my best friend."

Christ, even though true, putting the blame on the now-dead Gravel Valence sounded pathetic, and Martin's sneer told him the boy felt the same way. Kaine continued anyway.

"Eight days ago, I was on a fishing boat in the North Sea, under orders to field test a new piece of military equipment. My boss radioed me with the targeting coordinates and confirmed I was aiming at an unmanned drone. The bastard lied to me, Martin. I promise you."

Kaine broke off and tore his eyes away, unable to suffer the boy's angry stare any longer. Although he tried to study the route they'd taken to abseil down Zelda's Smile, his mind kept bringing back the horrific image of a fireball in the sky over the North Sea.

Martin twisted towards Kaine, eyes blazing. He grimaced with the movement.

"Why?"

"Sorry?"

"Why did your so-called boss want you to shoot down Matty's plane?"

Kaine took a deep breath and puffed out his cheeks, ignoring the discomfort. He couldn't blame the kid for the anger and antagonism, but Kaine needed ... something. His absolution?

"Long story, Martin, but it boiled down to greed. Money. He was paid to do it by ... the head of a company that produces arms and munitions. One of the passengers on that plane had a price on his head and the people paying my boss didn't mind how many people had to die in order to get to him. In the military, we call it 'collateral damage'."

"If all that's true, where is he now, your boss? Why didn't you just tell the police about him?"

Kaine shook his head. The boy's attitude showed the naïve innocence of the very young. At least he was asking questions and showing a willingness to listen.

"I'd drag him to the police by his hair if I could, but he's dead."

"You killed him," Martin said, shaking his head slowly. "So, that means everyone's right about you being a killer."

This time, his words came out as matter-of-fact.

"No, Martin, he was murdered by the people who put out the contract on the real target. They tried to kill me at the same time. I escaped, but I did learn the identity of the man who gave my boss the targeting code. A nasty individual called Rudy Bernadotti."

Martin frowned. "He sounds Italian. Are you trying to tell me the Mafia's involved?"

"No, lad. Bernadotti was a senior director of the largest weapons manufacturer in the UK. It turns out the company's chairman, Sir Malcolm Sampson, and Bernadotti were trying to force through a hostile takeover of another weapons manufacturer."

Kaine paused for another breath and Martin jumped in with, "Was? You said Bernadotti 'was' a director of this company. He's dead, too. Yeah?"

Once again, Kaine nodded.

"And this guy, Sir Malcolm, murdered him to stop him talking?"

Kaine relaxed a little. Martin's anger had disappeared, replaced by a kind of boyish wonder at the mention of industrial espionage and hostile takeovers. At least he seemed ready to believe Kaine's story.

Small mercies.

"Not quite. *I* killed Bernadotti. Gave him the chance to hand himself over to the police, but he chose not to take it. We got into a fight, and he wasn't as tough as he thought."

"Is that how come your face is all battered?"

"No. Bernadotti didn't land a single blow. I received this damage after breaking into Sir Malcolm's penthouse suite in London and …"

Martin showed excitement during the rest of the story and Kaine took extra time to explain how he'd entrapped

Sir Malcolm into confessing to his part in the disaster. The boy deserved the explanation, and Kaine felt some minor cleansing during the process.

"I was on my way to the police with a somewhat reluctant Sir Malcolm and a digital recording of his confession when I heard you were missing. I know this area quite well, and I decided to come find you."

"Really? Is that the truth?"

Kaine locked eyes with the lad. "On my word of honour as a Royal Marine and former-SBS officer. I swear it."

"SBS?"

Kaine sat up straighter. "Special Boat Service. We're the Royal Navy's version of the SAS."

"Like a Navy SEAL, you mean?"

"That's right, only with a British accent—and more … style."

He studied the boy's reaction and saw understanding and forgiveness. At least that's what he hoped he'd seen.

Martin grunted as he rolled onto his back and lay silent for a few moments before speaking again, a malicious smile creasing his mouth.

"What did you do with Sir Malcolm? I hope you killed the bastard slowly."

"Absolutely not. I don't murder helpless, old men. I left him trussed up in the back of a smelly, old van together with the evidence and told a police officer friend where to find him. Despite his millions, Sir Malcolm Sampson is going to spend the rest of his miserable life behind bars. Please believe me, Martin. I've told you the truth."

At least most of it.

As Kaine told his tale, he hoped for some kind of cathartic release, but found only more pain in the silent stare of a victim's brother.

He allowed a pregnant silence to stretch out forever and spent the time listening to the wind whistle through the crags and watching tears roll down Martin's cheeks, all signs of the previous anger gone. What must he think of the man responsible for his brother's death? Nothing but hatred probably, but did he believe the truth?

Martin sniffled and wiped his nose with the sleeve of his jacket. As Kaine had done before him, Martin studied the cliff face. He shuddered, no doubt remembering his time on the narrow ledge.

"Thank you," he said in a voice barely above a whisper.

"Finding you was a long shot, Martin. I got lucky."

"I meant, thanks for telling me what happened. Couldn't have been easy. And of course, thank you for saving me."

Kaine struggled to reply.

"You're welcome, lad," he managed, barely able to force the words out past the boulder-sized lump in his throat.

"So, why do you give a toss about an idiot kid getting lost on a school trip? Why not go to your cop friend and clear your name?"

"I'm … trying to make amends." Kaine ran a hand through his gritty hair. "Pathetic isn't it. I'll never be able to make up for what I did, but … I'll spend the rest of my life trying."

However long that might be.

Blinking away the tears, he squeezed the boy's good shoulder and pushed himself to his feet. It took some effort to overcome the pain and inertia of fatigue when he wanted nothing more than to stretch out and take a long, well-needed rest. On his way upright, his knees creaked, and a low moan escaped his lips.

"You're not leaving me are you?"

"No, Martin. Just making that call."

Wrapped in the gold space blanket with only his head and one good arm showing, Martin looked so young, still a boy, but with the maturity of an adult. No matter what happened, Kaine wasn't going to leave him on his own. He'd deliver him to his parents even if it meant ending up in a police holding cell.

He swallowed hard, raised the satphone, and punched the red button.

Chapter Thirty

Thursday 17th September – Gregor Abercrombie

**Kinross Farm MRC, The Cairngorms,
Aberdeenshire, Scotland**

"Oh dear Lord, no," Gregor said under his breath.

He closed his eyes for a moment, preparing himself for the emotional onslaught as the Princetons burst through the office door, Inspector Gaskell and an attractive, blonde constable in their wake. He hated the emotional stuff. If he had his way he'd ban the public from the building during emergencies, but he could tell from the set of her chin and the light of desperation shining in her eyes, a battalion of squaddies couldn't have held back Mrs Princeton.

She raced ahead of her husband and grasped Gregor's forearm, her grip strengthened by hope.

"You found Martin!"

How could he answer that? For all he knew, Kaine had located nothing but a corpse. He rested his hand on hers for a moment before easing his arm away.

"One of … my men spotted something on the north face of *Ben Craed*. It could be Martin, but we're not cert—"

"What do you mean 'could be'?" Mr Princeton interrupted. "How many teenage boys are lost in your mountains?"

The clear accusation in the words was illogical. The mountains were no more Gregor's than anyone else's. All he tried to do was find the missing souls. It wasn't as though he was responsible for placing them in danger.

As soon as the anger flared, it dissipated. Gregor could put himself in the Princetons' position. If either of his wee lassies disappeared, he'd have been inconsolable. He tried a different, more tactful approach. "He's unable to tell the condition of the individual."

"Why not?" Mr Princeton asked. "There's something you're not telling us, isn't there?"

Before Gregor could respond, the ST9 indicator flashed up on the big screen.

Thank God.

Gregor held up a finger and turned his back to the Princetons. He glanced at Gillian and tapped his headset, and she ran the feed through the closed system.

"*ST9 calling Kinross Farm. Are you receiving me? Over.*"

"Aye, we're here, ST9. Do you have any news? Over."

"*He's alive, Gregor. Martin Princeton is alive. Over.*"

The weight of the previous days dropped from Gregor's shoulders. He lowered his head and closed his eyes.

Praise the dear Lord.

"One moment, ST9." He gave Gillian the thumbs-up

and the sound boosted to the ambient speakers. "Repeat your last message. Over."

"*I said, I've found Martin Princeton, and he's alive. Over.*"

Mrs Princeton squealed, her hand flew up to her mouth, and she sagged against her husband. Joyous tears fell from two pairs of eyes.

Spontaneous applause rattled around the room. Huge grins and whoops of delight sounded out from hard-bitten men and woman recently returned from the field. Before the message, the room had been a silent, tense cavern of worry. Now, the delight was plain to see and hear. Pretty soon, they'd be able to start filling the whisky glasses and let the party begin, but not yet awhile.

Gregor flapped a hand for silence. The roar died but the high fives and back-slapping continued.

"What condition's he in? Over."

"*Head injury but, far as I can tell, there's no concussion. Dislocated left shoulder with some blood flow restriction to the arm. He might need microsurgery. He also has a broken or dislocated ankle. None of the injuries are life threatening. Over.*"

"That's excellent news, man. Is he conscious? Over."

"*That's an affirmative. Over.*"

"Wonderful, I have two people here desperate to speak to their son. Over."

"*Okay. I'll … hand him the phone. Over.*"

Mrs Princeton snatched a microphone from Craig and held it up to her mouth, her hand trembling.

"Martin? Is that you, darling?"

"*When you finish speaking you're … supposed to say 'over', Mum. But yes, it's me. I'm hurt, but safe now. How are you? Over.*"

"My boy, my precious baby."

"*Oh Mum, stop it. Please,*" Martin groaned, his voice weak. "*You're … embarrassing me. Over.*"

Hoots of relieved laughter rebounded off the walls and low ceiling. This time Gregor didn't try to silence his people. After working flat out for so long they needed to release some of their built-up tension.

Mrs Princeton's lower lip trembled and the tears returned afresh. She handed the mic to her husband and buried her face in his chest. He held her tight and stood taller, his upper lip as stiff as Gregor had ever seen.

"Hello, son. It's your father here"—he turned his head from the mic and coughed into a handkerchief, which came away spotted with blood—"I hope you're pleased with yourself. Lying around in the sun taking it easy while your mother and I were worried sick … Er, over."

The man tried to sound gruff, but his eyes shone bright, delight and relief written large on his haggard face.

"*Sorry, Dad. If it helps, I was cold and in pain the whole time. How are you? Over.*"

"Don't you worry about me, son. I've never been better. Over."

"*I was worried for you both. I'm … sorry. Over.*"

"I know, son. What happened? Over."

"*Can't tell you over the phone. Mr Kaine says—*"

"Who?" Mr Princeton asked. His bloodshot eyes shot up to fix on Gregor.

"*Ryan Kaine, Dad. He found me. Over.*"

"You can't mean—"

"*Yes, Dad. Ryan Kaine—that Ryan Kaine—saved me. Without him, I … I'd probably have—*"

Mrs Princeton pushed herself away from her husband, her face red, eyes wild. "Ryan Kaine? What's he doing there? The man's a murderer. A madman. He wants to hurt my baby. Oh God. No!"

Her knees buckled and she started to collapse, but

Gregor and Mr Princeton caught her and helped her into a chair.

"*It wasn't his fault, Mum. He's innocent. Someone set him up. He told me all about it. Over.*"

Gregor took the mic from Mr Princeton and said, "Sorry, Mrs Princeton, but I need to let my team know where to find Martin. We'll get him to you as fast as we can."

Mrs Princeton kept her head turned away, and her husband looked stunned, too stunned to take in what he'd heard.

"How ... How long will your people take to reach him?"

Gregor cast an eye over the big screen and ran a quick calculation.

"The first teams should reach Mr Bartholomew within the next thirty minutes or so. After that—"

"What's that?" Mr Princeton stiffened and sat straight up in his seat, but kept a consoling arm around his wife's shoulders. "Mr Bartholomew is on the mountain, too? Nobody told us. What on earth is going on here?"

Gregor scowled at Gaskell. What had he and the officious boor, Ingram-Howe, told the Princetons? Damnation. It wasn't up to him to do the police's job. He had enough on his plate.

"I thought Inspector Gaskell would have explained what happened here last night. Francis!" He beckoned to the tubby police officer with an index finger and a dark frown. "Perhaps you'd like to get over here and do your thing ... properly this time."

Gaskell hesitated, apparently wavering between approaching the couple and running away, tail between his fat legs.

Be generous, Gregor. The good Lord loves all his creations. Even fat, useless police inspectors.

Eventually, Gaskell stiffened and marched smartly across the room.

"I'll leave you to it," Gregor said, turning away from the distraught couple and focusing on the screens. "Craig, let the other search teams know the boy's alive and give them the location."

Craig's bright-toothed grin could have graced the cover of a dental hygiene magazine. "Already done that, Gregor. If you look at the screen, ST1 and ST6 are closest. I sent them to help, but they'll still take a couple of hours to reach Kaine and the boy. That okay with you, boss?"

He always knew Craig was more than just a geek with a love of electronics. Unable to match the wattage of the younger man's smile, Gregor didn't bother trying.

"Aye, good man. And Drew?"

"I held off calling him until you were ready. Thought you'd like to tell him yourself."

Gregor nodded and tapped his headset. "Give the Princetons access to Martin for as long as possible, and let me speak to Drew in private."

A couple of seconds later, his headset speakers clicked and Craig gave him the signal to speak.

"ST3, this is Kinross Farm, are you there? Over."

"This is ST3. Receiving you strength five. What's happening? Over," Drew asked, breathless.

He'd clearly been pushing hard. Gregor gave him the news.

"That's fantastic. Hold on while I tell the guys. Over." The speakers fell silent for a moment before reactivating. Ragged cheering drowned out Drew's next words.

"Repeat that, ST3. Over."

"*Can ye hear them hollering? Over.*"

"Aye, I can. Tell them to concentrate. That terrain's treacherous. I don't want to be rescuing the rescuers. Over."

"*Stop yer fussing, y'old mother hen. My men know what they're about. Where's the boy? Over.*"

"At the base of Zelda's Smile. Over."

"*Exactly where Kaine said he'd be. The man knows his stuff. Over.*"

"Aye. Seems to. How far from *Craed's Fist* are you? Over."

"*No more than ten minutes. From what Kaine told us, Bartholomew's in a bad way. How's the lad? Over.*"

Gregor outlined Martin's injuries as Kaine had explained them. "Bartholomew seems to be a lot worse off, but I'll leave you to assess the situation. Iona's on her way to the loch with her medical kit, but I've asked Inspector Elliott to make sure she stays there for now. Over."

"*Good idea. Any idea where the posse is? Over.*"

"None. Cody turned off his satphone after making his last report and hasn't checked in since. He could be anywhere on the mountain. Over."

"*Ha! Probably wandering around at Point Zero trying to pick up Kaine's trail. Tell Jock he did a grand job. I'll set him up wi' a wee dram or two when I get back. Over.*"

"Don't drop your guard, Drew. You know what Cody did down in London. The man's a hothead and I don't want any of my people getting in the way of one of his bullets. Over."

"*Whisht, man. That wee Englishman couldnae find his way up the mountain if we left him a trail of breadcrumbs. Wait … we're coming up on* Craed's Fist. *I'll report back when we've assessed Bartholomew. ST3, out.*"

The line fell silent and Gregor studied the blips on the

map. Kaine had left his satphone active, and the ST9 icon occupied the centre of the big screen, which displayed five other dots.

ST10 and DT1, Iona and Elliot's dive team, remained stationary at the loch. Gregor could only imagine what Lewis Elliott had to do to keep Iona from rushing headlong after her brother. He was happy not to be a witness to that particular pre-marital discussion.

He smiled at the imagined imagery.

Drew's team, ST3, was heading northeast and looked to be right on top of *Craed's Fist*.

The other search teams, ST1 and ST6, were on the south and east sides of the mountain, respectively. As usual, Craig's estimation was dead right. It would take them a good two hours to reach Kaine and Martin Princeton.

Things looked under control, but one question remained. Where in the good Lord's name were Buffalo Bill Cody and the rest of his posse?

Chapter Thirty-One

Thursday 17th September – William Cody

Ben Craed, The Cairngorms, Aberdeenshire, Scotland

Panting heavily in the thin, cold air, Cody pulled his water bottle from its pouch and sucked in a thirsty mouthful. His team had made good time, but at a price. The uphill slope and the rough going had taken its toll on their operational readiness. If they'd had a helicopter as they were supposed to, the bloody hunt would already have ended. But no, this fucking backwards country only had a couple of air-sea search choppers. There were plenty of others at the disposal of the oil companies to ferry workers to the rigs, but none available for the police. Pathetic. Fucking Scotland was nothing more than a backwards-looking joke. As far as he was concerned, they could have their independence and good bloody riddance to the lot of them.

The sooner he could end his enforced banishment and return to civilisation, the better.

Kaine's death would be his gateway home, and he wasn't going to fuck up what would probably be his last chance at salvation. If he had to kill Ryan Kaine with his bare hands, he'd do it happily, and he'd do it with a clear conscience and a broad smile. Might even laugh as he squeezed the life out of the murdering, terrorist arsehole.

Up ahead on point duty, Townes raised his right fist to signal a halt. The men dropped into a one-kneed firing stance, weapons at the ready, trained forwards. Cody rushed up the hill at double-time and dropped, gasping, into position beside his second-in-command.

"Yes, Sergeant?" he whispered between breaths.

Damn this fucking mountain.

Townes grinned at his discomfort. "You need to spend more gym time on the endurance equipment, sir. Those weights machines don't help much in this terrain."

"That's enough insubordination from you, Sergeant. What you got for me?"

Townes pointed up the hill to where a knife-edge of rock shot up from the side of a curved valley floor. It looked as though someone had taken a groove out of the side of the mountain with an ice cream scoop. Small rocks and pebbles dotted the hollowed-out floor, making a silent approach difficult, if not nigh-on impossible.

"Shit. Any way around it?"

Townes consulted the satellite image on his tablet. "Doesn't look like it, sir. But see that piece of rock jutting out of the ridge about halfway up?"

Cody followed the direction of the sergeant's pointing finger. Sure enough, a shaft of black stone stuck out from the rounded side of the cliff like a thumb of a boxing glove.

"Is that our target?"

"Yes, sir. Drew McTay's team is on the far side of that tor. According to the map, it's called *Craed's Fist*."

Cody nodded and pulled in another deep breath. "I can see why. Poetic lot, you mountain folk. Are you sure that's where they are?"

"Aye, sir," Townes said, spreading his fingers over the screen to enlarge the image. "The tracker stopped moving a couple of minutes ago, and I caught sight of movement on the ridge. That's why I signalled a halt. It's them all right. I reckon they're hard at work treating the kid."

"Good. They might not hear us coming."

"Your orders, sir?"

"Give the men a second to catch their breaths."

Townes looked at the others and smirked. "Unnecessary, sir. We're ready to go as soon as you are."

Cody blanked him.

You smarmy, Scottish git. Wait 'til we get back to base. I'll tear you a new one.

"Show me that screen again."

Townes turned the tablet so Cody could study it properly.

Fuck it. Townes was right. No direct alternative approach. They'd have to follow McTay's route and come up behind them.

Still on one knee, Cody turned to face the sorry-looking bunch of Celts. Christ, what wouldn't he give to have his London team. They'd know what to do. He'd hardly have needed to give them any orders.

"Okay. Listen up. This is where we earn our money.

McTay's team is up there the other side of that boulder. I've no idea what we'll find over there, but it looks like there's only one way up and one way down." He shot a look at each man in turn, holding their return gaze for a moment before moving on.

"Keep your wits about you and your weapons ready. And listen carefully. If Ryan Kaine *is* up there, he has access to hostages and we all know what he's capable of doing. Don't hesitate. Shoot to kill. Do I make myself clear?"

He waited a beat, half-expecting the gutless Townes to put up an argument, but for once, the sergeant kept his mouth shut. Cody drew back the charging handle on his C8. The rest followed his lead. Locked and loaded, and ready to hunt bear.

Now we're getting somewhere.

"Okay, men. Single file, I'm taking point. Move out."

CODY TUCKED his C8 tight into his shoulder, took a general aim at the mountain rescue team, and screamed, "Armed police! Armed police! Stop what you're doing!"

His men echoed his warnings in a cohesive display of "shock and awe". Some civilians on the wrong end of the tactic wet themselves. The power was awesome. Some, not Cody, might even call it orgasmic.

Two of the three volunteers spun to face him. Terror registered on their ruddy faces. The one on the right dropped his end of a cage-like stretcher, but his friend reacted lightning-fast and caught it before it could slip over the edge.

The third volunteer, a big one with shaggy hair poking out from beneath his safety helmet, kept his head down and continued working on a body that lay in a crevice formed between two rocks.

A spider's web of safety ropes held the Search and Rescue team and their patient in position on the precarious slope. Cody stood on a narrow shelf with one leg straight and the other bent at ninety degrees, leaning tight into the cliff face for balance. He'd had more stable shooting positions in his life, but his sightline was fair and he wouldn't miss any of the targets above him on the ledge. Townes stood on his shoulder, the only other man able to take proper aim.

Due to the awkwardness of the terrain, the rest of his men were bunched up behind, unable to make it past.

Their position was unsustainable.

Fucking Goddamned mess.

This wouldn't happen in a town. Bloody mountains. Bloody country.

Cody added a fraction more pressure to the trigger and engaged the first lock. The laser sight clicked on and punched a red dot between Shaggy's shoulder blades. Still the man didn't turn.

"Nobody move!" Cody shouted.

He pressed closer to the cliff, allowing Townes and the others to slide past while he kept the civilians covered. Before long, his men were crawling over the scene like ants on a pile of dung. As each one found a stable platform, he took aim again. Soon, red dots locked on the torsos of each of the three volunteers. Good operating procedure told each to take their lead from him—as they damn well should.

"You with the long hair. Stop what you're doing and put your hands up!"

The big Scotsman, Shaggy, stood slowly and stretched

out his arms, but for balance, not as a sign of surrender. His movement allowed Cody a sight of the patient. A grown man with blood-matted, blond hair and a beard. Not the boy!

Shit.

Clean-shaven, and at least five years younger than Drew McTay, Shaggy finally spoke. "Lower your bloody weapons. You're in Scotland now. This isn't the London Underground." He glowered up at Cody.

Ahead of Cody and off to one side, Townes sucked air between his teeth.

"Where's Ryan Kaine?" Cody shouted.

Shaggy's eyes narrowed into slits beneath his climbing helmet. "Who?"

"Don't try telling me you've never heard of Ryan Kaine."

"Aye, we've heard of him, but as you can see"—he waved his hands round the cramped scene—"he's not here and none of us is a criminal. Put those bloody popguns away and leave us tae carry on wi' our work."

Reluctantly, Cody removed his finger from the trigger and rested it along the guard. His red light disappeared, as did the other five. Townes lowered his C8 and snapped the selector to safety. The rest of the men followed his lead.

Cody lowered his weapon, but kept it live in case Kaine made an appearance. He'd put nothing past the slippery bastard.

Shaggy lowered his arms and allowed Cody a begrudging, "Thanks," before adding, "Can we get on wi' our work now?"

"What's your name and who's he?"

Cody pointed to the injured man who was wrapped in a

sleeping bag. The man not holding the stretcher took over from Shaggy and resumed bandaging the patient.

"I'm McGill," Shaggy said, "Michael McGill, and this poor fellow's name is Bartholomew."

The name activated a memory.

"The teacher?"

Cody shot a glance at Townes who shrugged. He didn't have a clue what was going on either.

"Aye," McGill said, "that's right and he's no' in a good way. So if you don't mind, he needs medical attention, and we're going to take him to it."

Why the fuck were all these Scots so fucking arrogant and obstructive?

"Where's Ryan Kaine?"

McGill shrugged. "No idea. As ye can see, he's no' hereabouts. How'd you find us?"

Cody ignored the question and studied the injured man cocooned in the sleeping bag. "Is he conscious?"

"Barely," McGill answered. "He's lost a lot of blood. How's he looking, Sandy?"

The man applying the bandages tilted his head. "Awake, but barely lucid. Needs a hospital right soon."

Cody grabbed a handful of McGill's jacket sleeve and pulled. He might as well have tried tugging at the side of the mountain. The man's arm didn't so much as twitch.

"What happened here? Did Ryan Kaine do that to him?"

McGill shook his head, an impatient scowl creased his face. He ripped his arm free of Cody's grip and took him by surprise. Cody toppled sideways, but McGill shot out a hand, grabbed Cody's arm, and stopped him falling.

"Take care up here, man," McGill said. "This isn't the place tae bugger about."

"Don't tell me what to do! Answer my question. Did Ryan Kaine do that to him?"

"That's ridiculous. Bartholomew would be dead by now if Kaine hadn't given him first aid and called in his location."

"So, you've spoken to the fugitive?"

"No, not directly. He called Kinross Farm and they relayed his message tae Drew McTay. Directed us right tae Bartholomew, but as you can see, neither Drew nor Ryan Kaine is here at the moment."

"Where are they?"

"Beats me," McGill answered, eyeing his teammates as though daring them to volunteer an answer.

The hairy fucker was lying through his teeth. Cody knew it and, judging from his expression, Townes knew it, too. But what the hell could he do about it?

Threats sometimes worked on the guilty.

"You know helping a suspected terrorist evade capture is a criminal offence?"

"Och, now," McGill said, "I'm quite sure it is."

McGill sidestepped closer to the cage. He took the teacher's legs, Sandy took the shoulders.

"Ready there, Sandy? Ready, Fergal?"

Fergal manoeuvred the cage into place alongside Bartholomew.

McGill continued his drill. "Okay, take the strain. One, two, three, raise."

They lifted a clearly dazed Bartholomew, while Fergal slid the cage under the body. Once lowered, they strapped the teacher into the stretcher, ready for the dangerous, and no doubt excruciatingly painful, descent.

Bartholomew groaned loudly.

Cody rushed forwards, avoided looking over the edge of

the cliff at the eager boulders below, and kneeled close to the man's head. He grabbed tight to the edge of the stretcher, daring the mountain men to move it away before he was done asking his questions.

"Mr Bartholomew, can you hear me?"

The teacher groaned before opening his eyes.

"Y ... Yes."

"What happened?"

He frowned and his eyes rolled up in his head before rolling back and fixing on Cody's.

"Kaine ... Ryan Kaine ... attacked me. Left me for dead ..."

Cody snapped his head up to glare at McGill. "I fucking told you! Kaine's a bloody killer." He returned his attention to the injured man. "Where's he gone? Where's Ryan Kaine now?"

Bartholomew licked his lips. "It hurts so much. I'm ... dying. Ryan Kaine's to blame. You ... have to stop him."

"Where is he?"

"Zelda, he's gone to ... Zelda."

Again, Cody looked at the Scotsman. "What's he saying? Who's Zelda?"

McGill shook his head. "No idea, man."

Bartholomew spoke again, this time with more force and clarity. "I-I think ... I think he might be looking for Marty ... Martin Princeton." He tried to lift his head, but the safety harness inhibited the movement. "He's mad. Mad, I tell you. I ... I think he wants to ... to kill Marty. Hurry. You ... have to find him first. S-Save the boy."

Bartholomew's eyes closed again and his head fell to the side. Cody fixed McGill with his fiercest glare.

"See what you've done? I told you Kaine's a killer."

McGill ignored him and nodded to Sandy. "Ready? Let's go."

Cody stood, barring McGill's way.

"What's wrong with you, McGill? You're letting Kaine get away. The boy's in danger. Where's Zelda?"

McGill took a moment to think before answering.

"Zelda's Smile is a climb on the north face of the mountain. Now answer me this, Mr Armed Response Officer. If Ryan Kaine's such a killer, how come Mr Bartholomew's still alive? How come Kaine applied a tourniquet and called in his location, eh? Saved his bloody life. Can you answer me that?"

Cody shook his head. "Of course not. How can anyone tell what's going on in the mind of a bloody madman?"

"And there's another thing. If Kaine wanted Martin dead, why did he no' leave well alone? He found the boy and called in his location, too. Why would he do that?"

"You bloody fool. Drew McTay's gone to help, hasn't he? Maybe that's what Kaine wants. Maybe the lunatic's trying to lure more people into his trap. As hostages! Have you considered that, McGill? Well, have you!"

For the first time, Cody detected doubt in the young Scotsman's manner.

"That doesnae make sense," McGill said, apparently shaking off the uncertainty. "If he wanted tae kill people, why not do it last night at the centre? There were plenty of easy targets for him tae murder in their beds." He paused to take a breath and resettle his load. "And he let Iona McTay go unharmed. The man you're talking about would have killed her and buggered off out of the area. And now, back out of our way. You've wasted enough of my time already."

McGill nodded at Sandy and took half a step forwards.

As he saw things, Cody had three choices. He could

shoot the man, allow the big goon to push him over the cliff's edge, or back down.

He leaned out of the way.

"At least tell us how to find this Zelda's Climb."

"It's Zelda's Smile, and you'll have tae find it yourself. I'm no' bloody sending a bunch of armed hotheads up the mountain. My friends are up there and I wouldn't trust you people any further than I could throw you." He made a great play of looking over the edge of the precipice before adding, "Although, one hundred and fifty metres isn't a bad toss, I'd say."

"Did you just threaten a police officer?"

"Who, me? No. Sandy, Fergal, did you guys hear me threaten a police officer?"

The men shook their heads and the team started walking. Sandy and McGill carried their patient, while Fergal held onto a rope that was fastened to the head of the cage, acting as a moving tether.

Inside, Cody boiled. He hadn't felt so helpless and frustrated since the incident in London. Had he been alone, he'd have screamed his lungs out. He tried the deep breathing exercises taught to him by the counsellor he was forced to visit after the London debacle. As usual, they were fucking useless.

Townes appeared at his shoulder. Cool as ever, nothing seemed to affect his mood.

"Why the hell are you so damn calm?" Cody demanded, forcing himself not to shout.

"Well, sir. I just thought you might want to go find Andrew McTay."

"And how are we going to do that?"

Townes grinned and waved the tablet under Cody's nose. "I put this away while we were climbing the scree and have only just taken it out again. McTay's still carrying the tracker. 'X' marks the spot!"

Cody suppressed a howl of delight. He clapped Townes on the upper arm.

"You absolute beauty. Let's go find ourselves a killer."

Townes screwed up his face in that way he had of suggesting doubt. "It'll not be that easy, sir."

"Why not?"

"He went that-a-way."

Townes pointed up one of the steepest climbs Cody had ever faced outside the rock wall in the gym. A bloody long one, too. He didn't like the look of it one little bit.

"So, Bunny's our best climber. Put him on point to lead the way. We'll be good. Ryan Kaine's not slipping through my fingers. No bloody way!"

"There is an alternative, sir."

"Which is?"

Townes tilted his head to one side and added one of his annoying shrugs. "We could always wait here and let Kaine come to us."

Cody worked through the options. "What if there's another route off this part of the mountain? An easier route."

Townes winced. "Hadn't thought of that."

"That's why I'm the inspector and you'll always be the sergeant. Okay, tell Bunny to take point."

"Yes, sir. Will do."

"And lose that frown, Sergeant. I'm only kidding. You're the best second-in-command I've ever worked with, and I've already put your name forwards for the next available command slot that opens up."

Townes' grateful smile was almost pitiful. "Thanks, sir. I appreciate that."

Cody nodded. It never paid to underestimate what a barefaced lie could achieve at the right moment.

Wally Townes a team leader?

Yeah, right.

Never in a million years. The lanky, Scottish arsehole was too damned gutless.

Chapter Thirty-Two

Thursday 17th September – Gregor Abercrombie

Kinross Farm MRC, The Cairngorms, Aberdeenshire, Scotland

Gregor ended the call with McGill, trying to quell the fury bubbling up from his guts. How dare Cody and his team point their weapons at his people?

He was angry enough to cuss, but would never resort to such behaviour. The pastor would never condone swearing, and the pastor was right. Swearing was the last refuge of the ill-educated and the feeble-minded.

Until receiving McGill's call, Gregor had been feeling rather pleased with the way things had been going, but the call had changed everything.

He tried to see it from the police point of view. After all, they were chasing a man charged with heinous crimes. But no, hang on, that wasn't right.

Ryan Kaine hadn't been charged with anything—hadn't even been arrested. Officially, the police had only identified him as a so-called person of interest. They wanted Kaine to "help them with their enquiries" into the crash of Flight BE1555. It was the media who'd added the "wanted terrorist" label, no doubt to spice up their copy.

Gregor was starting to smell conspiracy and, with a bunch of uniformed police running around his mountain, waving their guns in the air, he sensed disaster around the corner. Before their arrival at *Craed's Fist*, he'd assumed that Cody's men didn't know their way around the place.

At one point, Gregor had allowed himself to wallow in the imagined, but delicious irony, of receiving a call for help from the lost posse. But they clearly had their own satnav system so that particular situation would probably not arise.

Gregor nodded to Gillian. "Call Kaine for me, lass. He needs to know what's going on."

She hit a button and Gregor's headphones clicked to a different channel.

"ST9, this is Gregor Abercrombie. Are you receiving me? Over," he called, keeping his voice below the level of the room's background hum.

Kaine answered instantly.

"*I hear you, strength five, Base. Do you have an ETA for the rescue team? Over.*"

"ST3 should be with you within the next half hour or so. How's the lad? Over."

"*In pain, but conscious and looking forward to seeing his parents. Over.*"

"That's excellent news, ST9. I'll pass that message

along, but if he's out of danger, you need to get away from there. Over."

"*Why? Over.*"

"The armed police unit are closing in on your position. I think they're following ST3, and I don't think they're expecting you to surrender, if you take my meaning. Over."

"*I do, but I'm not leaving the lad. He's been alone for three days, and he needs my company. I'll wait for ST3 and offer whatever help I can. Over.*"

The main doors flew open and the oily-smooth Superintendent Ingram-Howe strode into the room, with a face like thunder on the mountain. Two of his lackeys—a sergeant and a particularly beefy uniformed constable—stood on either flank, but slightly behind the insufferable man.

Uh-oh, what's this now?

"ST9, standby for an update. Base, out."

Gregor gave Craig the pre-determined signal to blank out all the screens and turned to face the senior police officer.

"Mr Abercrombie, a word, if you please!" Ingram-Howe barked, his anger barely under control.

Take one step closer, and you'll see anger, you damnable pipsqueak.

Gregor held up an index finger. "One moment while I sort out this mess."

Slowing his breathing in a deliberate attempt to cool the fire raging through his belly, Gregor turned his back on the sputtering policeman and strolled slowly to the comms enclave. He took a spare chair and sat between Craig and Gillian, delighted to take the weight off his aching feet at last.

He leaned forwards and kept his voice low. "Thanks for killing the screens, Craig. Now, power them back up, but do it slowly, and make sure to hide Kaine's locator signal. I don't want that arrogant, jumped-up clown giving the cowboy any directions. Assuming he can read a satellite map."

Gillian snorted, and Craig played his fingers over the keyboard. One by one, the screens started flickering. Somehow, Craig made it look like they were having trouble with a weak signal. The young man mightn't be able to find his way around his own back garden, but give him a communications desk and a satellite hook-up, and he'd be an integral part of any rescue operation. The same was true of his diminutive partner-in-comms, Gillian.

"ST9, this is Base," Gregor said, hiding his mouth behind his hand and speaking quietly. "Are you still reading me? Over."

"*Affirmative. Over.*"

"Sorry for the break in transmission, annoying interference on this end. You maybe don't understand what I was telling you earlier. I'm worried the ARU are trigger happy. They'll not give you a chance to surrender. More to the point, I don't want my people anywhere near you if the shooting starts. Do you understand now? Over."

The line fell silent for a few seconds before Kaine replied. "*Yes, I understand. I'll leave the moment ST3 arrives. Over.*"

"Thank you. And if it means anything, I don't believe what the media says about you being a terrorist. None of my people think so either. We just wanted you to know. Over."

"*I appreciate that, Gregor. ST9, out.*"

"Good luck, Kaine. You'll need it," Gregor said under his breath.

He gave Craig the nod. The screens stopped flickering,

and the images once again became pinprick clear—minus the ST9 indicator.

Gregor removed his headset and put on his game face before swivelling his chair to smile at the near-apoplectic police officer. "Well now, Superintendent Ingram-Howe, what can I do for you this fine afternoon?"

"Do you have any idea of the penalties for interfering with a police investigation?" the man bellowed.

Gregor crossed his arms and leaned against the back of the chair. "No, I'm afraid not. I'm a Scottish sheep farmer during the day, not a solicitor. What about you, Craig? Gillian?" The two IT specialists shook their heads. "No, I thought not."

Gregor stood and addressed the room. "Anyone else know the answer to that legal question?"

When no one offered a response, Gregor smiled.

"What's this about?" he asked to stir the pot a little more.

Ingram-Howe eased his weight forwards and the heels of his highly polished shoes lifted from the floor. The leather squeaked loud in the near-silence.

"Are you responsible for those unfounded media accusations?"

"What accusations might they be?" Gregor asked, frowning, genuinely confused by the question.

"You know full well what I mean. Sky News is claiming that Police Scotland is running a shoot-to-kill policy. One online source is accusing me of putting a bounty on Ryan Kaine's head, damn it. Me! They referred to me by name. Did you leak that story?"

"Me? Don't be ridiculous, man. I've been in here all day."

Craig stared at the big screen, his expression wide-eyed

and innocent, and no melting butter anywhere in sight. Gillian stared straight ahead, stone-faced.

"Give me one good reason why I shouldn't close this operation down and put my men in charge."

Gregor laughed. "You could try, but what would be the point? We've already found the boy, and we're bringing another injured man down right now. I was just about to call off the search operation. Or would you be wanting to take over because the leaked story is true?"

"You found Martin Princeton?"

A small fraction of the man's bluster ebbed away.

"Yes. We have. Where've you been for the past half hour?"

"I've been trying to discover who released those lies about the Armed Response Unit. And given your people's actions to hamper our efforts in the search for Ryan Kaine, I've considered arresting you for interfering with a legitimate police operation."

As he delivered the threat, Ingram-Howe's eyes lit up, and his mouth bent into a cruel smile.

Gregor paused and searched the faces of his people as though worried by the thought of being dragged from the room in handcuffs.

He lowered his head in an apparent show of discomfort. "Do you mind if we continue this conversation in private?"

Ingram-Howe nodded to his men, his supercilious sneer telling them he had everything under control and they could stay where they were. He followed Gregor out of the office, through the kitchen, and into the corridor leading to the rear of the building. Shame-faced, Gregor opened the final door on the left and stood to one side, allowing Ingram-Howe to exit the corridor first and enter Gregor's private office.

As soon as he shut the door behind them, Gregor planted a hand between Ingram-Howe's shoulder blades and pushed him deeper into the room.

"What the—"

The policeman threw a hand out for balance and barked his fingers on the rough stonework. He spun and Gregor stepped close. Ingram-Howe flinched.

"What did you do that for?"

"Sorry, son, you must have tripped over a wonky flagstone. Hurt your hand, did you?"

The superintendent looked at the grazed fingers and raised the hand to his mouth to suck at the blood.

"You've just assaulted a police officer."

He made a move towards the door, but Gregor barred his way.

"The medical clinic is just along the way there. Why don't you come with me and we'll find a first aid kit?"

"Explain why I shouldn't have you arrested for assault."

"You arrogant arse." Gregor took another step forwards, backing Ingram-Howe against the wall. "Do I have your attention now, little man?"

Ingram-Howe's mouth opened and closed but no words spilled out.

"Now, you listen to me very carefully, *Superintendent* Ingram-Howe. I've had about enough of you throwing your weight around. That cowboy of yours, Cody, is running around out there pointing his guns at my people. *My* people, and I won't have it. D'you hear me?"

Ingram-Howe shook his head. "Inspector Cody and his team are highly trained, professional firearms officers. None of your people is in any danger from them. Even though you've been helping Ryan Kaine escape—"

Gregor stabbed an index finger under Ingram-Howe's nose and the man snapped his mouth shut.

"Repeat that accusation in front of witnesses," Gregor said, making his voice as deep and threatening as ever in his life, "and I'll have your warrant card."

Ingram-Howe finally found his nerve and tried to push himself away from the wall, but Gregor planted a hand square on his chest and drove him back. Years of working on the farm and climbing the mountains had endowed him with more strength of muscle and will power than the bean-pole policeman. The man would have struggled to stay upright in a light breeze.

"Now, what you're going to do," Gregor continued, "is call off your armed thugs and you're going to do it right now."

"Why on earth would I do that?"

"Because they are a menace to themselves and anyone else out on the mountain. I'm not letting you murder Ryan Kaine just so you can earn a few Brownie points."

"How dare you suggest—"

"Get over yourself, man. It's just you and me here. Ryan Kaine's done nothing but help Martin Princeton, and I won't allow your men to shoot him down as though he were a rutting stag. Deer hunting in the Cairngorms is strictly controlled. D'you *ken*?"

Gregor pressed a little harder on Ingram-Howe's chest. The thin man's Adam's apple bobbled, and his beautifully knotted dress tie danced a jig.

"Now, are you going to call Inspector Cody, or am I going to call a press conference?"

Ingram-Howe shook his head. "I'm sorry. That simply isn't possible."

"Why not?"

"Inspector Cody's gone dark. Powered off his satphone. There's no way I can contact him until he calls me."

"You don't have a failsafe or another way to call him off?"

"Short of flying over his position in a helicopter … and making a loudhailer announcement, no. I-I'm afraid there isn't," the superintendent said, stumbling over his words.

"In that case, little man, you'd better hope 'Buffalo Bill' Cody doesn't shoot anybody today or you and he are going to be looking at the inside of a prison cell, and I'll be the one helping to turn the key."

Chapter Thirty-Three

Thursday 17th September – Afternoon

Ben Craed, The Cairngorms, Aberdeenshire, Scotland

Kaine nodded, satisfied. Martin's colour had improved dramatically—at least the colour on his face, the only patch of skin not hidden by the space blanket.

How well the right arm would recover after so many hours of reduced circulation, only time would tell—time and a good vascular surgeon. Crush injuries had a tendency to create their own problems, and the sooner Martin could reach hospital, the better. Iona might be able to offer some remedial help, but the limb needed specialist treatment as soon as possible.

Meanwhile, the best thing Kaine could do for the boy

was to keep him calm and occupied. He adopted his most avuncular manner, but since he had next to no experience with kids, he doubted it would earn him any acting awards. Outside of boot camp training, the last time he'd been near a teenager had been at school, and he'd hated the whole academic experience. Sitting behind a desk absorbing facts, or trying to, was the closest thing he could imagine to purgatory.

He sat on a flat rock beside Martin, but downwind. He didn't want the lad to catch any of his ripeness. God, how he needed a long soak in a hot bath. A quick shower wouldn't really cut it.

"Did you hear that call, Martin? The rescue team will be here soon. In the meantime, anything I can get you? Warm enough?"

The boy offered up a pained smile. "Yes … thanks." He spoke quietly, his voice barely carrying over the whistling breeze that ruffled his hair.

"Any pain?"

Stupid question, Kaine. Of course he's in pain.

"My leg's throbbing, I can't move my right hand, and I … think my head's going to explode. Apart from that, I'm cool, thanks."

Martin's smile stretched wider. Kaine allowed himself to be impressed.

"Mind telling me how you got yourself in that mess?"

A frown creased Martin's face and he turned his head away.

Despite the boy's obvious discomfort, Kaine continued. "I mean, what were you doing trying a climb like Zelda's Smile without any protection? No harness, no ropes, no anchors."

The space blanket rustled. Martin freed his left arm and wiped tears from behind his closed lids.

"I wasn't …"

"You weren't what?"

"I … wasn't climbing …"

Kaine knew he shouldn't pry, but Bartholomew's story had been a load of crap and he needed an explanation.

"Did you mean to do it? Did losing your brother become too much?"

Martin pulled his hand from his face and stared at Kaine. "What do you know about anything?"

Kaine hated pushing, but Martin needed to talk. Bottling things up wouldn't help his emotional recovery.

"Mr Bartholomew told everyone you'd been depressed. He said you'd … well, run away and were going to hurt yourself."

Martin's lower lip trembled. "That's a lie. I'd never do that. Matty… Matty would have killed me for leaving Mum and Dad alone."

"So why did Mr Bartholomew try to convince everyone you'd thrown yourself into Kidney Loch?"

A ripple of confusion played across the boy's face. "Kidney Loch? Why would I want to go anywhere near that place? The water's freezing. Bastard …"

Again, he turned away.

"Who's a bastard, Martin? Me?"

"No, not you," Martin said. "You saved me. I'll always be … grateful."

Kaine really wanted to believe that.

Martin closed his eyes and spoke, almost to himself. "The Bart … Mr Bartholomew. Everyone at school reckoned he was a star, y'know? Being part of his crew was an honour,

333

yeah?" He took a stuttering breath before continuing. "He's a brilliant teacher. Best in the school. All the boys like him. Girls, too, but he doesn't choose girls for the geography trips. Something about not being able to find the right chaperone. Oh God, I'm such a fucking idiot. I should have seen through it."

Kaine reached out a hand to touch the boy's good shoulder, but thought better of it.

"Go on, Martin."

"We all knew he'd been this world-class climber. It was one of the reasons his geology camps were always so popular. We were all desperate to go, but there weren't enough places. Last year, when he chose me, I was ... Jesus, it was ace, you know? I was the youngest ever. The Bart normally only picks fifth and sixth formers, but I'd done all the coursework, earned extra credit. He chose me, right? Me. Couldn't believe it. My crew was dead jealous, but ..."

More hesitation. Kaine checked his watch. Drew was due soon and the team's arrival would end the boy's story.

"But?"

Martin blinked. His eyes reflected the blue of the sky. "Last year, I had to cancel the trip. Dad was taken into hospital. His chest, y'know? Lung cancer. He's stronger now, fighting it, but I couldn't go on a school trip with him in hospital, could I?"

More sniffles.

"The Bart chose me again this year. Gave me first refusal, y'know? I couldn't turn him down a second time—would never have been given another chance. Mum didn't want me to go, of course, not with Matty... well, y'know. But Dad said it was okay. Said he knew what it meant to me. Fuck, I'm such a moron."

"What happened, Martin? Did Bartholomew do something?"

The boy dipped his chin and squeezed his eyes tight shut.

"This trip, he sort of … latched on. Was extra nice. Y'know, supportive. Protective. At first, it was great. But I started getting some really bad vibes from Atko … Really bad vibes."

"Who? Gavin Atkinson, the teacher's assistant?"

Martin's upper lip curled into an Elvis sneer. "Teacher's lacky, more like. Whenever The Bart went off on a field trip with one of the others, Atko would go ballistic. I mean full weapons drawn, war-footing mode. Being really nasty to everyone. Snide comments, you know? Verbal bullying. I didn't have a clue why until the last morning."

More tears squeezed out from behind the closed lids.

Kaine struggled to take in the information. The boy was rambling but he couldn't lead the conversation too much in case Martin clammed up. His faltering delivery had more to do with the information's emotional effect than his physical condition. All Kaine could do was let him speak and hope he reached the point before Drew's team arrived.

Whatever the full story, he'd been right about Bartholomew. The teacher was involved right up to his thick neck.

"What happened that morning, Martin?"

"Do you know anything about ornithology?"

Okay, so he wanted to play twenty questions. Kaine sighed and pointed to his battered face.

"Don't let this ugly mug fool you, son. I might look like a nightclub bouncer with the brains of a claw hammer, but I've been to school. Been known to open a book or two in my day. Ones with words as well as coloured pictures. Ornithology's bird watching, right?"

The boy blushed. "Sorry. Didn't mean to offend."

"I'm kidding, Martin. Last time I read a book, it was a technical ... a crime thriller."

Christ, he needed some rest. He'd nearly blurted out that the last thing he'd read was the operating manual for the rocket launcher he'd used to shoot down Flight BE1555. That would have gone down well.

"Actually, ornithology is the scientific study of birds," Martin said, passing straight over Kaine's near blunder. "Nothing at all like bird watching, or twitching. Dad and I've been mad keen on birds since forever. Before he got ill, we'd spend weekends on the moors. I loved it, but Matty said it was like watching a TV soap. He was right into sports, y'know? All kinds. Rugby, cricket, hockey, golf, squash. You name it. He was good, too. Would have represented his university, for certain. Anyway, I don't suppose you've noticed the golden eagles, have you?"

Kaine's mind shot back to the imperious, yellow-eyed creature that allowed him to climb past her nest unmolested.

"Yes, I've seen them."

"Golden eagles, *aquila chrysaetos*. Gorgeous, aren't they? The way they catch the air. Majestic. Make flying look so easy. Well, the other night after supper, The Bart pulled me to one side and mentioned he'd seen a pair of eagles nesting near his climb."

Without looking at the rock face, Martin waved in the general direction of where he'd been trapped.

"You know that climb's called Zelda's Smile? The Bart named it after his mother. He was the first to climb it solo. He mapped out the route."

Kaine nodded. "Impressive."

"That's what we all thought. Anyway, I was dead excited about the nest."

"What about the other lads?"

"They wouldn't have given a toss. It was just me and The Bart. We had to get up before dawn, and the guys would only have been interested in having a lie-in. Lazy buggers."

His voice caught. He tried to swallow, but it turned into a grimace.

"More water?" Kaine offered.

"Yes, please. Don't suppose you've got any more food?"

"Sorry, no ... hang on. I should have a few pear drops left. Fancy one?"

"Yes, please. Boiled sweets? Is that how come you're missing a tooth?"

"No, mate. I lost it during the beating. And thanks for reminding me. Bloody tooth's been driving me nuts. I'd have seen a dentist yesterday, but you put the kybosh on that idea."

"Sorry."

"So you should be," Kaine said, adding a smile and a wink.

He helped Martin take a drink and handed him a sweet. He popped one into his mouth and revelled in the sugar hit for a moment before asking, "Okay?"

"Delish. Haven't had one of these since I was a kid. Can you help sit me up?"

"Best not, the rescue team will want you horizontal for the stretcher. Besides, any movement will hurt like stink. So, what happened next?"

He had the feeling Martin wanted to talk about anything other than the next part of his story, but Kaine needed answers and maybe Martin needed to put the truth out there.

"So, The Bart woke me early yesterday morning—"

"Sorry, Martin. That was Tuesday morning. It's now Thursday afternoon."

"Really?" He frowned in concentration. "Yeah, yeah, that's right. Two days ago. So long. Anyway, The Bart woke me before dawn and we left Atko in charge of the camp."

"Don't tell me he led you up Scooter's Chimney? That's a hell of a route for a novice."

"Chimney?"

Kaine described the route he'd taken after leaving *Craed's Fist*, but left Bartholomew out of the story entirely.

Martin shook his head a little too quickly and winced against the movement.

"No, we went a different way. The Bart called it *Craed's Bairn*. It's safer, but takes a lot longer. That's why we had to leave so early."

"Yes, I know the path."

He planned to use the *Bairn* as his escape route the moment Drew McTay arrived. Easy going with a fast getaway and plenty of cover from aerial recon if the chopper made a reappearance.

"Okay," Kaine said. "That makes sense. What happened when you reached the start of the climb."

Kaine looked up, but from their position, Martin's ridge hid the ledge where he'd belayed for the first abseil. He sensed Martin needed a little more time to gather his thoughts as they'd reached the sensitive point in the story, but the lad continued almost without pause.

"We … got there a little before six o'clock. It was a gorgeous morning. Crystal clear. We could see for miles. No sign of the eagles, but that was okay. Then …" He swallowed and stopped talking.

"Go on, Martin."

"The Bart started talking about Matty. Saying how sorry

he was and how I'd make him proud one day. That's when I broke down. Started crying. The Bart, he … he hugged me. It was okay at first, but then he put his hand on my thigh. Tried to … Christ, he tried to feel me up, y'know? I yelled at him. Pushed him away. Called him a fucking paedo. Then … then …"

"Did he push you over the ledge?"

"No, no. It wasn't like that. He apologised. Said he just wanted to comfort me. Told me I'd mistaken his intentions. Denied everything. It was pathetic. I told him to fuck off and leave me alone, and he did. He said he'd go back along the trail a bit and wait for me to calm down. Told me to take care and stay away from the edge."

"Really? He left you alone up there?"

"Yeah. Alone."

"What happened? Did you fall?"

Martin's tears flowed again and his nose started running. He wiped it clean with his sleeve and turned his eyes on Kaine, the pain within them clear.

"Atko turned up from out of nowhere and pushed me, and … I fell." He crunched on the pear drop. "Falling was weird, y'know. It was like flying. Like the eagle. Then I stopped falling and …" Martin's face creased at the memory of hitting the rocks.

Kaine had been prepared for Bartholomew's culpability in Martin's disappearance, but the teaching assistant's role came out of the blue. Damn it, things just kept getting worse.

"Atkinson?" Kaine said. "Are you certain it was him?"

"It's a bit fuzzy, but he screamed at me before pushing me over. Shouted something like, 'He's mine, not yours', but I …"

"What happened to Bartholomew?"

"I … don't know how long after I fell, but he came back. I heard them arguing. The Bart wanted to climb down to me, but Atko said I was dead and they didn't have any climbing gear. Then The Bart was screaming, crying, calling Atko a murderer. I … I don't remember much after that. It started raining, and I got so cold. Then, hours, days later, I saw this straggly, wet bloke with a battered face and a missing tooth crawling over the rocks. I … thought *Gollum* had come for me."

"So, let me get this straight," Kaine said, trying to take control over his anger at the way the teachers had treated Martin, "if both Bartholomew and Atkinson were here with you, who was supervising the others back at the campsite?"

Martin snorted. "Don't be daft, those morons would sleep 'til midday unless someone woke them. Useless they were. Didn't take anything seriously. Stayed up until late every night partying with The Bart and Atko."

"Partying? You mean alcohol?"

Martin wrinkled his nose. "Atko would pass around a bottle of whisky after supper to 'keep the chill off', he said."

"He got the boys drunk?"

"Yeah. Not me though. Couldn't stand the taste of the stuff. I prefer cider. Shit." He threw his hand up to cover his mouth. "You weren't supposed to know that."

Kaine let the confession slide but the anger still burned. "When Atkinson was passing the whisky around, what was Bartholomew doing?"

Before Martin could answer, a stone clattered in the distance beneath them.

A deep voice called out, "Kaine? Ryan Kaine? It's Drew McTay. We're coming up!"

Chapter Thirty-Four

Thursday 17th September – William Cody

Ben Craed, The Cairngorms, Aberdeenshire, Scotland

Cody struggled to suck enough oxygen from the air. Thirty minutes after leaving the obstructive clown, McGill, his vision had started to blur.

Up ahead, Bunny set an impossible pace, but Cody wasn't about to show weakness by slowing the team. He ignored the growing stitch in his side and pushed on, desperate not to let the gap between him and the others grow. He concentrated on watching Stedman's heels and drove himself forwards.

Within minutes of leaving *Craed's Fist*, the slope had increased so much, Cody needed to use his hands to help pull himself upwards. The footing changed from loose gravel to uneven rock.

Despite the hard exercise, Cody shivered as the moss-covered cliff face on their right threw out wave after wave of cold, damp air. He tried to ignore the perpendicular drop to his left, a drop that one misstep would have had him plummeting hundreds of metres to the rock-strewn valley floor below. He'd never suffered from vertigo before, but there was clearly a first time for everything, fuck it.

Why anyone would choose to scramble around in the Scottish mountains was beyond him. Fucking morons. The lot of them.

Stay home, put your Goddamned feet up.

Finally, with Cody seconds away from ordering a rest stop despite himself, Townes raised his fist to call a halt. Cody struggled forwards to where the narrow trail ended at the start of a false flat. The men hugged the side of the cliff as Cody slipped past each in turn, keeping his back to the drop. He took note of how fresh and relaxed the young sods all seemed.

Bastards.

As he scrambled past Bunny, Townes signalled for him to keep low and stay tucked against the vertical rock—as though he'd do anything else.

He dropped to all fours and crawled alongside his second-in-command. The narrow ledge didn't allow much room, but at least the waves of heat radiating from Townes showed he'd also worked hard during the climb.

"McTay's stopped, sir," Townes whispered, his eyes flicking between the tablet and the route ahead. "He's about two hundred metres up ahead. Around that next turn. And you'll never guess who's up there with him."

"Fucking hell, Sergeant," Cody said, still panting, but

just about managing to force out the words without sounding totally drained. "This isn't the time for a fucking quiz."

Townes' sweaty face remained expressionless. "Sorry, sir. I heard McTay call out to Ryan Kaine. The bugger's just around the next corner, sir."

Cody punched the rock with the side of his fist. "Excellent. What does the satellite image show?"

The wind picked up and blew dust into their faces. Cody used it as an excuse to remove his safety glasses and rub his vision clear, thankful the short rest had already allowed his breathing to recover. Pretty soon he'd be able to talk normally. Perhaps he wasn't that unfit after all.

Townes handed him the tablet. Cody worked the screen until the image showed as much detail as it was going to. He studied the topography. If he'd read the map correctly, McTay and Kaine were in a flattened valley boxed in to the west, south, and southeast by perpendicular cliffs. The remaining open segment ran downhill and directly towards Cody's position. The layout made the perfect kill zone.

Kaine couldn't have chosen a worse place to make his final stand.

Cody breathed deep, trying to calm his mounting excitement. So bloody close.

Not long now, Kaine.

He moved his finger to the right of the fixed marker and rested it on a tight band of contour lines running parallel to the flat shelf at the base of Zelda's Smile.

"See that?"

"Aye. Pretty steep. It'd take some time to climb. What are you thinking, sir?"

"Anyone at that point would be above Kaine's position.

It'd make a good sniper's nest. Do you reckon Bunny could climb that and take Patel with him?"

"Might be doable, but what's the point? According to the doctor, Kaine's unarmed. What's he likely to do against the six of us? The way he's been running since shooting down that plane shows he's hardly a candidate for suicide-by-cop."

"Who knows the fucker's motivation," Cody snapped. "I'm not taking the risk. Bunny's our best climber, right?"

"Definitely. Should have named him after a mountain goat, not a rabbit."

Cody signalled for Darren "Bunny" Prentice and Arjun Patel to join them. The two men arrived quickly, and they formed a tight huddle.

Cody addressed Bunny.

"Think you can get up there and take Patel with you?" He tapped the area on the tablet. "It'll command a good view of the takedown area."

"Pat's scared o' heights, sir," Bunny said, flashing a grin and showed the prominent front teeth that had given rise to his nickname. "But I reckon I could pull him up by his hair."

Patel sneered at the playful insult. "Bollocks. I'll race you to the top."

"Don't be an idiot," Bunny said. He shoulder-nudged his mate and spoke to Cody, his face serious. "During our climb I've been studying this here cliff, sir. There's a spot about fifty metres down the hill with good hand and footholds. It'll take us to the top of this bluff"—he pointed to the screen—"and give us an elevation on the target. I reckon even Pat could manage the climb, sir. Given help."

Cody nodded. "Excellent. Get into position as fast as you can. Go check your climbing gear. Pat"—he waited for the sharpshooter to lock eyes with him—"a word in your ear."

"Yes, sir?"

Cody fixed Patel with a cold stare. "If Kaine so much as twitches when we approach, take the shot. You have the green light. Don't wait for my orders, okay?"

Townes caught his breath, but said nothing.

Patel flashed a glance at his sergeant before returning focus on Cody. "Come again, sir?"

"You heard what I said. There were eighty-three innocent people on that plane. Kaine's a killer. I'm not risking any more innocent lives. Do you understand your orders?"

Patel dipped his head. "Yes, sir," he answered after a momentary hesitation.

"Good man." Cody clapped his shoulder. "Okay, off you go, and let me know the moment you're in position."

"Aye, sir. Will do."

As the two backed away, Townes coughed quietly.

"You have a problem, Sergeant?"

"Giving the kill order in advance of engagement is not a standard part of our operating procedures, sir."

"If you're worried you'll get into trouble, don't be. This operation has been sanctioned at the highest level. Understand? The highest level. We're protected."

Townes wiped his mouth with the back of his hand. "Is that what you and the Super were talking about before we went dark?"

Cody nodded. "Like I said, we're protected. No blowback, guaranteed."

"Right, sir. Understood. I'll make sure Bunny and Pat are good to go."

Townes flashed a quick salute and scrambled away down the hill. As he passed the men, he said something to each in turn. No doubt chivvying them along, offering words of encouragement. Despite his many shortcomings, Townes did have good rapport with his men. Cody gave him that much credit. Wouldn't do him any good in the long run. No one got ahead by making friends with the lower ranks.

Cody watched his sergeant check Bunny's climbing gear, ropes, harness, and other stuff, and couldn't suppress a grin. The end of his Scottish exile was fast approaching. Life would soon be back to normal again.

Bunny and Patel started back down the slope and Townes made the return trip.

"Everything okay, Sergeant?"

"Aye, sir."

"Right, let's take a look at what Kaine's up to."

Cody dropped onto his belly and crawled further up the trail. He advanced another fifteen metres until the trail flattened and opened up enough for Townes and the rest of the men to spread out along the ridge.

Ahead, the mountain shot up in two vertical cliffs, a wide cleft separating each. In the distance, the two crags merged and climbed to form the rounded summit of *Ben Craed*. Behind Cody, another sharp rise—the one Bunny and Pat were climbing—guarded their rear and their right flank. Empty space guarded the left.

Cody used hand signals to tell his men to stay put while he and Townes crawled further up the hill. Another five metres took them to the edge of the valley plateau. He peered through his field glasses.

Gotcha!

Ahead, at the foot of a cliff so sheer and glass-smooth it looked impossible to scale, were three men. Two stood off to one side, talking too low for Cody to hear. The third man kneeled next to what looked like a mound of crumpled gold.

"What's that?" Townes whispered.

Despite being close enough to hear him breathing and feel his heart beating, Townes' words—thankfully—barely carried across the gap between them. With the wind at their backs, Kaine would be able to hear them approach.

Not good. Not good at all.

"The gold?" Cody asked. "Looks like a space blanket to me."

Townes nodded. "Must be Martin Princeton. McGill wasn't lying. Kaine *did* find the boy after all."

Cody, his eyes fixed on the prize, said nothing.

"Why's he still here?" Townes asked, turning to look right in Cody's eyes, a direct challenge. "Kaine could have been miles away by now, but he stayed to search for the boy. Why would he do that?"

"Don't know. Don't care. We're taking him down. What's the distance to the target, do you reckon?"

"Fifty-five, maybe sixty metres."

"Yeah, that's what I thought."

Cody packed away his field glasses, unslung his rifle, adjusted the sights, and raised it to the firing position. The butt fitted snug against his shoulder like a dear, old friend. With his thumb, he clicked the selector from safety to single shot.

Uphill and with a tailwind, the shot wasn't particularly easy, but he'd make it nine times out of ten on the range. Good odds. Why wait for Bunny and Patel? Why not take the glory for himself?

"What are you doing?" Townes asked, his voice louder. Possibly loud enough to carry up the hill.

"Sergeant Townes, keep your fucking noise down."

"Kaine's unarmed and not offering a threat."

"I'm not telling you again, Sergeant. Shut the fuck up."

Cody adjusted the focus on the C8's scope. The fugitive stood out sharp and clear under the crosshairs. Perfect.

Cody blinked once, settled his breathing to slow his heart rate, and hooked his index finger around the trigger. He added a little more pressure until it activated the targeting laser. The red dot appeared in the middle of Ryan Kaine's chest.

Cody smiled and waited for his heart rate to slow further.

"Bye-bye, Kaine."

As he added more pressure to the trigger, Drew McTay stepped in front of the target. The red dot shifted and settled in the middle of the big Jock's lower back.

Fuck it.

Cody's earpiece crackled.

"Prentice to Team Leader. Are you receiving me? Over."

Reluctantly, Cody released the trigger and lowered his rifle.

"Team Leader here, Bunny. Receiving you loud and clear. Where are you? Over."

"We're in position and have the target covered. Over."

"Nice work, Bunny. Pat, can you hear me? Over."

"Yes, sir. Over."

"Remember your orders. We're about to move in. Team Leader, out."

Cody snapped the selector back to safety. Drew McTay moved away, leaving Ryan Kaine exposed and vulnerable once more.

A reprieve, Kaine. Only a bloody reprieve.

Chapter Thirty-Five

Thursday 17th September – Afternoon

Ben Craed, The Cairngorms, Aberdeenshire, Scotland

Kaine squeezed Martin's hand. "Here they are, lad. Soon get you out of here."

He stood, but the boy held on tight. "Thanks again, for … finding me."

"You know I had to, but you're very welcome."

Kaine stood and turned to the sound of approaching feet. The big man with the red hair and bushy beard climbed the hill, open mouthed, his teeth bared and shining bright against the dark mouth and the red facial hair. A safety helmet and huge backpack—half as big again as

Kaine's Bergen—threw Drew McTay's face into deep shadow.

A short, wiry man followed. He had a collapsible stretcher strapped to his back, its metal spars sticking up behind his head like antlers. They'd both been climbing hard, their efforts showing in laboured breathing and sweat-bedraggled hair.

Drew pounded up the hill, stopped two metres in front of Kaine, and eyed him with deep suspicion before shaking off his backpack and dropping it to the ground.

"Good to see ye, Mr Kai—er, Sidings," he said between breaths, adding an embarrassed smile.

Kaine relaxed a little. He'd half-expected the big man to be out for blood, considering the way he'd treated his sister.

"And it's good to see you too, Martin," Drew continued, turning to the boy. "You've led us a merry dance. How are ye feeling, lad?"

Martin managed a weak smile and a left-handed thumbs up. "Okay thanks to Mr Kaine."

"Afternoon, Drew," Kaine said. "Don't worry, I've introduced myself to Martin. He knows who I am."

Drew's eyebrows shot up to his hairline, but he took it as read and kept any questions he might have had to himself. Kaine appreciated not having to scratch at the scab once again.

"Only two of you?" Kaine asked, keen to change the subject. "I thought you guys operated in teams of four or five?"

Drew helped his mate to unclip the stretcher. "Aye, normally we do, but the rest of my team's down at *Craed's Fist* taking care of yer friend, Bartholomew."

"He's no friend of mine."

The big Scot smiled and shook his head. "No, and he

doesnae speak too highly of you, either. Well now Martin, are you hungry, thirsty?"

"Yes, starving."

"Never met a teenager who wasn't always starving," he said. "Bruce here's a paramedic. He'll give ye the once-over and, if he says it's okay, we've a high energy bar here with your name on it."

"I gave him a cereal bar and he kept it down," Kaine said, at the risk of upsetting their fragile *détente*, and added, "I checked him out. No signs of concussion."

"You'll forgive us for doing our jobs? Bruce knows what he's doing."

Kaine raised his hands. "Fair enough."

Drew stood aside while Bruce set to work and pointed Kaine to a spot out of earshot. They separated from the others.

"Have ye spoken to Gregor recently?" Drew asked, looking down at Kaine from his great height.

"A little while ago. You're bringing company, I take it?"

Drew nodded and looked at the trail they'd climbed before stepping in front of him.

"Bruce and I made good time, but Cody and his men cannae be far behind us. You'd best be away while ye have the chance."

"You're letting me go?"

Drew hiked his massive shoulders in what Kaine took to be either a shrug or a stretch. Whichever the case, it was an impressive sight.

"It's no' up to me to arrest anybody. I'm just here for the boy."

Kaine followed Drew's gaze and slowly shook his head. "Understood, I'll say goodbye to Martin, then I'll be on my way. It's a shame though. I'm sick of running. Truth is, I'm shattered. A night or two in a holding cell looks pretty good right now. Can't remember the last time I had a decent kip. Don't get me wrong, this is a beautiful part of the world, but sleeping rough in the heather is a young man's game."

Drew turned to face Kaine fully. The Scot cast a huge shadow, but it wasn't threatening.

"If you're still keen to hand yourself over to the police, do it back at the centre. No one would dare to take pot shots at you with all those media people around."

Drew made sense, and Kaine didn't take long to decide.

"Okay, I'll do that. Thanks. One question, though. Why are you helping me after what I did to Iona?"

"Good question. When you first laid yer English hands on her I wanted to tear ye apart, but she told me you chose her so you wouldnae have to hurt little, old me. Is that right, wee man?"

He expanded his barrel chest more as a challenge than to take in extra air.

Kaine looked into the giant's eyes. "And she believed me?"

Drew tilted his head. "Maybe one day we'll find out if you're full of crap."

Kaine stifled a yawn behind his hand. "I hope not, Drew," he said, adding a disarming smile. "I really wouldn't want to damage you."

The big redhead paused for a moment before letting out a huge, deep-throated, bellowing laugh.

"I like you, Ryan Kaine," he said after letting the outburst die. "You're a funny man."

"So I've been told. Let me fetch my Bergen and say goodbye to Martin."

"Aye, but make it quick. I don't know how much time you have left."

Drew followed Kaine back to his mate and Martin.

"Bruce, how is he?"

"Pupil reactions are normal. It's okay to give him a little food. His leg's stable so I'll leave it alone for now, but I don't like the look of that arm. We need to get him off the mountain right away."

"In that case," Kaine said, "you'll be needing my help. It's a long way down to the loch."

"We've already discussed this. It's too dangerous."

Martin stirred. "Dangerous? Why is it dangerous?"

"Descending a mountain with a stretcher is always dangerous," Drew answered before Kaine could say anything.

"Is someone after Mr Kaine?"

Drew stared at the boy. "Aye. The police are coming."

"You'd better leave, Mr Kaine. We won't tell them you were here."

Kaine squatted close to Martin and squeezed his hand.

"Don't go lying to the police, lad. It'll get you into all sorts of trouble, and I doubt your parents would approve."

"What they don't know won't hurt them," he said, smiling, face flushed.

"Trust me, Martin. Tell the truth and everything will work out fine. Be good, lad. Be safe."

"You too, Mr Kaine. And thanks again."

Kaine stood. By the time he'd reloaded and fastened his Bergen, Drew and Bruce had lifted the lad into the cage and were strapping him in tight.

During his transfer, Martin hadn't so much as whimpered, despite the fact that the movement must have been agonising. A strange feeling of paternal pride floated over Kaine at the boy's strength. He wondered how a fifteen-year-old Ryan Kaine would have reacted in the same situation. He'd probably have been a babbling, quivering wreck.

"I imagine you plan to use the *Bairn?*" he asked Drew.

"Aye. It's the only feasible route with the stretcher."

"The first part's narrow. It'll be tough with only the two of you."

"Don't worry about us. Help is on the way. Off ye go now."

Drew held out a hand the size of a small ham and they shook. Thankfully, the big Scot didn't try to crush his fingers as a show of strength.

Kaine turned to leave.

All around him, the air echoed with screaming voices and clattering boots.

"Armed police! Armed police! Do not move."

Chapter Thirty-Six

Thursday 17th September – Afternoon

Ben Craed, The Cairngorms, Aberdeenshire, Scotland

"Ryan Kaine, you are surrounded. Raise your hands and do not move!"

Raise my hands without moving? That'll be a good trick.

Kaine stood motionless, helpless, as the shadows flickered around him. Four men, ominous in their black uniforms, fanned out. Red lights shot from laser sights. One man, short and red-faced, kept screaming out counter-intuitive orders. "Shock and awe" they called the tactics, but Kaine was neither shocked, nor in awe. He was simply tired. Totally exhausted.

"What's it to be?" Kaine called out to the short man.

Even to him, his voice sounded surprisingly relaxed, given the circumstances. He'd always prided himself on being able to keep calm in a crisis. It marked him out from other military men. Some of his old unit commanders had worried about his apparent lack of emotion. One actually sent him for a full psychological assessment, but he'd passed it easily. Fear didn't help in a crisis. Stay cool and work the angles. Like playing snooker, or chess.

"Do you want me to keep still, or raise my hands? The second option is a tad problematic given my load. This Bergen's heavier than it looks."

"Shut up! Shut the fuck up!"

"Fair enough. Keep your hair on."

The inspector—judging by the cloth pips on his epaulettes—looked close to stroking out. His eyes bulged wide behind the clear marksman's goggles and spittle formed at the sides of his mouth. At his side, a taller man—a sergeant—seemed more in control, less jumpy. Kaine looked to him for some kind of sense and order.

The inspector rushed forwards and, although a mere three metres away, still screamed. "Raise your hands. Do it now!"

Drew stepped between them. "Inspector Cody," he said, his deep voice rumbling around the natural amphitheatre, "take it easy. Mr Kaine is unarmed. Tell your men to lower their weapons. We have an injured boy here."

Cody threw out an arm and tried to push Drew away, but the big Scot wouldn't budge. It didn't seem possible but, if anything, Cody's colour darkened. His blood pressure must have been off the charts. If things got much worse, Iona would have another patient on her hands.

Kaine coughed. "There's no need for this, Inspector. I'll come quietly. I'm going to put my hands up now. As Mr

McTay says, I am unarmed. Please ask your men to lower their weapons."

"Do it, Kaine. Don't try my patience."

Kaine lifted his arms straight out to the side, the better to maintain his balance.

"Now," the inspector said, lowering his voice a little, "very slowly, remove the backpack."

Kaine followed the instructions and lowered the Bergen to his feet. He let it fall, then raised his arms again.

"Good," the armed cop shouted. "Keep those arms up, turn around, and take five paces to your left, away from the boy."

Kaine complied, scraping his boots along the ground. The last thing he wanted was to trip over a rock and give Cody an excuse to shoot.

On his fourth step, something punched him in the back, and a boot kicked his ankle. He stumbled.

"Patel!" Cody yelled. "He's got a gun. Fire!"

Kaine turned his fall into a forward roll and twisted mid-flight. He tucked in his head as he hit the ground, barrel-rolled to his feet, and spun to face his enemy. No way would he let them shoot him in the back.

Eyes scanning the scene, he tensed. Waiting for the pulverising thump of bullets.

None came.

Cody screamed again. "Shoot, Patel, shoot! What the fuck's wrong with you, man?"

Martin screamed, "No! Don't. Please don't!"

Drew jumped in front of Kaine, shielding him from Cody in the bravest move Kaine had ever seen a civilian make.

The inspector raised his rifle. "Move, you fucking idiot. Kaine's dangerous."

"Lower your weapons!" Drew shouted and threw his arms wide, making himself an even bigger target.

"Drew, don't be such a fool," Kaine said, easing away from the man, drawing a single laser spot with him. "That was the stupidest bloody thing …"

Kaine couldn't have been more impressed with the big Scotsman. If they made it through the situation unscathed, he'd either box the man's ears, or buy him a drink. Maybe both.

Cody stood in front of them, feet apart, arms so tense they shook. The muzzle of his C8 trembled as his twitching index finger hooked around the trigger. The time drew out, second by second. Kaine stopped moving.

Fifty metres away, on the ridge high above and behind Cody, a man in a black uniform clambered to his feet from a prone position. He cradled a sniper's rifle in his arms, the muzzle pointing to the ground. The disobedient Patel, Kaine assumed. He transmitted a telepathic "thank you" to the man. A second uniformed officer jumped up and stood beside Patel. This man also had a rifle, but carried it in the "port arms" position, hugged tight into his chest with the barrel pointed at the sky.

In front of Kaine, the armed officers stood in a wide semicircle. Two constables split their attention between Cody, their sergeant, and Kaine, clearly uncertain what to do. Each had a rifle in hand, and a holstered sidearm, but the only one pointing his weapon at a target was Cody, and it was aimed at Kaine's fast-thumping heart.

Slowly, Kaine stood taller, raising his arms to the side again. "Let's take stock here. I don't know what's happening, Inspector, but this is wrong. I'm unarmed and surrendering to you. Sergeant," Kaine said, dragging his gaze away from Cody, "you know this is wrong."

The rangy sergeant closed on Cody and whispered something into the inspector's ear. Cody's head snapped around and the two men eyeballed each other, in a silent battle of wills that seemed to stretch out forever.

Kaine stood stock still. He'd been in difficult situations before, but rarely alone and without weapons. The six heavily armed men he faced had the advantage, no doubt about it. What had prevented Patel from taking the shot? A conscience? Basic humanity? God? Whatever the reason, Kaine had escaped Death once again, but the Grim Reaper had passed bloody close by and had stayed in the neighbourhood.

Things could still go badly wrong, but the tension eased with each passing second. Something in the sergeant's attitude, the way he carried himself, the way he edged in front of Cody, adding a second human shield to bolster Drew's brave stance, told Kaine he had another ally. If not an ally, then at least someone he could trust to escort him down the mountain to the relative safety of a holding cell.

While the two police officers faced each other and the rest awaited the outcome, the wind whipped around the space, creating dust bunnies that danced at their feet.

Then, as though stung by a cattle prod, Cody jerked to attention. He raised the muzzle of the C8, and released the charging handle, making the weapon safe. At no time during the procedure did he take his eyes from the sergeant. He kept the selector switch in the "single shot" position.

"Okay, we'll cover this in the debrief," Cody said, nodding as though he still maintained control over the proceedings. "Take over here, Sergeant Townes."

Kaine let out his breath. Alongside Drew McTay and the distant Patel, he now had the name of another man to whom he owed his life that day. The debts kept piling up. Debts he'd probably never be able to repay.

Townes raised a hand and spoke into his wrist mic. "Pat, Bunny, you can come down now. Quick as you like. There's a young lad here who needs to see the inside of a hospital."

Cody turned his back to his men and took a few paces away, head lowered, dialling numbers into a satphone. He raised the device to his ear and paced as he spoke quietly.

Kaine lowered his arms and nodded when Townes stepped up to him.

"Thank you, Sergeant. I guess you just saved my life."

"Aye, perhaps so, but don't get too comfortable, Mr Kaine. It wouldn't take much to make me change my mind," Townes said, speaking loud enough for everyone in the valley to hear. "The only thing stopping me from throwing you off this mountain is what you did for the boy."

He leaned in and lowered his voice. "That and the fact none of us can stand that arrogant prick. Buffalo Bill Cody" —he almost spat the words—"never a truer nickname. Bloody cowboy. Why he isn't banged up in a rubber room I'll never know. Probably has friends in low places. If you get my meaning."

"I take it you had something to do with Patel not taking that shot?"

The gangling sergeant turned sideways, keeping his body between Kaine and Cody, and looked up at the now-empty promontory where the sniper had made his nest.

"Aye," he said. "None of us joined the police to shoot unarmed men, even if they are mass-murdering terrorists."

Kaine took a breath, but chose not to respond. The truth about his part in the disaster would stay hidden from them for a little longer. One thing's for certain, Kaine wasn't about to rake over any coals so soon after the abortive firework show.

"Now I'm left with a wee bit of a problem," Townes said. "What the hell am I gonna do with you?"

He raised a finger to halt Kaine's intended response.

"There's no point handcuffing you with your locksmith skills. And how would you climb down wearing bracelets? You'd likely fall and kill yourself and I don't need the paper-work. Will you give me your parole, Captain Kaine?"

What? Have we just time-warped back to the Napoleonic wars?

Kaine frowned and shook his head, trying to clear the fog.

"Come again? My parole?"

"Aye, man. Give me your word not to attempt an escape until we're off the mountain, and I'll let you help carry the stretcher. Despite everything that's happened, the lad seems to like you."

Stunned, Kaine couldn't think of any reason not to agree.

"Yes, you have my word. I will not try to escape while we're on the mountain."

Christ, did the sergeant actually wink at him at the same time as saluting? Weird, but Kaine wasn't one to query the dental hygiene of gift horses.

Townes spun away and barked out his orders. "Men. Let's get the lad off this mountain. Mr McTay, do you mind taking the lead? I'm sure you can show us the safest way down. And the fastest."

Drew's big, red beard stretched and rippled, partially hiding a relieved smile.

"That I can, Sergeant. I'll call my sister to meet us at Point Zero. It's an easier route from here than making for the loch. They'll reach it well before we do. I'm assuming your big, strapping police officers will give us a hand carrying the stretcher. Or are they going to keep glaring at this poor, wee Englishman?"

Kaine matched Drew's grin, although his eight-day beard didn't hide it half as well as the Scotsman's bushy monstrosity.

"Keep calling me 'wee man', McTay, and I'll forget my promise not to smack you down, despite the fact I owe you big time for that show of lunacy. Stepping in front of a loaded gun? Wait until I tell your sister."

Drew tried to clap him on the shoulder, but Kaine dodged the friendly blow—a dead arm wouldn't help him to carry the stretcher.

Despite the immediate relief of not being shot and of the relative support of the sergeant, Kaine couldn't afford to relax. During the descent, he'd have to keep Inspector Cowboy in view. The last thing he needed on a narrow mountain trail was another ankle tap.

Chapter Thirty-Seven

Thursday 17th September – Afternoon

Ben Craed, The Cairngorms, Aberdeenshire, Scotland

Kaine rolled the tension from his neck and shoulders before kneeling at the head of the stretcher. Martin had acquitted himself well and shown his resilience, traits he'd need given the months of rehab he faced if the surgeons managed to save his arm and put his ankle back together.

"Okay, Martin?"

"That got a bit scary for a moment, Mr Kaine."

He dismissed the boy's concern with a one-shouldered shrug. "You did well to stay so calm."

Once again, Martin blushed. The added colour looked good on the lad.

"Want to take the first stage, Bruce?" Kaine asked the paramedic.

Drew's partner, who'd spent the whole episode crouched beside Martin, trying to keep the boy safe, shook his head. Face pale, breathing hard, it took a while before he spoke.

"Sorry. I'm not used to all these guns. How the hell do you keep so calm?" he asked, looking at Kaine.

"You should have seen me the first time I came under fire. Nearly wet myself."

"Yeah, right. Don't believe that for a minute." Bruce stared at his trembling fingers before shaking out his hands and making fists.

Drew stepped up and dropped a hand on Bruce's shoulder.

"Rest here awhile. I'll take the first go. Follow us down later. Okay?"

Bruce shook his head firmly. "No, I'll be right. I'll no' leave my patient."

Drew scratched the furry creature wrapped around his chin. "Fair enough. You good to go, Kaine?"

"What do you say, Martin?" Kaine said. "Ready?"

Martin returned his smile. "Yes, please. I've had more than enough of this place."

"Which way are we heading?" Sergeant Townes asked from his position down the hill, beside Cody.

"Back the way we came in. There's a split in the trail at the top of Scooter's Chimney. It takes us a couple of miles out of our way, but the trail's a lot easier with the stretcher, and Iona's going to meet us with the ambulance. Kaine, you can take the head end."

"Good idea," he said, and knew exactly why.

Kaine squatted, slipped the stretcher's rear harness over his head, and worked it into position around his neck and on his shoulders. Satisfied he could never make it any more comfortable, he grabbed the handles and waited for Drew to do the same.

Drew called the timings. "One, two, lift."

Kaine took the strain in his quads, glutes, and lower back, and straightened. The combined weight of Martin and the aluminium cage put more strain on his fatigued arms and legs than he expected. The quicker they descended the mountain, the better for all.

They moved out.

To begin with, Kaine had to bend his elbows and lift to keep the cage horizontal, but the moment they reached the path, the downhill slope levelled their height difference and gave Martin a more comfortable ride.

"How are ye doing, wee man?" Drew shouted to Kaine after they'd trudged no more than a few dozen metres.

"Pretty damned fed up with your 'wee man' jibes, but apart from that, I'm tickety-bloody-boo. Never better." Kaine lied through his teeth.

The powerful Scotsman barked out a happy laugh, clearly finding the physical task undemanding. Kaine, on the other hand, struggled. His shoulders, arms, and lower back screamed for rest, and his palms, red-raw from climbing the rasping granite, burned. The physical exertions of the previous few days were taking their toll. He managed a further three hundred metres or so before his grip strength finally gave way and he had to call a halt or risk dropping the stretcher.

"Sorry, Drew. I'm done."

They lowered Martin gently, and Kaine collapsed to his knees. Townes detailed the shortest of his men, Stedman, to take Kaine's place.

Before they set off again, Bruce checked Martin's condition. "The rocking's put him to sleep. Lucky for him."

Townes stood over Kaine. "You're done in. We'll rest here for five, but everyone else keep going. Bunny, you're in charge, but take your instructions from Mr McTay. Sir"—he turned to his unexpectedly silent superior—"is that okay with you?"

Cody scowled at Kaine, but grunted his agreement.

Townes continued. "Pat, Bunny, and Stedman, take turns with the stretcher. Get the lad to the doctor as fast as you can, but take care. Porgy, you stay with us."

Porgy, a middleweight with a dark complexion and intelligent, brown eyes nodded, peeled away from his mates, and took up a position behind Cody.

The medivac team set off and soon dropped out of sight when they reached the first bend in the trail.

Kaine kept his eye on Cody. If Townes' intervention had been an elaborate setup, there wouldn't be a better time to spring the trap. He searched the surroundings for a way out, but found none. His hands couldn't have chosen a worse place to let him down.

The three of them were perched on a narrow trail worn into the side of the rock, wide enough to walk without crabbing sideways, but not enough for two people to pass without brushing each other. Bare rock face to the left, and a perpendicular drop to the right. One misstep would mark an end to his life's dark struggles.

The wind, which until that point had provided a constant background wail, chose that moment to die. Only their heavy breathing broke the unexpected silence.

"Is this where it happens?" Kaine asked, addressing Townes, not Cody.

"What d'you say?" the sergeant demanded.

"Is this where I have an unfortunate fall?"

The sergeant looked puzzled, but Cody lowered his head in what … embarrassment?

"What are you talking about?"

"Someone punched me between the shoulders and ankle-tapped me back there, when Patel was supposed to kill me. The inspector was the only man close enough."

"I know. I saw it," Townes said. His face darkened and he turned to Cody. "You are a fucking arsehole … sir."

"Don't talk to me like that, you jumped-up, Scottish moron!" Cody screamed, his face red, fists raised, and his whole body quivering. "That's insubordination!"

"You're out of control, man. Porgy," Townes said, addressing the man who still stood behind Cody with his hand resting on the grip of his sidearm, "relieve the inspector of his weapons. I'm taking command here."

Porgy stood still for a moment. "Are you sure, Sarge?"

"Certain. Go on, I'll take full responsibility."

From his position on his knees, Kaine watched the drama unfold. So many things could go wrong from that point forwards and he had to be ready for all of them.

"Sir," Porgy said, stepping closer to his inspector. "Please hand over your rifle."

Cody spun to face the younger man. "What? Are you fucking serious?"

"Yes, sir. Please don't make this any more difficult than it already is."

Porgy reached for the weapon.

Cody took a step backwards, moving closer to Townes and Kaine.

"Don't you touch me, you ignorant fuck-up. I'm in charge here. Arrest Sergeant Townes. He's the one out of control. Do it, man! What are you waiting for?"

Porgy moved even closer, a wounded expression forming on his weather-worn features. "Please, sir?"

Cody jerked away and swung an arm wildly. He lost his footing and his balance.

The man teetered on the edge of the void, eyes wide, arms flailing.

Screaming, he toppled backwards into empty air.

Chapter Thirty-Eight

Thursday 17th September – Afternoon

Ben Craed, The Cairngorms, Aberdeenshire, Scotland

Kaine sprang forwards and wrapped his arms around Cody's left ankle but the man kept falling. His back and head slammed against the cliff. The jar loosened Kaine's grip.

The foot slipped from his grasp.

Cody fell.

He fell, screaming.

Arms flailing, legs kicking, howling all the way until he crashed into a jutting boulder. The scream cut off, abruptly. Blood exploded from beneath a crumpled helmet, arms and legs crushed and floppy—a mannequin without strings.

"No," Kaine yelled. "Damn it, no!"

The body tumbled and bounced, down and down, until it hit the valley floor and disintegrated in a pile of bone, blood, and gristle.

Kaine lay, arms dangling over the ledge, watching the man who'd have happily killed him die a horrible death. One more death witnessed, one more life cut short, wasted.

He twisted to look up at Townes. "You saw that, didn't you? I-I tried to save him."

Townes nodded. "I saw. You did all you could." He made the sign of the cross and stepped back from the precipice. "It was damned stupid, though. He could have dragged you over with him."

Kaine let his arms flop.

"Goddamn it. Another death they'll blame on me."

Two pairs of hands pulled him back and propped him against the cliff face.

Townes squatted at his side, concern on his face. "We saw what you did, Captain. It wasn't your fault. Nothing but an accident. The inspector got careless. Never was worth squat on the mountain. He's been holding us up the whole way."

Kaine leaned forwards and peered into the valley. Cody, what was left of him, lay on his front, safety helmet broken and crushed, blood and brain matter splashed red and grey over the boulders. No chance of him having survived. Not with those injuries.

Porgy stepped alongside Townes and leaned out, too, his face pale.

"Shame, but he'll not be missed."

"Porgy!" Townes snapped. "That's someone's son."

"Sorry. Didn't mean nothing by it. Just telling it as I see it."

Townes scratched the side of his nose and nodded. "Went out for a drink with him when he first arrived on station. Tried to make him welcome, you know? Only did it the once though. Mean bugger hardly put his hands in his pocket the whole night. Told me he was an only child and both parents were dead. I doubt we'll find many tae grieve over him, although the brass will probably give him a big send off. Brave officer fallen in the line of duty. Y'know how it works. The press office loves that sort of story. Good for the image."

Townes made the sign of the cross again. Kaine didn't. Neither did Porgy.

Kaine took a swig of water from the bottle Townes gave him. His hands trembled. He tried to steady his breathing.

Porgy coughed. "I suppose you'll be sending Bunny down there after him?"

Townes shook his head. "No point. Recovering the body's a job for the S&R team."

"What about his weapons and ammo? We can't leave it unattended."

Townes leaned further out, holding out his inner arm to counterbalance his shift in weight. "Take a look at that terrain, Porgy. See how isolated it is? Difficult to traverse. It's a safe bet nobody's going to stroll by and help themselves to a broken C8, and a SIG covered in blood and guts. But since you made a good point, why not stay here and keep guard until Mr Abercrombie organises a recovery team?"

Porgy looked around him and then down at the corpse. "Is that an order, Sarge?"

"No, it's not, but since you volunteered, I'm happy to accept your offer. Thanks a lot."

Townes smiled at his man's look of resignation and took

a computer tablet from his pack. He tapped the screen and showed it to Kaine. "I've just bookmarked these coordinates. It'll give the S&R team a location for the body."

"Aren't you going to call it in now?"

"Nope. Can't acquire a signal," he said, without confirming it on his satphone. "Besides, Cody's not going anywhere, and he's got Porgy to keep him company. Right"—he backed away from Kaine and offered his hand—"are you fit to stand?"

Kaine ignored Townes' hand. "Mind if we take a moment? Don't imagine I'll be back this way for a while and that view"—he looked out, not down—"is stunning."

Flanked by Townes on his left and Porgy on his right, Kaine soaked in the atmosphere. Porgy broke an energy bar in half and handed a piece to Kaine. They relaxed and picnicked like old friends on a day out in the mountains.

———

TOWNES TWISTED the wrapper of his food bar into a tight coil and stuffed it into his pocket.

"Okay," he said, standing, "time you and I weren't here, Captain."

Kaine struggled to his feet and had to lean against the cliff until the head rush cleared before giving Townes the nod. "Ready when you are, Sergeant."

"Take care, Porgy," Townes said, nodding at the firearms officer, who remained sitting, "I'll send Bunny back to keep you company and make sure you don't take a tumble and end up alongside the poor inspector. Losing one member of the unit might appear unfortunate, but losing two would be careless."

He put on a pompous, English accent for the last sentence and chuckled, clearly an Oscar Wilde fan.

"Thanks, Sarge. You're all heart."

"After you, Captain Kaine," Townes said and threw out his arm like a waiter pointing Kaine to his table.

Kaine started walking, but stopped after a few steps and threw up his head. "Damn it."

"Problem?"

"I left my Bergen up there"—he nodded at the path they'd recently descended—"at the foot of Zelda's Smile."

Townes shook his head. "Don't fret yourself, Captain. One of my men is portering it for you. You'll get it back, but not until after we've searched it for weapons."

"You'll find a Swiss Army knife and nothing else. But thanks for letting me know."

It took them less than twenty minutes to catch up with the slow-moving medivac team and for Kaine to be reunited with his Bergen, but not before it had been emptied and repacked, under Townes' supervision. The sergeant confiscated the knife, but ignored Kaine's false papers—the ones identifying him as Staff Sergeant Sidings—before handing it back. Kaine didn't have the energy to question Townes' apparent lapse in security, and saying thanks might have earned him a bullet.

During the descent, Kaine searched out Patel, who'd strapped his rifle over his shoulder and was using one hand to steady himself against the cliff.

"Thanks for not taking that shot earlier. Why didn't you, by the way?"

Patel slowed and allowed Kaine to draw alongside on the widening path.

"The sergeant told me not to shoot unless you showed a weapon or did something aggressive, and you did neither.

Besides, unlike some," Patel added, lowering his voice and adding a scowl, "I'm no killer."

He stopped and forced Kaine to walk ahead.

For the rest of the descent, the prickle in the back of Kaine's neck stood as a constant reminder of the sniper dogging his trail.

Chapter Thirty-Nine

Thursday 17th September – Early Evening

Ben Craed, The Cairngorms, Aberdeenshire, Scotland

The climb down the mountain seemed to drag on forever, but Kaine wasn't in any hurry. He locked his gaze on the heels of the man in front, Stedman, and concentrated on placing his feet with care, trying to block out anything in his peripheral vision.

Slowly, almost imperceptibly, the pitch of the slope beneath his feet levelled out. The rocky trail changed from granite to dirt, and then to moss. Eventually, and with Kaine almost asleep on his feet, Townes called a halt. Stedman stopped, and Kaine walked straight into the back of him. The man grunted, and Kaine snapped awake.

"Sorry, son."

"Watch where you're going, pops!" he said, without malice. "Wouldn't want old Pat to think you're trying to escape, now would we?"

His smile confirmed the joke and, from behind, Patel's snigger and backslap made the moment completely surreal.

"Relax," Patel said. "We're here."

Kaine looked up. He had to shield his eyes from the blinding, white light of the early-evening sun reflecting off something in the valley below.

A row of vehicles caught the sunlight and threw it into his eyes. Kaine recognised one of the cars as the ancient Land Rover he and Iona had commandeered ... when? Hell, was it only that morning? It seemed like weeks ago.

Four other vehicles accompanied the Land Rover—a giant Mitsubishi sporting "Kinross Farm Mountain Rescue Centre" and ambulance decals and three shiny, new police Range Rovers. All faced down the hill, their tailgates open in wait.

A dozen uniformed police officers huddled in small groups, no doubt waiting to throw a blanket over Kaine's head and drag him into the back of one of the Range Rovers the moment he reached them.

It didn't matter. Kaine couldn't summon the energy to give a damn. In fact, the dark interior compartments with their padded seats promised such comfort, he considered running off down the hill and collapsing into their soft embrace. The only things stopping him were the distance— three hundred metres at least—and the worry that Patel might mistake his desire for rest as an escape attempt. Truth was, he could barely stand, let alone run.

Apart from the addition of the people and the vehicles, the school campsite, with its semicircle of tents, remained largely unchanged from the morning, although the early-evening sunshine added a more welcoming vibe than the morning's grey drizzle.

Kaine stood still, awaiting instructions, while Townes and his men gathered around him, preventing him moving towards the camp. Drew and Bruce, apparently unaware they were alone, marched on with Martin between them in the cage, still asleep.

What now?

Townes and his men were probably getting ready to handcuff him and march him triumphantly into the valley. No doubt someone in the camp would have a camera to mark the occasion when the brave, Scottish police officers captured the evil terrorist after the useless, bloody English had failed.

Kaine relaxed his taut shoulders and soaked in the beauty of the Scottish Highlands for what might be the final time.

A cloudless sky, the clearest and bluest it had been since he'd crossed the border, smiled down on him. The pink, red, and grey granite, the dark green moss, and the multi-coloured heather threw out the colour palette an artist would have been proud to call their own. Despite his imminent incarceration, Kaine couldn't help smiling.

Drew and Bruce closed on the vehicles, and still Townes hadn't given the order to move out. The men by the cars, police and civilian volunteers, cheered their approach.

Before long, Iona, dwarfed by her brother, was leaning over the side of the stretcher, stethoscope pressed to Martin's chest. A few seconds later, she nodded, smiled up at Drew, and signalled him to load the cage into the ambulance. The audience fist-pumped, high-fived, and slapped each other's backs.

After the cheers died, the throaty roar of a powerful, diesel engine broke the hushed silence.

Kaine and his captors turned towards the sound.

Another police Range Rover bounced over the rough terrain, speeding towards the gathering. It pulled to a halt beside the ambulance. Almost before the wheels stopped turning, the passenger doors flew open. A slightly built, middle-aged woman jumped out from behind the driver's seat. She ran to the ambulance and leaned over the stretcher. Seconds later, a man of similar age followed her from the rear of the SUV at a much slower, more laboured pace. The woman grasped Martin's good hand. Even from a distance, her cries of delight reached Kaine's ears. Martin's father stood beside his wife and son, hand covering his mouth, shoulders shaking. He staggered, but Drew reached out a steadying hand.

Kaine blinked hard to clear his vision. He smiled along with Townes' men, unable to hold back the sense of achievement. He'd done something good. Something to be proud of.

Finally.

Townes took a pace forwards and stood directly in front of Kaine, blocking his view of the family reunion. Kaine leaned to one side, desperate to keep watching, but Townes matched his move in an awkward, two-step shuffle. Behind him, Townes' men closed rank and turned their backs to the campsite.

"Well, Kaine?" Townes said. "What are you waiting for?"

"Yes, I gave you my parole. Take me in, Sergeant."

Kaine held out his hands ready to accept the cold steel of handcuffs, but Townes pushed them away.

"That's not what I meant. I only asked you not to try to

escape until we were off the mountain. Well, here we are, off the mountain. Away you go now, sir."

He made a dismissive gesture with his hand.

Kaine froze. "This isn't some kind of excuse to shoot the prisoner while he's escaping, is it?"

Townes sighed heavily. His men swapped glances with one another, but made no move to intervene.

"Haven't we proved ourselves to you yet? Go man. Get outta here."

As though to emphasise Townes' point, Patel unslung his rifle, removed the magazine, dropped to one knee, and started stripping it down. The other men also unloaded and made their weapons safe.

Still, Kaine refused to move.

"Ah for goodness sake, come wi' me, man," Townes said.

He marched past Kaine, retracing the route they'd just taken. Doubtful and still on alert, Kaine followed until they reached a point where the path ducked behind a large slab of dark red stone. Townes stopped and waited for him.

"I thought you'd appreciate seeing the family reunion. Without you, Martin would have died. Now, off you trot."

"How will you explain my disappearance? Do you want me to punch you in the face or something?"

Townes dipped his chin. "And end up looking like you? Hell no. I'm happy to remain handsome and unmarked."

Unable to believe his luck, Kaine still couldn't move. "Any preference for which direction I should take?"

"Reckon you can find your way to Kidney Loch from here?"

"Of course."

"Away with you then."

"What'll I find there? Patel's brother with another sniper rifle?"

"Don't be ridiculous, man. If I wanted you dead, I'd have let Buffalo Bill do the dirty. Haven't you twigged yet?"

"Twigged? Stop with the riddles, Sergeant. I haven't slept properly for over a week. I can't sit a pop quiz."

Townes broke out an irritating smile. "DCI Jones sends his regards."

What?

"You know DCI Jones?"

"Not personally, but one of my colleagues, DI John McDougall, Big Jock, used to be part of his Serious Crime Unit down in Birmingham. Aberdeen is a small place. I doubt there's a police officer in the city who doesn't know Big Jock McDougall."

"Big Jock McDougall? Jeez, is every second man in Scotland called Jock? ... No, don't answer that." Kaine slapped his forehead with the heel of his hand. "Oh, wait a minute. Back on the mountain, you let it slip that you know I can open handcuffs without a key."

Townes' knowing smile confirmed Kaine's suspicions.

"You've seen the video evidence clearing me?"

"No, I haven't but DCI Jones has, and the minute he learned you were in Scotland looking for Martin Princeton, he contacted Big Jock, who told me. I, of course, told my men."

"Not Cody, though?"

"No way, that barmpot—God rest his black soul—wasn't interested in justice or the truth. You saw what he was like."

Kaine wiped the sweat from his face with his raw hands. "Okay, I believe you, but why don't we end this now? You take me in, and I'll have a nice rest while the legal wheels are turning."

Townes' smile dropped. "That won't work. I spoke to Mr Jones while we were on our way here from Scooter's Chimney." He took a satphone from his pocket and waggled it under Kaine's nose. "Didn't know I had one of these, did you? Neither did Cody. Anyway, Mr Jones mentioned the possibility of there still being a large reward for your head. He's worried you won't make it to the cells, or to a court if it comes to that."

Kaine nodded.

"I'm starting to feel the same way."

"And Cody's death has done you a big favour, by the way."

"Really?"

"Aye, without him, and with Bartholomew being so discredited, no one need know you were ever here. I'll talk to Martin and his parents, and the few people who actually saw you. None of my men will talk to the press."

"I don't want people getting into trouble on my behalf."

"They won't. At the worst, your presence here will become one of those urban myths like Nessie—who does exist, by the way." He tittered. "Listen, there's no time for any more jabber. Get going and good luck."

Townes offered his hand and Kaine grasped it tight, ignoring the discomfort.

"You said I should head for Kidney Loch. Why, who's there?"

The sergeant shrugged. "Beats me. Mr Jones said something about a horse doctor and a salty sea dog."

Kaine spun on his heel, yelled his thanks, and started jogging, the happiest he'd been in days.

Behind him, Townes laughed and shouted, "Hey, was it something I said, wee man?"

Chapter Forty

Thursday 17th September – Evening

The Cairngorms National Park, A9, Aberdeenshire, Scotland

Kaine lay across the back seat of the Mercedes G-Class—a more expensive, if soulless, replica of a Land Rover Defender—struggling to keep his eyes open, but massively content and smiling.

When possible, he focused on Lara's profile. She'd tied back her long hair, and it allowed him a wonderful view of her slim neck and high cheekbones. Absolute perfection. He doubted a portrait artist could have done her justice.

He hadn't stopped smiling since arriving at the muddy trail above *Dubhaig Loc*. Despite his bone-deep exhaustion and the weight of the Bergen, he'd refused to ease his pace and completed the punishing, downhill, six-kilometre yomp from the campsite in less than an hour.

Lara ran the last thirty metres to meet him and they stopped a few paces apart, unable to decide on the proper way for relative strangers to greet. His heart nearly burst when she broke the deadlock by rushing into his arms, ignoring what must have been the foulest-smelling, sweatiest embrace she'd ever endured. He ached to kiss her, but she didn't offer him the opportunity.

Rollo leaned in the crook of the car's open driver's door, arms crossed. A cheesy grin split his angular and weathered face.

Kaine ignored him for the moment and held Lara tight, breathing in the fragrance of her shampoo while trying to ignore the stale sweat wafting from his every pore. After a short but delightful lifetime, Kaine forced himself to push her away, but he held her at arm's length, unwilling to lose contact.

"Your poor face," she said, reaching up to his cheek.

Her touch was feather light.

"Don't think I'm unhappy to see you, Lara, but what the hell are you doing here? It's not safe."

If she was upset by his gruff words, her unflinching smile didn't show it. "We'd better get a move on then, hadn't we."

Kaine scowled at Rollo and clenched his jaw. "Sergeant, I told you to keep her safe."

David Jones' "salty sea dog" raised one well-muscled shoulder and let his smile drop. "You try stopping this woman from doing something she wants. Short of locking her in her room, what could I do?"

"A locked cell would have been better than allowing her to blunder into a dangerous situation."

"Sorry, sir. I did try, but—"

Lara interrupted Rollo's statement for the defence. "You do know I'm right here, don't you? I can hear every word you say." She waved a hand in the air. "We can either stay here gabbing and risking arrest, or jump in and go. Your choice."

"See what I mean?" Rollo asked, ducking into the car and firing up the G-Class' powerful engine. "A real harridan. Don't know how you'll put up with her."

He hit a button on the SUV's dashboard and the rear door popped open. Kaine dropped the Bergen into the luggage compartment, stumbled around to the offside passenger door, and flopped gratefully into the rear seat.

"So much for DCI Jones keeping you out of trouble," he said to Lara, who climbed into the front passenger seat and showed him her stunning profile.

Rollo selected drive and pointed the car down the rutted track. Within seconds, the rolling movement had rocked all the fight out of Kaine.

Rollo flashed a glance through the rear-view mirror.

"If you must know, it was Mr Jones who suggested we should come up here and pull your nuts out of the fire," he said, smiling

Kaine yawned and waved a hand over his lap. "As you can see, I remain burn free. I didn't need your help."

"There's gratitude for you, eh, Doc? After we've come all this way to give him a lift back to England."

Lara's light reply soothed more of Kaine's anxiety. "Maybe we should head to Kinross Farm and leave him here to face the Scottish police?"

"Good idea. All I need to do is turn left at the bottom of the hill, not right. Which way, sir?"

"What's this, a new double act? What am I going to do with you two?"

Still facing forwards, Lara answered. "You could start by taking a shower. You stink."

Kaine turned his sting-tired eyes on the back of Rollo's head. "Did you hear that, Sergeant? Charming, eh? In the past few days I've been beaten to a pulp, spent the night outdoors in a thunderstorm, scrambled up and down a mountain, found a lost teenager, and faced a lunatic police officer out to kill me. Oh yes, and I faced down the attack of a golden eagle, and all she can say is 'you stink'. Ruddy marvellous."

"Golden eagle? You didn't hurt it, did you?" Lara asked, ever the concerned vet.

"Now would I? They're a protected species." Kaine settled deeper into the soft, leather seat. "Damn thing nearly gave me a coronary, though."

"Okay, Ryan. Try to rest. I'll book us into a nice hotel across the border so you can take that shower." She lifted a brand new mobile and started tapping the screen. "Any preference for location?"

"You have the internet on that thing?"

"Of course, full roving access. Why?"

"Can you look up the address of Martin's school?"

She turned her head so fast her hair splayed into a dark halo. "Oh hell. What's wrong now?" She frowned in concern.

Dear God, but you are beautiful.

"Nothing much and it won't take long. Once we've found a certain teacher's assistant, a couple of hours, tops. I need to encourage him to find his way to the nearest police station."

Rollo lifted his chin to look at Kaine through the rear-view once again. "Care to explain why, sir?"

"Long story, Rollo. I'll tell you after I've had some sleep."

"And a shower?" Lara asked.

"Nope, not a shower," Kaine said, shaking his head.

"What?"

"A bath," he added, widening his grin. "A nice, long, hot soak. After that, and after the stop off at the school, you can choose a holiday destination. I think we could all do with a break in the sun. I'll pay."

After a few moments, Lara said something that could have been, "Dublin dance," or "trouble in France," but Kaine didn't have the strength to ask her to repeat it.

With Rollo behind the wheel, Lara Orchard safe and within easy reach, and Martin Princeton safe with his parents, all was suddenly right with the world. Kaine untied his boots, kicked them off, and sank further into the soft upholstery.

France? Now there's a great idea.

Chapter Forty-One

Friday 18th September

BBC Radio News

"…*shock business news, SAMS Chairman, Sir Malcolm Sampson, was arrested and charged with seventy-four counts of tax avoidance. A leaked government document suggests that Sir Malcolm personally owes the Exchequer hundreds of millions of pounds.*

"*The news broke after the FTSE closed last evening, but international stock exchanges including the Hang Seng, Dow Jones, and Nikkei saw the company's share price plummet. Billions were knocked off the company's value. There is no doubt that the UK's leading aerospace and technology conglomerate is in serious financial trouble.*

"*A SAMS spokesman announced that an emergency stakeholder meeting would be called early next week. In the meantime, the current board will take over Sir Malcolm's duties and business will, and I quote, 'continue as usual'.*"

The newsreader, Barry McWhirter, shuffled some papers and cleared his throat.

"*In our Cambridge studio, Professor Grant Whittingstall, an expert in the international armaments industry and Chair of the Tactical Studies Unit, St Anne's College, Cambridge University, has an interesting perspective on events.*

"*Professor Whittingstall—*"

"*Please, call me Grant,*" the professor interrupted, his American accent smooth, his delivery relaxed and confident.

"*Ah, yes, Grant. You have a different perspective on the story. Is that so?*"

"*I do indeed. Let me tell you, Barry, I have the ear of a number of very senior members of the British government. You'll understand I can't name names, but they are serious players. I won't be speaking out of turn if I tell you that the UK government sees Sampson Armaments and Munitions Services Plc in the same way they saw the banks during the recession in '08. In effect, SAMS is far too big and too important to fail.*"

"*Really? That seems rather a bold statement. Do you have any corroborat—*"

"*Let me put it this way, Barry,*" Whittingstall interrupted. "*SAMS has contracts to decommission all of the UK's '50s-era nuclear power plants. They are providing most of the targeting systems and armaments for the Royal Navy's next generation aircraft carriers, and they are also providing the bulk of the servicing personnel for the Trident nuclear deterrent. On top of which, the prime minister recently announced SAMS as the preferred bidder for DUCA, the proposed Defensive Umbrella for Civilian Aircraft. A project she announced in the wake of the tragic destruction of Flight BE1555.*"

Whittingstall paused for a moment before continuing. Someone in the studio shuffled papers.

"*No, Barry, I can assure you. SAMS cannot be allowed to go to the wall, and I have some even more interesting information. It would appear that the instances of tax avoidance are the least of Sir Malcolm Sampson's illegal activities. A source close to the prime minister told me that he'll be facing a bunch of other charges. Charges that, due to the Official Secrets Act, will never be discussed in open court.*"

"*That is really interesting,*" McWhirter said, dryly. "*Are you able to elaborate?*"

The American academic scoffed. "*Sure I can. A senior member of the SAMS board was murdered earlier this week and some sources have pointed the finger at everyone's favourite scapegoat, Ryan Kaine, but I happen to know diff—*"

"*One moment, Professor Whittingstall,*" McWhirter interrupted, excitement speeding his words. "*This is an incredible coincidence. I'm receiving some breaking news relating, in part, to the fugitive you mentioned, Ryan Kaine. We're going to Angela Strange, our Scotland correspondent. Angela, can you hear me?*"

"*Yes, Barry. I can hear you.*"

"*I understand you have news on the once-missing schoolboy, Martin Princeton.*"

"*I have indeed. I'm speaking from outside Aberdeen Royal Infirmary. Five minutes ago, hospital authorities provided an update on Martin's condition. Doctors say he underwent a nine-hour operation to repair damage to his leg and help improve circulation in his right arm. In time, he is expected to make a full recovery.*"

"*Angela, that is wonderful news.*"

"*But that's not all, Barry. You will be aware that last night, Mr Bartholomew, the teacher in charge of the school party from which Martin disappeared, claimed to have seen Ryan Kaine at the mountain rescue centre. As you know, Mr Kaine is seen as a 'person of interest' in connection with the downing of Flight BE1555.*"

"*Interesting you should say that, Angela, we've just been discussing Ryan Kaine in relation to another story entirely.*"

"*Well, Barry,*" Angela Strange said, breathless, "*it would appear that Mr Bartholomew may not have been telling the truth. The local police have arrested him in connection with Martin's disappearance. Furthermore, after receiving a statement from Martin Princeton himself, Police Scotland has issued an arrest warrant for a Mr Gavin Atkinson. The charge is likely to be the attempted murder of Martin Princeton.*"

"*Extraordinary. This story is moving quickly. Who, may I ask, is Gavin Atkinson?*"

"*Ah that's where the story becomes even more bizarre. Mr Atkinson is Mr Bartholomew's teaching assistant at St Thomas' Grammar School. And it would appear that Ryan Kaine might never have been in Scotland at all. Mr Bartholomew may have made that claim in an effort to obscure his part in Martin's disappearance.*"

"*And where is Mr Bartholomew now?*"

"*He is under police guard, here at Aberdeen Royal. It seems that he, too, suffered a fall.*"

"*Would this be an example of poetic justice, Angela?*" McWhirter asked, his voice dripping irony.

"*Quite possibly, Barry. Quite possibly. One final, and stunning, piece of news just in, is that Mr Atkinson walked into his local police station less than thirty minutes ago with his solicitor, Mr Gareth Patterson.*

"*On camera, Mr Atkinson confessed to pushing Martin off the cliff with the intent of murdering the poor lad in a fit of jealousy. I have to say, Barry, while making his confession, Mr Atkinson was rather pale and kept looking over his shoulder ...*"

Chapter Forty-Two

Monday 21st September – Midday

The Villa, La Forge, Nouvelle-Aquitaine, France

Kaine couldn't remember a time when he'd been happier.

The Bay of Biscay spread out ahead of him, the waves gently lapping at the silver sand. Flat calm and empty of boats, Kaine hadn't seen anything as beautiful since Lara ran towards him at *Dubhaig Loc*.

Fresh salt air filled his lungs for the first time in weeks. How he'd missed the sea, his powerful, supportive enemy.

"What first?" Lara asked. "Explore the villa or find somewhere local to eat?"

"Swim first, food later."

Kaine dropped his suitcase and the Bergen on the

balcony, peeled off his clinging polo shirt, and nodded at the beach.

"Fancy joining me?"

"Later," she said. "I'm not much of a swimmer."

Kaine pressed his hand against her cheek before giving her a smile. "That's going to have to change. Consider me your swim coach for the next few weeks."

She untied her headscarf and allowed her hair to fall free. "I'm here for rest and recuperation—a holiday. Not a training camp."

"Swimming with friends can be fun. Back in a few."

"Don't forget, you have a dental appointment in three hours."

"Fantastic. Can't wait." And he really couldn't.

He kicked off his shoes and sprinted over the hot sand.

The second his toes hit the cool surf, Ryan Kaine knew he'd found a home.

The END

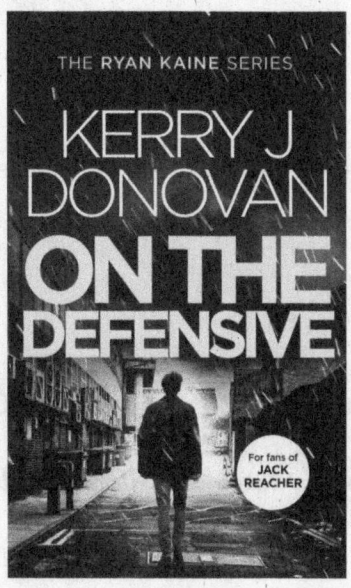

On The Defensive: Chapter One

Wednesday 30th September – Justina Constantine

Bistro Mykonos, Tower Hamlets, London, England

Justina blinked as the sun flickered between the fast-moving clouds and shot bright, yellow beams through the Bistro's big windows, highlighting the dirt and the grime sprayed by passing traffic. Orestes, her darling Ore, had promised to clean the glass before the evening service, but, as usual, he would need another reminder. The forgetful man always needed one more reminder.

Her eyes stung, in part from chopping strong onions, and in part from worry over their financial troubles, but mainly from the loss of Papa Onassis. Three weeks after her father-in-law's untimely death aboard Flight BE1555, the tears still bubbled up when she least expected them. Such a dreadful waste of a wonderful human being.

Eventually, the pain would fade, as it had done when her own dear parents passed, but it would take time. The loss of Papa Onassis was still so terribly raw.

Justina sniffled and dried her tears with a tissue.

How long could they survive? How long would it be before the bank forced them to close their doors forever?

What had once been a thriving, family business, now struggled under the weight of falling sales and crippling debts. Where once the business generated a small, but steady profit, she and Ore now owed thousands of pounds to the bank and yet more to their suppliers. The darling man tried to hide the worst from her, but the business was in terrible trouble, that much could not have been more obvious. It could not be ignored.

Although he tried not to show it, she could tell Ore was scared. The official-looking letters—the ones he hid from her—made matters much worse. Every time she asked about them, he snapped at her, and Ore never did that. Not her calm, steady, loving husband. Not her Ore. And she could do nothing to help.

All she really knew was that their business would soon fail, and when it did, the family would lose their comfortable, little, upstairs apartment. They would be left homeless.

Sighing, she dabbed away another tear, scraped the finely diced onion into a plastic container, and placed it in the half-empty fridge ready for that night's service.

In the hope that dear Ore had added bookings without telling her, Justina checked the diary. Nothing. Not a single reservation for the evening, which was unusual, even for a Wednesday.

Preparing the rest of the vegetables and the meat could

wait. Why waste ingredients that might otherwise keep for one more day?

Justina had plenty of other tasks to keep her occupied while waiting for Ore to return after collecting the girls from school. Her little darlings would be hungry. They always were after school. Ravenous. She smiled in anticipation of hugging them tight. The quiet family time before evening service always was the very best part of Justina's working day.

She washed her hands, enjoying the warmth of the water and the aroma of lemon-scented soap—the only preparation that could take away the taint of garlic and onions.

Justina took a clean dishcloth from the drawer next to the sink and rolled the heavy canteen trolley into the dining room. It bumped over the slight lip between the hard kitchen floor and the dining room tiles, causing the cutlery to rattle and the glasses to clink. Happy sounds, she always thought—the sounds of friendship and hospitality. The sounds of joy.

As usual, she began at the four-setting table in the corner furthest from the entrance and worked her way towards the centre.

She smoothed the white, cotton tablecloths, set out the cutlery, folded the plum-red serviettes into attractive, serrated fans, and polished each glass to a shine before placing it in its correct position in the right hand of each setting. Finally, she added the centrepiece—a small, glass vase with its posy of fresh flowers. With only ten tables, Bistro Mykonos could never be described as large, and might not boast a fancy Michelin star, but no one would ever find fault with the food, or the front-of-house ambience. The *atmósfaira*.

In such things, Justina could still take great pride. She loved the precision of each table decoration.

The bell over the front door jingled.

Unexpected and harsh, the noise shocked Justina out of the familiar, mindless actions that had become her meditation. Her heart leaped. She placed a hand flat to her chest and turned. Two men, strangers, stood inside the open doorway.

She must have forgotten to flip the sign from "Open" to "Closed". But surely, she had locked the door? She never left it unlocked with the restaurant closed. Never. Perhaps Ore …?

The wall clock above the entrance showed half past three. Ore and the girls would not be home for at least twenty minutes. She stood alone against them.

"Excuse me, gentlemen," she said, surprised at how weak her voice sounded despite the relative quiet. "We are closed."

Being alone in the restaurant did not usually worry her, but something about the intensity of these men made her uneasy. The way they glowered at her. The way they carried themselves. It sent a shiver through her body. Ore, born and raised in London, would have called it a "bad vibe". In Greece, her homeland, it would have been given a different description. In her native Greek, it would be *"to simádi tou diavólou"*—the sign of the devil.

She stood behind the trolley, gripping the dishcloth tight. The trolley offered little security, but it acted as a barrier and hid her trembling knees.

"We do not open until seven o'clock," she called, forcing the words through a tight, scared throat.

The first man stood tall and straight. He had wavy, blond hair and the lean, athletic build of a soccer player.

With his smooth, angular face, strong jaw, and high cheek-bones, some women might have considered him handsome, but only if they ignored his hard, lifeless, blue eyes. He carried a shiny, metal briefcase in his left hand and moved quietly towards her, lips bared in a wide smile that exposed sharp, white teeth—the movements of a wolf closing on its prey. Circling. Hunting.

Again, Justina shuddered, and she gripped the dishcloth tighter.

Although the blond man was intimidating, his partner was worse. A dark-skinned giant, he had to turn sideways and duck to fit through the doorway. The expression on his tattooed face shouted anger. His eyes were as dark as his skin, the eyeballs yellow rather than white. Muscles bulged and rippled beneath a stretched T-shirt, and his grey, two-piece suit, although well-tailored and expensive-looking, seemed out of place on so square and large a body.

Justina's heart thumped faster, and she shuddered under the monster's fixed gaze. The dishcloth she had been wringing slipped through her sweaty hands.

The big man with the tattooed face shut the door and turned the lock. She *had* turned the sign to "Closed". He stood with his back to the door, feet apart, arms folded across his barrel chest. A man on guard. A rock. Immovable. Terrifying.

Dear Lord! What is this?

Beyond the windows, the world continued as normal. Cars still crawled past, but more slowly, and pedestrians still tramped the opposite pavement, but no heads turned towards her.

She stood alone. Helpless. Vulnerable.

The clouds chose that moment to break apart once again, and the sun burst through the windows. The monster cast a huge shadow into the room, but somehow, with his tattooed face darkened and hidden by the glare, his ominous presence became even more terrifying.

The blond man stopped in front of her, keeping a table and the trolley between them.

"Good afternoon, Mrs Constantine," he said quietly. "Or may I call you Justina?"

He knows my Christian name!

His voice carried a heavy, East-End-of-London accent and had the guttural rasp of a man who had smoked cigarettes for many years. The voice sounded older than his looks.

"My name is Alfred Lovejoy, but you can call me Alfie." Again, he smiled, but it was equally as chilling as the first. "It's always nice to call people by their first names, isn't it? Much more conducive to pleasant conversation. My rather large friend over there is known as Tugboat, for obvious reasons, but I call him Tuggy. It's much nicer, don't you think? Gentler. Friendlier."

The fact that Lovejoy stood over her, menacing and scary, was bad enough, but that he did not mind telling her his name seemed somehow worse. It showed he did not care that she knew.

"W-Who are you, and what do you want?"

Lovejoy's smile melted away and his cold, blue eyes drilled straight through her.

"Weren't you listening?" he said, his tone aggressive, harsh. "I just told you my name. Clear out your fucking ears, bitch."

Her mouth dropped open. She backed away until stopped by a table, but Lovejoy stayed where he was, his upper lip peeled back into an animal sneer.

"Yes," he said, nodding. "I thought that would get your

attention. I hate resorting to foul language. Swearing is the last resort of the ill-educated, don't you think? But sometimes, the shock value helps drive the message across. So, what do I want? Hmm. I'll tell you what I want." He hummed a familiar tune, jiggled his hips, and chuckled. "Ah, the Spice Girls. Lyrically brilliant, weren't they?"

He swung the metal briefcase, slammed it on the table, and pushed it towards the middle. Justina jumped. Glasses smashed and cutlery scattered. The centrepiece vase broke. Water spread over the tablecloth and dripped to the floor.

A long-stemmed wine glass, the final one, wobbled. Justina's arm twitched involuntarily. She wanted to rush forwards to catch it, but Lovejoy's presence locked her in place. Frozen in terror.

The glass toppled and fell slowly from the table. It hit the tiled floor and smashed into a dozen pieces. Only the stem and base remained intact.

Dear Lord, the mess.

Insurance would not cover such a small loss, but how could they afford to replace the broken glasses and the vase? A flash of anger pricked Justina's bubble of fear. How dare he do such a thing? She had only just finished setting the table!

She ground her teeth but kept quiet and lowered her gaze. The trolley's cutlery drawer was part-way open, showing her the wooden handle of a wickedly sharp steak knife. It lay within easy reach. She only had to stretch out a hand and take it.

Without removing his eyes from her, Lovejoy snapped the clasps of the briefcase, opened the lid, and removed a document bound in a clear, plastic cover. He dropped it on the table amongst the shards of glass, the flowers, and the crushed napkins.

"W-What is that?" she managed to say, lifting her gaze from the steak knife to stare at the document.

Lovejoy lowered the briefcase lid, secured the clasps, and placed his hands together as though in prayer.

"That there," he said, back to his smiling, quiet worst, "is a contract for the sale of this … shithole."

For the first time since entering the Bistro, Lovejoy dragged his gaze from her and scanned the dining room through half-closed lids.

"Jesus H Christ, what a pitiful excuse for a restaurant. Not worth half the price we're offering, but the boss is a generous man. Too fucking generous if you ask me. He recognises the challenges involved in 'uprooting young families from their homes'. His words, not mine. I don't give a fuck."

He snorted and shook his head.

"If it was up to me, I'd torch the place one night with you, your hubby, and your sweet, little girls still inside." He jerked a thumb over his shoulder at the monster blocking the door. "Tuggy there's a dab hand with a Molotov cocktail. Aren't you, Tuggy?"

The giant did not move or make a sound.

Lovejoy continued. "Trouble is, that wouldn't give the boss what the lawyers like to call 'ownership with vacant possession'. Get me?"

Justina shook her head.

She had no idea what the horrible man was talking about.

"Stupid cow. It's all hubby's fault. He keeps refusing to sign the papers we send him. Damn it, the bastard didn't even acknowledge receipt of the fucking things. Didn't answer or return our phone calls neither. If he'd have responded, the boss might have been prepared to negotiate an even better price, but … Ah well, water under London Bridge. Too fucking late now. Much too late. Time's short and a new deal's out of the question. Orestes has caused too much irritation. Do you understand me now, Justina?"

Despite his supposed explanation, Justina did not comprehend any of it. Ore had kept so much from her, telling her things like they had to "soldier on" and "stay afloat until the good times returned". Sometimes, even after nearly nine years of marriage and ten years of living in London, Justina still had no idea what Ore was talking about. Although she spoke good English, and was proud of her ability to converse easily with the customers and the suppliers, some English expressions sailed way above her head like the wind over the Aegean.

What did money and papers have to do with one of the bridges over the river Thames? No sense. No sense at all.

"The rude bitch isn't listening, Tuggy. She isn't paying attention," Lovejoy said and sidestepped the table. As he rushed towards her, she stood transfixed, shaking, any hope of reaching for the steak knife gone.

He jerked the trolley aside and stopped within arm's reach, staring down at her. Even taller than she first thought, Justina had to tilt her head up to look at him, but she did not want to stare into the harsh, dead eyes. She wanted to scream for help. She wanted to run, but there was nowhere to go. Nowhere to hide. No one to save her.

She shuddered under his evil glare.

Lovejoy leaned closer. Justina's nose wrinkled in distaste at his overpowering, spicy aftershave.

"Let me make this perfectly clear, so even you can understand, you thick, Greek bitch."

The sweetness of his peppermint breath freshener made her gag.

"If your hubby doesn't sign the contract, Tuggy's gonna pay you a visit one night. You like playing house with sweet, little girls, don't you, Tuggy? Yeah. You love it."

My girls? My girls!

"Do not touch my babies!" she screamed. "I will kill you!"

Justina lunged forwards, clawing for his face. She wanted to scratch and tear, gouge the eyes from his head.

Laughing, Lovejoy dodged to the side. He caught her flailing arms and crushed them together, holding them by the wrists in one big, powerful hand. He slapped her so hard with the other, the blow rattled her teeth, and lights flashed behind her eyes. Her knees buckled, but he held her up by her arms and stopped her from falling.

Lovejoy grabbed her hair and tugged, snapping her head back. The skin stretched tight across her vulnerable neck. She was totally at his mercy.

Justina stopped struggling. Stopped fighting. He was too strong. His powerful grip hurt her wrists and her scalp stung where he pulled at her hair so hard. Her eyes watered again, more tears flowed. Her stomach churned. She fought the desperate need to throw up.

"Tut tut," Lovejoy said, his face millimetres from hers, his spittle wetting her chin. "Now, that's a rather aggressive way to react to a legitimate business proposition. And all because I mentioned Tuggy in the same breath as your offspring. That's likely to hurt his feelings. Don't let his size fool you. Tuggy has feelings, don't you, mate? I call that unjustified, Justina. Unjustified."

He laughed again. A horrible, cruel laugh, it turned her stomach. Loud sobs erupted, unbidden, from her mouth. She could not help herself, could not fight it. The thought of her babies in the clutches of these creatures tore her insides apart, but she could do nothing but struggle impotently against the powerful grip of the evil man.

Lovejoy turned towards the glowering monster and stepped to one side, lifting Justina's arms above her head, displaying her to the creature—a piece of meat for his approval.

"See what I did there, Tuggy? Justina—justified? That's what's called a pun. So, what d'you say, mate? Fancy paying a night-time visit to a couple of frightened kiddies?"

The monster tilted his head to one side as though appraising Justina. After a moment, he nodded and pointed a massive finger at her.

"You want this scrawny bitch, too? Yeah, you can have her if you like. Don't see why not."

Tugboat's lips peeled back. White teeth gleamed against the dark and brooding background.

Lovejoy pulled Justina's head close to his again and whispered in her ear. "Insatiable, he is, Justina."

Her cheek still throbbed from his slap, but her vision had cleared, and his dead eyes skewered her so badly, she could not look away.

"Tuggy's a dynamo, you know," Lovejoy continued. "Women have told me he can go all night. How would you fancy a man that huge on top of you hour after hour?" Lovejoy leaned away and shook his head. "Nah. He'd probably break a little thing like you. Wear you out from the inside."

The brute released her hair and her wrists, and pushed her away. Justina staggered to the side and stumbled against the trolley. She held on tight to the handle. She would not fall—they would not make her grovel in her own place of work, in her own home.

"On the other hand," the braying man continued, "I

could be wrong. A woman like you might enjoy Tuggy's attention. What do you reckon, Justina? I bet the thought turns you on, doesn't it! I bet you're wringing wet right now, hey? I wonder."

He stepped back and looked her up and down, undressing her in his mind.

"You know what? Despite everything, you aren't a bad looking bit of scratch. Quite tasty, in fact. Decent-sized tits and they still look firm despite having been used to feed your spawn. Flat stomach, too, and a nice, round arse. Wonder what you look like without that baggy apron and that daggy dress? Maybe I should find out. How about it? Fancy stripping for me and bending over that table? I can help you with the buttons if you like."

Justina's chin trembled, she gripped the trolley tighter, and prepared to strike for the steak knife. This time, she would grab it. No doubt. No hesitation. If he made another move towards her, she would stab him in the throat and run out the back way. She avoided looking directly at the part-open drawer and waited.

A car horn broke the near-silence. In the street outside, a man shouted something, and another, further away, laughed. Beyond the windows, traffic continued to rumble.

Clouds returned to block the sun, the shadow faded, and warmth bled from the room.

Lovejoy sighed and shook his head once again.

"Nah, don't worry, darling," he said. "Only kidding. I don't need to force myself on a bitch even if she is a bit of a MILF. Just making a point that there's no one to save you. And don't bother calling the cops. They'll do nothing. I can find fifteen friends and the barman who'll swear that Tuggy and I are in the pub, see? Right now, we're knocking back Belgian beers and telling bad jokes. The till receipts will show me using my credit card and everything. Got it all covered, see? In short, we're protected, and you aren't."

Lovejoy straightened his tie and smoothed back his blond hair before grabbing the handle of his briefcase and lifting it from the destroyed table. More pieces of glass fell to the tiled floor. He laughed again.

"You have 'til the end of next month to sign those papers. That's midday, October the thirty-first. Hallowe'en. Got it?"

He stopped talking, probably waiting for an answer, but she refused to give him one.

"Five weeks ought to be plenty of time for you to clear this place of your garbage and fuck off out of it."

Lovejoy pointed at the contract.

"Don't forget what I said. Sign and deliver those papers by midday, Hallowe'en, or we'll be back with a dirty, great 'trick' for you and a Tuggy-sized treat for your spawn."

The evil smile returned to his face.

"Now," he continued after a short pause, "we're going out the way we came in. And remember. If we hear you've gone blabbing to the filth—and we will hear it, believe me —all bets are off. You, your hubby, and your pretty, little daughters, are fair game. Right?"

He stared at Justina and held the look until she nodded. Only then, did they leave.

The moment they'd gone, Justina rushed to lock and bolt the front door, and collapsed into a chair. She buried her face in the crushed dishcloth and sobbed.

During the whole terrifying episode, the monster, Tugboat, had not uttered a single sound, which was perhaps the scariest part of the whole nightmarish incident. Not a sound.

Justina did not know how long she sat crying, but a

rattling on the door made her jump. She spun towards the sound, preparing to run, but found her beautiful, smiling girls tapping gently on the glass.

"Rena, Kora!" she cried again. "My darlings."

She jumped up, tore open the door, and swept the girls into her arms, squeezing tight. She absorbed their smell, their wriggling warmth, their love.

"Too tight, Mama," Kora said, squirming. "You're hurting me."

"Sorry, *moraki mou*," Justina said, easing the pressure but not letting go completely. "It is just that I missed you so, so much."

Rena ducked out of Justina's loosened grasp and darted inside. "Mama, did you have an accident?"

"I … tripped. Stay away from the table until I pick up the broken glass. It is dangerous. You will cut yourself."

Rena shuffled closer, her eyes narrowed, staring hard.

"Mama," she said, "your eyes are puffy. Have you been chopping onions?"

"Yes, my darling girl," Justina said, unable to stifle a laugh. The relief at seeing and hearing her babies was overwhelming. "That is exactly what I have been doing. And garlic. Do not forget the garlic."

Justina picked up Kora, locked the door, and carried her past the damage.

"Rena, come away from there. I told you it is dangerous!"

"Sorry, Mama."

"Now, upstairs and get changed while I clear the mess. I expect you are hungry?"

"Starving, Mama," Kora said.

Rena nodded and slid the satchel from her shoulder. "Yes please, Mama. School dinner was horrible."

Justina ruffled Rena's hair. "Help your sister change out of her uniform and, just this once, you can watch television before doing your homework, okay?"

She shooed them up the stairs to the apartment before rushing back to the kitchen in time to meet Ore, who had parked the car around the back as usual, off the busy street.

Before he had the chance to step fully into the kitchen, she flew into his arms and poured out her heart to him.

For the longest time, they clung to each other.

Ore listened, stroking her hair and whispering soothing words. Eventually, she recovered enough to let him clear the damage and make supper for the girls.

With Ore in charge, she ran upstairs and stood under the shower until it ran cold, scrubbing her skin raw to remove the stench and the feel of a man called Alfie Lovejoy.

She cried for a full hour.

————

LATER THAT NIGHT, after they closed the restaurant—six covers all evening, barely enough to cover the night's electricity bill—she and Ore sat in their living room. The girls were fast asleep and blissfully unaware.

They read the new contract together. She found the legal wording difficult to follow, but Ore snorted at the document's promised to pay them the full "independently assessed market value" for the leasehold of the building and the goodwill of the business. To Justina, the total purchase price—laid out in words and figures at the bottom of the final page—looked impressive.

"It ain't enough," Ore said, holding her close and gently kissing her bruised and swollen cheek. "After paying off the mortgage, we'd barely have enough to clear our other debts. There'd be nothing left over for a deposit on a new home. And worse than that, far worse, we'd both need to find new jobs straight away."

Despair wrapped around her, choking her, making it difficult to breathe.

"Ore, what are we going to do?"

He threw the contract on the coffee table and turned to face her, holding her hands, and kissing her wrists where the marks from Lovejoy's grip still showed red and sore.

"I don't know. I've been trying to find a way out, but …" Ore squirmed in his seat, creating a gap between them. "Before he died, Papa and I had a blazing row. He was planning to sell a share in the Bistro, but I hated the idea. The Bistro is the girls' inheritance, their future. Papa thought the money would tide us over until after the development company had finished renovating the block."

"Is that why Papa was on the flight to Amsterdam?"

Ore lowered his head. "Yes. He knew a man in The Hague, a rich man who owed him a favour. Darling, Papa died thinking I hated him."

Ore wept quietly and, even though she imagined herself all cried out for the day, tears also filled Justina's eyes. They held each other.

"Papa knew you loved him, Ore. He knew it."

They kissed and hugged, and for a moment, things were better.

Eventually, Ore leaned back on the sofa, his arm draped around her shoulders. Justina rested her head against his chest, listening to and feeling the slow, steady beat of his heart. The soft rise and fall of his chest lulled her, helping to calm her involuntary emotional and physical twitches.

"After Papa's funeral," he said at length, his soft words

vibrating through his ribcage, "I found the contact details of the man in The Hague, but … it's too late. He didn't want to help me. He said the debt he owed Papa died with him. Darling, I have no idea what to do."

She had no idea either and they sat in silence for hours and hours.

On The Defensive: Chapter Two

Thursday 22nd October – Morning

The Villa, Gironde, Nouvelle-Aquitaine, France

The late-autumn sun flared off the water and sliced into Ryan Kaine's eyes, but the light breeze made the day pleasant. A cloudless, azure sky, miles of fine, silver sand, and the blue-grey Atlantic painted a picture-postcard beauty that would change by the day and with the seasons and never grow old. The villa and the Gironde Coast made a great base of operations. Comfortable, isolated, easy to defend, and with multiple means of ingress and egress.

In short, the place couldn't have been better.

The Bay of Biscay, calm in the autumnal stillness, stretched out to the gently curving horizon. The silence interrupted only by the breeze, the breakers wearing the sand into a finer powder, and the discordant cries of Audouin's gulls as they bickered over seaborne scraps. There were no ships or boats to spoil the sea's rolling majesty.

The view was stunning enough, but the smells wafting up from the sun-baked land, the salt-water ozone carried on the onshore breeze, completed it for him. The air held the tang of sun, sea salt, and marram grass. A fragrance no perfumer could capture in a bottle.

Kaine was in his element. For the first time in over twenty years, he could almost relax. The location made him as content as was ever going to be possible given the heavy load his conscience carried. The load he would carry for the rest of his life. However long that would last.

"Are you ready?" Lara called from the office.

He reached a hand to his left side and allowed his fingers to trace the raised, twenty-centimetre scar running along his rib cage. One of the most recent additions to his unwanted collection of body art. A legacy of the knife wound he'd suffered the morning after he'd shot down Flight BE1555. The gash had been serious enough for him to seek out the nearest medical treatment. Luckily for him but, as it happened, unluckily for Lara, his internet search had pointed him to her veterinary clinic.

She'd stitched together a rough and bloodied stranger without complaint and without a thought for herself. Saved his life. No doubt about it. He'd be in her debt forever but, in the weeks since their first traumatic meeting, things had changed. He'd started to feel more than gratitude—much more.

The growing emotions were wrong, inappropriate, forged in battle, and fostered by a sense of responsibility to her and his innate loneliness. He could never act on his feelings and worked hard to draw a professional but friendly line in the sand between them.

"Everything set up properly this time?" he asked, playing for enough time to roll himself out of his comfy chair and plaster on his game face.

"Yes, and it has been for the past five minutes."

"Is Sabrina online?"

"Yes, and has been—"

"Yeah, yeah. For the past five minutes?"

"No. She's been taking me through the system for the past hour. Get your backside in here, right now!"

And there it was, her patience threshold breached. Not saintly, but still beautiful. Angelic.

Kaine grunted as he rolled off the recliner and onto his feet. He hadn't been resting all that long, and the aches and pains from the early-morning workout had eased, but he'd have preferred more recovery time. His first training session of the day—a two-mile swim, keeping close to the shore, within sight and easy access of the villa, a thirty-minute run over the nearby dunes, followed by another thirty minutes spent throwing weights and punching bags—was the barest minimum, maintenance only. It took it out of him, and recuperation took longer than it used to—the cost of an aging body. Growing older could be a nightmare. On the other hand, it beat the alternative.

He snorted to himself.

Sabrina was doing them a huge favour and it would be wrong to keep her waiting any longer. Reluctantly, he turned his back to the sea and its gently rolling waves and padded barefoot across the hardwood deck into the cool shade of his whitewashed safe house.

He'd bought the single-storey, Mediterranean-style villa ten years earlier for cash—strike that—he'd picked it up for peanuts at the depth of a banker's recession. The original owner, a snot-nosed, London fund manager, needed a quick sale to help pay his legal fees and keep him out of prison, and he wasn't too keen to leave much of a paper trail. As a result, Kaine acquired the part-built property with its three bedrooms, open-plan kitchen-diner, and subterranean *cave* —wine cellar—set on acres and acres of dunes overlooking the sea as a retirement home. He'd since spent a fortune upgrading it into a self-contained, off-the-grid fortress, complete with its own triple-redundant renewable energy source—tidal, solar, and wind—and a bespoke satellite service.

For security, he'd used non-local artisans for separate parts of the project. As a result, no single firm, or single individual, had a comprehensive knowledge of the completed structure.

Although not averse to the odd glass or two of wine, Kaine didn't require a dedicated wine cellar, but did need a home for a secure communications hub and a state-of-the-art surveillance system. To that end, he'd called on the services of a couple of military engineer friends to help him convert the cellar into an office that could double as a panic room. They also spent a week deploying a security net of motion sensors and surveillance cameras—both standard and infrared—to protect the whole property.

Finally, before furnishing the place in a clean, minimalist style, Kaine added a hidden exit to the panic room. Only he, and now Lara, knew of the back door's existence. Kaine wasn't about to allow anyone to trap him or Lara inside a concrete cell, no matter how apparently secure it might appear.

What some might have described as paranoia, he'd seen as a healthy concern for his long-term personal safety. How right he'd been, and now he had Lara to protect, his extensive preparations had proven more than justified.

As an added security measure, since making the villa their temporary base of operations, Kaine, with Lara's help, had calibrated the surveillance system to react to any human-sized approach from land, sea, and air. They'd streamed the surveillance feeds through the comms hub in the office and each had access to the system via mobile phones and waterproof, military-grade, smart watches. As long as they had satellite access, mobile phones, and wore the watches, both he and Lara could monitor the villa and its surroundings at any time, and from just about anywhere on the planet.

Despite all the electronic wizardry, Kaine never forgot the human factor and regularly patrolled the area, often taking Lara with him as both cover—a loving couple out for a stroll—and to hone her surveillance skills. There were no real substitutes for human eyes and ears. Or for human intuition.

To complete the whole defensive arrangement, Kaine spent two hours each afternoon coaching Lara in what she had once jokingly referred to as "The Way of the Warrior". She did, however, take the training extremely seriously and, being bright and physically strong from her work with large farm animals, she made an ideal apprentice. In the few short weeks since their arrival at the villa, she'd developed a good grasp of military fieldcraft and had taken nine minutes off her fifteen-hundred-metre swim time. Kaine had rarely coached a more willing and able trainee and, he'd definitely never coached one as damned good looking.

He secretly loved the time he spent with her and looked forward to each session, but he knew it couldn't last. One day, they would clear his name and confirm that no one wanted to use her to get to him. On that day, Lara would be free to return to her quiet, normal life, and they'd never see each other again. Until then, he could never leave her alone and vulnerable. If ever he had to leave, there were people available at a moment's notice—men he trusted—to guard her in his absence.

He hoped neither day—his leaving on a new mission and her returning to her old life—would ever come, but knew, deep down, they must.

Grab your copy...
vinci-books.com/onthedefensive

About Kerry J Donovan

#1 International Best-seller with *Ryan Kaine: On the Run*, Kerry was born in Dublin. He currently lives with Margaret in a bungalow in Nottinghamshire. He has three children and four grandchildren.

Kerry earned a first-class honours degree in Human Biology and has a PhD in Sport and Exercise Sciences. A former scientific advisor to The Office of the Deputy Prime Minister, he helped UK emergency first-responders prepare for chemical attacks in the wake of 9/11. He is also a former furniture designer/maker.

kerryjdonovan.com